Redempt

CW00433279

Andrew Murrison

Table of Contents

Prologue

I

Westminster
January 1649

A cruel east wind with nothing to warm it from Siberia to the flatlands of East Anglia slammed into the sheer face of the Banqueting Hall. But it was not the weather chilling the delicate figure stepping from the hall's boarded-up gloom into the raw winter light. An extra shirt had made sure of that.

No, the cause of the King's discomfort was the apparatus of bloody public execution.

He took just a moment to check himself, not so much as anyone would notice, he was sure of it. He was in the middle of the scaffold now, scanning shame-faces, eyeing feet shifting uneasily on the sand-covered planks.

There was the coffin, pitch pine, lid off. Was he really so small? He saw the iron staples in the deck and the heavy rope and pulleys that would prostate him if he proved unwilling. How little they knew him.

The better sort had long since elbowed a decent view at every window and parapet but the King was grateful for the canvas screen. At least his despatch to the gates of St Peter would be lost to the common people, his agonies hidden if the headsman botched the job.

Charles peered at the beings pressing forward to catch the bloody talisman that would soon drip, drip between the boards. But something was missing. 'Sweet Jesus.' Relief thawed the King for a crazed instant. 'The poor boobies in their funk have clear forgotten the block!'

'Sir?' The novice executioner had not anticipated a conversation with the condemned man.

'Well, I mean, where am I to go?' said the King. 'You've mislaid your equipment.'

The man squinting from his slitted mask pointed at the log hidden in straw between the iron staples. The King tensed, hard-won composure slipping. 'It's much too low, man,' he spat. 'I'm to kneel, not *crawl*.' The last prince to be done in like this; his sainted grandmother, had knelt serene before they cut her.

The executioner swallowed hard. 'Can't be helped, Sir.' The condemned was allowed a short speech. Then he would do it, with the uncertain axe and his unpractised arm.

The King, a drop forming at the end of his chiselled beak, caught mild blue eyes behind the mask and soft west-country vowels. He sniffed, feeling for the note, clearing his throat. But now halberdiers were poling people clear. His thin voice would not be heard by the crowd. Irritated, he turned to the party pinned against the Banqueting Hall.

The King spotted the scribe, crooked back, withered arm, standing at the window, poised to scribble his words. Slavering at their value to the news books of London, the scribe twisted forward, His Majesty waving him in. A weak cough and the King began his school-masterly performance. 'I shall be very little heard of anybody here.' He flopped a gloved hand dismissively towards the mob. 'So I will speak a word to you. Indeed, I could hold my peace very well, but keeping silence would make some men think I submit to the guilt as well as the punishment.'

'Oh, that's good, *very* good,' muttered the crooked-backed scribe, scribbling furiously, measuring each word by the shilling. 'Sing, sing, Cock Robin.' He winked at the headsman. 'Sing your spavined heart out.'

The executioner dropped his gaze, bowels turned to water. The stinking gear of his borrowed profession would hide him, wouldn't it? Yes, yes, pray God, even from the devilishly cunning scribe whose cruel arts he knew so well. Because retribution, even viler than the punishment he was about to administer, would come to him if, with the fall of his axe, the Parliament's fragile polity was stillborn.

I see you, farm boy, the scribe mused, sucking thin cheeks, and *you'll wear the Mark of Cain for this.*

The King was nearly done. 'You see, I am an innocent man.' A snatch of cloth slipped from his fingers. The executioner bent low, shaking straws from the black embroidery, offering it to the King. Plucking another stalk from the cap, Charles turned in his grey hair. 'Does my hair trouble you?'

The executioner hesitated; laying a finger on the King was a serious matter. He fumbled the errant strands beneath the cap, baring the monarch's neck.

Throwing away his cloak, the King crouched awkwardly against the block. The executioner stepped up, mouth dry as the Sabbath day.

Charles Stuart gave his last command and the soldier pulled at the unfamiliar weapon.

At street level the common people fell silent. White upturned faces saw the blade rise, wink in the winter light and fall below the screen.

Out of sight, the King's head fell deftly away.

The new republicans froze. Maybe the bloodied axe would rise again as it had to finish this man's grandmother. No, here was the headsman stepping forward like he had been told to. Treading the fallen nightcap into the gore, he thrust the severed head, dripping, above the parapet like a night watchman's lantern, parading it around the scaffold.

And, oh, the most hideous, Stygian groan that ever sprung from a body of men. 'Behold,' the headsman's burr was strained beyond recognition, 'the head of a traitor!'

At half past three o'clock, the head of the King of England dropped into a pauper's coffin as the devil-birds of London rose to blacken the sky.

Wiping bloody paws down his apron, the executioner staggered round the twitching corpse, past the scribe, falling into the hall's dark refuge.

'*Cruel cock sparrow, the cause of their grief,*' the scribe eyed the retreating assassin, '*was hung on a gibbet next day, like a thief.*'

Shielding the journal from the party pressing back into the hall, he scratched the gentle executioner's name...

Part One – World turned upside down

II

Brook Farm

Whitsuntide 1643

Nathaniel Salt left the party for no particular reason, taking the dusty chalk and flint track winding up and round. 'You there, Billy Burrows?' A rustling back round the bend. Nat grinned, a good-natured face, west-country broad and flat, a shadow already at his jaw and lip. Tall enough to duck at his threshold, the loose chemise billowing in the light air covered a build on the heavy side of average. In a market day crowd, kind blue eyes and an easy smile won him a second glance. 'Billy, you rogue, what're you up to?' Silence. Nat passed a hand through his thick black mane 'Daft bugger.' He fired a pebble into the bracken to flush out the watcher. 'Gotcha!'

Poor bent Billy Burrows shambled down the track. 'Aw, come here, noddlepate. Got you something.' The man turned, twitchingly curious. 'Here.' Billy took the sugary treat warily, rolling it, sniffing it, licking it. 'Good?' Nodding vacantly, Billy perched on a grassy knoll, sucking noisily.

'In one ear, out the other, eh Billy boy?' Nat grinned. 'I was thinking about my old Pa, walking up here. You remember his tales?' The lop-sided gummy face peered up, smiling gormlessly. 'No, course not. After supper, wintertime, when there was no work outside, I used to sit at Pa's feet with the wind howling and the rain whipping off the downs. King Henry kicked Bishop o' Sarum's fat arse, Pa said, aye, and the she-devil Abbess o' Shaftesbury's rump too.' Nat had grown strong sucking legend from a puritan teat. 'Then he gives us Salts our little farm. Lusty nipper me, Widow Banks says, when I came into the world down there. Long hot summer it was, 1616, crops withering and cattle dropping with the rinderpest. Ain't much though, is it? Mud, horse hair and cow turds on a wildwood frame, topped off with a bit of thatch. But see that?' He nodded at the pond behind the house fed through a slip in the chalk and the stream dancing towards the village. 'That's what makes it special.

Spring water, see. Kept us safe up here, all those years, with all the village in the plague pit.' Nat jammed hands on hips. 'What d'you make of that then, Billy? Well Nat, you says, lesson is bloody well keep out of it. And that's what I'll do in this war that's brewing, Billy-boy!'

Nat searched his pocket for another treat. 'She's been dead five years now you know, my missus.' Tossing Billy a sweet, he nodded at the twins, Nicholas and Eliza, horsing around in the farmyard. 'Childbed – it's a bugger.'

The warm breeze brought fiddle music from the house across the strip fields. 'Bloody hell, what a racket,' grinned Nat. 'Still you're missing the party, Billy Burrows, up here with me blathering on.' Billy picked his nose, examined his finger and sucked.

Nat plucked a stem of barley, playing it between his teeth. 'Me and Effam used to come up here, before her mother found out and packed her off to London.' He threw the stalk like a dart. 'You know, Billy, Euphemia Farrington, squire's daughter.' The sparky, strong-willed Farrington girl had easily given her governess the slip to liaise with Nat in the long, languid summer of 1631. 'Gutted I was, Ned. If she'd stayed here, the London pox wouldn't have mashed her pretty face, eh? But then she'd have some toff like her mother wanted. No chance for a randy little farm boy either way.' He turned his back to piss against the boundary oak. 'Now I hear she's sweet on Erasmus Carew. What d'you think of that Billy? Carew – I ask you!'

Billy warned him, bolting across the ditch ringing the wood. Nat had to shade his eyes but the silhouette was unmistakable. 'God give you good day, Mr Carew. We were just talking about you, weren't we, Billy?'

'You're a damned poor host, Nathaniel Salt.' Carew jabbed his crop at the farmhouse. 'Eh?'

'Revels for my sister, Dorothy.' Nat's eye was drawn to black leather gauntlets with intertwining 'E' and 'C' in heavy silver thread. *Erasmus Carew*. 'Left a maid, returned a wife.'

'Indeed! Hope you fixed a decent match.' He was removing the gloves now, tucking them carefully in his waistband. 'Lots of money, eh? Mistake splicing for anything else.'

Nat shrugged. 'A love match, I think.' He wondered what Effam saw in him, apart from the merchant's moneybags.

Carew snorted, uncoiling from the beast. 'Hold, Billy Burrows.' Twitching, Billy took the reins. 'Not from round here, your new brother?' Carew stroked the whiskers of his narrow face sculpted like Van Dyke's new portrait of the King he had so admired at Whitehall.

A traveller on the downs would say Carew and Salt were like chalk and cheese. *And be wrong.*

'He's called Le Roux,' replied Nat. 'Etienne Le Roux, apothecary, merchant of Cheapside.'

'Ah, merchants.' Carew applied a pinch of snuff to the base of his thumb. 'What's he peddle, your Le Roux?'

'Devon pilchards, Canary wines, ginger, sugar from the Indies, fancies for the goodwives of London.' Nat sucked his teeth. 'Wiltshire wool for the Dutch.'

Carew's nose twitched. '*Etienne* Le Roux, Frenchie, eh?' He applied each nostril to the snuff. 'A moment.' Whipping a large silk square from his sleeve, he buried his exploding sinuses in the fabric. 'My word, that's a mighty fine cut. Where were we?'

'Frenchies.'

'Frenchies *and* merchants, damn their eyes! Well, here's the thing, neighbour. Poor saps like you and me scratching a living from these flinty fields while city men woo our pretty maids with their fancies and deep purses. What d'you say, Nathaniel Salt?'

Nat looked askance. Cloak-bag breeches tied at the knee with red ribbons, leather doublet slashed with a rich crimson lining. Not to mention the gloves. All for a dusty climb on a hot summer's day? 'Well, neighbour, reckon all England'll be richer on the backs of city men like Etienne Le Roux.'

Carew scowled. 'Don't see any of it round here. All I see is your showy London merchants with their fast money spewing out beyond city walls, winkling old families from their seats. Ghastly, vulgar people.' The man shuddered, plucking the elaborate gloves from his belt. 'In any case, the King's daughter's married to the Dutch Stadtholder and those continentals are mighty jumpy. Can't see trade with the Low Countries being served by Parliament's buffoons up-ending the King's peace. Eh?'

'I hear the King's left London,' shrugged Nat. 'Gone to Oxford.'

'Yes, yes but how long will those Dutchmen haggle for *Monsieur* Le Roux's cloth?' He jerked his crop at Nat's sheep. 'If Parliament unsettles Holland, that'll be mutton.'

'Etienne reckons with Parliament in London and the King safe in Oxford, trade'll be just fine,' said Nat. 'Anyway, no reason why all those high blown goings-on should bother us here, eh?'

Carew bent low, stroking the horse's neck. 'You're wrong Salt.' He sat up, choosing his words as he stared across the field strips towards the village of Hinton Helions a mile down the track and his own slab-faced brick mansion straight from a draughtsman's book.

'You ever met King Charles?' Nat stroked his stubbled chin. 'I have. Passing through, on one of his progresses.'

'Eh?'

'Down our lane, with my father, gave me a silver penny. Didn't spend it. Still got it.'

'Ah.' Carew's face cracked a smile. 'Well, since you mention him, Nat, where d'you stand in the matter of His Majesty, eh?'

So that was it. 'Le Roux says the King's sending gentlemen from Oxford to raise regiments of Englishmen to kill Englishmen.' Nat squinted at the figure in the sun. 'Is *that* why you're here, Mr Carew, climbing this hill in the heat of the day?'

'God's blood!' Smack, smack, Carew's whip strapped burnished boot leather. 'You mule-headed yeomen,' he slapped a fly from his neck, 'all the same, irksome as these foul creatures bedevilling all living things.' On the side of a low Wessex hill, two estates of a dividing country stood in silent debate, pondering change. And for an instant, Nat glimpsed something new in the merchant's eyes. He saw fear.

'Bah!' Snatching the reins, Carew put his boot into Billy Burrows. 'Oh get away, you spavined creep!'

'Easy there!' Nat hoisted Billy to his feet. 'There's no call for that.'

The horse stepped up, forcing Nat aside. 'I'll tear through this county, arseworm, like a fire through brushwood, flushing traitors like cock pheasants.' Carew bent low over the beast's haunches. 'Remember, *yeoman*, there are plenty here who'll be mighty pleased to see you brought down.' Nat smelt hot, sour breath. 'Who's buying hereabouts, eh? You bone-headed peasant. Whose writ'll run? And I'll brook no traitors!'

'Now you look here, *Mister* Carew. I don't owe you anything and you're on my land.' Nat's eyes fixed on Carew's newly minted badge, the crescent moon burned into the gelding's rump that, with a shake of his purse, had turned the merchant into a gentleman. 'And here's your answer. You'll not have my arm in any quarrel that's not mine.'

Carew turned in the saddle. 'You're a disobliging, insolent cur. I came for your support as a friend. What flattery!' The horse slipped a few inches, sending chalk screed rattling down the escarpment. 'But I'll have it in any case. Aye, I *will* have it.'

'Will you now? Well, I'm thinking you've no more call on me than I have over this tree. This one, here, the one I just pissed on.' Nat ploughed on. 'Now it's a fine boundary oak. But it grew up inside the wildwood, before your man cut into it.' Where the merchant stood Nat saw the whoreson Bishop and the parasitic she-devil Abbess, even William the Bastard himself. 'That tree marks common land, underwood that's fed and warmed families you robbed. Men'll gladly shake off the yoke of your kind, *Erasmus sodding Carew.*'

Carew found his voice, choked and dry as dust. 'Just watch yourself, Nathanial Salt, or you and your Cheapside fellow'll learn I make a dark and terrible enemy. Cross me, Salt, and your sedition will reap a bitter harvest.' He dug his heals hard into the beast, taking off down the hill.

'That's done it Billy Burrows.' Nat slumped against the wood bank, staring glumly at Carew's dust trail. 'Lord love us, what drew me up this damned hill, eh? No good'll come of it.' Wearily against a reddening sky, he kicked his way back. Halfway down, he stooped to pluck some of the pale crimson betony from the bank. 'Keeps evil from the house, maybe Erasmus Carew, eh? Perhaps I'll send some to Effam.' He grinned at the silent companion shambling at his heels like a spaniel. 'What d'you think, Billy Burrows?'

'Papa!' A girl in white cotton with a bow in her hair and a sturdy miniature yeoman in a leather jerkin clung to his legs like limpets. He ruffled their hair dislodging the bow. 'Oh, Papa, look what you've done.' She readjusted the silk band, preening. 'Aunt Dorothy brought it. From Cheapside, that's in London. *Very* expensive.'

'Lovely princess.' He prised the boy from his leg. 'Off now. Got things to discuss with Uncle Etienne.'

Perched on a staddle stone, Etienne Le Roux was fussing with a long clay pipe. Plainly dressed, the tight hood of his calling, fixed at the throat with drawstrings, made him look like one of the Squire's sporting birds. '*Zut, mon ami,*' Le Roux rose stiffly, 'you've a face as long as a Baptist's sermon!'

'Aye well,' Nat shrugged unhappily, 'had a set-to with the moneybags who's buying up the village.'

'Ah, will that be the whisker-faced pitching pole who wanted to know where you were?'

'That's him, the merchant Carew, raising a regiment of ploughboys for the King's army against Parliament,' said Nat. 'The man called me traitor, brother. Me, a traitor!'

'Then call me traitor, too.' The apothecary tamped the hot bowl of his pipe, drawing air through the shag in short bursts, puffs of blue smoke pressing from the corner of his mouth. 'London's happy day, *mon frère,* when Charles Stuart buggered off.' He grinned, venting smoke through his nostrils. 'Went down to Parliament, he did, to arrest five unquiet members. But they'd long since shipped off downriver.' A version of the story had already been round the parish. '*Le Roi Charles*, he looks across the chamber. "I see the birds have flown," says he, and commands the Speaker to tell him where they were. The old man was having none of it. "Oh, Majesty," he says, "I fear I cannot, for by your leave I've neither eyes to see nor tongue to speak in this place save as the House is pleased to direct me." Well, imagine how he took that!' He jabbed the air with his pipe stem. 'Not well at all! Just think of it *mon ami*, all those Members lining up behind Mr Speaker's pluck, leaping to their feet. "Privilege! Privilege!" they hollered.' He shook his head. 'Can you imagine it, screaming like that, at the *King*?' Nat, still turning over the encounter on the hill, shrugged and said nothing. 'So, Charles gathers his dignity, bangs out of the chamber and takes off round London after the missing gents.' Le Roux snorted. 'Didn't find them, naturally, but made such an arse of himself the City quite took against him.' He sucked noisily at the pipe. 'Within a week King Charles and his French papist wife were shaking the dust of London from the heels of their pretty Parisian slippers. And I say good riddance!'

Nat, chewing on the local consequences of the King's rift with Parliament laid bare on the hillside, was hardly listening.

'Sounds like Mr Carew had you sized up for his company o' foot, *mon frère.*' The merchant waved his pipe at a knot of Nat's farm hands. 'Perhaps he wants these poor boobies too. What d'you say, *mes amis?*' Now Dorothy Le Roux was beating towards him to put a stop to his subversion. 'Will you take up arms in Captain Carew's pitchfork militia? Will you strike the heads from traitors and stick 'em on long spikes at London Bridge to frighten old women, eh?' He glanced sideways at Dorothy. Too much sun and ale she would tell him later. 'And will you watch as Tower crows peck out their eyes and sparrows make nests of their hair, bleached by the sun and the salt of the Thames? Will you do that, eh?'

'No, Sir!' A toothless ploughman staggered to his feet solemnly raising a leather jug. 'But we'll follow Master Nat to the ends of the world. King or Parliament, makes no odds.'

Le Roux put an arm around his wife's tensing midriff. *'Voilà, mon frère,* clay in your hands, once you've cast your hat in one ring or the other.'

'Or neither.' Nat watched the twins bounce across the yard.

'I'm looking at you,' Le Roux shrugged, 'but don't see a royalist with plumes and feathers.'

'Now, that'll do, husband.' Dorothy wriggled free. 'Brother, don't you go listening to hotheads like him.' She shot the apothecary a warning. 'You keep out of this war, Nathaniel Salt. Carew'll cool his heels, you'll see.'

'You mark my sister, Etienne Le Roux.' Nat smiled ruefully. 'She's a well o' wisdom, aye, more than's good for a morte.' He met her scowl with a wink. 'Remember King Charles coming through here, Dorothy?'

'Oh, I do, brother. What a sight!' The young King's progress had been the talk of the parish for years. 'All those gentle mortes in silks and laces. You still got that silver penny?'

'Aye. Mother said it was like touching for the King's evil, only on account, since I wasn't ill.'

'Nathaniel.' She took his arm, abruptly serious. 'Rich men like Carew fill their heads with politics because they've nothing else to mither about. Middling folk, our folk, burgesses, yeomen, godly men *and women*, well, we're different.' Nat saw fear in her eyes. 'Have no part in this war, brother. Wait for the storm to blow out. Storms do you know, even the worst of them.'

Her husband shrugged wearily. 'Aye, *mon ami*, sit tight if you can, live quietly, hold those twins tight.' He shrugged wearily. 'But London's for Parliament and no monarch can last without city money. Gold'll flush the King and his Catholic maw from their Oxford rat-hole, Carew with them.' He dropped his voice conspiratorially. 'Survive this brother and filch Carew's land. Either way, tell me you'll not be seduced by that pig-dog Charles Stuart and his canting cavaliers. A man must be true to his kind.'

A man Dorothy did not trust twitched forward with his opinion. She nudged her husband a warning.

'You should keep your counsel, Sir, if you'll take the advice of a friend.' The gangling, bat-eared relation smiled comfortlessly. 'Carew's man came banging on my door. Wanted to know where I stood.' He passed a ragged sleeve across his nose. 'Well, says I, His Majesty's the Lord's anointed and that's that.'

Nat took the leather jug from his cousin. 'Now, Thomas, off home or we'll be having one of our fallings out, eh?'

'Home?' Thomas belched, waving his arm at the farmhouse. 'This is my sodding home.' He turned on the guests. 'Robbed of our inheritance we were. But I'll get even, you'll see!'

'Etienne, for pity's sake watch your tongue,' hissed Dorothy. 'I'm thinking these days we can't always rely on kin, particularly *that* kin and especially kin that may not be kin at all, if you take my meaning.' Arms folding, she stared daggers at the back of the contested relation. 'Still, who's to say who's born on the wrong side of the blanket?' She glanced anxiously at Nat, sending the thought back to its dark place.

'Grandpa's tribe are all solid, broad-faced coves,' mused Nat.

'All except one,' Dorothy agreed.

'Gossips say half the women in the parish spread their legs for Carew's father.' Nat chewed his lip, eyeing Thomas staggering down the lane. 'Maybe he palmed his tenant off with a bastard?' But he had his own demons, conjured by hushed voices in the dead of night behind his parents' door.

And the demons whispered, '*Who are you?*'

Ignorant of the Salt siblings' anxieties, Le Roux was developing his argument in a circle of blue smoke. 'Look at them, wife, innocents on the brink of catastrophe.' He waved his pipe stem at the revels, rough ale gilding the cadences of his adopted tongue. 'See those pretty maids eyeing up the shallow pool from which it's their poor lot to draw? Dorothy wished he would not drink. 'How many will huddle together in the evening of chaste and bitter spinsterhood, eh? So many inconvenient and unloved old women robbed by war of the warmth of their own hearth, living in shadows under the sufferance of nephews and the grudging, icy charity of wives or, worse, the parish. Eh?'

'Oh, buck up, husband.' Dorothy was feeling the cold, wanting her bed. 'Haven't we enough to mither with pilchards pegged at eight and six a thousand?'

'Well, I said we paid too much for those pilchards, *ma chérie.*' He smiled sadly. 'And where was the sense in shipping indigo at five shillings a pound with London awash with it and all my apothecaries buying at four?' Le Roux shivered theatrically. 'Cold isn't it? I've brought a bevy that'll warm us up, Nat.'

'And don't forget that parcel of wort you made up, husband.' Dorothy, wary of Nat's dark moods that came and went like clouds on a spring day, whispered in his ear. 'And make sure you take it. Shorten the leash on that old black dog, eh?'

Nat put his shoulder to the back door, stamping into the parlour. The cavern was dominated by a stone hearth big enough for a man to stand in. To one side a boxed-in staircase poked through the ceiling to three rooms under the thatch. On the other side a wood-slat door, ajar, led to the kitchen and Ma Rudd's cackling cronies finishing the party.

'Place wants for a woman's touch, brother,' sniffed Dorothy. She trailed a forefinger the length of the heavy oak table leaving a long dark strip. 'See? Wants a cloth, with muscle behind it.' Light shafts danced through dust onto old oak, pewter and brass. 'I'll do what I can whilst I'm here.'

'Don't go on, Dorothy,' Nat groaned. 'Mother Rudd's slowing up with only the girl to help.'

'She'd get a move on if she had a mistress.' Dorothy pulled the kitchen door shut. 'People are talking, Nathaniel.'

He sighed, combing fingers through his hair, waiting for her sermon. 'People do.'

'Twenty-eight next birthday and penned up here without a wife. And showing no signs of getting one, or wanting one. Well, you know.' She folded her arms, mouth pinched, challenging him. 'And don't be wasting your time on that pox-faced morte Euphemia Farrington. Far too posh for the likes of us *and* no spring chicken.' She prepared her broadside. 'There are rumours, you know.'

'What rumours?'

'Oh, stop it, wife. Don't listen to her tittle-tattle, Nat.' Le Roux flipped open a leather satchel. 'Here, this'll raise your spirits.' He gripped the neck of a squat blue glass bottle. 'Quite the thing among the London gentry.' Dorothy scowled at the thick red liquor generously poured. 'Fired wine.' Le Roux tapped his nose. 'Cut with brandy by my Gascon cousins so it travels better. Stronger too. *Bon, n'est-ce pas?*'

'Aye, good.' Nat smacked his lips. 'Like Mother Rudd's elderberry, sweeter though.'

'You keep your parlour brew, Nat.' Le Roux re-filled his own glass, spilling some. 'Here, I've brought one more. Hide it safe to celebrate a young 'un, eh?' He winked lewdly. 'When you've snagged your morte.'

The twins tumbled down the stairs. 'Aggh, they're drinking blood. Is it the King's blood?'

'*Non, mes petites*, for that would be treason.' Le Roux stubbed his finger in the spilt wine. 'But it *is* Mr Carew's.' He dabbed their foreheads like Jesuits on Ash Wednesday. 'And mark it well, for this day you've been bloodied. For Parliament!'

III

The Wildwood

Euphemia Farrington spat shot down the barrel and poured black powder into the pan. Turning the musket in its fork rest, she breathed in. Crack!

The lead ball carried its message in a heartbeat. For an instant, the bailiff Jessop thought it was a miss. Unusual that, and she'd blame him for the weapon. But the lady had no doubt. Sinking to its haunches, her quarry tipped its head, glimpsing the sky one last time through the canopy.

'Good one, lady.' Bloody was, too.

'Wheel-lock's stiff as a board,' she barked. 'Fix it.' Heaving the weapon at the bailiff, she crashed towards the beast. 'Stock needs a drop of linseed too, Joe Jessop. I've splinters in my neck and you to thank for it.'

Stooping low, she stroked the noble head, searching wild eyes like black marbles, hot dying breath against her hand. Now the bailiff was panting at her shoulder leaning low with his knife. 'No.' She snatched the blade and, tenderly, opened the stag's neck, the monarch's blood spilling across the forest floor. 'Want his antlers mounted in the hall, Joe Jessop, on the screen so father sees them from his place.' She stood, wiping blood spots from her face.

'Squire had a few pops at him, y'know.' Jessop eased the wheel-lock, blowing in the pan. 'Ain't nothing wrong with this musket.'

'Father hasn't the eye,' she said casually.

'Right enough, lady,' conceded Jessop. 'Piss-poor shot, the Squire. What'll I do with the carcass?'

'You butcher it, Joe Jessop. I haven't the stomach.' Deftly flicking over the blade, she offered him the pommel. 'Take a haunch to the kitchen. And there's meat for the paupers' hodgepodge if you knock up the beadle.' She straightened her back drinking the cool still air of the forest, cut with the kill.

The bailiff stiffened like a pointer. 'Jessop?' He was unclipping his musket. 'What's up, man?'

'Trouble, lady.' Jessop nodded into the forest, towards the track. 'Carew's men. Big fella's Ezekiel Rich. Young 'un's his brother's boy.'

'Well, now, looks like we've bagged a couple o' poachers.' The braggart Rich was smacking a gnarled club in the palm of his hand. 'What's this, Joe Jessop, thieving with yer doxie now, eh?'

'Watch your tongue in front of a lady arseworm.' Jessop did not see the second ruffian moving in fast.

'Lady, is it?' Rich spat, his accomplice, thick arm round Jessop's neck, hauling the bailiff to the ground. 'All I see's a thieving bastard and a tart dressed like a boy.' Rich clamped his heel on the side of Jessop's head, forcing his face into the bloody leaf mould. 'What's yer name, *boy*?'

'Hold there.' The horseman's face was creased with amusement. 'The lady's name is Euphemia Farrington of Helions, *Effam* Farrington isn't it?' She said nothing. 'Well, I'm your servant, madam.' Erasmus Carew swept off his hat. 'Have I your permission to teach this oaf his manners?' An elegant finger beckoned the man Rich who slunk up, cringing for the blow. The cane came down hard across his shoulders. 'Stand up.' The weapon fell, again and again.

Effam Farrington stepped forward. 'Enough, now, Mr Carew.'

The assailant smiled thinly, uncoiling from his horse. 'Madam.' He jabbed his crop at the stag. 'Your work?'

'Of course.' She retrieved the musket, springing the dog arm to inspect the mechanism and, satisfied, slung the weapon across her shoulder. 'Please have your oaf remove his boot from my man's head.'

'My stag though.'

'Not so.' She was sweetness itself. 'But *you're* trespassing, Mr Carew.'

'A matter of dispute,' smiled Carew.

'If you like,' she shrugged. 'But at least we can share the meat.' She intrigued him, her manner simultaneously disarming and defiant. 'Dine with us, tonight.' Carew raised an eyebrow. 'Dine with us.' She was a clever morte this one, asking him to share his venison at the table of his quarrelsome neighbour. 'Oh dear, Mr Carew, forgive me.' She raised a hand to her face, exploiting his hesitation. 'You think I'm forward, don't you?'

'Yes I do,' said Carew. 'But I'm also thinking of your father's apoplexy, with me at your table.'

'Squire's gone to Westminster.' She screwed her nose. 'My cousin Norrington's staying with me.'

Carew nodded, mounting up. 'I know Tobias Norrington.' He pointed at Jessop moaning on the ground. 'My fellow's made a mess of yours but I think he'll mend, m'dear. If not, I'll find another that'll do just as well.' He picked his way round the bailiff shaking his head, tut-tutting. 'Bad show, bad show.' He bent low with his cane, poking Jessop in the ribs and guts. 'Now, m'dear, is the villain fit to see you home?'

'I see myself through the forest,' she snapped.

He did not doubt it. 'Very well, tonight then.' Carew turned the horse, raising a hand. '*Au revoir,* lady.' Piss poor, ugly as sin. Damn good pedigree though and *convenient.* An alliance would even fix the forest dispute without blood-sucking lawyers. Oh yes, the Farrington girl was worth a second look.

Ezekiel Rich stuck his boot in Jessop's guts. Squatting low, he hissed his venom. 'Next time, whoreson, next time.'

*

She watched him from the solar window, starting up the drive, taking his time, hand on hip, fresh horse, arrogant. 'Where's Mr Norrington?'

'In bed and snoring, madam.' The maid Sarah screwed her nose. 'Sleeping off the master's brandy wine.'

'Good.' She had told her cousin to be ready for eight and sent a note to Carew for seven. 'I'll be a painted courtesan if the county's busy bodies get it into their small minds that Euphemia Farrington's taken to dining alone with gentlemen. Mr Norrington'll save my reputation, but he needn't be conscious!'

Crossing the shallow moat with its little stone bridge, ducks and weed, Erasmus Carew scanned Helions' wrinkled facade. 'Ah, the old families, how studied they are in their neglect,' he mused. The slab-faced Carew mansion was going up as fast as his pockets filled with money from the teaming port of Bristol. New money. Helions spoke of antiquity and legitimacy, a heady brew that had not yet reached the thin lips of the trade-rich Carews.

'Welcome to Helions, Mr Carew.' Effam curtsied, Sarah behind her.

Dismounting, Carew tossed the reins at the boy. 'It's a fine evening, lady, and your house is looking grand.' She less so, he thought, though she had scrubbed up well. But had she been as alluring as her house she would be married, not flirting with a middle-aged widower from a questionable family.

She led him through the screen into the great hall, a space he had not seen for a decade. It looked shabbier. He guessed forty foot long, half as much wide and high, half panelled in plain linen-fold oak with a screen forming the passage and a gallery above. Shallow hipped roof, carved beams and bosses, simple plaster tracery, all very restrained. High up on the right, four arched windows and, opposite, on either side of a great stone fireplace, oriel windows with groined stone ceilings, a later addition, floor to ceiling. A predictable manor house, he mused, nestling in the bosom of its acres.

'Glass of sack, Mr Carew?' He noted the long oak table, black with age, its unfashionable deep carved high back chairs, all set for dinner at the near end of the hall. She drew him to the stone fireplace with its delicate spandrels and dusty filling of herbs and wild flowers. Old chairs and settles, poorly stuffed, set round the dormant hearth and two watchful lurchers. Carew counted three places at the table.

'Norrington's in his room.' She hastily plumped an oversize tapestry cushion coving a tear in the largest settle. 'He's, um, indisposed.'

'Ah, Tobias had a skin-full, eh?' Taking a glass from Sarah, Carew selected the settle and made a show of pulling together the edges of the ripped fabric. 'Your furniture's spilling it's stuffing like a cockbird's entrails madam.' He sipped, scanning the Farrington nest. Portraits, bits of armour, swords, guns, the sedimentary layers of a family as old as the Conquest, God rot them. His house contained the same sort of things, better things actually, but there was the rub. His stuff was a job lot from another man's estate. Erasmus Carew's eyes flicked between the lady and the portraits lining the hall, the Farrington stable book in oils, hatchet-jawed military men. Their descendant turned out dog-ugly, of course, but under those skirts he would likely find comfort on a cold winter's night. And in the bedroom with the candles snuffed out a face like a monkey's fist wouldn't matter, would it? Sooner have a doxy that looked like a dog but would whelp well than a fancy piece with doe eyes and an empty womb. Euphemia Farrington had the look of a morte that would pop sons like she was shelling peas from a pod.

She saw Norrington swaying at the screen. 'Damnation.'

'Ah.' Carew was on his feet. 'Tobias, how are you?'

'The better for seeing you, Erasmus.' A jowly bull of a man, around thirty, all bugger's bars and broken veins, loped towards Carew, getting as far as the drink. 'Here Carew, Farrington's wine ain't much better than badger piss but what's a man to do, eh?'

Effam beckoned the girl Sarah. 'Now we'll eat.' Norrington was making for the head of the table. 'That's my place,' she hissed. 'You're there.'

Carew's lips twitched. He was enjoying her company and the possibilities fitting together in his mind.

'Whole thing's beyond me, Carew,' belched Norrington.

'Oh, how's that?' Carew was plucking white doeskin gloves from his slender hands. She noted the delicate floral motifs picked out in gold and silver.

'Well, half my neighbours with the King, the other half with Parliament. Country's split like a withy and nobody knows why.' Norrington tipped wine from the glass and food from his mouth.

'King Charles is God's anointed, remember,' sighed Carew. 'Parliament'll bend the knee, or answer on Judgement Day. '

'What's that?' Norrington wagged a finger. 'You're forgetting Edgehill. Eh?'

Carew sucked his teeth. 'Edgehill was the very touch paper of war.' The battle, though indecisive, had left 3000 dead and smashed the King's aura of invincibility. 'Each man must now declare for himself. Where'll you stand Tobias Norrington, in this war between brothers?'

'At home, Sir, minding my business.' He tapped his nose. 'Until we see which way the wind's blowing.' He shook his head, chops swinging. 'But here's the thing, Carew, after Edgehill we all know, don't we?' He grinned at Effam. 'Charles Stuart, well, he ain't the Conqueror, is he?'

'Have a care, Norrington,' snarled Carew. 'Remember my commission.'

'Ah yes, raising county gents in support of the King. Well, I'm hearing it ain't going too well, old boy. Reckon they're watching and waiting, like me. But after Edgehill...'

Carew snorted like a mare on a hot day. 'A pox on all rebels.'

'Cousin Farrington's declared for Parliament.' Norrington supported his big head in his hands. 'So, you're supping at a rebel's table. Y'know that?'

'Well, Tobias, I'm thinking gentlemen should conduct themselves decorously however they're fixed politically.' Carew was tapping the bowl of a serving spoon into his palm with a thud, eyeing the demur, confident woman at the head of the table. His interest in her was fermenting like a barrel of ripe cider apples. 'And when this *unpleasantness* has passed Miles Farrington and I will still pass the time of day, as we do now.' As candlelight danced on the portraits of her ancestors he imagined what she might have been if the smallpox had not made such a mess.

She smiled at him sardonically. 'You mean grudgingly, through gritted teeth.' Eyes black as sloes drilled hers. 'Or do you mean it at all, Mr Carew?' The gathering storm carried risk for the old families but opportunity for his type; fast, new men busting with ambition. It chilled and intrigued her.

Carew said nothing, simply raising the claret to his lips on which, she noticed, a thin residue had formed. Sinister. Tapping the glass against his teeth, he was eyeing her like a sow on a quarter day, though she knew he would not know one end of a pig from another.

Sarah passed between the diners with the wine, her skirts whispering across the flagstones. Carew noticed her – pretty thing. Farrington' tannic wine was beginning to warm him and, stroking his lip, he began to undress the lady. High born bints like her blushed and set their eyes in their laps. They did not go measure for measure. But this one did.

Effam was wondering if she could live with the man, share his bed. She tried to imagine it. He was hardly a beau. She noted the over-large signet ring with its crisp crescent moon device. Effam's withers remained stubbornly unwrung by Mr Erasmus Carew.

There was, of course, a man she felt drawn to, physically, just one. Sarah brought snatches of village gossip about the yeoman of Brook Farm, packaged as small talk, watching for her ears to prick. But there was no good in it. Erasmus Carew was rich and available and that was that. And what he wanted was plain as a pikestaff. He was computing sons she could bear him (since men always want more) and the social advantage of absorbing the last Farrington into his ascendancy. For such a man could not resist the elusive lick of old money, in her case perilously little of it but what there was very old indeed.

And what did she want? A wise woman peddling homilies at the kitchen door once said war quickens the menses, said it was nature's way. All she knew was that she wanted children, above all, children before time robbed her of the opportunity. Three strapping sons trooping after Carew in church on a Sunday were testament to his qualities in that respect. Oh, and she wanted money, enough to pay off the moneylenders and, after her father, preside unencumbered at Helions. She wanted to see her children dance and caper in the hall of their ancestors.

Dim-witted Norrington was reviving. 'Edgehill, what, what?'

She sighed. 'Oh, do be quiet, cousin.' Carew was how old, forty? Job done, he might not live long. Think of it, a wealthy widow, *with children*. Better than an impoverished old maid in a Salisbury alms-house. She would have to endure the act of course. But that would be preferable to a wedding night with Tobias heaving and slobbering, and if she closed her eyes....

Norrington's watery gaze lobbed between the two. 'Need a piss.' The oaf rose unsteadily, heading for the midden.

'Poor Tobias,' sighed Carew, picking his teeth. Pushing his chair from the table, stretching long, thin limbs, he smiled predatorily. 'It's a fine, clear evening for a stroll by the moat.' He was on his feet, slapping the doeskin gloves in his palm. 'Will you walk with me, lady?'

She chewed her lip, turning over his loaded invitation. 'Aye, Sir, I rather think I will.'

IV

Sat on the edge of his bed, there was just enough moonlight for Nat to read the letter Dorothy had brought from London.

Cheapside 14 May 1643

Dear Nat,

I hope you're well.

Uncle Abiel says I did fine at the wedding standing in for you but it was a trial for me with Etienne Le Roux inviting so many of his grand friends.

Brother Etienne's a godly man who keeps the Sabbath and helps the poor. It's a good match even if he's near twice her age. She'll see him right for you know her way with figures and things.

Etienne's mighty vexed by riving Dutchmen and Turkey pirates in the narrow seas. Says his ship can't stick its nose out of Harwich for fear of being struck off. If only our Protestant cousins in Holland stopped messing with our herring boats off the Dogger and turned on the Barbary pirates we'd be alright.

Abiel Biles reckons the troubles will be the ruin of his foreign trade. But here's the odd thing brother – our uncle Abiel gets richer as all others in the trade fail, even landing up in the Clink with their debts. Why do you think that is?

Anyway, I've joined the militia got up to defend London against Laudians and the King's evil counsellors, God rot them. After the Edgehill and Turnham Green fights we must all make ready.

Our company has a red banner the size of a coverlet that says Jehovah Providebit. It means God will provide.

I sail on the evening tide aboard uncle's ship Deliverance. She's fast, well armed and insured.

God rest you dear Nat and may the Lord keep you. Remember brother – Jehovah Providebit.

Your loving brother,

Edward

Whatever had passed between their parents in this room had sent Edward to London and limited Nat's horizon to Salisbury market on a quarter day. Cursing the birthright of a yeoman's elder son, he fingered the twist of bitter herbs, Etienne's potion to bring the black dog to heel. *Twenty-eight next birthday and penned up here without a wife.* Dorothy's bolt had hit its mark. *And don't be wasting your time on that pox-faced morte Euphemia Farrington.*

Nat closed his eyes, whispering the Lord's prayer, but Le Roux's wine and the wort made the room buck and his guts heave. He reached for the piss pot.

*

'Look out!' Squire Farrington's coach crashed down the lane forcing Nat's household into the hedgerow. He glimpsed Effam in a heartbeat.

'There's one no better than she should be.' Dorothy plucked twigs from her church clothes.

'What?'

Dorothy pursed her lips. 'You haven't heard?' She glanced over her shoulder. 'Well, you know I'm not one for gossip brother, but that Effam Farrington has a *reputation.*' Nat stared blankly. 'You tell him, Mrs Rudd.'

Ma Rudd was regretting the elderberry wine that had loosened her tongue to Dorothy. 'Well, nothing definite, mind,' she wheezed. 'Only my sister helps out at the big house, see.' Nat waited. 'Well, apparently, the Lady Euphemia's taken to entertaining men folk, when Squire's away in London.' She shrugged, adjusting her lace cap. 'Anyway, the goings-on at the manor have got around and that's why she's not hitched already. No man wants a morte that's already been bedded, especially one with a face like a sow's arse.'

*

The benefice of St James at Hinton Helions had two patrons. The first, Sidney Sussex College Cambridge, cauldron of the righteous, had spawned the new Rector, the Reverend Daniel Markham. But obscure country livings generated little income and a lot of bother. So the Fellows relied on the second advowson, the manor lord, who by happy chance was a member of the college: Miles Farrington, magistrate and Member of Parliament for Hinton.

Farrington had gone up in 1616 with an obscure scrap of the shabby gentry, Oliver Cromwell, both lamenting declining families. By the time Farrington left Cambridge, the cloth-rich Carews had begun acquiring the mortgages on his land.

But it was still Squire Farrington and Effam in the front pew on the right. Carew and his three sons filled the corresponding left hand rank below the pulpit, the arrangement forcing them to crick their necks to glimpse imperfectly Farrington's placeman the Reverend Markham.

Further back the seating arrangements were causing discomfort of a different sort.

'What's she doing there?' fumed Dorothy Le Roux. The clerk Jeremiah Norris had installed himself in the Salt pew with his new wife.

'Dorothy, don't go on.' Nat disliked standing on dignity. 'She's been planting herself there for a while. Mother Rudd had a quiet word.' He sighed heavily. 'Apparently Mistress Norris believes she's as good as anyone and will sit where she damned well pleases.'

'Brother, where's your shame?' Dorothy boiled. 'You'll have to move them,' she hissed. 'Now, or we'll leave.'

Nat peered into the shadows at the back of the church where the usual collection stood, patiently, for the weekly ordeal. There was poor Billy Burrows, twitching quietly by the font, alone because of the stink. Nat waved him over. The poor sap hobbled across, pathetically grateful. Dorothy raised her nosegay, Nat issuing his instructions. 'Now, Billy, I want you to sit in my place and keep Mrs Norris company. Do that for me and there'll be ale and a bit of mutton for your supper. Yes?' The mute's twisted face broke into a gummy parody of a smile.

The Norris woman's shriek shattered the congregation. All eyes turned on Billy Burrows grinning at his victim, a malodorous cloud blanketing the contested place.

Laughter rippled through the church. 'Reckon that's job done. We'll have our place back next week.' Salt folded his arms, nodding at the absurd little man swinging round ruddy faced. Norris must know who had done it or there would be no point. 'Meanwhile Mrs Norris will have to endure Ned for two hours of Markham.'

Two hours became three. Markham, crow-like in a carved tree, glared at the sea of pale upturned faces, pinning the Norris couple. 'Colossians chapter three, verse 18: *Wives submit yourselves unto your husbands as it is fit in the Lord.* And the prophet Isaiah chapter three verses 16 to 17; *Moreover the Lord saith, because the daughters of Zion are haughty and walk with stretched forth necks and wanton eyes, walking and mincing as they go, and making a tinkling with their feet: Therefore the Lord will smite with a scab the crown of the head of the daughters of Zion, and the Lord will discover their secret parts.* Scolds will be punished in this life, but pity their husbands. Oh yes, for they'll answer on judgement day!'

But there was a much bigger fish to fry than Jeremiah Norris. Markham gripped the parapet of his eyrie, knuckles whitening. 'And brothers, there are those that do wild Moorish dancing and May Poles and lewd, drunken Whitsun-ales.' He had practised this moment from the day of his induction. 'Popery, idolatry, *fornication.*' Spittle-flecked Daniel Markham was bringing his tirade to its rabid, dangerous climax. A long forefinger, fired towards the north window, quivered with rage. 'And that *blasphemy's* nothing but the devil's work!'

Carew had no need to shift his gaze from the pulpit. He knew Markham's fury was directed at the glazed image of the Madonna and Child installed in his father's memory. And he did not have to look for the author of his discomfort. Yes, of course, the inscrutable Miles Farrington was very much enjoying the theatre of his firebrand priest.

'Satan stalks this land sowing his popish superstition, stoking the flames of hell for those that profess it.' Markham trained his black eyes on the parvenu Carew. 'Yea, even as the acolytes of bloody Queen Mary are burning now for the agonies of Protestant martyrs. I say to each, regardless of estate, to each without distinction, turn to the true religion or burn in hellfire, commoner – *or King!*'

A gasp like wind through rushes swept the congregation. The Vicar of Hinton Helions had attacked God's anointed King of England.

'So,' muttered Carew to his eldest son, 'the puritan storm ripping our country apart has finally reached Hinton and Farrington's ten pound priest is its disciple.' He patted the youth's shoulder. 'Come on.' Carew stepped into the aisle, clawing the ornately carved finial at the end of his pew. Bowing deeply at the altar, he turned his back on Markham to address the astounded congregation. 'All those that speak treason against the Lord's anointed, even in this holy place, will answer for it. And the penalty for treason is death.' His footfalls on the hard encaustic tiles echoed through the church followed by the rustle of his family and followers.

*

'Disgraceful,' hissed Farrington in Effam's ear. 'If your mother had found you entertaining that whoreson in my house, you'd have been horse-whipped.'

'You make me out to be some doxie, father.' It was the first time they had spoken since Farrington returned to Helions and news of the dinner party. 'You know very well Norrington was there, Sarah too.'

'Well what about poor Jessop, eh?' carped Farrington. 'Whipped by Carew's cat pizzle in *my* forest.' Joe Jessop had been milking his injuries. 'Markham says your dalliance with Erasmus Carew's all round the village. Well?'

There was a rustle of taffeta behind. Effam cursed ear-wigging matrons, dropping a hand to her father's knee. 'He's rich and sires males.'

'Pah!' Farrington hugged his arms.

'Well, maybe it hasn't occurred to you father but the prospects for your line are retreating faster than Darius from Alexander.'

'I'd sooner have you spliced with the midden-man,' snapped Farrington.

'How about Tobias Norrington?' She whispered sweetly. 'Yes, maybe I'll rut with him.'

'Oh, do as you please.' Enviously, he eyed Carew's sturdy sons leaving the church. 'You always do. Like your mother.' Miles Farrington also had a plan, though one that would raise his late wife from the dead. No tongues would wag over an alliance with Carew. Effam could easily stoop to this merchant with a purse deep enough to justify the thinning of her bloodline. But the match Miles Farrington had in mind would be a scandal.

'Huh!' Effam resented the comparison. 'Where are the young men mother said would come sniffing like boars round a sow on heat then father? Tell me that?' She wove her arm into his, patting his hand. 'Come, now.'

In the porch Farrington took the parson's arm. 'God's blood, Reverend, hope Bishop doesn't get wind of *that* lecture!' He turned to the yeomen filing out. 'Bloody good sermon!'

Released from parish communion and fired up by the parson's rant, the village lads had begun destroying Carew's window. Farrington hung back. 'Ah, Nathaniel Salt, can I have a word with you?' The Squire took Nat's arm. 'What an extraordinary performance, by Carew.'

'Never seen the like, Sir,' Nat agreed. 'But he was provoked.'

'A *gentleman* keeps his temper.' Farrington steered him through the tilting headstones. 'What d'you think of Markham's sermon?'

'Didn't like it, Sir. No, not one bit,' said Nat. 'Reverend gentleman was plain cruel. Cruel to poor Norris, I mean.'

'Norris?' Farrington sighed. 'Oh, yes, of course, Norris. But what about Carew?'

After the hillside encounter with Erasmus Carew, Nat was not about to be drawn into a feud between the gentry. 'Mr Carew can answer for himself. Norris can't.'

'Quite.' Farrington was not interested in Norris. 'But why d'you think I appointed Mr Markham?'

'Don't know, Sir.' He tipped his head at the smashed window. 'But I don't hold with that.'

Farrington cleared his throat. 'Markham's views were too much even for Cambridge. Giving him refuge in Hinton Helions means I've trumpeted my politics as clearly as Carew with his piece of theatre today.' Farrington turned to face the farmer. 'And now I'm wondering where the master of Brook Farm stands in the matter of the King?'

Nat shrugged and looked away, preparing his evasion. 'He came here once, the King.'

'Yes, twenty years ago.' Farrington rubbed his chin. The royal party had fallen on Helions House like a plague of locusts. 'You've a good memory Nat.'

'Not every day a King trots past your gate,' said Nat. 'Father snatched my cap off, forced me to my knees, pushed my head down. But I squinted up at this young man on a dark horse. I remember his face like it was yesterday – a narrow face, it was, with a sharp nose.' If he could keep it up perhaps the Squire wouldn't press him like Carew on the hill. 'But y'know what I remember most, Sir?' I remember the King was sad, so very sad. Mother said I wasn't to be so daft because, what with palaces and horses and all, Kings must be the happiest people alive. D'you think I was daft Squire?'

'No, Nat but…'

'Well, the King leans over, low across the horse's neck. "What's your name lad?" he says. "Nat, Sir, Nathaniel Salt, your honour," says I. "Well Nat Salt, here's a keepsake with my head on it. Remember, eh?" Then he tosses me the coin and they were gone with only the dust to say they had ever been.'

Farrington laid a pinch of snuff at the base of his thumb. 'That same King's been parleying from his Oxford rat hole with Frenchmen, papists and Irish cut-throats; plotting against his Parliament, the people and the true religion.' Farrington sniffed noisily, one nostril and the next. 'England hangs in the balance.'

'Sir, you know me. I'm a yeoman, that's all. And there'll be the harvest to bring in. Lords knows it's been hard enough these past years.' He stared at his feet in the rich moss. 'My brother-in-law, that's him with my young 'uns at the gate, he weighs my situation and says I'm Parliament's man for sure. But I've no time for politics.'

'Obscurity's the luxury of women and mute addle-pate peasants cowering in hovels, not the yeomen of England,' Farrington hissed. 'Too many good men died at the Edgehill bloodbath last October for that. I'm thinking by Lammas day all men who want to look their sons in the eye must be resolved – for King or Parliament.' The Squire drew Nat conspiratorially behind a flying buttress. 'You know Carew's been sent by King Charles to raise a cavalry troop in the south of the county?'

'Yes Sir. Invited me to join his company, or whatever you call it. He was very persuasive, Sir.'

'And were you persuaded?' Nat winced. Digging his cane into the moss, the Squire leant back against the buttress. 'No, of course not.'

Nat nodded at the twins playing among the headstones. 'Sir, I must go.'

Farrington turned, sneezing into a square of red cotton, wondering if he had the measure of the man. 'Sir William Waller, General Waller, wants soldiers for Parliament's army.' He shrugged. 'Felt sure I could rely on you.'

'Squire, my musket's for bagging a coney for the pot or a fox in the hen-house.' Nat shuffled awkwardly, treading a glass shard into the turf. 'Not some poor bugger caught in a fight between his betters.'

Farrington was picking at crenulated medallions of yellow-white lichen on the wall, absently easing a fingernail beneath the plaques. 'You're more than you think, Nat. But I won't press you, not now.' He turned, gently squeezing Nat's arm. 'Just promise me, when the storm breaks, you'll call on me. Promise me that, Nathaniel Salt?'

Nat beamed in his broad, good-natured way, as pleased as a fingerling slipped from the hook. 'Aye Sir, I will that.'

'Ah, here you are.' Effam appeared at her father's side. 'Oh, and here's Mr Salt.' Affecting disappointment, the antidote to a beating heart, she gave Nat the very hint of a smile.

Blood burned his cheeks. She had him squirming, a fumbling adolescent wrestling with a tithe barn of awkwardness that put her beyond reach. Now she was mocking him. He contorted a bow.

Effam's mouth twitched as she began to press the Squire back to the path. If only her head could allow some license to the secrets of her heart. But she was Euphemia Farrington, last of her line. It did not matter that the yeoman she teased before leaving for London and the smallpox had her now, with barely a word, swooning like a love-sick milkmaid. Nobody would see and that was all that mattered. 'According to my maid Sarah,' she whispered to Farrington with a half glance back at Nat, 'wittering in her revolting earthy peasant way, that Adonis in broadcloth is the damp delight of the parish. Reckons village matrons with daughters to settle think he's the bull's eye, the dog's bollocks, even with two children snapping at his heels.' But Sarah could not say why the man remained a widow, impervious to her giggling associates, pug-faced farmer's daughters in the main. 'Maybe he's got the hots for another,' Sarah had opined, far from casually.

'Oops!' A small boy bowled into Effam. 'Sorry, miss.'

'You're the lady Euphemia,' challenged Eliza. 'Do you like my ribbon?'

'Away now both of you.' Nat twitched his head towards the gate. 'Don't bother Miss Farrington.'

Effam saw the pride in his smiled apology. 'You like pretty things?' Eliza nodded solemnly. 'Would you like this?' She looked at Nat. 'It's just a fairground trifle. I hope it's alright?' She unclipped the tin brocade from her skirt and pinned it to the muslin of the girl's dress.

Eliza looked at her father and then, adoringly, at her benefactrix. 'Do you like my Papa? Aunt Dorothy says he needs a wife.'

'Eliza!' Nat felt the blood throbbing in his temples. 'Miss Farrington, I *am* sorry.' The girl smiled winsomely, skipping away to brag about the broach.

Effam hid a smile. 'We should leave, father.' She looked anxiously towards the churchyard wall. 'Sounds like there's more rough business afoot.'

Ma Rudd wheezed down the path. 'It's a skimmity-ride got up by the Reverend's rant. That Master Norris, he's got longer horns than our old cow!' The old servant had not forgiven the Norris couple for squatting in the Salt family pew. 'Time that man controlled his wife and her fancy ways. Everyone says so.'

Nat combed a hand through his thick mane. 'Oh, let them be, for goodness' sake.'

The parson's hectoring had whipped up a dozen parishioners from the shadows at the back of the church. Having smashed the Carew window, they were now turning on Norris. A pair of ram's horns mounted on a pole bobbed above the church wall to shrieks and beaten kettles and pans. Hanging on the coat-tails of the tawdry procession, the diminutive Reverend Markham was hopping like a black crow.

'This isn't right.' Nat appealed to the Squire.

'I agree.' Farrington stroked his chin. 'You sort it out Nat.'

'Hell's teeth!' Nat turned on his heels, stamping through the lynch gate and past village wives at their thresholds enjoying the day's second defenestration. 'Reverend, Sir, your sermon's done this.' Norris's pale face appeared fleetingly at his window before the first stone flew. 'Speak up Sir, won't you? Poor sap doesn't deserve this.'

Reverend Markham waved a finger. 'Colossians 3 verse 18...'

'Yes, Sir, you used the Apostle in your sermon.' Markham was bending scripture to terrorise Norris. 'But Paul says in verse 25; *He that doeth wrong shall receive for the wrong which he hath done and there is no respect of persons.*'

Scowling, Markham scampered after the ram's horn posse striking off down the passage to lay siege to the cottage from the back.

'Come on, Norris, let's be having yer, useless streak of piss.'

Norris was at his threshold, white as a sheet, eyeing the protesting donkey being edged forward. And there was graceless Thomas Salt, in the thick of it. Nat's heart sank. 'Get away, Thomas, you oaf.'

Waving a bottle, Thomas grinned stupidly, spinning round to torment the Norris couple. 'You stay put, missus. But your man'll learn his manners!' The woman flinched as the bottle smashed against her home. Grabbing Norris' collar, Thomas forced him against the ill-tempered donkey. 'Up and face its arse or it'll give you a right good kicking.' The Skimmity ride moved off towards the green, shame and bitterness in Norris's eyes fixing Nat like a lamped rabbit.

Nat was back at the schoolroom. He was the child alone at the window watching helplessly, horrified, fascinated. In the corner of the yard, his cousin, Thomas Salt, trousers down, standing in piss. His tormenters showed no mercy.

'Stick him, the lanky bastard. Bastard'

'Look 'e's pissed himself. Ha! Ha!'

'You're a bastard, ain't you Thomas Salt?' A cuff to the head. 'Ain't you?

'Bend over, Salt, you whoreson.' The larger thug came at him with a bat. 'Say, it piss-head, Thomas Salt's a bastard!'

Through stick legs Thomas saw Nat, guilt-ridden, in silent, helpless witness to his shame, and hated him. 'Thomas Salt's a bastard,' the boy sobbed. 'I'm a bastard.'

Spilling out of the Lamb and the Angel, drinkers were enjoying the spectacle. Nat grabbed Thomas Salt. 'Stop this, cousin.'

'Sod off, *cousin*.' Thomas shook free. 'Remember who started it.'

'Markham did!'

'No, fool, you did, setting Billy Burrows on 'em in church. Eh?' With a yelp, Norris was in the horse trough and Thomas was punching hard. 'That'll sodding learn you!'

'That's enough!' Nat seized his collar, spinning him round. Thomas raised his fist, taking Nat's full in the face.

Thomas staggered back dabbing blood. 'I'll sodding kill you, Nathaniel Salt.' Nat's fist raised again, he turned and ran, laughing accomplices rolling away towards the Angel.

'Here,' said Nat, hand outstretched.

'Bugger off,' snarled Norris, struggling out of the water.

Nat watched him slink away. 'What's that poor man done to deserve such a drubbing?'

'Apart from allowing his missus to pinch *our* pew?' Dorothy was unsympathetic. 'Well, it's rough village justice Nathaniel, but a man must be ruler in his own house.

Nat sucked his teeth. 'D'you rule yours Etienne?'

Dorothy's elbow silenced Le Roux. 'Old Mother Rudd says we need a cucking stool for the likes of Mistress Norris with a pond to dunk her in. And she's right!'

Clouds, glowering black, sped behind the church tower where the sexton and his boy were already boarding up Carew's broken window. 'Weather's changing,' said Nat. Hinton Helions had taking a cruel turn. He felt the lowering menace of it, cold and portentous like the first gale of winter. 'We're in for a storm.'

V

'What with the world turned upside down and no good likely to come of it, a poor body hardly knows what to do, or what to think.' Mother Rudd poured another beaker of elderberry wine, shaking her head mournfully at the twins and the girl Emma across the kitchen table. 'Yer daddy'll be home soon, sweet hearts.'

There were hooves on cobbles, lots of them. 'Who's that then?' Mother Rudd hauled herself up. 'Ain't your pa, Lord love us.' She was at the window, screwing her eyes in the fading light. 'Aw, it's that good-for-nothing Ezekiel Rich.' Carew's henchman was swinging into the yard with his thugs. 'Say nothing, let nobody in,' she rasped at the girl, hauling her aching bones up the stairs to hide the twins. Crouched low in the eaves, she followed the villains closely. 'Keep still now, dears, and quiet as mice.'

'Salt, you whoreson, show yerself!' Rich, very drunk, had his orders.

The girl Emma cracked open the window. 'There ain't nobody in, Master Rich, Sir. Them's all away to Sarum, see, an' I'm to let no one in, 'specially soldiers.' She slammed the casement shut.

'Well, missy, yer master shouldn't 'ave left a milky maid on picket duty, eh boys?' Belching, swaying in the saddle, newly attested Ezekiel Rich. 'Right lads, kick 'is door in.'

Emma had spirit. Slipping the dogs, she seized a fire-iron pointing it at the door as it splintered. The great, grey beasts, paced the flagstones snarling, but kept their distance.

'I hate dogs.' Rich steadied himself at the door. A man cocked and fired, folding the first beast. The iron fell, clattering to the flagstones. The trooper fired again flaying the second animal's rump, its hind quarters collapsing in gore that washed black against the grey stones.

Rich turned on the girl. Through her fingers Emma saw his gormless kinsman, the scar-faced Jethro Rich and Robert Mann, another scraping from the village. 'Where's me brother's boy?' Jethro edged forward. 'Here he is! Didn't yer old uncle say he'd rid the family o' virgins by

Lamastide?' Nodding at the girl, he leered at the youth. 'There, sow your oats in Salt's doxie dell. Pox free, fresh as a spring meadow.'

Rich lunged at Emma, hissing in her ear. 'Be nice to 'im and you'll be alright.' In her sanctuary Mother Rudd covered her charges' ears and prayed. Jethro gulped, fumbling hopelessly. 'Come on, do it, you cocknocker.' Rich's lip curled. ''Ere boys, 'e can't manage it!' He pulled Jethro off. 'Had yer chance, queer boy! Come on, Robert Mann, show us a real *man*.'

The slobbering peasant was spent before he could touch her. Finding her strength, Emma brought her legs up hard. Mann gave an unearthly groan, creasing up, gasping for air. 'Bitch!' Fists clenched, purple with rage he smashed into the girl.

The maid fell back hard against the oak board, Mann arching across, poised to strike. 'Bitch!' Again and again he pulped her pretty face, pulling back sucking his knuckles. Now her head flopped towards the assailant, big eyes fixed and reproachful.

'Jesus, Robert Mann, *Jesus*,' Jethro spluttered, eyes fixed on the corpse. 'You'll swing for sure, sick bastard.' The murderer's bowels turned to water, supper joining the dogs' gory mess.

'Now then, there'll be none o' that.' Ezekiel Rich was sobering up fast, pointing at the brands in the hearth. 'I want the place fired.' He looked around. The girl had said she was alone, hadn't she? 'And not a word about this *accident*. Right lads?' The drop-jawed ruffians nodded. 'Look sharp now.'

As the fire-setters saddled up, the flames were already making easy work of the tinder-dry wattle and daub.

Below the thatch, Old Ma spied the horsemen pulling away. 'Not long now, dears.' But the twins began to cough, smoke inching under the door. 'Dear God.' She threw open the casement, screaming into the night. 'Fire!'

From the henhouse, poor Billy Burrows watched in wide-eyed horror. Twisting into the yard, crouching low, he began to rock, hands pressed against his ears.

'Billy Burrows, that you?' Mother Rudd was leaning out of the tiny window now, smoke billowing. 'Dear man, for the love of God!'

Billy knew he must save Old Mother Rudd and the twins, rescue them for Mr Salt. But the box staircase was already in flames. At the top through heat and smoke he spied the old woman, children pulled close. Blindly he forced the fired stairs, falling back, flesh charred. Now Mother Rudd was lifting Eliza, shrieking at him above the cacophony. 'Catch her, Billy, for pity's sake.' She prised the last plump finger from her arm and the bundle fell screaming towards him. He fell to his knees, feeling for her. 'God love you, Billy Burrows' rasped the old woman, hoisting Nicholas. Billy held out his arms. He would be ready this time.

Crack! An oak brace split taking away the stairs. When Billy looked again, Ma Rudd and the boy were gone. Blinded, he pawed the ground; he would save the girl for Mr Salt. Crack! Another beam exploded, crashing down. Heaving, he tumbled into the sweet air at the moment the upper floor collapsed with a roar. Sobbing gently, noble Billy Burrows hauled himself towards the wooded hill above the field.

*

'King's soldiers do not rape.' The elegant figure turned his gelding to face the wretch standing cap in hand. 'They do not butcher women.' Slowly, he raised a gloved hand at Robert Mann, index finger like a dart. 'There's a field punishment for what you've done.' Carew lent down, hissing in Ezekiel Rich's jaw-dropped face. 'Do it now, or the constable will and you'll join him.' Rich's mouth opened and shut but the only sound was a low moan from the condemned man, pissing himself. 'God's blood.' Carew seized the bridle and reins from Rich's horse and with his sword cut and knotted the leather straps. Freezing the prisoner like a snake pinning a mouse, he dangled the makeshift noose. 'Round your neck.'

Blubbing, Robert Mann did as he was told. Carew took a soft, silken cloth from his saddlebag, pressing it between the noose and the youth's skin. Pulling the slip knot firm, he led Mann to the unbridled horse. 'Up!' Carew bound his wrists, bringing the beast under the bough of the boundary oak. 'You boy.' Jethro Rich jolted from his stupor. 'Shin along that bough.' Rich inched along the branch until he sat above the condemned man, catching the rope's end. 'Tie it off, quickly now.' He made the rope fast. 'God have mercy.' Carew laid the flat of his sword across the beast's rump. The leather snapped tight, Mann's bulging eyes on the smoking scene of his crime. Carew stepped forward quickly to pull down hard and strong, snapping the second cervical vertebra like a twig.

Carew, turning his back on the corpse, squinted at the farmhouse. 'Thank God there was no one home,' he muttered, pulling his beard, 'apart from the maid.' Ezekiel Rich looked over his shoulder at the ruin, the dead girl's reassurance ringing in his head; *There ain't nobody in, Master Rich, Sir. Them's all away to Sarum, see.* 'That's right ain't it Rich?'

'Aye Sir,' spluttered Rich. 'The maid said they'd all gone to town.'

'But, Ezekiel', lisped Thomas Salt, 'I met my cousin on the Sarum road.' He turned to Carew. 'Nathaniel Salt, Sir, was quite alone.'

*

Nat on the drove road catching the red glow above his home dug his heels in hard. What he found was a charred shell.

'Dear boy.' Squire Farrington was exhausted. 'Done everything we could. Christ's blood, I'm sorry.'

'Twins?' Reverend Markham mumbling at the wreckage and the Squire's hard man Joe Jessop sobbing like a child gave him the answer. 'Where are they?' Nat looked around like he had stumbled into a moralistic play, the sort put on outside the cathedral on a quarter day to frighten sinners.

Farrington looked away, gulping, shaking his head. 'The men found four; two children. With everything so dry, these things, well, I mean, a spark from the fire, a candle...' He put a hand on Nat's shoulder, squeezing gently. 'God's wounds man. I am so, so sorry.'

One by one the men drifted away, heads bowed, taking the news to waiting wives. Nat nodded dumbly. The chaos of Brook Farm was no mummer's play, forgotten by the nearest alehouse. He sank to his knees and howled at the sky.

*

Nat's vigil was broken at dawn by the watchman down from the hill. Billy Burrows, burns bound with dock leaves, looked for a way to tell Nat what he must know. Crouching low in the ash, he waved Nat in. Slowly, deliberately, his finger made two broad sweeps in the dust. The crescent moon. 'Ca, Ca...'

'Carew?'

Billy shook his head vigorously.

'Carew did this?'

Nat stood quite still for a moment, waiting.

43

Waiting for the hammer of hell.

Blind fury, blood red, slammed like a storm tide. And there was Carew spitting venom on the hill. *Cross me, Salt, and your sedition will reap a bitter harvest.*

Nat turned his face to the racing sky, calling down vengeance on Erasmus Carew whose destruction was now the sole purpose of his being. Arms open to the blackening firmament, he tipped his head back in dark communion. '*Damn you to hell*, Erasmus Carew.' Nat's heel smashed the crescent moon, the herald's badge that made Carew a gentleman. 'I'll snuff out your line for this day's work.'

A sentinel crow rose in the lowering sky above the watching seer, old as time. 'Come heavens crack and split like the veil of their temple. Send your balm, cool the spitting embers of the pyre.' Through the rain, the gypsy woman eyed Nat collapsed to his knees. 'But I'm thinking the day's mischief won't be so easily quenched.'

*

Erasmus Carew at his desk fingered the note, scowling at the delivery man. 'You're the cove my man chastised in the forest, ain't you?'

'Aye, Sir.' Joe Jessop rubbed his chest. Salt's servant Emma, his Emma, was dead and he was looking at the murderer.

Carew plucked the fingers of his delicately embroidered doeskin gloves, pressing them gently against the document on his desk. 'Well, that villain's no longer in my service.'

'Heard that.' But, thought Jessop, whilst Ezekiel Rich lives, four innocents lie unavenged. '*Five* innocents.'

'Eh?'

Jessop smoothed his face. No point in spilling Emma's secret now, whispered behind the church on Sunday. Carew had the blood of five on his hands – Old Ma Rudd, the twins, Emma ... and Emma's unborn child, *his* child. 'Squire wants an answer.'

'The whipping's done nothing for your manners.' Erasmus Carew pursed his lips. 'Your master whistles,' he flicked Farrington's invitation, 'and I'm to scamper to his side like a grateful spaniel. Is that it?' He toyed with the signet ring with its crescent moon device that had so recently elevated his family.

Jessop shrugged. 'Squire said I was to deliver his letter, that's all.' Grimy nails dug deep into his palms. In a heartbeat he could be across the desk snapping the man's neck like a pullet.

Scratching his name, Carew tossed the reply across the table. 'I'll call tomorrow forenoon.' He nodded at his clerk hovering at the door, dismissing Jessop with the flick of a hand.

Carew picked his teeth, watching the bailiff's back. A summons to Helions could mean only one thing. He began turning over the wedding terms. 'Wait.' Carew had the smile of a lizard. 'Squire's daughter. She's at home?'

'Yes, Sir.' The maid Sarah had whispered their mistress was sweet on Carew. Careful Joe, she said, he'll likely be master of Helions, Squire after Mr Farrington.

'And she'll be at Helions tomorrow?' He was manicuring his fingernails studiously with a bone-handled knife.

'Ain't said otherwise. But I'm not her minder.' He cleared phlegm from the back of his throat, wanting to spit.

Carew brushed away the nail clippings and tossed the knife across the desk. 'Not capering through the wildwood then?'

'She hunts when she pleases.' The interview was turning into an interrogation. 'When she's a yen for it, I'm ready.'

Carew leant back, frapping the gloves against the table, screwing his thin lips. 'I'm sure you are.' The peasant was close to her, useful perhaps. Long fingers dipped into the purse tied at his waist. A fistful of coins, counted one by one. 'Here.' He tossed a month's wages across the table.

'What's that?'

'For your trouble.' Carew returned to his papers.

A down payment, the bailiff thought. 'Squire pays me, nobody else.' Jessop turned on his heels, clapping the clerk on the back. 'Yer boss thinks I'm bleedin' Judas mate.'

'Disagreeable oaf.' Carew made a funnel of the document, tipping the coins back into his purse. 'Now let's have that lawyer's boy back.'

John Gaskell, clerk to Carew's Salisbury attorney, padded in. 'The conveyance reflects your instructions Sir?'

'You're to hand it to Nathaniel Salt with my remittance.' Carew smoothed the paper. 'Salt mustn't know the purchaser. Understand?' He scratched a figure.

The clerk gulped. 'Sir, that's far too much.'

'You think so?'

'Oh yes Sir! I'm sure my master would say so. You see, Nathaniel Salt's in no position…'

'…And for two pups not yet cold in the ground,' Carew was already turning the key in his strongbox, 'how much for them, my young friend?'

*

Erasmus Carew arrived at Helions late, deliberately. It was a short ride, but enough to firm up the arrangements in his head. A quick marriage, times being what they were. No fuss.

Jessop answered the door. Dear God, did Farrington have no other servants? No wonder he was palming his girl off. And here was the decrepit and his interesting daughter in the peeling hall of their ancestors waiting to be rescued. Only neither of them looked like petitioners. 'A good day, madam, and a pleasure.'

'Never mind that.' Farrington was making him feel as welcome as a Welshman in Hereford. 'Cut to the chase, Carew. Brook Farm. Your doing, weren't it, eh?'

Carew blanched. 'Hold on, neighbour!' He had come to talk matrimony, not murder. 'You sent an invitation, not a summons. I don't appreciate being summoned.'

'I'm a magistrate,' Farrington shrugged. 'The gravity of the case demands it.'

'Well, I challenge your authority. But, I've already dealt with the miscreants under military law, being enlisted soldiers, and that's an end to it.' He pulled distractedly at the cuffs of his gloves, kidskin this time, she noted, with 'Es' and 'Cs' intertwined in gold.

Farrington pursed his lips. 'I see our jurisdiction's contested, like the wildwood.'

'Until this war's run its course, yes.' Carew sucked his teeth. 'But *gentlemen* should remain above the fray in parochial matters, eh?'

'*Quis custodiet ipsos custodes?*' said Effam.

Carew's lips twitched. 'Who will guard the guards themselves? Then you associate me with the Brook Farm conflagration, lady.' He fiddled

46

with the sword, mark of the King's commission, badge of authority that trounced the rebel Farrington.

'Enough to leave a heavy pall of suspicion above you,' said Effam, 'that can only be lifted in a court of law.'

'Your daughter should be called to the bar Farrington,' snapped Carew. 'I'll not be cornered by a morte needing a lesson in holding her tongue.'

'My daughter's a scholar, and much else too,' barked Farrington. But not a wife and mother, she thought, dispassionate eyes lingering for an instant on her suitor's crotch. *Not a woman in the fullest sense.*

'Ah,' lisped Carew, 'much more, indeed. You take a particular interest in Nathaniel Salt, Miss Farrington, don't you?'

'Oh, for the love of Christ have pity, man,' barked Farrington. 'Salt's young 'un's dead.' The maid Sarah reported that Nat was living alone in a woodsman's cottage beyond the village. 'The man's made destitute, and you ask if she cares?'

'Pity's fine, care needs to be more *tangible*, eh?' What would she say if he told her about the small fortune he had just offered Salt for his farm? 'Look Farrington, I'm offering marriage to your daughter and redemption of your bankrupt estate, maybe even the lengthening of your line, God willing. It's a good offer,' he shrugged, smiling at Effam. 'What dear lady are the alternatives? Taking up with the poor sisters of the cathedral close or Tobias Norrington. Neither palatable.'

'Did you order the burning of Brook Farm, Mr Carew?' she said.

'No madam, I did not.'

*

'At last,' said Effam, eyeing him critically. 'Moses comes down from the mountain.' She knew Nat would come eventually from his borrowed cottage on the edge of the wildwood. The Squire's churchyard call to arms had become his opportunity for vengeance. 'But there's been more tears sprung from those eyes than the Book of Lamentations, I'm thinking.'

At the destruction of Brook Farm when everyone else had drifted, awkwardly, to their beds, Squire Farrington stood to as Nat's world fell apart. From his carriage he stared through the rain and bore witness to the distraught soul's compact with the devil.

Filthy from fire fighting with the rest, another had kept watch from the shadows that night. The lady watched him now, her childhood friend jaw-clenched, ready to splice vengeance with Parliament's nobler cause. 'Carew's for King Charles, Sir,' rasped Nat, 'so I'm for Parliament.'

Had she not been Euphemia Farrington, she was sure this man would have completely disarmed her. In her mind's eye it was 1631 walking with him for the last time by the chalk stream. Deaf to the farm boy's mumbled plans for an impossible future, she was unpicking her first love, conjuring excitement beyond boorish Hinton Helions. When she came back, nothing was the same.

'Carew's an upstart, Nat. You don't have to delve far into that pedigree to find a harlot rutting with a saltpetre man,' growled Farrington. Parliament's tawny-orange sash knotted around his waist, it suited him to stoke Nat's hatred of his neighbour and by extension the King. 'For all his affectations, Erasmus Carew's the son of a poxy turd-churning tanner. And blood will out,' he huffed, pacing the hall, scuffed bucket-top boots clicking the worn flagstones. 'Carew'll answer to the Lord for his crime. May God grant your wish and make you the instrument of his retribution.'

Nat nodded solemnly. 'And your office Sir, as magistrate I mean, Brook Farm was a …'

'Misadventure, Nat?' Farrington raised his palms hopelessly, letting them fall against his thighs. 'Yes, if that's what you want'

'Aye, I do,' insisted Nat. 'Poor Ned Burrows'll keep his counsel. Only the three of us, Carew and his men know the truth. I'll be rat-catcher, just me.'

'Well, things being as they are, I can hardly arrest Erasmus Carew, can I?' Wincing, Farrington raised a hand to his shoulder, massaging the joint. 'King's pikeman caught me a glancing blow. General Fairfax put me on the sick list.'

'Lord Fairfax did me a great service in returning to his hearth a stubborn old man that should never have left it,' snapped Effam pouring three glasses of claret.

Farrington snatched the wine, grumbling. 'From field officer to recruiting sergeant in the jab of a pikestaff.'

Effam passed Nat his glass, fingers brushing. The maid Sarah gossiped about his admirers in the village. Well, thought Effam grimly, without another woman's children, brooding Mr Salt would now be even more of a catch.

Over the rim of his glass, Farrington eyed the poised young woman and awkward, dishevelled widower. In normal times what he had in mind would have been impossible, the gulf unbridgeable even though smallpox had made a ploughed field of her complexion. The pox had lowered his expectations and expunged her mother's to the point of spinsterhood. But they were not normal times and land, marriage's master greaser, was an illusion in his case. Any bridegroom would take a spavined mortgage for a dowry, a poor hook for the pampered dolts that darkened his doorway from time-to-time in their randy search for a well-born woman with which to farrow down and produce more idiots. They came in eager anticipation and moved on quickly, laughing into their sleeves at the prospects of an opinionated, pox-marked daughter of man with a grand name but no money at all. His recent injuries at the Adwalton fight made him mortal. But, although there was no pleasure left in life, he could not die without resolving the conundrum that robbed his sleep and punctured every waking hour. *What would happen to Effam?*

The acquisitive Dean of Salisbury knew what. Over a glass of Madeira the reverend money-grubber proposed that the Helion estate should pass to the safe keeping of the Chapter House. Effam would have a pension and lodge with the poor sisters of the Close. Two stout alms-houses would be built with the Farrington arms above the door. So, his line would end with an old maid and a couple of stone cottages.

Events spiralling beyond the old man's control were making him impatient. But as the old certainties tore and ripped along England's fault lines, he began to devise a plan that might restore order to his world.

*

Sarah hummed gently, pulling the brush through her lady's hair. Effam watched in the mirror enviously. She would be thinking of her young man and swapping an old trout rotting quietly in her chilly manor for a troupe of youngsters in a cosy cottage. 'That's enough,' Effam snapped. 'Pass me the looking glass.' She snatched the silver backed mirror, turning her face this way and that. The powder obscured the worst. Plaster on any more and she would look like a china doll. 'The blue gown, the hooded one, and my silk collar.' She sighed heavily, casting a gloomy eye round the solar. None of it – heavy oak furniture, tester bed, tapestries – had changed since her grandfather's day. Although the morning light dancing through the tall windows did its best, the big room was as dowdy as she felt. In her mind's eye she saw an old woman in the plump high bed drawing her last, alone. Euphemia Farrington, last of her line. She shuddered. 'I'm sorry, Sarah, if I was short.'

The maid busying herself about the room, straightening curtains, smoothing the coverlet, smiled nervously, humming to still her nerves. The penalty for what she was up to would be severe. Alone in her room beneath the eaves by candlelight she had crafted and recrafted two messages. One in Effam's hand, the other in her own. Satisfied, she tiptoed to the kitchen and, waking the boy, entrusted him with the letters, the first addressed to Erasmus Carew and the second, Nathaniel Salt. The maid knew her lady's mind and was sure it was for the best.

Sarah was now preparing the second part of her subterfuge. 'Joe Jessop, that's *Sergeant* Jessop, says the militia's mustering at the butts today. Pretty sight it'll be I reckon 'cos most of the village is for Parliament on account of Squire Farrington. Apart from Mr Carew and his men what's going off in another direction, so to speak. More's the pity 'cos my man Arthur's with 'im on account of his old dad being Carew's bondsman.' She gave Effam a sideways glance, getting to the point. 'Joe says Nathaniel Salt'll be there.' In the glass she thought she could see the small muscles of her mistress's face tighten. 'Poor man. Do him good. Can you imagine it, madam, them sweet children all done in like that?' She thumped a feather bolster, sending up a cloud of dust. 'Nice rally down the butts, just the job.'

Effam smudged a pinch more chalk around her cheekbones. She stood for a while at the window watching the sheep in the park, early sunlight cheering her up. 'We're going to the butts Sarah. Only to be seen, mind.' She seized the looking glass, tearing a strip of precious Spanish paper to add the pink blush of cochineal to her cheeks. 'The fur trimmed cape I think and sensible shoes. Ah, and pearls, the longer string.'

They both smiled privately at their ruse. The parade was an excuse to see Nathaniel Salt, a proposition that, if plainly put, would be unthinkable.

*

The track into the village skirted the wall Carew was building around his house. The apprentice mashed the mortar, his master slopping it on the bricks, scraping them with a rasp and tamping down. The pair straightened up as Nat approached but it was not the farmer on his nag that had caught their eye but something much finer further down the track hidden from Nat by the brick wagon.

'Hold now.' Carew raised his arm, bridle-gauntlet glinting in the sun. His troop, a dozen dragoons, pulled up at the brick wagon.

Blood thundered in Nat's temples but he was lost for words.

'Salt.' Carew's right hand jammed on his hip, closing on Sarah's forged letter through the stiff buffcoat. 'The lady gets the better man, is it?'

Nat's brow creased. Sarah's letter to him had said something different. Now he just wanted to tear out the devil's throat. But he would be cut down if he moved a muscle. 'Off to war, Carew?' His throat was as dry as dirt. 'You murdering bastard.'

'I've nothing to say to you.' Carew pulled ahead but Nat forced his horse against the wagon. 'Don't be a fool, man.' He flicked his head casually towards the dragoons, the first already drawing his sword, pushing past easily on the larger horse. Nat swung his fist, catching Carew beneath the chin. Two dragoons forced through heaving Nat onto the boards of the brick wagon in a cloud of red dust, pinning him with half the troop, slamming his head down hard. Through the red haze he saw the corporal straddling him, laughing faces crowding in and Carew's bemusement.

Water fell like rain, splashing his face. God's blood, the corporal was pissing on him. Nat backed off against the wagon's frontboard as the troopers split their sides.

'Why?' Nat's brow creased.

Erasmus Carew clamped Nat's chin with the metal gauntlet. 'Look, you bone headed peasant, I do not attack women and I don't kill children.' He gathered a fistful of brick dust, weighing it in his palm. 'Be thankful I consigned the man who did to a heavenly court.' Opening his hand, he blew the red dust into Nat's face. 'And let that be the end of it.'

*

Euphemia Farrington, last of her line, stepped out with Sarah. She wore a swatch of Parliament's orange cloth across her shoulder and a bolt of the material tied as a broad ribbon around a wide-brimmed hat, attracting a buzz of patriotic admiration from the rustics assembling at the butts. Squire Farrington, Lieutenant Colonel, trotted across under his sky blue banner with the cross of St George in the top corner flapping bravely in the care of buff coated Joe Jessop. A dozen irregulars armed with pikes and farm tools braced up as the officer rode past, pleased with the pale blue armbands distinguishing Farrington's company of foot. Their corporal, veteran of the continental wars, held his cutlass at the salute and a boy with a drum beat a ragged tattoo. But the main action was in the centre of the field where the parish's better sort, the dozen farmers owning a nag and a musket, were assembling with their gear. They were the yeomanry and Nat would be there. She squinted at the figures in the sun. There was the Reverend Markham in cassock and clerical hat blessing everything he could find, but she could not see Nathaniel Salt.

An old soldier with an antique Cabasset helmet was doing his best to drill the horsemen, bellowing instructions. 'You'll 'ave to use yer own muskets for now. That's why you're fancy dragoons and them over there's men o' foot.' He nodded at the far side of the field where large circular targets of red cloth had been pinned against straw bales. 'Let's see what damage the King's army can expect.' The farmers lined up, grinning. The veteran spat. 'Bugger all, that's what,' he muttered. 'Gawd help us.'

*

Only Sarah's crumpled note kept Nat from limping back to the cottage. A matron in the knot of village women elbowed her companion. 'Look at him, poor love.'

'Aw, ain't it a shame? The old bag agreed. 'Still, allow 'im the bottle's solace, young 'uns in the ground just six weeks an' all.'

Sarah on the lookout tugged Effam's sleeve. 'Oh, it's Mr Salt. I expected you on parade.' Effam nodded at the yeomanry. 'But all I see's a ruffian who looks like he's been fighting already.'

'I'm an irregular, Miss Farrington, not sworn, not attested.' Nat doffed his hat, brick dust falling like dandruff. 'Suits me, suits the Colonel.' He flicked the red dust from his coat. 'And, aye, I've had a brush with the enemy.'

She wrinkled her nose. 'Mr Carew?'

'Aye, lady.' The yeomanry gave fire, the series of cracks and cloud of black, acrid smoke drawing huzzahs from the villagers. 'Looks like I've missed the action.' He thought he saw the maid Sarah wink. 'Pity.' He chanced his luck. 'Walk with me Lady?'

'Walk with you Mr Salt?' Where was the fumbling farm boy now? Changed, she thought, by his great loss. Yes, after *that* there was no place for tongue-tied embarrassment or for a strong man to turn to jelly any more before a show of ribbon and lace. She took a moment, glancing at the crowd, but it was preoccupied with the militia. 'Yes, if you like, you can see us home.'

Picking up her skirts, Effam pondered their last encounter. The Farringtons had stood in the rain at the edge of the churchyard as two shockingly small coffins bumped into a watery hole. She had hidden her tears as Nat hunched over the cloven earth, black mane dripping wet.

Markham wasted no time over the grave and the sexton began shovelling. Nat folded, falling to his knees. Instinctively, she had pressed forward but Farrington held her back as a big village woman smothered him, leading him away sobbing into his coat.

'I hear you've sold Brook Farm.'

'Aye, what's left of it.' He wondered if Farrington had told her, surely he had. 'I'm truly grateful to the Squire for his goodness.'

Effam's brow furrowed. 'I hope you got a good price.'

'You don't know?'

'Why should I?'

'Well, I mean, the sum was many times what my poor farm's worth.' He passed a hand over his chin. 'Lady, I *am* really grateful.'

'I can see you would be.' She would get Sarah to find out from the gossips who the benefactor was. 'Can I speak plainly, Mr Salt?' she said, staring at the ground. 'I've been reflecting, on what you said to my father, about enlisting, *why* you're doing it.'

'You mean Carew?'

'No good will come of it,' she said. 'You know that, don't you?'

Over his shoulder he saw Sarah hanging back. 'D'you know what's kept me alive Miss Farrington, kept me from taking a musket to my brains or tipping into the weir?' He shrugged, smiling tightly. 'Hatred, miss, red and raw, more than air, or food or water.' His eyes misted and she knew she had gone too far. 'If it wasn't for that, I'd be dead too.' Effam opened and closed her mouth. 'There now,' he wiped an arm across his face, nodding ahead, 'nearly home.'

The manor's stone stanchions loomed at the gap in the park wall. But she was in no hurry, not wanting to lose him, wandering what to do.

Falling.

'Madam!' Sarah bolted forwards. But Effam was already in his arms.

'Damned conies.' She cursed the imaginary rabbits whose excavations had tripped her up.

For a second he held her, like a lover, and she prayed it would last. But now he was holding her off, as if he was checking an injured child. Eyes, deep blue oceans of pain, bored into hers and she did not need to feign the weakness in her legs.

Enough now. Wasn't she Euphemia Farrington, last of her line, or some bitch on heat? 'Oh, poxy rabbits!' She waved the maid across, testing her foot. 'No harm done. Sarah can take me from here.' Leaning on the servant, she turned with the trace of a smile. 'So, will I see you before you leave, Nathaniel Salt?'

*

Farrington's dozen prepared to mount up at first light, moisture heavy on the breath, thick air muting even the raven's cawing. Nat jerked the mare's girth strap tight, snatching a final glimpse of Helions.

But he saw nothing as she shrank from the window.

*

Farrington led the troop across a low stone bridge. Squinting against the noonday sun, he nodded at a squat-towered church, rasping instructions. 'Rest up, Sergeant Jessop.' He pulled over, walking his horse down the shallow chalk stream.

Dismounting by the churchyard yew, Nat unclipped the unfamiliar broadsword that had chaffed and rattled him to distraction, hurling it against the bank. Men were sinking their heads into the cool water. Nat flicked his hair back gratefully, combing thick wet locks with his fingers.

Bookish John Gaskell should have stayed at his desk in his master's Salisbury chambers. 'I expect you've seen heaps of action, sergeant.'

Joe Jessop crouched low, filling his canteen. 'Action eh? Yeah, suppose, what with night raids 'gainst poachers and the like.' The big man grinned at the crestfallen lawyer's clerk. 'No mate, we're county militia, me and the Squire, I mean Colonel.' He nodded at Farrington standing on the bridge. 'Marching up and down with bills and pitchforks of a Saturday afternoon, that's us. Oh, and scaring nippers and old dears with yarns of murdering Scots n' Irish.'

'My brother Edward's joined the London trained bands,' Nat remarked absently. He did not really know Joe Jessop, Farrington's bailiff-turned-Sergeant, but they had the same height and frame, same west-country face, broad and flat. Jessop, a few years older, had a reputation as a lady's man good at holding his ale. Nat knew the bruiser had been walking out with Emma, Brook Farm's murdered maid. It was said there had been an understanding between them. When they buried Emma, Nat remembered Jessop hovering on the edge of the party, choking, staring at his feet, fists clenching a bunch of hedgerow flowers.

'Seems whole bleedin' country's in arms Mr Salt, don't it?' Jessop reckoned the farmer must know what was going on.

'Aye, but what're we to do, Mr Salt, eh?' Gaskell had been conscripted by Farrington on his arrival from Salisbury with the Colonel's will. But he knew Nat from the purchase of Brook Farm by, though he could not divulge it, Erasmus Carew.

'Sergeant says we're to join Sir William Waller's force at Devizes.' Nat knew there was no certainty that General Waller would be there. However, Farrington hoped that by moving north his troop would eventually connect with a sizeable Parliamentary force. 'That's about right, isn't it, Joe?'

'Aye, right enough,' Jessop said. 'Colonel's got a cousin in Lavington, up Devizes way. Name o' Tobias Norrington.' He spat his opinion. 'Gen'leman's billeting Waller's staff, so Squire's heading over there to get 'is orders.'

'But if the King stays in Oxford,' said Gaskell mournfully, 'we'll have no fighting.'

'Only His Majesty won't stay in Oxford, friend, now will he?' Jessop crouched low, cupping water across his face. 'Ain't much to be King of in Oxford.'

'Right you are, Joe.' Nat tossed a pebble in the stream. Gaskell's boyish enthusiasm for the war repelled him. 'With no silver, I'm thinking King can't any more sit on his haunches in Oxford as leave it.'

'Yes, yes! And now all the liverymen and merchants are declared for Parliament, he can't be dipping his fingers in London's money bags.' Gaskell's fresh face brimmed with excitement. 'We'll find some royalists, quick dust up, home by Michaelmas. Proper heroes, pick of the doxies, eh?'

Markham scowled, hitching his cassock to paddle. 'Except the whore-Queen Mary's been passing the begging bowl round the papist Princes of Europe,' he called from the stream. 'But after the Edgehill fight they're waiting to see which way the wind blows. Ha, ha!'

'Well, if they don't pay up the King'll be bankrupt, won't he? Then Gaskell here won't get his war.' Nat took a swig, eyeing a fierce red-faced man in a grimy surplice beating towards the stream.

'Get out, get out. No soldiers here. Get out, damn your eyes.' The man was raving, face in Nat's. A crowd of labourers returning home across the bridge began to look like a mob.

Jessop was up in an instant, pushing the cleric's shoulder, forcing him back. 'Mind yer bleedin' manners, Laudian prig.'

'Steady,' Nat hissed, eyeing the scythes and billhooks. The cleric fell back hard. There was a low murmur from the tightening group of rustics. Nat bent over, arm outstretched, but the man, stinking of piss and ale, brushed him away. Raising his palms, Nat stood off. The curate backed away, tripping against a low headstone. He rose and fell again, comically, limbs waving like a beached crab, surplice riding up.

One of the peasants pointed at the priest's embarrassment. 'There you are, big Mary, reckon that's the only prick in the village you ain't had the pleasure of.'

The woman Mary, arms thick as hams, jammed horny fists into ample hips. 'Well, that's 'cos it's the only privy parts what's never been used!' She grinned toothlessly.

'Aw, Reverend, Sir,' Nat tried again. 'No harm meant.' He pulled at the surplice to restore the man's modesty. 'Here, now, let's get you up.'

'Damn you, damn you all, bastard sons of Satan!' The curate clawed at Nat drawing near-upright and with his free arm thrashed blindly at the soldiers. 'Fall ye like the godless swine of Gadara into the pit that is bottomless.'

The mangled, spittle-flecked oath fell like water on a camp fire. Nat felt his stomach knot and his grip fail. The curate fell back, half turning in a ghastly pirouette. Down he went, hard against a split tablestone. Twitching, head skewed like he was gawping at the stream, a dark shadow edged from his nose and scalp, advancing slowly like a flow tide across the stone.

'Reverend?' Nat was on his knees, shaking the man's shoulders. 'Oh, Lord love us!'

'He's gone,' observed the woman Mary flatly, bending stiffly, smoothing the cleric's bloody mop, gnarled thumbs pressing his eyes shut.

Jessop stepped forward. 'Accident, right?' There was a ready murmur from the troops, silence from the dark-eyed mob. 'Right?' He snarled at the rustics.

'Constable must be called.' A greybeard pressed forward. 'Aye, and the Crowner.' The death of a priest was a serious matter.

'God's blood,' Nat muttered, weighing the gathering insurgency, searching for Farrington. The soldiers began to square up. Ignoring the greybeard, Nat turned to the crowd. 'Curate fell, pissed he was. Couldn't be helped.' Seizing Gaskell's gown, he pulled the bug-eyed clerk to the front. 'This man's a lawyer.' Gaskell reddened. 'And he'll take sworn evidence from each man here for the Sheriff in Salisbury.'

The swains, eyeing the youth sceptically, lowered their equipment. Satisfied, Farrington watching from behind the bridge kicked on. 'Mr Gaskell!' The clerk, fretting with his stool and satchel, tripped across. Farrington lowered his voice. 'Now then, Gaskell, I don't expect to see the marks of this illiterate rabble scratched under any *disobliging* evidence. Understood?'

'Perfectly, Sir.' He nodded at greybeard. 'I'll wager foreman's the only one that knows his letters. Rest'll set their marks to whatever I write.'

'Capital! Sergeant Jessop, two men if you please and a corporal to stay with Mr Gaskell.' He glanced at the crowd. 'Good men mind, well armed.' Swinging in the saddle, he bawled towards the stream. 'To me, Mr Salt, quick as you can.'

Nat on the bank was rubbing the curate's blood from his hands. 'I'll fetch him Colonel.' Jessop marched across the churchyard. 'Mr Salt?' He hovered awkwardly. 'Beg pardon, Mr Salt, Colonel says to get going.' Stifled his embarrassment, the gamekeeper crouched low beside the farmer. 'Got to go now, Mr Salt.' Nat splashed water across his face, saying nothing. 'Gawd Almighty, know how you feel. Had a nipper, same age as yours. Other side o' blanket of course, but gutted I was when she died. Lost me brother too. Last year. Edgehill fight.'

'Nathaniel Salt!' Farrington was impatient, hurting from the ride.

'Beg pardon, Colonel, Mr Salt and me'll catch up.'

Farrington nodded, wheeling the troop away.

'I found 'em, yer young 'uns.' Jessop checked then laid a thick arm across Nat's shoulders. 'At Brook Farm. Laid 'em out, best I could. Them and my poor sweet Emma and Old Mother Rudd, what was left of 'em. He sniffed moistly, passing a sleeve across his nose. 'Thing is, I found my Emma, me an' Billy Burrows, all done in like, 'cos the flames didn't have her poor body like the others. Don't see how no candle or cinders from the fire could've done all that. Told the Colonel but he just looks at me queer-like and tells me it were an accident. But Billy tells me straight 'cos my Emma was kind to him, see.' He turned away, staring off downstream towards the bridge. 'Christ, Mr Salt, now you've got me blubbing too. Couple of beldames, eh?' Clearing his throat, he spat into the water. 'Anyway, point is, we're sort of in this together, you and me.' Jessop squeezed hard. 'Come now, before we lose this light.'

Saddling up, Nat eyed the big woman supervising the removal of the priest to the church and the first witness standing in front of Gaskell. 'Bad business.'

'Bleedin' priest's fault,' Jessop shrugged. 'Anyways, ain't no sense mithering.'

Nat jerked the horse's head, turning onto the Salisbury road. 'Back there, Joe.' Nat chewed his lip, staring straight ahead. 'Should've bottled it. I mean, well what I mean is, *thank you*.'

The man said nothing but, on the banks of the Wylye river, Joe Jessop had become Nat's confederate, bound together in the destruction of the devil Carew.

VI

'What did he mean about them swine?' Joe Jessop rubbed his chin. 'The papist, what did mean about them pigs falling in a pit?'

Markham's ears pricked up. 'Gadarene swine, friend,' he boomed over his shoulder. 'At Gadara Jesus found a man possessed by demons fearful of being sent back to hell. The demons asked the Lord to be cast into a nearby herd of pigs instead. He agreed. The beasts, duly possessed, took off, hurling themselves off a cliff into the Sea of Galilee.' He grinned at the Colonel, pleased with himself. 'There you have it, story of the Gadarene swine.'

Nat leant across to Jessop so Markham could not hear. 'That curate thought he was casting out demons, Joe. He wanted us to burn in hell. But those swine didn't fall into the pit. Jesus saved them, see. So the preacher was all wrong. Mr Markham too.'

'Blimey, you know your scriptures mate.'

'Aye, that and not much else, friend.'

North of Gore Cross where the high ground of Lavington Down joins the featureless expanse of the Black Heath was a hillock called Gibbet Knoll. The justices had chosen the spot well, a dire, joyless scrap, the home of fly-blown sheep and silent, watchful crows. The rise had been selected to catch the traveller in each direction and to hold his attention for a long stretch.

The hanging tree stood out gaunt and black. From it, strung up like a pheasant was a priest, long cassock torn and shredded. The noose, poorly sited, cocked the man's head so the corpse turning in the breeze puzzled as it followed the travellers. From the priest's mouth, thick and bloated like an ox, lolled the sermonising tongue that had been his downfall. 'Jesuits.' The Reverend Markham was unmoved. 'The very devil.'

'God's blood, have we come to this?' Nat wanted to throw up. 'Reverends rotting by the road like thieves.' He turned to share his disgust with the Sergeant but Joe Jessop was made of sterner stuff.

'Beg pardon, Colonel,' Jessop cleared his throat and spat, 'don't reckon there'll be none of them prickless God-botherers left before long!'

Farrington scowled. 'God rest all sinners, even papists.' He kicked on, hard.

*

The house at Lavington was not much of a manor. But its owner was not much of a Squire. Captain Tobias Norrington, well into his cups, was steadying himself at the threshold. Kitted out like Farrington, Parliament's orange sash strained across his midriff and was tied on the left in an elaborate bow.

'Don't trust that cove, friend,' Joe Jessop hissed at Nat. 'Norrington's thick with them royalist cavaliers. But here he is all trussed up in that tawny-orange sash like a bleedin' spatchcock chicken. Make's you wonder, don't it?' Nat heard that some gentleman wore their allegiances lightly, waiting to see how the wind blew.

'See you've taken to wringing the necks of papists, cousin.' Farrington dismounted painfully. 'Not pretty, Sir, not pretty at all.'

'Damned Jesuit, begging your pardon, Reverend,' smirked Norrington. 'That holy man jigged around for a good while I can tell you before my man stopped his galliard by swinging off his ankles.' He clapped Farrington on his injured arm. 'Who cares about papists anyway, eh? You and the reverend'll be gagging for a glass o' sherry wine.' He grinned at Markham who brightened up. 'See, parson, I've nothing against priests in general, just the whore-mongering acolytes of Rome.' Norrington slapped the back of the hovering elderly servant. 'My steward here'll billet your people. Any here good enough for the house?' He cast a sorting eye over the company. 'No, barn'll do Obadiah.'

Mutton-chopped Obadiah Cotton made his own assessment. 'You boys'll bunk down with Captain Norrington's dragoons. My missus'll fetch you over summut presently.' He held the yeoman back. 'This way, friend, we've a flock bed that'll suit you better than the barn.'

In the kitchen an elfin-faced serving girl bobbed fleetingly, fair unmarked skin, pretty features that laughed in the warm, dancing light of the fire, cracking and hissing in the man-sized hearth.

'Ale for our guest, girl,' ordered Cotton, 'and a plate of that smoked ham. Now, sit you down, Sir.'

The girl fetched the brew in a pewter tankard with a lid. Kneeling, she pulled away one boot and the next. The steward Cotton, drawing deep on a long clay pipe, settled at the long pine table facing Nat. A buxom woman was supervising food for the house and its impromptu garrison. 'Mrs Cotton?' enquired Nat.

The steward grinned sheepishly. Two maids, one badly marked from the pox, the other a dumpling, giggled excitedly, labouring under Mrs Cotton's eye. The matron had the look of one that knew all about soldiers and what might pass between them and a brace of silly girls.

'Devizes was a right pickle, friend.' Cotton had apparently witnessed the royalist commander Sir Ralph Hopton arriving in town badly injured after scrapping with his old friend Sir William Waller at the battle of Lansdown Hill. 'Anyhow, thought I'd better find out what I could. Gather intelligence like, for my master.' Nat listened politely, eyeing the girl. 'Well, before long Hopton's men begin to close the town down. Obadiah, says I, time to leave, so I makes my escape. Just in time!' He beamed at his guest. 'Cap'n Norrington said he'd send my report to General Waller. Said it would help Sir William lay siege. What d'you think of that?'

The women and the elfin girl had cleared out of the kitchen. Nat wondered what Mrs Cotton would do to protect the servants from a house full of soldiers. Obadiah Cotton droned on. 'Of Course, *Captain* Norrington – seems odd calling him that but he's most insistent – was especially interested to hear I'd seen Mr Erasmus Carew in General Hopton's force.'

'WHAT?'

'Well, yes. D'you know Mr Carew then?'

'Oh, I *certainly* do.'

'Then maybe you know Captain Norrington and Mr Carew are thick as thieves. Linked through marriage somehow or another. But don't ask me how.' Cotton took two drags from the pipe, pumping blue smoke from the side of his mouth. 'The war's slammed a cleaver through many friendships, hasn't it? Still, my master and Mr Carew stay best of pals.' Cotton smiled like it was a game of ninepins. 'Well, of course, I could hardly make myself known to Mr Carew. Can't be too careful these days, can you? But he was there alright, riding up and down in the square, all fine and dandy with his crew. I heard tell in the Bear that Hopton promoted him Major. That didn't please *Captain* Norrington, I can tell you!' He punched the air playfully. 'Them being sparring partners and all.'

'Who was with him?' Nat could not believe his quarry had been delivered so easily. 'Maybe two villains called Rich – Ezekiel and Jethro?'

'Well, brother, there was a gaggle of bawdy looking coves snapping at the gentleman's heels but I couldn't tell one from the other,' blustered Cotton. 'I was keeping to the shadows see, being on reconnaissance and all.'

'Sir, I've made the gentleman's bed.' The elfin girl gave Nat a look that would stir the loins of Edward the Confessor. 'I'm to show him the way.'

'That'll do, girl.' The old bag barged through with a candle 'I'll show our guest to his quarters.' Mrs Cotton's fist squeezed his arm. 'I've heard about your great loss,' she whispered. 'You've all my prayers, you poor man.' She turned to bark her instructions. 'Obadiah Cotton, you've exhausted Mr Salt with your stories, to bed with you. I'll be along presently. And girl, you remember how lightly I sleep.'

Nat glanced at the elfin girl, quietly, passively seductive. It had been a long time. 'No, Mistress, I'll bed down with the men.' Mrs Cotton's eyes flicked slyly between them. Nat raised his hand. 'No, really, it's the stable for me.'

The old woman screwed her face. 'As you wish.' She would have to be vigilant. 'Show our guest the way, Obadiah.'

'No need, madam, there's a full moon.' He brushed past the girl, sap rising. 'Goodnight.' She would have to contrive a way to slip through the old trout's net.

Across the yard shining like burnished gunmetal, Nat strode towards the yellow tallow light of the stable block. 'Over here, Mr Salt!' Jessop, in his cups with the dragoons, was pleased to see him. 'Thought you'd found comfier lodgings.'

'I'd sooner spend the night with my mates, Joe.' Jessop looked at him doubtfully as he passed a leather jug of Cotton's brew house ale. 'Alright, well it ain't no feather bed but there's hay, soft an' sweet.'

'Tell me about Effam Farrington.'

The bailiff's forehead creased. 'What's to tell?'

Nat shrugged. 'Heard she was stepping out with Carew.'

'Did you now?' Jessop took another swig, passing the back of his hand across his lips. 'Aye, well so she is, in a manner of speaking, though Squire don't like it. Got her mother's steel, see, and a yen for Carew's moneybags.'

Nat drained his jug and wandered outside to piss in the bucket. There was movement in the shadows towards the house. Too big for a fox, too fast for a badger. He cut round the side of the yard. 'Got you!'

'Ooo Sir, what are you like?' It was the pock-marked parlour maid.

'It's late to be out, miss, particularly in this company.' He nodded at the barn.

Giggling, the girl put a finger to her lips. 'Oh, Sir, what larks!'

'Best I return you to Mrs Cotton.' He sucked his teeth. 'To save you from the soldiers.'

The girl paled. 'Oh no, Sir! The old cow'd skin me alive.'

He smiled sadly at her poor, scarred face. She would be even less of a catch if a quick poke put her in the family way. 'I'll forget about Mrs Cotton if you show me the blonde girl's room.'

She sighed, disappointed. 'We're together, us three, up there in the attic.' The girl nodded at a small gable window. 'But she's the only one asleep tonight!'

He had to twist to navigate the box staircase. At the top, knocking gently, he pushed the plank door ajar.

'Come in quickly, before Mrs Cotton hears you,' whispered the elfin girl. Moonlight streaming through the casement illuminated the space under sharply sloping eaves. 'You took your time.'

Deep in the bowels of the house the ears of a slumbering old woman pricked at the cry in the night.

*

Picking through the snoring troopers, Nat found a place in the straw. He lay back and forced a prayer. God would understand. *Jehovah Providebit.* For the first time since the fire he slept through the night.

*

Mrs Cotton glanced from her breakfast, nodding at the girl with the poor complexion. 'She'll find you some bacon, if you've an appetite. And there's fresh drawn milk in the jug.' Nat hesitated, looking around. 'It's no good, really it isn't.' The woman caught his eye, sighing with a look of weary disappointment. 'She'll not be back, whilst you're here. You can be sure of that, *young man.*'

'I just came to thank you for your hospitality, Mrs Cotton.' The maids giggled and, blushing, he made for the door. But, passing the pock-faced girl, he felt a paper pressed into his hand.

*

Captain Norrington rode part of the way, piloting Farrington's troop to the east of Devizes where Sir William Waller had put his heavy guns. From a temporary redoubt of earth filled gabions built on a low hill, General Waller's sakers and demi-culverins were inflicting heavy punishment on the town.

Resting against a gabion, Nat plucked the note from his sleeve.

I'll wait, if you want. Return safe, please God.

But she had not signed her name and he realised shamefully that he had not asked. He chewed his lip, thinking how better it would feel if it was Effam writing him notes. But hadn't Joe Jessop confirmed that the enigmatic lady of Helions had set her sights on his adversary? Carew, black heart, deep pockets.

The battery commander pointed north towards Bagdon Hill. 'General Waller's up there, off the Oxford road.' He covered his ears as the saker pressed five pounds of iron into the tower of St John's. 'Above Roundway village.'

Captain Norrington decided he had seen enough action. 'Huzzah, Colonel Farrington.' Waving his cousin towards Bagdon Hill and the downs rising above the scrappy hamlet of Roundway, he pulled his mount over.

'There goes my cousin.' Farrington allowed a small show of contempt. 'High-tailing it back to his hearth and India gown.'

'Aye Sir,' said Nat. 'I'm thinking Captain Norrington's the kind of soldier that's best left at home.'

'All arse, no bottom, that's him,' quipped Joe Jessop. 'Beggin' yer pardon, Squire.'

Companies of buff-coated pikemen and musketeers were sweating up Bagdon Hill. Oxen and clapped out nags kicked up dust, vying for space, heaving their gear up the track under the eye of the Wagonmaster General. 'God's Blood!' Farrington pulled back as two huge beasts dragging an overloaded cart slipped. 'Brake man, brake!' Too late. For a moment the wagon teetered, agonisingly, on the edge of the track. Just in time, the carrier leapt clear. Ball and kegs of powder, spewing from beneath the tarpaulin, took off down the slope. A quartermaster set about the hapless carrier with his switch, entertainment for the company of foot wheezing up the hill.

'Worse than Salisbury on a quarter day,' said Nat, 'and just look at that lot.' He nodded at the legion of camp followers dotted along the escarpment. 'King's cavalry'll make mincemeat of them.' Women tended skillets slung over camp fires, ragged children barefoot, blacksmiths jostling with tinkers and wheelwrights.

The escarpment chaos had not prepared Nat for the panorama of Roundway Down. 'Bloody hell!' There were more men than Nat had ever seen.

Colonel Farrington reined in, fumbling for his perspective glass, briefly sweeping the downs. 'God's Blood! Need your young eyes, Salt.' He thrust the instrument at Nat. 'Tell me what you see.'

Raising the exquisite piece as the Colonel had done, it was as if Nat could reach out and touch the horizon.

'Well, *well?*'

'Parliament's got five thousand at least,' said Nat. 'General Waller's drawn them up east-west. There, Sir, across that poor track running through the downs.'

On the right, hard up against the rise of Bagdon Hill, Farrington could see unaided Waller's own horse brigade, its troopers struggling to control their animals in the tight space. He pointed to the left flank where the sun was glancing off the breastplates of heavy cavalry. 'What's that?' Nat shifted the glass

'Parliament's horsemen. Breastplates and helmets with long tails like mares.'

Farrington nodded. 'That'll be cuirassiers. Sir Arthur Haselrig's famous lobsters. Haselrig's horse to the left, Waller's to the right.'

Nat swept the perspective glass again. 'Waller's drawn up his infantry in the centre, pikemen formed up behind the musketeers.'

'They'll dig their pikes in at the slope and stick the King's cavalry before they fall on our infantry.' Jessop sucked his teeth. 'Job done.'

'The horsemen have to get past our guns first. We've got six pieces at least. Look like big 'uns.' Nat smacked a bluebottle from his cheek. 'Looks like the gunners are ready to fire already.'

'What about the enemy?' Farrington had heard that Lord Wilmot was racing from the King at Oxford to join the fight. Nat retrained the glass towards the Wansdyke. 'Two miles off, royalist cavalry, two thousand, I reckon. There're a couple of guns but no infantry at all.'

Farrington was satisfied. 'That'll be Lord Wilmot. Keep hold of the perspective glass, Nat. Be my eyes. From your account Sir William Waller has deployed in the traditional manner. I would expect nothing else.' He squinted towards the enemy. 'But with an inferior force Wilmot must play by the rules, and lose, or be audacious.' He shrugged. 'Waller has a winning hand, a heavy burden for a commander. History won't be kind to Sir William if he fails with odds like that. They call him "William the Conqueror", you know. We'll see.'

The troop cantered down the road towards the centre of the line, reining in behind the wall of pikemen. They were big, swaggering brutes already sizing steel-tipped lances, the height of three men, to level with a horse's head. But musketeers made up the bulk of the force cosseting their precious matchlocks. Some had uniform coats of deep red but most wore little more than the broadcloth on their backs when their women kissed them goodbye. A few had the thin protection of scuttle-butt or pot helmets, the rest made do with a woollen Monmouth cap. Their few possessions slung in canvas snap-sacks, each musketeer carried a bandolier with flasks of powder and bags of shot. The force had looked a great deal more impressive through the perspective glass.

'Old men and boys,' said Jessop. 'Look like scared rabbits.'

'Too many of those officers look like they've learnt fieldcraft from drill books,' muttered Farrington, chewing his lip.

A black clad parson, bible clutched firmly, shuffled past. Markham glared malevolently and let rip. 'Brother, a closed bible's a useless bible, even one as big as that!' The hedge priest reddened, scampering away, disinclined to treat with another godly firebrand. Markham bellowed at the assembly. 'Won't anyone offer a prayer?' Cursing, he jumped down, rummaging in his saddlebag for the book, elbowing to the front. Taking ten paces forward, turning his back to the enemy, little Daniel Markham stood. The front rank hushed, baring their heads, silence spreading to the rear. Slowly, deliberately, the Reverend Markham began to finger the well-worn pages for his place.

The prophet Micah cut the warm summer air.

Now gather thyself in troops, O daughter of troops: he hath laid siege against us: they shall smite the judge of Israel with a rod upon the cheek.

Nat's lips moved to the familiar incantation.

Thine hand shall be lifted up upon thine adversaries, and all thine enemies shall be cut off.

The breeze died away, the little man's big voice crashing around chapter 5.

And I will cut off witchcrafts out of thine hand; and thou shalt have no more soothsayers:

Thy graven images also I will cut off, and thy standing images out of the midst of thee; and thou shalt no more worship the work of thine hands.

Spit-flecked Markham reached his zenith. *And I will execute vengeance in anger and fury upon the heathen,* his arm flew out wildly towards the royalist lines, a gnarled talon digging at the air, *such as they have not heard.*

His lungs heaving like bellows, Markham slammed the book shut. From the left flank a voice struck up, deep and strong; *All people that on earth do dwell* ... Psalm 100, The Old Hundredth, weapon of war on the side of the righteous, thundered through the ranks, a defiant bulwark against an ungodly King.

'Yes!' Nat thrilled to be part of it. 'Pity the King's men over there, Joe Jessop, with no more cover than a couple of round barrows. Don't hear anything from them, eh?'

Markham's voice rose on the dying notes. 'Lord, you know how busy I must be this day. If I forget thee Lord, do not thou forget me.'

*

'That lot,' said Farrington pointing at Haselrig's oversized staff cantering up and down the line, 'look better suited for a caper through Richmond Park than a pitch battle.' He kicked on. 'Come on!'

'Huzzah Colonel Farrington.' Sir Arthur Haselrig, Colonel of Horse, acknowledged Farrington's salute. 'Capital day for it, ain't it, eh, eh?' Sir Arthur peered at Farrington's yeomanry. 'Light horse Sir, *light* horse? Haselrig valued weight, particularly breast-plated heavy cavalry, his famous Lobsters. 'Still, stay close to me, Colonel Farrington. I may need your speed of sweet Achilles before we're done.' Haselrig stood in his stirrups raising an eyeglass towards the enemy. As an afterthought, he swung round to examine the terrain at his back. 'Buggered if I understand this poxed country.' What he thought he saw was a line of scrub with fields rising innocently beyond. 'Where's Farrington? Ah, Colonel, your stomping ground ain't it? What's the lie of the land, Sir? Local knowledge, Sir, eh?'

Farrington squinted at the horizon. 'Colonel, Wiltshire's north and south are as chalk and cheese. I know no more than the track that brought me here.'

'Yes, yes, but you know these damnable Wessex hills, don't you? Had your eyes shut these fifty years, eh?' Haselrig swung the glass left to right, peering at the scrub that did not quite seem right. 'Come, Sir, should I worry about that hedge, the hedge Sir, eh?'

Steadying his horse, Farrington could just make out a thin line of bush a mile off with high ground beyond. 'Tall trees, sculpted by the wind. Unusual.' His mind was tumbling to the significance of what he could see through the clouds in his eyes.

'Well, Colonel Farrington?' barked Haselrig.

'Looks clear enough Colonel.' *Sotto voce* he hissed, 'Even your tin-chested plough boys could clear that fence with a troop of lifeguards snapping at their heels.' Squinting, still uncertain, he beckoned Nat. 'I'll send a scout, to be sure.'

'No!' thundered Haselrig. 'God's Blood, Sir, do you want me to peg out a line of retreat? We mean to advance, Sir, not retire, like a parlourful of beldames!' A Cornet pulled up, saluting Haselrig, fumbling in his saddle bag. 'Come on, come on.' The boy dropped the paper. Jessop leapt to ground, flicked dirt from the dispatches and handed them up to the Colonel of Horse.

Farrington nodded at his man. 'Light horse, Colonel. Light afoot too!'

Haselrig snatched the paper, breaking the seal, quickly scanning the heavy script. He tapped the instructions against his breastplate then thrust them at Farrington. 'What d'you make of that, Colonel?'

'Sir William expects Lord Wilmot to present the royalist horse to the pike and musket of our infantry.' He reined in his skittish mount. 'He then requires our cavalry to sweep round to embrace his Lordship like the two horns of a bull. In this way Sir William expects us to engage in a classical set-to as if our armies were dancing a Volte, measure-for-measure.'

'And if you were standing in Wilmot's place?' growled Haselrig.

'I would depart from Sir William's dance, Sir, since its outcome would be, um, predictable,' said Farrington. 'Lord Wilmot would be annihilated, even by our company of blood-shod farm boys.'

'Quite. If he's wise he'll wait for Hopton's Cornishmen to leave Devizes and attack our rear. We'll still have numerical advantage but a fight on two fronts would narrow the odds.' Haselrig swung in the saddle. 'Gentlemen, General Waller wants us to hold our position until Lord Wilmot engages our centre. Let us pray for a great victory. And a chastened King!'

Nat retrieved the perspective glass from his sleeve, panning towards the enemy lines. Against Parliament's massed ranks, the King's force looked puny. As if to emphasise the cavaliers' impotence, the royalist light artillery at such long range had been sounding off ineffectually. But now they fell silent.

''Ere we go.' Jessop turned the quid round his mouth once more and spat it into the dirt.

Now the King's horse was moving ahead at the trot.

'Stand to, stand to!' A crush of cussing, elbow-jabbing foot soldiers; pikemen jamming butts of sharp-tipped poles into flinty ground, musketeers, all fingers and thumbs, pulling at powder flasks and shot bags.

Waller's heavy pieces began pounding iron into horseflesh but the cavalry's ordeal was short lived. At a thousand yards the charge split, the two parts fanning across the field.

Haselrig grinned at Farrington. 'Ha! We were right, Colonel, you and me.'

'Yes, but you didn't need to be Hannibal to work it out,' muttered Farrington. 'Given the choice – impaled like a stuck pig on Waller's tooth picks or a sword fight with his peers – any cavalryman would do the same.'

'Stand fast the Lobsters!' Haselrig's bark was lost in the cannonade of horseflesh bearing down.

Waller's infantry with their redundant pikes and muskets looked on helplessly from the centre, Wilmot's cavalry crashing into Parliament's horsemen on each flank.

And there was Haselrig posturing in front of his cherished Lobsters, quickly catching the attention of Royalist Captain Richard Atkins. With his Cornet, Atkins swerved, making straight for his enemy, pulling up within 200 yards of Haselrig's party.

'Who's that cocky devil?' Haselrig stared at the royalists levelling carbines at him. Nat saw his horse rear up and Haselrig slump to the left, wheeling off from his party down the line. Atkins was barely 100 yards from his target.

'Come on, Joe Jessop!' Nat dug his heels in.

But Atkins was quickly overhauling Haselrig. His sabre sliced the rump of the Colonel's horse like beefsteak. The wide-eyed beast fell to its knees, tipping Haselrig over its mane, helpless as a baby in his armour. Raising an arm to fend off Atkins's sword, Haselrig saw his Lobsters besieged by Wilmot's nimbler horsemen. 'Bloody light horse.' His epiphany was completed by Farrington's featherweights galloping towards him. But they were too far off. 'Too late, boys.' He shook off the cuirass, Atkins rounding for the kill. The two royalists slashed at the grounded Colonel, missing their mark, giving Nat and Joe Jessop time to intercede. Captain Atkin's well-aimed blow glanced off the heavy sword of a Wiltshire farmer drawn in anger for the first time.

Atkin's Cornet poised for the coup de grace. Nat kicked on, thrusting his weapon hard at the young man's chest, blade slipping in easily and deep, skewering the royalist's heart. First kill, quick kill. A bloody rivulet ran down the grooved blade wetting Nat's hand and sleeve as the dead man fell away.

Atkins took off. 'Go on. Bugger off.' Jessop hit the ground. 'Had it in for you, Sir Arthur, no mistake.' With covering fire from Farrington's troop, Nat and the Sergeant pulled the Colonel of Horse across Nat's beast. Colonel Farrington drew up, a bloody hand clawing his side. 'Bravo, man! Now get Sir Arthur out.' He caught Nat's eye 'Here, take it.' The Squire was thrusting a small parcel at him. 'Take it, man, and God be with you!' He struck Nat's horse hard with the flat of his sword, turning to lead the advancing line of Parliamentary cavalry.

Nat took the Devizes road down the southern escarpment until he reached the encampment where a piquet stood to. A man in a blood-soaked leather apron briefly examined the day's highest ranking casualty. Haselrig fell from the horse, deathly white. 'Tell Colonel Farrington I doff my hat to his lightweights, damn his eyes.' Touching his bonnet to the commander, Nat wheeled round, pressing the horse back up the hill.

'God's blood!' Waller's line had been forced westward with the royalist cavalry pressing home their attack on both flanks. The hapless Parliamentary horse was now in full thunderous retreat. Nat panned the perspective glass on the low green rise of Roundway Castle beyond the retreating cavalry. 'The Lobsters'll regroup around those earthworks, surely.' It still seemed the refuge was divided from the battlefield by just a thin strip of brush and a line of small trees. 'Then they'll turn and Lord Wilmot'll get what's coming to him!'

The right edge of Haselrig's cavalry was now just five hundred yards from the hedge. Riderless mounts had already made it to the scrub but veered away along its line. A mare flew past towing a cuirassier, screaming, his foot caught in the stirrup. Parliament's infantry stood fast, pikes at the slope in a giant hedgehog, waiting for the eddying cavalry to test itself on the spikes. Fat chance.

Nat snapped the perspective glass shut. 'Shit!' Two horsemen were closing from Bagdon Hill. Fast. Unclipping the gun, he primed and took aim. The leading horse fell, a lucky shot. He unsheathed the sword in time to meet the second man, thrashing out wildly, missing the man but not the mount. Great vessels flaying opened, the horse fell to its knees in a cloud of dust and pool of gore. Reloading the carbine, Nat took aim at the wide-eyed soldier whimpering behind the beast twisting and snorting in the dirt. 'Aw, sod it.' Shifting his aim, Nat dispatched the animal then dug his heels in angrily.

Nat struggled to regain a sense of the battle. Through banks of smoke and dust the Parliamentary cavalry was disintegrating on both flanks, dangerously exposing Waller's red-coated infantry. 'Dear God, they'll be slaughtered for sure without the horse.'

The retreat of Haselrig's precious Lobsters was in danger of becoming a rout. Below the escarpment Nat prayed the unprotected baggage train had withdrawn or it would be overrun. And the Royalists had a reputation for savagery.

With the route to the south blocked, the Lobsters were being forced towards the broad fields that appeared to open out in the west and which Farrington had squinted with the perspective glass, beyond the hedge. Nat pushed into the mêlée, seizing the bridle of an officer's horse. 'Hold, Sir! Hold the line, Sir, damn you, and save the day!'

'Save the day be damned,' bawled the man. 'Waller's quit the field. Save yourself, brother!'

Nat reined in, cutting across the flow towards the stranded infantry. Farmer Salt, not a soldier at all, would keep faith with his mates. And there, in the thick of it, a parson, black stick on a black horse hard against the colours. 'Bloody Markham!' The vicar of Hinton Helions was in his element. 'You tell 'em, Reverend!' Markham, barking mad, hurling the Old Testament at lambs to Cornish wolves, crack troops that would surely now be making their way out of Devizes to fall on the remnants of Sir William's army of the west.

Nat screamed along the line, searching for a clearing in the thicket of pikes. 'Markham, Reverend Markham!'

'Nathaniel Salt?' Markham nudged his horse into the pikemen. 'Let him in, brothers!'

The human stockade cracked open, just a bit, swallowing Nat in the press of men and swirling mist of acrid smoke and dust. 'Zounds Reverend, looks even worse from here.'

'Not so, Salt!' Wide-eyed, spittle-flecked, Markham was in no doubt. 'See, the King's horsemen have cleared off. Hallelujah!'

'Bleedin' God-botherer,' intoned a familiar voice. 'Parson's mad as a March hare.'

'Joe Jessop!' Nat slapped the grinning bailiff's back and jabbed a finger at the cavalry. 'Thought you'd been swept up in that hell-for-leather.'

'Not me. Didn't much like the look o' Waller's escape route.' Jessop tipped his chin towards Bagdon Hill. 'But it ain't too clever here neither, what with Markam's spavined sermonising an' that flaming great wall of cavalry coming to sweep up.'

'Oh, Lord love us.' The second wave of Lord Wilmot's cavalry was hammering towards the square. The pikemen had seen it too. Nat could smell their fear. Looking round for their officer, he saw only the ranting cleric and the drained, upturned face of a wide-eyed puppy with an orange sash. 'Sodding hell.' He snatched at the reins, turning the horse's head round. 'Stand to, lads!' He was not trained for this. 'Muskets to the front.' A shambles of musketeers pushed through the pikemen. 'Fire!'

The ragged volley destroyed a dozen of Wilmot's horse. Job done, the musket men scurried back behind the wall of pikes. But the King's men kept coming on. 'Steady lads. Spike 'em like faggots.' It was an optimistic command. In good order and from a safe distance, the dragoons fired their weapons into the square.

Nat pawed at a slap of blood and brains. 'God be praised!' His heart missed a beat. Buried in a cordon of dragoons stood a man of rank. '*Jehovah Providebit!*' Crazed, Nat dug at the mare, spurring her through the mêlée, clumsy, blooded sword pointing the way. 'Carew!' Unmistakable, even through the choking, blinding fog.

Breaking against the wall of steel, Nat saw Carew's thin lips curl. 'Nathaniel Salt?' A basket hilt smashed into his face. 'Hold there, trooper!' He reeled and, dimly, waited for the coup de grace.

'Sod off you bastards!' A familiar voice and thick arm pulling him up. 'Hold on, Mr Salt.'

'Joe?' Nat was bowling westward in the great press towards the hedge that Haselrig had so easily dismissed. He kicked on, ready to jump, but the beast stalled.

Still expecting a level field beyond the hedge, Nat dug his heels into the animal's flank, launching forward. 'O dear God!' The wide-eyed animal twisted and bucked, bellowing at the void, ground falling away steeply. Too late, Nat realised the low scrub beyond the hedge was not scrub at all but the crowns of beech and ash cascading downwards. He saw broken trees, men and horses extending far away to the right. A trooper, limbs flailing, was impaled on a broken pole of ash like a stuck pig, black gore spilling down the trunk. 'Bloody priest!' The curate's curse was playing out:

Fall ye like the godless swine of Gadara into the pit that is bottomless.

The Parliament's horse tumbled and twisted into the ravine. Nat flew past trees snapped like reeds and, stretching deep into the gorge, a presentiment of hell. His chest straddled a ravaged beech, ribs like greenstick. Barely conscious, he hit the ground, hard. As the cream of Parliament's army continued its descent, Nathaniel Salt blacked out.

Nat came to with his fingers lodged in a tacky mess of blood and bulging thigh muscle and no time to examine the wound in the path of the cavalry crashing down the ravine. Shuffling to the downhill side of the beech tree, he could see that he must stop the haemorrhage or expire. The blooded orange sash of the corpse within arm's reach would do. He pulled. A pistol jammed into the boy's waistband fell away. The youngster's face was a mash of bone and blood. 'Russell. You poor little sod.' It was Waller's delivery boy, the pup whose trembling hand dropped the dispatches at Haselrig's feet as the parliamentary army's preening commanders anticipated their easy victory.

The sash made a tourniquet twisted with a stick. Nat eyed the pistol. He hesitated. 'I'll take it to your father, boy, to ease his grieving heart.' He took the gun and untied the little sack of powder and shot clipped to Russell's belt.

'Zounds!' Nat pulled back against the beech tree, a man breaking cover like a fox in a spinney. With a whoop another two leapt ahead, vaulting through the undergrowth. The first man stumbled, just feet away. Pushing up, he launched forward too late, the royalist boot pinning him back in the dirt. The man's scream echoed round the gully, a thin blade entering his chest between the fourth and fifth ribs. The assailant ground his heel into the man's back, heaving the blade out with a grunt and a bloody spray.

'Bleedin' paupers an' god-bothering shop boys.' The Cornish assassin began his examination. 'Ain't sod all on this one.'

'Nah, come on, matey, I've 'ad a belly full,' said his accomplice. 'Rest'll be dead by morning an' save us the trouble.'

Sobbing like a child, punching through the pain, Nat inched his way up the slope through the charnel house of Haselrig's fallen cavalry. Hopton's Cornishmen had scoured the steep woodland and, he guessed, the scrapings of Devizes would shortly be picking through what was left.

At the top of the ravine the deceitful Siren hedge had been cut to pieces by the tumbling parliamentary cavalry. Keeping low, Nat retrieved Farrington's perspective glass.

Looters were rooting like dogs among the wimpering remnants of Waller's army. Hopton's ill-disciplined Cornish bandits and the rest of the King's army would be fanning out across the country to exact bloody retribution.

'Please God you still draw breath, Erasmus Carew, you bastard.' He reasoned that few of the tortured corpses seen with the perspective glass would be royalists, fewer still officers. '*Jehovah Providebit.* God will provide.'

*

Nat tumbled back down the ravine, falling into a sunken track. Glancing up and down the road, he knew he had to move quickly through country that was now hostile. He took the flintlock from his waistband, weighing it. It was a beautiful thing, finely balanced, superb even to his untutored eye. The gunsmith crafting such a piece would want his name on it. He flipped it over. 'William Upton of Oxford, eh? I'm thinking you're worth a pretty penny.' It was easily hidden, but not the cutlass. Unclipping the rough leather belt, he thrust the parcel deep in the thick hedge. 'You'll hide there 'til the crack of doom.' Unburdened, he checked himself up and down. 'Where to?'

Bristol. Declared for Parliament, it was the sort of place to hide a fugitive. He could take ship, find a new life in a quiet, godly corner. 'Americas, aye, that's it, Massachusetts.' Nathaniel Salt, assuredly civilian, contemplated the possibilities of a new life.

It would be dark soon, much safer to move. The King's thieving, leaderless rabble would be in their cups, toasting victory into the night. Nat staggered into the road but at every turn fell into the soft bank, checking ahead.

His caution was rewarded.

Above the hedge line, 200 yards off, the unmistakable red and gold colours of a company of foot emblazoned with the crown of the King of England and the dull, crump-crump of well-shod troops. 'Bloody Life Guards!'

Earth banks rising man-high on either side had hidden him well, but they were now his prison. Pitching at the embankment, he clawed uselessly at thick, barbed blackthorn. He fell back, bloodied. *Crump-crump*; the winding road twisted the column within yards. The King's standard flapped overhead. A final desperate lunge, thorns tearing, Nat bludgeoned through the hedge. Forcing his face down, he squinted at the young man whose feathered bonnet he had seen with the standard above the hedge. A patrician's chiselled profile, but the gods had been cruel. It was as if oxblood had been spattered across pale skin stretched over high cheekbones tight as a drum.

Nat held his breath as two dozen pikestaffs filed past. 'Zounds, that was close.' He rolled into the field. There was a good stand of ripening oats and barley and a thin light winking in the distance. Closer in, a tethered dog sounded off and a bent figure was quickly at his door. 'Who's there? Go on, get out of it.' The cottager was an ancient with a pitching fork.

Nat stumbled on, arms half-raised in mock surrender. 'Put up, father, I'll not hurt you.' He took a guess at the man's sympathies. 'Just a traveller, godly and true.'

The man shrugged, lowering his guard, bellowing into the hovel. 'Another poor scrap from the Parliament, Martha. We'll have a whole ragged regiment billeted here afore long and me dancing at the gallows tree for it.' He nodded wearily towards the barn.

'Yer mates are in there with my food an' drink. But if them royalists come,' he spat, 'I ain't seen nothing, right?' The rustic turned. 'And you'll be away first light. Eh?' The old man slammed his door. Nat limped towards the cracks of light spilling from the barn. He paused at the great door, fingering the Upton, listening to men rustling like rats in a hayloft.

He inched inside. And there, leaning against the barn's cruck-frame, was Sergeant Joe Jessop.

'Well if it ain't Mr Salt! Hadn't reckoned to see you again and that's the truth.' Beaming, the Sergeant loped towards him, gripping his shoulders. 'Made it past the old get and his moll then?'

'He wasn't pleased to see me.' Nat winced. 'Can't blame him.'

'Bleedin' hell, just look at you! Need some scoff and a kip.' He tipped his stubbled chin at the straw. 'Lodgings ain't cosy as yer last mind. No serving girls to warm a poor body. Just these poor scraps I picked up along the way.'

Nat squinted into a void lit by a single tallow lamp. He counted half a dozen youths, jaundiced in the yellow light, startled to their feet like weaners. Two of them snatched greasy Monmouth caps from tussled heads, the rest shuffled about uneasily, staring at the ground.

'Cheer up, lads, Mr Salt's one of us. Ain't no bleedin' officer on parade.' Jessop glanced at Nat, uncertain on both counts. 'Londoners they are, Trained Bands. Here, Master Salt, see if you can stomach some of this muck the old lizard's given us.' The Sergeant slopped something into a wooden bowl. 'Best downed in one.'

Nat cupped the bowl gratefully. 'What's your plan, Joe?' He tipped the liquid down his neck, wiping his lips with the back of his hand.

'Ain't planned nothing,' shrugged Jessop, spooning more broth. 'Thought we'd rest up here a bit then take off all civvy like.'

'Colonel Farrington?' Nat sprinkled a twist of Le Roux's wort into the broth. The bitter herbs that had failed to lift his spirits could season his soup. 'Well?'

'Dead.'

'Squire's dead?'

'Proper dead.'

'How?'

'Caught in the 'umbles by a ball from that poxed assassin what had a go at Colonel Haselrig.' Pulling a straw from the stack, Jessop began picking his teeth, passing his tongue round, sucking noisily. 'Knew he was worm's meat, I reckon, so tells you to get Colonel o' Horse away then leads the sally 'imself. Still, better than dying o' green rot or the surgeon's knife. Lord save all soldiers from that.'

Nat's bruised memory tumbled to his last, hurried exchange with Farrington. His fingers closed on the Squire's package. Weighing it, he flipped it over a couple of times, sensing the plain red seal, breaking it. A heavy signet ring and a locket fell away. Nat passed his thumb over the shallow device etched in both. Five letters, one each to Effam, the Sheriff of Wiltshire and himself and two addressed to Captain Norrington. Each closed with wax carrying the Farrington badge.

'Weren't pretty, were it, Mr Salt?' Jessop wanted to talk.

'No.' Replacing the letters and gold, Nat stuffed the pouch into his sleeve. 'What happened to you, with Markham and the infantry?'

'You don't remember?' Jessop peered at him. 'That'll be yer bang on the 'ead,' he nodded. 'Aye, that's it. Well, after you'd steadied the line, bleedin' good that was, you breaks out, sparring with them dragoons see. Must 'ave wasted dozens of 'em.' Jessop turned to his audience of Londoners. 'Bleedin' spectacular! Aye, all thrashing about like a tusked boar in the wildwood. Anyhow, one of the buggers cracks you over the 'ead. Thought you was a gonner.'

'All I remember's Carew, his dragoons pinning me down, thinking I'm going to die, before getting *him*.' Brow furrowed, Nat fought to remember. 'But I'm not dead. How's that, Joe?'

The Sergeant winked, tapping his nose. 'Yer guardian angel, that's what. Then you tips up here and right glad we are too.' He beamed at the Londoners. 'Anyhow, after the tussle with them dragoons I fell back in with our infantry and them cavaliers clears off like they was after a fox. But some berk left our cannon to the enemy; unspiked!' The Londoners had suffered the consequences. 'Them royalists turned the pieces round and start banging away at us, didn't they, lads? Then up comes Hopton out of Devizes all fresh like with his bastard Cornishmen an' them royalist cavalry lining up to finish us off, easy as you please.' He passed a hand over his face, chewing his lip, scanning the downy upturned faces. 'Last thing I remember's our crazy bloody parson bawling out psalms from his horse. Then I gets knocked down and wakes up with me nag dead on top and all me mates in a better place.' He sucked his teeth and shrugged. 'Played dead for a bit. Weren't difficult in that company. Face down I was, in the dirt, among all that gore. Oh the stink of it, the bleeding racket.' Jessop turned away, scratching the dirt with a stick. 'Royalist bastards set about them poor cunts where they'd fallen. Stripped 'em, flayed 'em with butcher's knives, quick or dead, made no odds. Screams of them poor souls'll be with me 'til judgement day. God rest them.' He passed a grimy fist across his eyes.

'There was this crabbit old woman with a big arse and a sack that went from one to the next harvesting like she was pulling turnips. She finds an officer what was breathing. So she puts her bag down, ever so dainty like, plucks out this great club and beats his bleedin' brains out. Then she puts the stick away, cool as you please, strips off his coat, all covered in gore, and sticks it in her bag.' He paused, breathing deeply. 'The old cow's about to move on to some other poor body but sees gold on his finger. There's a great tugging and pulling, but it won't budge. So she gets a rock and smashes his knuckle what's caused the obstruction and off it comes.' The soldier spat in the dust. 'Well, I weren't waiting to 'ave my brains spread across that poxy field so I legged it. Angel o' death looks up from her work and hollers like. One of their musket men takes a pot at me. Too quick I was. Vaulted over that hedge what the cavalry jumped. Bleeding hell, what a sight! Fell rest of the way.'

'That'll be the cliff I tripped over,' said Nat.

'Aye, well I met this sorry crew at the bottom.' Jessop tipped his chin at the Londoners. 'Only there was more of 'em then. Three slipped away like and we lost two when we got jumped by a company o' dragoons.'

'Life Guards.' Jessop had done well to save any of the Londoners from them. 'They were King's Life Guards.'

'Yeah? Well, right glad you've shown up 'cos I'm buggered if I know what to do with these boys.'

Nat took a closer look at the militiamen. He guessed the best had cleared off, preferring to take their chances on the London road. One lad stood out among the frightened shop boys. 'Where're you from soldier?'

'London, Sir.' The soldier swelled with pride. 'Colonel Jellicoe's Regiment of Foot, Sir, name of Porit, Sir, Will Porit of Bethnal Green, Sir, 'prenticed butcher and slaughterman, Sir.'

'You're a long way from home, lads, and you'll not be marching back with colours blazing.' Nat shook his head. 'There'll be no tin whistles on the London road.'

The soldiers looked at one another. 'Serg said he'd sort us out,' Will Porit piped up. 'Said he'd see us back home.'

'Well, you can take pot luck on the road, boys, but I'll give odds you'll fall in with more of those Life Guards,' said Nat. 'Nearly got my own head on a pikestaff back there.'

'What'll we do then?'

Nat looked at Jessop. The Londoners were the Sergeant's responsibility, not his. 'You lads get your heads down.' Nat pointed at the door. 'Sergeant and I will have a quiet word outside.'

'Country's crawling with King's men, Joe.' Nat doubted Jessop understood the precariousness of their situation. 'Murdering bastards'll fall on your nursery like a dog fox in a hen-house.' He nodded at the cottage. 'And you'd better mind that old goat and his beldam.'

'Aye, can't trust nobody.' Jessop snorted and spat. 'I've set a piquet down the track case he goes for a Mosey. Can't stay here though. What'll we do, Mr Salt?'

'I *was* heading for Bristol.' Nat tapped Farrington's enigmatic package against the wall. He should have kept to the road, avoiding Jessop and his crèche. 'And Massachusetts.'

'What about us?'

Nat shook his head. 'You're the sergeant, sworn and attested.' Nat realised it was not just a helping hand the big man was after. 'I'm not even a private soldier, just a farmer.'

'Did bloody well today for a farmer,' muttered Jessop. 'Holding the line with them infantry about to scarper. Aye, man, reckon you can call yerself soldier, much as any of us.'

'We all did *bloody well*, Joe Jessop. You, me, those boys in there. How many of the Parliament's men d'you think were in a battle before today? Huh?' A few score, I reckon, among thousands.'

Jessop screwed his face, scratching his head. 'That's not why we lost though, is it, Mr Salt?'

'I'm no soldier, Joe Jessop,' shrugged Nat.

'Soldier?' Jessop snorted. 'You don't 'ave to be no bleedin' soldier. We lost 'cos our commanders don't know their arse from their armpit.'

Nat smiled thinly. 'And Lord Wilmot does.'

'Aye.' Jessop kicked the barn door. 'And there's the friggin' rub.'

Nat let Joe Jessop calm down. 'Well, what's to be done then, eh?' He ran a hand through matted hair. 'I'm thinking a dog-leg back to Lavington. Offload your platoon on Norrington. Then I'm for Bristol, and Massachusetts.'

Jessop cleared his throat. 'Ah, Lavington, *hospitable* place Lavington. Bit of comfort waiting for you there, eh Mr Salt?"

'If you've a better plan, friend, let's hear it,' snapped Nat. 'Or shut it, eh?'

'No offence, Sir,' muttered Jessop. 'Lavington it is then. I'll tell the lads Sir.'

'Joe.' Nat leant against the barn. 'I'm sorry – didn't mean to snap.'

'Nah.' Jessop grinned. 'We're all knackered, that's all.'

Nat tipped the contents of Farrington's packet into his palm. He replaced the first four letters, the locket and the ring and played the fifth letter between his fingers before breaking the seal.

Lavington

12 July 1643

My dear Nathaniel (if I may),

If you see this I will be with the Lord. Rejoice, since I do not fear death, simply the manner of it and the leaving of my dear, sweet Effam. And it is on that account in the last hours of my life that I write to you.

She is a fine young woman, cruelly struck down by her illness and on that account a spinster. I see your affection for my child and, in her way, hers for you. Be patient. Her stern manner is for the avoidance of further hurt, a defensive position. To you alone, my daughter has shown a chink in her armour. Exploit it.

Grand persons like my wife, God rest her, may say a yeoman is unfit. They are wrong. I would be honoured to call you my son in place of the heir that God has denied me but I hope will grant you both. My fervent wish is for you to wed and take with my daughter all I hold, though it's precious little.

I enclose a letter to Effam in personal terms and two to Captain Norrington. Of these two, one is marked with a small ' X' in the corner. It seeks my cousin's assistance in the proposal I put to you. Deliver this to him only if you are in agreement with the terms I have set. The second I hope you will be able to destroy for it is an entreaty to take in my poor Effam. He is her only kinsman and last resort if you fail me. The last letter is my testimony dealing with the death of the curate that will deliver you from the scaffold though not, I fear, from the violence of papists, recusants, Laudians etc.

Finally, the locket is for my daughter and the ring with my device is for you.

God bless you both.

Miles Farrington

Nat jammed the ring on his fifth finger. Stretching his hand, he studied the worn engraving, twisting it gently round and round.

He felt for the two letters addressed to Norrington, replacing one and tearing up the other, watching the pieces carry away on the breeze like autumn leaves.

Back in the barn, Joe Jessop was squatting on his haunches with the ragged platoon. 'I've put an extra guard on the track with a clear view of the cottage. Two hour tricks 'til dawn.' Jessop scowled and spat. 'We've lost one lad already. Said he was going for a piss. Never came back.'

Nat shrugged. 'The provost'll deal with him, if he makes it to London, which I doubt.'

'Sorry about that little tosser, Sir.' The butcher's boy, shuffled awkwardly, staring at the ground. 'Better off without him and that's a fact.'

The man was the best turned out of the six, well built, commanding their respect. 'Porit, isn't it?'

'Aye, Sir,' said the boy, drawing himself up. 'Will Porit, butcher an' slaughterman, remember?'

'Yes, I do.' Apprentice, Nat mused, but a veteran too. His own mother would not recognise him. 'Your calling's steeled you well for today, slaughterman.'

The boy looked stunned. 'No Sir, not at all, Sir.'

'No, suppose not,' said Nat. 'There's nothing in creation to ready a poor soul for that knacker's yard.'

'Now then, philosophising at this hour ain't healthy,' said Joe Jessop. 'Porit, you and yer mates'll stand piquet, two hour tricks. Keep awake mind 'cos them cavaliers'll be mopping up out of Devizes once they've drunk it dry and 'ad the last of its maidens, if they find any in that heathen place.'

'Aye Sergeant.' The boy looked pleased with his commission. 'What do I do if I see a royalist?'

'What d'you do, what d'you do?' Jessop leered at him. 'You shoot the bastard's 'ead off lad!'

The boy shrugged. 'What with, Sergeant?'

Nat realised that apart from Jessop's matchlock the only serviceable gun was his borrowed pistol. And he planned to keep that hidden. 'I expect, Sergeant Jessop, he's to sprint back here quiet as he can, raise the alarm.'

Jessop nodded swiftly. 'Aye that's it, Sir, so we can scarper before we're marched down the square in Devizes, lined up in front of The Bear and shot for rebels.'

*

Jessop's litany of oaths woke Nat with a start. Will Porit was bundling in their host and his woman. 'I was sat where you told me Sergeant and guess what tripped past, yacking like it was May Day at Moorfields?'

'Well, bugger me!' roared Jessop. 'Why's the gruesome twosome stepping out upon the devil's dancing hour?'

The woman let rip.

'Sergeant Jessop!' Nat caught Jessop's raised hand.

The old man pressed forward. 'Sir, it's not what you think. I was frightened them cavaliers would string me up if they found you here. So me and the missus figured we'd lodge a while in Devizes with her sister. Ain't that gospel truth, Martha?'

'But you weren't talking about no sister when I found you, were you?' quipped Porit. 'Him and his missus were counting the pretty purse they'd get in Devizes for ratting on us, Sir.'

Nat towered over the wretch. 'You're a lying old goat. Thank the Lord it was Sergeant Jessop and his gentle men that fetched up here and not the King's Cornish cut-throats.' He nodded at Joe Jessop. 'Reckon you've put him in a fix. Me, I'd fire the place with you in it.' The wretched couple gawped, bug-eyed. 'Lucky I'm not in charge. Maybe my Serg'll let you off with a penalty.' The old man nodded pathetically. 'Only guessing, but if your missus finds her manners and raises a proper breakfast? None of that putrid slop you palmed them off with yesterday, mind. How about a side of that bacon I caught a whiff of at your door last night?' Nat smacked his lips. 'Small beer to slake the lads' thirst would be good. Aye, and whatever else you've got stashed away that takes the Sergeant's fancy. Yes?'

The old devil's pig eyes shot between Nat and Jessop. 'Aye, I get it.' He packed away his woman to prepare the richest feast she had ever served, under Will Porit's watchful eye.

VII

Boxed with ancient dogwood, blackthorn and elder almost touching overhead, a man could pass the deep, lush green hollow-way unseen on either side.

'That breakfast was a fine idea of yours, Joe.' Nat congratulated Jessop from the back of his borrowed donkey. 'Those Londoners talk of nothing else.'

'Poor saps ain't had scoff like that for a while, nor likely to for a bit.' Jessop grinned at the ragged troop. Full bellies lifted morale. 'The poor man's hodgepodge ain't hardly seen a lick o' pheasant or partridge these past few winters.'

A few paces ahead, Will Porit put out his arm, raising a finger to his lips. 'Look, turkey bird,' he whispered.

'Nah, it's a bustard. Lord, and it's a biggun. Bleedin' oversized chickens, bustards, twice as stupid,' Jessop winked, 'twice as tasty.' The bailiff unslung his musket, feeling for power and shot. 'They're slow and bold as brass, which is why there ain't many left.' He shook his head wistfully. 'But reckon he's safe enough with this poxy matchlock.'

'This any good?' Reluctantly, Nat passed the Upton.

'Lord love us! You kept this little beauty quiet.' Jessop spun the flintlock between his fingers. 'Rifled job. Can't miss with a thing like this.' He played his thumb over the inscription.

'It's an Upton.' Nat doubted Jessop could read the maker's mark.

'Yeah? William Upton?' He made a low whistle. 'Fella makes tools fit for Prince Rupert himself.' Jessop had the gun primed and loaded in an instant, raised it and fired, winging the bird. 'Beauty.' He wiped the gun with his sleeve, caressing it like a woman, handing it back just as reluctantly. 'And not a bad shot at this range, even with this lovely. Off you go, Porit, show us what an Eastcheap butcher can do.'

Snapping the bird's neck, Will Porit plucked twine from his napsack to bind its legs, hauling the creature onto his back.

'Fine cock bird like him did well to live so long what with the country crawling wi' thieving soldiers, all with guts against their backbone.'

Lowering his voice, Jessop nodded at the pistol. 'William Upton makes guns in Oxford for cavaliers with thick purses. Begging yer pardon, Sir, how does a farmer come by a thing costing ten years of a working man's life?'

Curious or suspicious, Jessop was probably both. Nat jammed the piece in his waistband. He would return it to the dead boy's father at the first opportunity. 'We'll draw lots for the drumsticks.'

Jessop cleared his throat and spat. 'Good place for your kitchen, Porit.' He pointed at the chalk stream forded by flat stones. 'Get cooking, Will.' Before long, the smell of Will Porit's camp fire was drifting across the stream.

'Hello.' Joe Jessop was the first to see the mutt lurking at the water's edge. 'Here.' The half-wolf took off. 'Miss Effam had a dog like him at Helions years ago after some mongrel jumped the wall. Squire's missus, hard nut she was, told me to drown the pups.' Jessop grinned through his mouthful of bird. 'But Miss Effam got this 'un before I came with me sack. Her mother was bleedin' furious, but it was weaned by then, so Colonel said keep it. Always gets her way, that morte.'

Nat ignored Jessop's sideways glance. 'Your dog's back.' The creature sidled towards the morsel, scoffing it, brown eyes fixed warily.

'Here.' Jessop held out another scrap. The animal, tail down, nose down, inched across the stream, sniffing for the meat. 'Good boy.'

'Careful Joe, look at those teeth!' Nat would sooner hurl a stone.

'Nah.' The animal took the treat, skulking off to watch from a distance. 'I knows the ones what'll bite.' Jessop picked fibres from his teeth. 'Course when she went away Squire's missus made me slit the mutt's throat. Told 'er it died o' natural causes.'

Will Porit snapped off the breastbone, handing it to Nat and Jessop. 'It's the wishbone, though much bigger than the turkey bird's. You make a wish, don't tell mind. Then you pull it, like this…' he hooked his little fingers round the limbs of the bone '… and the bloke that gets the bigger bit gets his wish. Simple!'

The bone snapped in Nat's favour. Jessop clapped him on the back. 'And what's Sir wishing for?'

Nat said nothing, in his mind's eye the body of the Jesuit creaking in the wind. Only when the corpse turned, the bloated face and lolling tongue had gone. Instead, staring down, neck snapped like Porit's bird, were the bemused, aesthetic features of Erasmus Carew.

*

Captain Norrington strutted the hall like a coxcomb. Poring over maps, fretting over dispatches, busy, important Tobias Norrington had no time for farmers. Turning his back, he pocketed Farrington's letter. 'That'll be all, Salt.'

Nat glanced round the makeshift HQ marvelling at the number of gentlemen hard at work administering Waller's defeat.

'That'll be all, Salt!' Norrington's bark silenced the room. But Nat had seen too many good men die to suffer the lily-livered poltroon with his pins and papers. Fists clenched, he towered over the Captain who had run away.

'Tosser.'

Staff officers sniggered into their sleeves, Norrington spinning round. 'Eh? What's that?'

'I think Salt should have his wounds tended, Captain Norrington.' An officer Nat knew, Major Henry Wagstaff of Warminster, was pushing forward. 'Sir Arthur won't be pleased if you upset his rescuer now, will he?' Wagstaff seized Nat's arm, steering him away. 'Keep silence,' he hissed, slamming the door. 'God's blood, Nathaniel Salt!'

Nat shrugged 'Man's an idiot, and a coward.'

'Agreed.' Wagstaff jammed his hands on his hips. 'Which means he isn't worth a flogging.'

'I'm civilian,' Nat countered truculently. 'Not eligible for flogging.'

'Christ Almighty, you've a packet to learn, young 'un!' Wagstaff sucked his teeth. 'Look, friend, irregular you may be, but this piss-awful war makes you a soldier like all the rest, and a private soldier at that. Insubordination means a flogging to add to your great well of misery.' He took a few moments to weigh the headstrong yeoman. 'Here's the thing: Sir Arthur owes you. He may reward you. Don't let an arse like Tobias Norrington screw it up.'

*

In the kitchen Nat learned Sir Arthur Haselrig was recuperating upstairs. 'Proper poorly,' said Obadiah Cotton, 'and mad as hell with Sir William Waller.'

86

'Needs to mend fast. Take charge of that lot.' Nat jerked a finger at the chaotic HQ. 'Major Wagstaff says Sir Arthur'll want my account of General Waller's disaster. Don't know why. Reckon he'd sooner put a farmer's jottings through the flame of a candle than use it to read them,' Nat sighed. 'Have you got a pen and some paper friend?' He scanned the room looking for the elfin girl.

Mrs Cotton was keeping her eyes on her needlework. 'I know what you're after, young man, but she's not here.' Needle and thread, up and down, reproachfully. 'Mr Jessop, your friend's beat. Looks feverish.' Joe Jessop, playing with a kitten, glanced up, grinning. 'He'd best stay here. Rest of you to the stable, same as before,' she sniffed. 'But make sure your Londoners steer clear of my girls.' With a glance, she silenced the two maids giggling over root vegetables. 'Captain Norrington's off to his house on the Strand. Needed in London, being so important and all. Wants the plate, linen, furniture and what's left of the liquor when those locusts have cleared off,' she nodded at the ramshackle HQ, 'sent to London so as the papists don't get the benefit of it.' Mrs Cotton rapped the table. 'There are the two baggages I'd like to pack away. No doubt the King's men *will* have the benefit of them, little trollops, given half a chance, which I intend to deny them.' She shook her head. 'Though why they'd want it, I really don't know.'

Nat signed his report. 'There, done.' He threw the pen down, wiping beads of sweat from his brow. 'Though I reckon Sir Arthur'll take as much time with my scratchings as the opinions of the Bishop of Rome.' He sprinkled sand, jerking his head towards the hall. 'Anyhow, no doubt his flunkies'll make sure it gets nowhere near him.'

Tapping his nose, Obadiah Cotton slipped Nat's paper under the Colonel's restorative and padded upstairs.

*

Major Wagstaff pored over the table with its map and coloured pins, glancing over his shoulder to check Norrington had gone. 'See here, Salt, our host reckons the King'll press home his advantage; says he's sweeping the county already, but I find no evidence of it.'

'Agreed. These positions don't exist.' Nat ran his figure over the territory crossed by his makeshift troop, plucking out Norrington's red pins. 'There, that's better.'

Tobias Norrington returning from his nap scowled at the little pile of pins, spying the Upton pistol jammed into Nat's waistband. 'That's a fine piece. Show me?' Nat handed him the pommel of the gun, Norrington examining it with a master's eye. 'How d'you come by it?'

'Keeping it safe, Sir, to return to the family of a brave man who did his duty on Roundway field,' Nat towered above his host, 'while others stayed at home.'

'Mind yourself, churl,' Norrington snarled, jabbing Nat's guts with the weapon. 'This magistrate cleaves hands from thieves.'

Colonel Sir Arthur Haselrig watched the performance from the door, fingering Nat's note. 'Mr Salt, likely I owe you my life, Sir, for your service yesterday.' He waved the report at a wingchair. 'Sit you down, Sir, sit you down. As for this,' he eased himself painfully into his chair, 'I have no issue with your analysis. But I'm wondering how a farmer turns Quartermaster General in the space of a week.'

'A civil war's a civilian's war, Colonel.' He looked round the room to illustrate his point. 'But I reckon the enemy has an edge on you.'

Haselrig winced, staring at the yeoman, stroking his lip with a forefinger. He nodded at Nat's bound leg. Despite Mrs Cotton's best efforts, blood and pus seeped through the dressing like juice through the crust of a blackberry tart. 'We've both been bloodied, Sir.' Haselrig grinned approval. 'Major Wagstaff says you were practically lieutenant to my friend Miles Farrington, God rest him.' He jabbed a finger at Nat. 'Well, that's a damn good 'prenticeship for a field commission, Mr Salt!'

Nat gawped, Norrington spinning round, purple faced. 'Oh, no, Sir Arthur, that won't do at all.' He lowered his voice. 'Well, I mean to say, I hardly think Sir William would consider Salt *suitable*.'

'You're nothing but a damned snob, Norrington. Look at him, he's been cut about abominably.' He nodded at the sodden binding. 'Zounds, this man's stripes are fresher than a fishwife's fancy! Best keep your counsel, you great booby, lest some unkind soul draws an inventory of your service these past few weeks. Innkeeper, that's all you've been. For all the good it'll do when Hopton clears you out.' He winked at Nat. 'Not suitable, my arse.'

Sir Arthur's officers were enjoying their host's discomfort, Nat feeling the full heat of Norrington's enmity, fanned by Farrington's letter. 'Sir Arthur, I'm no soldier, certainly not an officer.'

'Or a gentleman,' Norrington rasped.

Nat scowled at Norrington, lowering his voice so only the Colonel could hear. 'I've a sort of private war, Sir, score to settle. I can't be distracted.'

Haselrig's eyes switched between Norrington and the young man. 'Understand you topped one of their priests, Salt.' He tut-tutted, wagging a finger. 'Norrington kills priests too. *Don't you, Norrington?*' His lip curled, revolted by the killing at Gibbet Knoll. 'But only Jesuits, and he's a magistrate. You're not, so the Bishop of Salisbury will want your balls for breakfast. King'll probably settle for your neck.'

'Curate's death was misadventure.' Nat protested. 'I've witnesses and sworn affidavits.'

'Well, I doubt that'll do much for you. World's gone topsy-turvy and peasants are biddable witnesses, encouraged by silver, or cold steel. What d'you say, Foxwood?' Haselrig bawled into the shadows.

'I've always found cold steel most effective, Sir Arthur,' lisped the pale-faced clerk twisting forward.

'Ha!' Haselrig slapped his knee. 'There you are, and Foxwood knows about these things, don't you, Foxwood?'

'Sir's too kind.' The little man rubbed his hands. 'The late European wars did foster certain *arts*, Sir Arthur.' But his roving eye had found a far prettier mark than Sir Arthur Haselrig.

'Gentlemen, Foxwood has come among us from London to spy for our superiors,' announced Haselrig. 'Ain't that so, Foxwood?'

'No, Sir.'

'Yes, Sir!' barked Haselrig. 'But that's alright, if you take John Pym a good account.'

Foxwood's eyes were still fixed on the young farmer that nature had assembled so handsomely. 'Thank you, Sir Arthur.'

Wagstaff leant across. 'John Pym runs Parliament. After the King, he's the most powerful man in the country. King Pym they call him.' He nodded at Foxwood. 'That crook back's got Pym's ear. See, even bluff old Haselrig's wary of him.'

'Salt, you're enlisted in Sir William Waller's army of the west,' snapped Haselrig. 'Remain here as private soldier or accept my proposal as Captain.'

'God's blood, Sir Arthur!' Norrington threw up his podgy arms. 'The correct field commission is Ensign, Lieutenant at a push, though either under the circumstances seems excessive.'

Haselrig brushed him away. 'You wanted to send scouts south. I can think of no better scout, can you, Captain Norrington?' The man shrugged unhappily. 'We're away to Bristol to help General Waller shore up that damned miserable God-botherer Nathaniel Fiennes against Prince Rupert of the Rhine. Prince'll lose no time besieging the port after the Devizes fight.' He beat a tattoo on the arm of his wingchair. 'Take two or three good men, *Captain* Salt, sweep south of the plain. Godly folk are being harassed by recusants. Christ's blood, man, you know all about that.' Wagstaff had told him about the fire at Brook Farm. 'Pep our people up, you know.' He paused for a moment, measuring his words carefully, glancing briefly at Foxwood. 'I shouldn't incite you to banditry, Nat, but I'll wager there's no better way to cheer up the godly than a little mischief on their papist neighbours.' Nat caught a smile chasing across Foxwood's thin lips. 'Will you put a bit of stick about for me, Nat?'

The newly minted officer did not share his Colonel's appetite for pillage and knew no orders would ever be written for the actions Sir Arthur had in mind. He would exercise his commission sparingly in respect of all recusants, except one. 'Aye, Sir Arthur.'

Chewing his lip, Haselrig beckoned Nat close 'Understand, Captain, you now hold Parliament's Commission. That's a serious matter. Cross me and it'll not just be the King that's after your neck.' Haselrig lowered his voice in a kindly, conspiratorial way. 'I know about Norrington's crony, that turd Carew, what he's done. But vengeance is a dish best supped cold, boy.' He gripped Nat's forearm like a vice. 'The army demands malignants be brought to book on the triple tree, at the snatch of a rope. Deliver your tormentor to me without the dignity of a soldier's death.'

'Sir, if God wills it, I shall.'

*

Norrington spitting tacks, Captain Nathaniel Salt, Joe Jessop and Will Porit chose the best of the horses and moved out.

'What's that?' The dog Jessop fed on bustard gristle was padding along warily twenty yards behind. 'Damme, Joe, it's your mangy wolf-dog, isn't it?'

'Ain't mine, Cap'n. Just kept following, see.' He raised his arm. 'Go on, get out of it!' The mongrel slunk back, out of sight.

'Gawd.' Jessop covered his nose, rounding Gibbet Knoll downwind with Norrington's Jesuit still swinging.

'Good sign,' said Nat. 'If the enemy was here they'd have likely cut their papist from the nubbing post.' A crow scratching at an empty socket rose noisily. 'Pound to a penny, the King's men turned west to move against Waller at Bristol.' He nodded at the corpse. 'God's blood, do something about that won't you, Will Porit?' Pulling up his neck cloth, the Londoner took a knife to the hempen rope. 'All God's creatures deserve a pinch of dignity, puritan or papist.'

Jessop shrugged. 'Dogs and the gallows' mandrake'll have your parson, Sir.'

'Better than bluebottles and carrion crows.' Nat steadied his horse. 'Remember man, could be you, or me, or Will Porit swinging in the wind, laying down stink for miles around.'

Jessop sucked his teeth. 'Porit's already 'alfway there!'

Will Porit nodded at the shadows. 'Well, it looks like your dog's back, Sergeant.' The hound was following its nose to the corpse.

Nat cursed. 'Sort it out man before it violates the Jesuit. Best pile some of those stones on him, you and Porit.' He was short, cracked ribs giving him grief. 'Catch up when you're done.'

Clear of the downs, Nat drew up at the Salisbury turnpike, waiting for his men behind a blackthorn hedge. He did not want another encounter with royalists on the road. 'Heard you coming, jabbering like a couple of beldames.' Nat's greeting had a hard edge. 'It's as well I'm no King's bloody Life Guard.' His gashed thigh was throbbing, temper shortening by the minute. 'And I told you sergeant, get rid of that mutt. It's not a flaming pet.'

'Aw Sir, thing is, felt proper bad about Miss Effam's dog.' Jessop looked mournfully at the animal. 'You know, all them years ago like I told you. Couldn't do it again, what with this 'un being practically its twin, now could I?'

Nat scowled, pointing his horse west, mood darkening with each step. 'Hold back, Will. Cap'n's with his thoughts, poor bugger.'

The companions of Nat's tortured sleep, four charred forms bound tight in white cotton laid out side by side, were more vivid with each step. Heart racing, he tugged angrily at his neck cloth, wringing wet, burying his face in the cool rag. His broken chest hurt like hell, each laboured breath rattling like a miller's lungs.

'Alright, Sir?' Joe Jessop pulled alongside. 'You look like shit.' He reached across to steady Nat's horse. 'Here.' Jessop winked, reaching in his saddlebag, teeth uncorking the half-empty bottle with a pop. 'Brewed from juniper berries by old man Cotton.' Nat took a drag. 'Easy Sir!' The raw spirit seared his gullet. 'Knock your bleedin' head off.'

Nat dug his heels in hard.

*

Euphemia Farrington watched the horsemen swing past the emblazoned stanchions of her drive, the dozy picket sent to spy on her startling away. Framed in stone at her threshold, she greeted Nat formally, scanning his face for confirmation. 'How did he die?'

'Quickly, madam, leading a cavalry charge.'

She turned first to the darkening sky and smiled, then to the strong young soldier shifting awkwardly at the foot of the steps. 'Oh blast, you expect me to grieve,' she sighed. 'You reckoned to make a wailing doxy of me with your news, didn't you, Mr Salt?' She peered at the spot vacated by the sentry. 'Well, you've upset the goblin at the gate. Scampered away to raise the alarm, I expect.' She looked cross. 'If you've drawn down trouble, I'll need your muskets, so you'd better come in.'

'Thank you, lady.'

'See you've taken a dog, Joe Jessop.' Her mouth pinched tight as a purse string. 'Like mine; the one you took a knife to when my back was turned.'

Jessop coloured. 'Died o' natural causes, lady.'

'Don't lie to me Jessop,' she snapped, smiling quickly at the animal before turning to the practicalities. 'My maid Sarah will take care of your men, Mr Salt. You come with me.' The mistress of Helions spun on her heels. 'I'll need a full report.' She led him through the atrium and the oak screen to the hall. 'You're confused, aren't you, Mr Salt? You're wondering what sort of woman takes her father's death so lightly.'

'Lightly, Madam?' He passed a hand through his thick hair, a habit of his she noted. 'Doubt it.'

The faintest, mocking smile as she poured two glasses of claret. 'And who are you to doubt it, Mr Salt, when you don't know me at all?' She hesitated with the wine. 'Oh, I'm sorry, how thoughtless. I'll send for beer or cider or something, if you prefer. I don't know what you people drink.'

He took the glass without a word. 'Grief comes to us according to our nature.'

Good, she thought, quick, apposite. Her father had been right to rate him. 'On grief, I suppose you're right. But losing a parent's a natural thing, ordained, like the turning of the tide. The death of a child, though?' Effam looked for a reaction. 'Well, it's enough to crush a person.' She carried on down the hall, plain taffeta gown rustling. 'Died at the head of his men you say, leading a charge?'

Nat wondered what romantic picture was forming in her head. 'Yes, madam, but Joe Jessop saw it better than me.'

She smiled grimly, satisfied. 'God be praised then.'

'God, lady, had nothing to do with it.' He shook his head wearily. 'God forsook the godly on Roundway Down. And I'm truly sorry for your loss.'

'Don't be, and you're not to think me callous either, Mr Salt.' The lady drilled into his eyes. 'But I see you do.' She shrugged. 'My father was dogged by the past. Can you understand?' Portraits of warriors glared down in support of their formidable kinswoman. 'His father followed Buckingham to France, his grandfather was with King Henry in Flanders and his great grandfather was knighted by Henry Tudor after Bosworth. Farringtons were at Crecy, Poitiers and Agincourt. D'you see?' Effam searched his face. 'My father spent his life at home.' She glared at the paintings. 'Poor booby, he tended his lands like a husbandman, watching them fail year on year. His greatest fear was that he should die in his bed.' She pointed at a hard-backed seat by the hearth. 'Sit, if you want.'

'Colonel said to give you these.' Nat reached inside his doublet for the Farrington letter and locket. 'He wrote me a letter, Captain Norrington too.'

Ignoring the locket, she took her father's note with puzzled hesitation. 'He left this with *you*?' She read quickly by candlelight without expression then played the note into the flame. 'And how did you find cousin Norrington?'

'I believe he found me wanting.'

She did not doubt it. 'Are you surprised?'

'Likely saw himself as your protector,' shrugged Nat. 'But Colonel, didn't, did he? I'd feel disappointed, in Captain Norrington's shoes.'

'Gentle soul,' she whispered.

'Madam?'

'Do *you* think I need protecting Nat?'

Blood burned in his cheeks. 'Colonel decided we should marry, that's all.' There, he had blurted it out like a clodhopper, treating the lady like some milky maid, the sort to spread her legs and be grateful.

'Indeed.' She smiled, still playing her game. 'And what have *you* decided, Nat?'

He shrugged, recognising an unequal tussle. Effam changed tack as skilfully as a pilot navigating a shoal.

'Your man called you "Captain"?'

'Field commission.' Nat was beginning to think Erasmus Carew and Euphemia Farrington were well matched. 'Madam, I have to check on my men.'

'A *Captain*!' He would not get away so easily. 'Oh, my word, that makes you even more of a catch. I heard tell Nathaniel Salt of Brook Farm was already the twinkle in the eye of a score of village lovelies. Just imagine the dash you'll cut with all those insufferable matrons that fancy their daughters young ladies when they learn you've come back an officer.' Brushing away the ash of her father's letter, she silenced his protest. 'So, Sir, with such fine prospects why bother me? No Sir, listen to me, you're to farrow down with some fresh faced farmer's girl and I'll smile from my pew as you shepherd your brood every Sunday.'

'Why, madam, d'you suppose I've not done that already?' He drained his glass. 'Remarried, I mean?'

'That's no concern of mine. But you should know my fortune isn't any more in my purse than in my face. A grand name's all I have and that's cheap enough in a world turned upside down.' She paused, framing her face with her hands. 'As you see, my fine Captain, I'm no Aphrodite. Now, let's have no more of my father's nonsense.'

He rubbed a hand over black stubble. 'Lady, I heard an understanding had passed between you and Erasmus Carew...'

'If so, no business of yours,' she snapped.

'He'd provide for you better than me,' said Nat. 'I withdraw happily knowing that.'

'Withdraw from what? I'm not a lot in Sarum market for men to bid against on a quarter day.'

He blushed. 'I meant, madam, my presence could stand you into danger. I meant Carew, things being what they are, would protect you when I can't.'

'Then know this.' She prepared to give an inch, see how far he went. 'What you've heard is gossip. I never had an arrangement with Mr Carew, and never will. Have you been ear-wigging, girl?'

'Oh, no, madam.' Sarah was standing at the screen.

'Huh! I think you have. Anyway, it was Sarah who told me about the wagging tongues whose tittle-tattle you swallowed.' She glared at the maid. 'Oddly enough I haven't been bothered by Mr Carew since the day of the butts when you turned up looking like a scarecrow.'

Nat caught Sarah's eye and was sure the colour in her cheeks had nothing to do with the heat.

'Off you go, Sarah,' snapped Effam.

Carew's bitter invective as the two men faced off by the brick cart thundered through Nat's head. *The lady gets the better man, is it?* He felt Farrington's note in his pocket. *To you alone, my daughter has shown a chink in her armour. Exploit it.* He sat stiffly, staring at the floor, once again the awkward, rough-hewn adolescent condemned to sneaking glimpses of her on a Sunday. 'Then I'd be honoured beyond words to have you as my wife, lady. I believe I've loved you since I first set eyes upon you.'

His uncut sincerity was the perfect antidote to her sophisticated cross-examination. She looked away, blinking, biting her lip, struggling to maintain the hauteur perfected as her own special defence against a world of silly young men. Her poor father entertained them all; coxcombs that put a heavy price on beauty and boorish arrivistes yearning to strengthen a toehold in society. Flawed creatures, all of them.

She sent them away and let it be understood that Miss Farrington of Helions would stay a spinster. But Nat's soft words caressed her like a warm summer breeze. The reply tumbled from her lips. 'Oh poor, simple, darling boy, that's the loveliest thing, ever.' But she was Euphemia Farrington, last of her line. 'The locket was my mother's. My father found it a comfort and kept it with him, always.' Her words were clipped again, guarded, patrician. 'Sir, I give it to you now in the hope that I will be a better wife to you than she was to him.'

'I have one condition,' she snapped. 'Take my name. I'll not take yours.' Lord, she ached for him. With her mother's hot blood it was a wonder she remained a virgin. In the forest alone with Joe Jessop she had thought about it. The bailiff would have been easily seduced and silent as the grave for a few coins. But she was her father's daughter.

His brow creased. 'Colonel didn't ask for it.'

'No, but I do.' She brushed past him to the window, scanning the park. 'Take it or leave it, up to you.'

'Then I will.'

'Very well. Salt for now, Farrington from our wedding day. Now, look at that.' She nodded at the gate. 'Carew's goblins have been swaggering about out there for days. They've held off until now. Maybe they think I'll run.'

'Effam, sweet heart.'

'There'll be no *sweet heart* if Carew has his way,' she snapped. 'Right now I need a soldier, not a panting lover.'

'Carew's back?'

Effam's handbell brought the maid Sarah too quickly. 'Sarah *who listens at doors* is sweet with one of Carew's men. Tell the Captain what you told me girl.'

'Well, Sir, it's like this. King's told Mr Carew to get him some soldiers. So he's formed a company. They call it Colonel Carew's Bluecoats. That's what my Arthur says.' She paused, biting her lip. 'My Arthur, that's Corporal Clegg, he's a good man Sir, really he is. It's just Mr Carew's his landlord see, so he's got no choice really, no choice at all, like most of us poor folk.'

'It's alright, Sarah,' said Effam. 'Go on.'

'Well, Mr Carew, he's got himself a new Constable and you'll never guess who it is! Oh, Captain, I don't know how to tell you, but it's best you know. Mr Carew made *Thomas* Salt his Constable!' She nodded furiously. 'Well, *Mister* Salt came round yesterday demanding to see my mistress. Wasn't going to apply at the kitchen, you understand, like any decent person, but came banging on the front, bold as brass. "Back door," says I, but he weren't listening.' Hands on hips, she was enjoying the audience. 'Tells me he was here "in his capacity" and that my lady was to see him right away. My lady to dance attendance on the likes of him! The very thought of it. "Well,", says I, "the mistress can't be disturbed as any *gentleman* should know."'

'My cousin Thomas is Carew's tenant so he can't be blamed for taking his side,' said Nat. 'But I'm sorry about his manners. Did Arthur say where Mr Carew was, Sarah?'

'Not here, Sir. Arthur says he's raising his regiment and in the meantime Mr *Thomas* Salt's in charge. But they're to join Prince Rupert in Bristol.' She preened herself. 'Arthur says he might have something to say to me before he goes. Oh, what do you think that might mean, madam?'

Effam replied coolly. 'How many men does he have, Sarah?'

The servant pouted. 'Well, there's half a dozen billeted at The Angel. Keeping watch, so as we don't come to no harm, Arthur says.'

Nat leant against the cold stone of the south oriel to rest his septic leg and smashed ribs. From the great window jutting into the carriageway, he tried to focus on the moonlit approaches and the perimeter wall beyond the moat.

'You'll be a corpse before you're a bridegroom,' Effam said, wrinkling her nose. She plucked a napkin from her sleeve and, for a moment, he thought she was going to wipe his brow. 'Here.' She thrust the cloth at him. 'Sarah will fetch a dish of wormwood and rue. You'll take it with small beer for the fever.'

Nat coughed thick green phlegm flecked bright red into the cloth, the exertion ripping the back of his head. Now Sarah was tripping through the hall touching a taper to the candles, haloed lights piercing his eyes. Staggering towards the midden, Effam's ancestors bucked and heaved, and his legs fell away.

*

'How long?' Nat guessed it was mid morning from the light edging under the woollen drape pinned to the casement. He realised with a start that he was naked beneath the sheets.

Effam was matter-of-fact. 'Two nights and a day.' On her toes to free the curtain, she cracked open the decayed window, fresh air flooding in. 'Fever's gone. Leg stopped oozing pus but I'd rest, if I was you.' He squinted at the window and when he looked away she was gone.

'Good morning, Sir.' Sarah tapped on the door with a tray. 'Mistress says you're to take this.'

'Sergeant Jessop asleep?' Ignoring the wormwood, he tore a strip of heavy bread to dip in the warm milk.

'Sir?' She was tipping a jug of water into a basin by the bed.

'Well, poor man, must be exhausted nursing me for best part of two days.' The milk hardly softened the bread.

'Oh bless you, Sir, wasn't Joe,' she giggled. 'Eat that bread, mind. It's tough old tack but my lady says milled flour ain't good for invalids.' She wiggled a finger in the bowl. 'And here's warm water for a nice freshen up.'

His brow creased. 'Will Porit then?'

'Sergeant Joe and Will Porit dragged you up here after you was taken queer, then my lady took over.' She pushed Nat forward to plump up the pillows. 'Said stock was stock, two feet or four. Not been out the room since. That be all, Cap'n?'

Feeling good in his cleaned and pressed gear, Nat banged down the stairs, humming gently. He stood for a moment at the screen admiring Effam at the south oriel washed in blue-green light refracted by the great window. She did not look up, threaded needle rising and falling from his torn buffcoat in mild rebuke. 'I told you to rest.'

He smiled, stretching gently, life returning to his beaten body. 'Nursing's no work for a lady, madam.'

'Sarah has an incontinent tongue,' she said tartly. 'Anyway, you were ranting with the fever. Said things I'm sure you wouldn't want a servant to hear.'

'What things?'

'Enough for a window into a troubled mind,' Effam said softly. 'But never mind that now. I'd given you up for worm's meat. Since you're not, you'd better make yourself useful.' She jabbed a finger at the south oriel window. 'Our friend's back.'

Nat saw the bundle of rags squatting against the gatepost beneath a wide-brimmed hat. 'Need a lookout. Is there a way onto the roof?'

'Of course there is,' she sighed. 'Your Sergeant, my bailiff's, up there, awake I hope. I've set watches with Jessop, Porit and father's old manservant. Four hour tricks. Hope that's satisfactory, *Captain*.' She picked up the needlework. 'I'd take my turn but, as you've gathered from Sarah blabbermouth, I've had other duties. Ah! Bloody needle.' She tossed Nat's buffcoat away, sucking her finger. 'Well, come on then.' She led him to a door at the side of the fireplace hiding stairs carved into the thickness of the wall, winding steeply counter-clockwise. He stopped to catch his breath. 'Foolish man. Didn't I tell you to rest?'

At the top the sun turned her long flaxen hair into threads of gold. Wheezing, he stepped onto the roof to a beauty profiled in the light.

'Back with us, Cap'n?' said Jessop. 'Still look like shit.'

Snatching the perspective glass from Jessop, Nat wedged himself against the stack, scanning the low buildings and hedgerows close to the Hall. He counted three sentries. 'Carew's Sergeant knows his business.'

Jessop, hands behind head, stretched with a grunt. 'Aye, and he doubles up after nightfall.'

Nat trained the glass at the wood abutting the wall. A breech in the masonry was covered, sentry staring at the house cradling his musket. The trees fell into a fold twisting south. 'Carew will be at us sooner or later.' Snapping the glass shut, he squatted against the chimney, weighing their chances. 'A garrison of three men, two women, an old serving man and his grandson, poorly armed, very little shot.' He coughed, spitting into the lead gutter. 'And food for how long – a week?' We're ill prepared for a siege and there's no chance of relief.' He paused to catch his breath. 'Madam, Carew's left you alone because he can take Helions whenever he likes.' He nodded towards the blackened remains of Brook Farm. 'He's no use for a farmhouse. But this?'

Effam shrugged. 'My father would expect me to burn Helions before surrendering it.'

Nat shook his head. 'But it's mortgaged to the merchants of Bristol.'

She was annoyed he knew that. 'Carew, money lenders or conflagration, my father would choose the flames.'

'And you?'

Head tossed back, Effam smoothed her hair, gazing south over land that was Farrington once as far as the eye could see. Conjuring children, tripping through the hall of their ancestors, she turned to him. 'I, would not.'

VIII

Nat's plan relied on Sarah's intelligence that the royalists commanded by his cousin Thomas would be called to Prince Rupert's assault on Bristol. He scratched a note.

Dear Thomas,

Colonel Miles Farrington has asked me to protect his house and its mistress against disaffected persons. I request your help as Constable.

Please attend at your earliest convenience.

Yours affectionately,

Nathaniel Salt

Captain

From the south oriel, Nat watched the lad Toby skipping down the drive to the piquet with his note. 'Not much older than the twins,' muttered Nat.

Toby prodded the bag of bones with the stiff paper, bolting back to the house. The spy, glancing angrily at Nat in the window, straightened his hat and limped off to find his chief.

Nat did not wait long for Thomas Salt to come twisting through the gate.

'Constable to see Mr Salt, young woman,' squawked Thomas.

Sarah giggled, edging the door open.

'Hello cousin.' Nat, in the broad tawny-orange sash of Parliament's commission, advanced on Carew's misshapen placeman. 'I see you've done well.'

Pawing a week's stubble, Thomas eyed him suspiciously. 'Passingly, for troubled times.'

Nat smiled thinly, wagging his finger 'Passingly, *because* of troubled times, cousin.'

'Take my opportunities where I can.' Thomas nodded at the sash and the sword dangling at the Captain's left side. 'As I see you've done…'

'Piece of cloth and a borrowed cutlass, Constable,' scowled Nat, 'are a poor swap for two dead children, a burnt out house and being cut like a knackerman's dole.'

'Cousin, I'm sorry, I didn't mean, that's to say...'

'Well, Constable, you say you're *sorry*,' Nat's contrivance found its mark, 'whilst serving my tormentor.' He waved a finger at the Constable's head. 'Hat's off for the lady, Thomas.'

Thomas snatched at the absurd item, agonies of a spurned relation that everyone thought was a bastard welling up. 'Look here, Nathaniel Salt, the King's peace round here's my responsibility,' he gulped. 'Sheriff says you'll answer charges for that curate you did in, see. Oh, and Helions is forfeit on account of the traitor Farrington.' Thomas puffed his chest. '*And* all in arms against His Majesty are to be arrested. That's you, Nathaniel Salt.'

'Oh, calm down, Thomas,' said Nat. 'I've a note from a magistrate who saw the curate die through his own stupidity.'

Thomas could hardly speak. 'I challenge the authority of your magistrate who's a rebel and a traitor.'

'Well, I question your Sheriff who's a malignant papist. And I question you.' Smiling, Nat offered the Constable claret and a high back chair. 'Let's speak plain, cousin. Your war's about getting rich; mine's killing, slitting the throats of butchers that did for my children. Eh?' Behind the chair, he leant down, spitting in the Constable's ear. 'But I've the devil's contract.'

'God forgive you, Nathaniel Salt,' gasped Thomas, the scar Nat had given him at Norris' Skimmington ride throbbing red.

'Oh, he will.' Nat slopped more claret into his cousin's glass. 'Meanwhile, what d'you plan to do with us, *Constable*?'

'Obey orders.' Shrinking into the chair, Thomas guzzled the wine, oblivious of his cousin's ruse. 'Deliver you to the Sheriff and seize Helions.'

'And how d'you mean to carry out your orders, Thomas?' Nat smirked, refilling the glass. 'Surely not with that bag of bones at the gate?'

'I've a dozen troopers at my command,' blustered Thomas.

'Two dozen?' Nat had reckoned less. 'But bound for Bristol, don't deny it. And you've orders not to raze this house because Carew wants it.' The Constable's reaction confirmed his suspicion. 'He can't have the squire's daughter but thinks Helions'll raise him up among the gentry anyway.' He winked at Effam. 'And the lady Euphemia. What'll you do with my lady?'

'Not my problem.' Thomas shrugged. 'Her father's estate is forfeit 'cos he offered violence to his Majesty. But she's free to go.'

Thomas' voice was slurred. Nat wondered if he had slopped too much brandy into the wine. 'Forfeit by whose order?'

Thomas turned in his seat, watery eyes narrowing. 'His Majesty's Court of Array for the county of Wiltshire.'

'Is the order signed?'

'It will be.'

'Is it signed?'

'No.'

'Then *Constable* read your law books. Colonel died two days ago. When your order's signed, Helions will belong to an innocent woman, the lady Euphemia,' he prepared his bluff, 'under the stewardship of her kinsman.'

'What kinsman's that then?' sneered Thomas.

'Why, Captain Tobias Norrington of Lavington of course. Cross that gentleman, Thomas, and it'll be like the Book of Revelations was written just for you.'

Thomas' jaw dropped. 'Oh cousin,' laughed Nat, 'look at you. Brow like a field on Plough Monday! Mr Norrington is your master's best mate, don't you see?' Nat pressed his face into Thomas'. 'And what about my farm then?' Nat straightened up, arching his back. It was time to spring the trap on poor, witless Thomas Salt. 'Your master killed my children and he'll pay. But Carew didn't light the torch, Thomas, did he? And, *cousin*, didn't I smack you good and proper at that Skimmington in front of all those folk? Oh, and you gobbing off about Brook farm being rightly yours. Hanging judge likes a motive...'

'Weren't me Nat,' gulped Thomas. 'Loved those young 'uns, like they were my own, didn't I?'

'But you were there, Thomas,' said Nat. 'I've a witness.'

'Who's that then?'

'Ah.' Nat tapped his nose. The witness Billy Burrows would be laughed out of court. 'That would be telling, wouldn't it?'

'It was Ezekiel and Jethro Rich,' Thomas stuttered. 'Ezekiel mostly, and Robert Mann, but he's dead.'

'Aye, and Carew's rough justice on the hill puts it all to rights, eh?'
Nat shook his head, wagging a finger at the Constable. 'You tell me what
stone Ezekiel and Jethro crawled under and I'll winkle them out.'

Thomas sniffed the unexpectedly strong wine, eyeing Nat's untouched
glass. 'They're with the trash o' Warminster Common,' he mumbled.
'Likely sweating sickness'll take them, if liquor don't.'

'Thanks, Thomas.' Nat smacked the Constable's back sending wine
down his grey chemise. 'But what's the blood price for your part in this,
cousin?'

'You can't bully me, Nathaniel Salt, but what d'you want?'

'Not much,' said Nat. 'We want to leave safely, with my lady's stuff.'

'Not bloody likely!' spat Thomas. 'I'll take my chances with your
allegations.'

'Trouble is, Thomas, Miss Farrington's about to torch the place rather
than hand it over. You know what the old gentry's like.' Thomas' jaw
dropped. 'Come and see the faggots Joe Jessop's stuffed the roof with if
you want,' shrugged Nat. 'Shame, what with Carew wanting the place so
much and your orders, not to mention Captain Norrington…'

'Och, Mr Carew's orders say nothing about capturing soldiers.'
Thomas rose, unsteadily. 'Clear off by dusk. I'll see you safe to the
Warminster road.'

'Swear it?'

'I do.' The Constable spat in his palm. 'Here, on grandad's bones I
swear it.'

From the edge of the south oriel Nat watched the Constable shambling
down the drive, twisting at the bridge, pale face sneaking an eyeful of the
prize he must deliver to Carew intact.

*

Muskets primed, the party headed for the gate and the Constable that
had given his word. The cart jarred on the bridge, pitching a portrait into
the moat. Face up, the likeness sliced through the slime.

'Leave it' Effam barked, seeing who it was.

'No, lady!'

'I said, leave it.' Effam watched dispassionately, her mother snarling
one last time.

Now Thomas Salt was waving his arms like a windmill, whining across
the divide. 'What's going on, cousin? Come on, *come on*!'

Crack! Thomas Salt's neck flayed open. He twisted to his knees, gore pulsing between his fingers. A King's soldier leapt through the gap, smoking musket held high. 'TRAP!' Casually, the royalist sergeant took aim. The man kept coming. 'Get out!'

'Arthur!' The girl Sarah implored, 'Oh, please don't shoot him.' The sergeant fired, winging the man, but he kept on.

'Thomas Salt, you lying bastard.' Nat shrieked at the man bleeding out. His cousin's last deceit vindicated the gossips and confirmed his parentage. '*Bastard*!'

Half a dozen infantry forming up at the gate prepared to fire. The household took cover behind the wagon as Corporal Arthur Clegg sprinted the last few feet to the redoubt.

'Fire!' Nat saw two royalists fall, the rest taking cover behind the wall. 'Good shooting, lads!' He grinned at Jessop. 'Three deaths and a desertion. Tidy bag for a short action. Now I need a sharpshooter.'

'That'll be me then.' Jessop, the bailiff, was a crack shot.

'I want to fall back with covering fire. Get to the roof, Joe. Shoot anything that moves.' But they had not reckoned on Effam.

'Jessop stay put, I'm the better shot.' He shrugged, it was true. Effam hitched her skirts, running for the house. At the chimney she steadied her musket against the stack. 'Crack!' She reloaded, fast. 'Crack!'

Falling back, Nat took stock with Jessop in the south oriel. The royalists had reached the wagon. 'We'll not hold out long,' said Nat. 'Not with them coming at us from all sides and the light going. I'll have to negotiate.'

'No!' Effam glared defiance from the screen.

'Carew'll leave you alone,' said Nat. 'Especially with Norrington.'

'God's blood!' Effam shook him off. 'Better dead than submit to Carew or that lizard's pizzle Norrington.' She put a finger on his lips. 'If you surrender, Nat, you know you'll hang?'

'Won't come to that.'

'No,' said Effam. 'It certainly won't. Now, what d'you think of this?' She grabbed the edge of a heavy hunting scene tapestry.

'Eh?'

'You see my old house hides many secrets.' Effam pulled back the heavy fabric putting her shoulder into the linen-fold panelling behind. 'Come.' The panel parted from the wall on its mechanism, a rush of cool air fanning from the pit. Sarah thrust a tallow lamp into the void lighting a flight of steep stone steps.

'Blimey,' said Nat. 'You're full of surprises!' At the south oriel, he could see figures pressing up the drive. 'Let them have it, Clegg.' The leading man caught it full in the chest, the other two diving into the wagon. 'Bull's eye! Maybe that Sergeant isn't so clever, eh?'

'It's a bleedin' feint!' Nat spun round to Will Porit tearing down the stairs. 'They're round the back. Ten of 'em.' Nat bundled the servants down the hole followed by Effam, Porit and Clegg.

'Leave it, man.' Nat hissed at Jessop.

With studied ease, Sergeant Jessop at the south oriel poured powder into the pan and spat shot down the muzzle. 'Shift yer arse then, daft bugger.' His target was standing drop-jawed over the twitching corpse. 'Froze like a friggin' rabbit.' Jessop pressed the wad home and flicked out his scouring rod. 'Too sodding late.' Shot ripped through the man's thigh. 'That'll learn you!'

Nat grabbed Jessop's collar, pirouetting to unclip the mechanism as the two tumbled into the void. The panel clicked back. Just as the King's men burst in.

A dozen steps curved to the right and a cell five foot square blocked by a heavily studded door. Effam seized a jemmy from a staple in the vaulted stone ceiling. 'Here, we'll need this, Joe Jessop.' She jammed a large iron key in the lock, putting her shoulder into the door. 'Queen Mary called my grandfather a heretic. Praise God, the spavined witch died before he went to the stake.' She thrust the tallow lamp through the void, flames dancing on dripping walls and startled rats. 'But here's Grandpa's tunnel used at last like the Red Sea parting, huh?' Roots thick as bell-ropes tumbled like hanging vines. 'Must be at the park wall, where the woods start.'

Nat brushed soil from his shoulders, looking anxiously at the roof. Someone was shuffling around directly above. He raised a finger, Effam dousing the light.

'Get yer skiving arse back 'ere, Penhaligon.' A soldier's muffled curse then footfalls retreating towards the house.

'*Penhaligon.*' Jessop hissed. 'Bleedin' Cornishman.'

'Likely we've escaped a detachment of those cut-throats from the Devizes fight,' said Nat. 'God be praised. Those devils take no prisoners.'

Effam felt forward. Her palms slapped a plane of cool slate. 'Jemmy, Jessop,' she snapped. 'Give me that, idiot.' Slamming the crowbar in the jamb, she put her weight behind the lever, prising the stone in a rush of dirt and fresh air.

'Quiet now.' Nat saw trees sweeping down towards the grey drove road and, behind, through the crumbled park wall, the hall's flickering lights. 'Stay low, keep quiet.' He reached down to pluck the boy out.

'Well, now, Captain.' Effam ignored Nat's helping hand. 'What now?'

'Sweet heart,' he whispered as she glared back at the occupied house, 'I've got orders to join Haselrig in Bristol.'

'Rot. Bristol's your magnet because Carew's there.' She sniffed dryly. 'I was privy to your chat with the Constable, remember.' She shook him off, smiling thinly. 'Do not, Mr Salt, treat me like an idiot.'

'Alright,' Nat shrugged. 'But we have to find safe lodgings.' And, before my leg gives out, he thought. 'Norrington's?'

'Never.' Her eyes burned. 'Oh, I can fend for myself,' she huffed, wringing out the hem of her skirts. 'They'll need billeting though.' She nodded at her household. 'But not at Norrington's.'

'Warminster then.' Nat did business in the market town on quarter days, under The Bell Inn's stone colonnades. 'It's a God-fearing town. I'll ask Major Wagstaff to take you in.' She looked at him suspiciously, Nat wondering if she sensed the town's comforts like Haselrig's orders were not the main consideration. The Warminster road ran through the Common and Nat had an account to settle in that thieves' kitchen. 'The Devizes fight has made the King's men cock-a-hoop. They'll be all over the place. But it's black as hell and if we keep an eye out we'll be safely with the Wagstaffs by breakfast.'

'There's a good road through the valley,' said Jessop pointing at the deep slash of chalk tracking northeast in the moonlight.

Rubbing his leg, Nat was tempted. 'Can't risk another tryst with the King's men.'

'Cross country then,' shrugged Jessop. 'Bit lumpy, but alright this time o' year. And no chance of bowling into them cock-sucking cavaliers.'

The fugitives took the white path, crossing the river where it ran shallow over chalk like black ink.

'You take to this like a backwoodsman, madam,' said Nat.

'Don't patronise me, Sir,' snapped Effam.

'I mean to say…'

'You've a dim view of women, Mr Salt, haven't you? ' He opened his mouth, but Effam was too quick. 'Oh, I think so.' She nodded at Jessop. 'Ask him.' His eyes told Effam that her sharp tongue had found its mark. 'The gamekeeper, *your sergeant*, ask him, about me.'

Effam watched him walk away. 'Nathaniel.' He turned, mouth tightening. 'Smashed ribs, bloody spit and fever.' She was biting her lip. 'It's a widow's triad.' She beckoned him close, whispering in his ear. 'And I don't mean to die a virgin.'

He clenched his teeth, turning to find Jessop. 'Been talking with your mistress.' The sergeant grinned. 'She mentioned you.'

'Raising me wages, is she? No?' He shrugged and spat. 'Well, I'm not holding my breath. Tough as old boots that gentry morte and I ain't expecting no easy time now she's in charge.' He leered at Nat. 'You got the hots for 'er, ain't you, Sir?'

'Tough, you say, but she's gentle too.' There was no reason Jessop should know about the engagement. 'That dog you were telling me about, remember?'

The bailiff shrugged. 'Well, I just see tough. But then Colonel never did have no sons, see.' He sucked his teeth. 'Used to say his daughter got the balls. Bleedin' right!' He glanced back. 'You know, a handier forester I ain't never met, man or woman. Jesus, that morte can bag a coney rabbit, skin and draw the bleeder, make a scoff of it and shit it out faster than you can say the Lord's prayer.' He lowered his voice. 'Don't get me wrong, Cap'n, she's a tidy broiler, face like a cowpat, of course, but all woman. Reckon she'll whelp like a good un if any man can get his leg over.' He cleared his throat and spat. 'All about bloodlines, see, matching this ewe with that ram. Trick's avoiding the obvious. That's where gentry go wrong, see. If you run your prettiest sheep with the sire with the biggest shoulders, pound to a penny, you'll end up with duds.' Euphemia Farrington and the newly minted captain, he mused, now that *would* be a matching. Splice them for champions, no question. 'Bleedin' top news she ain't getting hitched to that arseworm Carew though, and there's no mistake.'

'I asked her to marry me,' Nat said casually, wanting to tell the world but finding only Jessop.

'No!' The sergeant recovered with a grin and a shrug. 'Still, no harm done, eh?' He clapped Nat on the back. 'Cheer up, Cap'n, womenfolk make addlepates of the best of us!' Cheeky bugger, he thought. 'You'll get over it.'

'She said yes.'

Jessop's jaw dropped, colour running from his face. 'Bloody hell.'

'Congratulations would do.'

'Congratulations, eh yes, that's it,' the sergeant spluttered. 'Look, all that stuff I said, meant no harm.' He grinned sheepishly. 'But you an' Miss Farrington, who'd have thought, eh?' Sucking his teeth, Jessop dug his commander painfully in the ribs. 'There away, that house'll take our baggage train.' Nodding at a dark smudge against the horizon, the sergeant grinned broadly. 'Though I'd sooner keep Euphemia Farrington in the order of battle.'

*

'Hold!' A musket punched from an upstairs window. 'What d'you want?'

'Captain Nathaniel Salt, Colonel Haselrig's staff. Put up your weapon, Mr Wagstaff.'

'I see you, Nathaniel Salt.' Major Wagstaff's querulous cousin peered down. 'Been robbed by royalists, damn their eyes.'

'Well, Sir, I've got Miss Farrington here who's been thrown out of her house. Can you shelter her for a bit?'

'Thieving whoresons made off with my animals, not so much as a broiler left. Sent for relief but there's been none and now you come upon me with a company of refugees. Is there no limit to the torments a poor body has to endure?' The tenant shot back the bolts, waving the party into his bleak little hall. 'I'm sorry for your loss, Nathaniel Salt. Young 'uns, you know, awful business.' He peered at Effam. 'Miss Farrington, you say? Colonel Farrington, damn good man. God rest him.' He shrugged unhappily as he climbed the stairs. 'My house and maidservant are at your disposal, madam, until you're better suited.'

The girl Sarah and Arthur Clegg edged away in the dark.

'Be quick about it, Clegg!' Jessop leered, nudging the Londoner. 'Come on, Porit, best leave Sir to it an' all.'

Glaring at the Sergeant's back, Nat pulled Effam aside. 'Sweet heart, there's not much time.' Staring at his feet, he fumbled for the talisman. 'Don't have much, but there's this.' Seizing her hand, he pressed it urgently into her palm. She played with the thin gold band, brow furrowing. 'My mother's. A token see, kind of pledge, that I'll call for you, soon as I can.'

She reached up, running her hands through his hair, pulling him to her for a first kiss, just one, on the forehead. 'Do not expect me to wait long, Nathaniel Salt.'

IX

'Gawd, ain't it queer?' said Will Porit unnerved by the still, black night punctured by the creak of partridge and the corncrake's low, mechanical rasp.

Clegg cuffed him playfully. 'Got the shits, 'ave we, city boy?'

'Noise down, wits about you,' snapped Nat, leg putting an edge on his temper. 'Sir James Thynne rules here, England's richest malignant. His patrols'll be back at first light. I want clear of this road.'

The track crossed a muddy brook at a hovel with a hay cart and wolf-dog pegged to a stake. 'Bugger off or he'll rip yer throat out,' the cottager snarled from his door.

'Easy now, brother,' Nat protested, half raising his hands.

The man spat. 'Rum time to be travelling, master.' A woman clutching an infant peered from the door. 'Go on, get in.' He shoved them inside, pulling out a cudgel.

'Nice cart.' Nat nodded at the wagon. 'Will it take us to Warminster for a shilling?'

The man silently palmed the club-end.

'Aw, behave yerself, man,' said Jessop, unslinging his musket.

'Wait, Joe,' said Nat. 'Now, friend, you can take us to town and get a shilling or we'll take your cart for nothing and you'll have to fetch it back.'

'You ain't the first, coming round here causing trouble. Last lot said they'd torch the place if I didn't feed them,' spat the peasant. 'Whoresons scoffed everything and me with a nipper and missus what's near her time. Bleedin' royalist vultures.' He stuck out a grimy paw. 'Ere, let's have a look at that shilling.'

With a flick of the coin, King Charles glowered from the Parliament officer's palm. The man licked his lips. 'Climb up. I'll not ask your business, though it's plain enough. If we're stopped, you forced me, right?'

The cart bumped down the hill towards the Common. 'Fuckin' 'orrible place.' The carrier laid his switch across the nag's back. 'Don't matter if you're King or Parliament, yer writ don't run in this godless dump.' But Nat had important business on the Common. The man cleared his throat and spat, shifting in his seat to grin at the soldiers hunched in the back. 'Beak came out of Sarum t'other week to do the judging. Gets one of them criminals before him, see.' He nodded into the gloom. 'Gawd, says 'is honour, thought I'd necked all them cut-throats from the Common years ago!'

Banks of fog eddied and swirled throwing a gappy pall over the waking shanty. The cart lurched drunkenly, tipping into another pot-hole. Nat swore, leg thumping raw. 'Pull up, man. Now, lend me your cloak and wait.'

'I will not.' The carrier drew the garment tightly across his shoulders.

A knife at the ribs did the job. Re-sheathing the weapon, Jessop gripped Nat's arm. 'Whatever happens 'ere, we've both got *interests*, eh? Remember my poor Emma.'

'Aye man.' Teeth clenched, Nat eased himself off the cart. Snatching a length of rope from the back and throwing the carrier's filthy blanket round his shoulders, he melted into the gloom like a wraith.

Nat threw back the flap of the first hovel, pressing the cloak to his nose. 'Here, my friend.' Nat tossed two silver pennies at the peasant. 'Two tossers called Rich, new here, young man pox-scarred, and his uncle. Show me?'

The man half rose, sidling towards the flap, braced to fend off the devil's blow. Jabbing a crooked finger towards a shack beyond the road, he grinned. 'Rich.' But cankered fingers were also closing on cold steel glinting at his waistband. Nat seized the man's wrist, snapping it back. The peasant squealed like a girl, the hunting knife jabbing into the dirt.

'Just the job.' Nat tested the blade on the flap. 'Inside, now, turn your eyes. Or I'll be back and gouge them out.'

Melting into the thickening fog, Nat steeled himself for the kill.

*

'Who are you?' croaked the condemned man.

The soldier towered above the two waking drunks. 'Can't you see, Ezekiel Rich?' The bloodshot eyes of Ezekiel and Jethro Rich widened. Crouching low, their tormentor, black as Old Nick, beamed malevolence.

'Weren't us.' Jethro Rich backed away on his arse.

The intruder stepped up, effortlessly flooring both. 'Wasn't what, Jethro Rich?'

Scarface began to blub. 'Robert Mann. It were 'im, and Mr Carew.' He nodded his head vigorous, glancing at his uncle for support.

'And who else?'

'Nobody, honest. But Tom was there.'

'Thomas Salt died yesterday.'

The two gawped as their assailant weighed his knife. 'One of you'll join him today.' He threw a coin at Ezekiel Rich. 'Heads you live. Go on arseworm, toss for it.'

Bewildered, Ezekiel fumbled for the coin, flicking it in the air. 'Heads!' The boy Jethro launched forward.

The assassin spun round, knocking him senseless. 'Now bind him.'

Ezekiel quickly did as he was told. 'I won the toss,' he grinned at his tormentor.

'You won nothing.' The dark man thrust his contorted face in Ezekiel's sending his guts into spasm.

'You promised,' whined the older man. 'Your promise...'

'... depended,' snapped the intruder, 'on those given it being halfways human, which they ain't, and on the elder begging to take the place of his brother's son, which he didn't.' The executioner glared at the snivelling Ezekiel Rich with renewed contempt. 'I'd have let the boy go. But you hadn't the balls.'

The man's eye flicked towards the opening. But the soldier was ready. Effortlessly, he sheathed his knife in Ezekiel's guts. Feeling its point scrape against the man's backbone, he twisted the instrument in an arc of bowel and blood. 'How's that feel then Ezekiel Rich?' he spat into the man's face. Pawing at his belly, Rich fell back against his nephew. With a countryman's practised hand, the tormentor flipped the knife, tipping Jethro's chin. The instrument crunched through cartilage, crudely dissecting the man's windpipe, silencing him. 'Bleed out and choke, you bastards.' The dark butcher delivered his last rites to the dying pair. 'But pains o' this world'll be nothing to the fires of the next, for what you did.'

The old woman crouched low over her skillet barely noticed the bloodied man plucking a brand from the fire, touching it to each corner of the hurdle. 'Go on, burn, you bastards, light up the sky.'

113

Then he walked away, fire at his back, smiling stupidly and without a care as if the filthy Common had become a field of wild flowers, Ezekiel's agonal screams the sweetest music in his ears. Out of the fog, Nat bowled into him.

'Too late.' Joe Jessop held Nat in his gory arms. 'Poor souls.'

Head cocked, the sentinel crow surveyed the scene and made its report. Of the hanging tree's five guilty men, only the principal still drew breath. The confederates were resolved that Erasmus Carew should not die in his bed.

*

As Nat ducked into the tap room, The Bell's convivial buzz faded like a breeze on the downs. A dozen billeted Roundheads stirred self-consciously, eyeing the tawny-orange sash of Parliament's commission.

'Welcome, Mr Salt!' The landlord beamed at Farrington's sword. 'You are *most* welcome.' A pair of smocked regulars shifted from the settle by the fire, the landlord flicking his cloth to accommodate Nat. 'King's troopers crashed through Warminster two days back but found these fine boys.' He nodded at the Roundheads. 'Beat a hasty retreat, I can tell you, and not a shot fired.' He wiped big hands on a beer-stained apron. 'I'll find a chamber for you, Sir, though your men must kip where they can.'

Nat grinned at Jessop. 'Looks like you three'll be sleeping in the parlour then.'

'No, Sir, I ain't bunking down with them,' said Joe Jessop, 'when I've a doxy dell in Warminster that'll keep me warm tonight.'

Biting his lip, Nat pulled Jessop aside. 'What's up, Joe,' he nodded at the knot of farmers and troopers, 'with them, I mean?'

Jessop passed a hand over his face. 'Well, reckon it's like this.' He knew Nat would not like it. 'When you comes in here last quarter day you was one of them. Now you ain't.' He peered at the officer, wondering if he understood. 'Don't do for likes of us to be supping with gen'lemen an' officers, even them what's been freshly made up, like.' Jessop sunk the rest of his ale, smacking his lips. 'Aw, don't take it bad, Sir, lads like you well enough.' He shrugged and belched. 'Best you find Major Wagstaff, Sir.'

*

At the threshold of the Chapel of St Lawrence, Nat paused to remove his battered sword and hat.

'Welcome, my son.' Nat had not seen the cherub in the shadows. The priest smiled. 'A friendly word to ease a troubled soul? He gestured at the silent interior. 'As you can see we're quite alone.'

Nat followed the saintly figure to the altar. 'Confession's a popish practice.'

'Indeed, but easing the mind of a fellow creature isn't and you're no penitent, I'm thinking.'

Nat chewed his lip, weighing the priest. 'Two men died on the common this morning.'

'By your hand?'

Nat shrugged. He could find no remorse for the verminous Ezekiel and Jethro Rich, none at all, not even in God's house. 'You've heard of Brook Farm?'

'Brook Farm?' The atrocity had scandalised the county. 'Ah, yes, my son, I understand.'

'Do you?' Nat sucked his teeth. 'Well, I went to destroy the men who did it.' He swallowed hard. 'There was fog. Couldn't see. By the time I got to them, my sergeant had done the job.'

'Thoughtful of him.'

'Yes,' said Nat. 'But Joe Jessop had equal cause, see.'

'Ah.' The priest reached out, gently turning Nat's face, reading it like a book. 'There's more, my son, isn't there?'

'Aye.' The bloodletting had redoubled Nat's zeal for the fulfilment of his dark vow. 'The dead men's master lives. I'll not rest until the bastard's in the ground.'

The priest pursed his lips. 'Erasmus Carew?'

'How d'you know that?'

'I watch, I listen, my son, I interpret.'

'And what's your interpretation?' Nat rubbed the stubble on his chin. 'I'm damned, aren't I?'

The priest smiled, shaking his head. 'No, my son, you are to be absolved for what you've done, *and what you have to do*. Aye, before the end, you will be absolved.' He gripped Nat's arm. 'This I know.' He nodded at the door. 'Now, I think that young man wants you.'

'A good day, Sir.' The youth waiting in the porch handed over Nat's hat and sword. 'Major Wagstaff presents his compliments and asks that you call on him at home, when you're ready, Sir.'

'Thank you, Mister...?'

'Wagstaff, Sir, Edward Wagstaff, Major's son.' The bashful youth swallowed hard. 'You won't remember, but we served together, at the Devizes fight.'

'Devizes, yes,' said Nat, clipping on the sword. 'You did well, I'm told.'

'Aw, no Sir, that'll be my brother, Jehu.' Edward Wagstaff flushed. 'Family hero.'

'Ah.' Nat jabbed his thumb. 'It's a neat and godly prayer house, Mr Wagstaff.'

'Aye, Sir,' smiled the young man. 'Our chapel's named for St Laurence.'

'Roasted on a gridiron.' The story of St Laurence was a puritan staple.

'Uh-huh. My father's fixing the place in memory of latter day martyrs.' Edward Wagstaff smiled sweetly. 'Burned by that papist bitch Mary Tudor.'

'And you've a godly parson.'

'Sir?'

'The man I was talking with.'

'You were alone Captain.'

Nat stepped back into the chapel. 'No, Wagstaff, you're wrong.'

'Captain?'

The chapel was empty. 'Let's go, Edward,' said Nat, blaming the chill on his poisoned leg. 'Major Wagstaff'll be waiting.'

The Major opened his door to the head strong protégé he had saved from Norrington at Lavington. 'You're right welcome, Captain.' He tapped his nose. 'You and the Farrington girl, providential match, well done.'

For a yeoman, you mean, thought Nat. 'News, if nothing else, travels fast in Warminster Sir.' But, after his reluctance to accept Haselrig's commission at Lavington, Wagstaff surely did not have him down as an opportunist elbowing his way into the gentry. 'Don't know about providence but you're right, I am lucky. Lucky in love.' He probably sounded prim. 'Helions is in the hands of malignants. Barely escaped with our lives, but I'm hoping your company'll help?'

'I'm a honeypot for gents with busted estates.' Wagstaff puffed his cheeks. 'Still, I mean to turn the tide on these riving cavaliers, Sir, and I will. But here's Mrs Wagstaff who'll make us eat first.'

'Servants, Sir, they're the very devil. Seems we run a charity for the relief of idle girls.' The round-faced matron halted abruptly, tight lips softening. 'Ah, now this must be the famous Mr Salt.'

Nat bowed stiffly. 'Madam, I'm here to ask for your help with Miss Farrington who's been put out of her house. She's staying with your cousin.'

'Well, I doubt she'll do well with that old curmudgeon! We keep a simple and godly house, Captain Salt, but Miss Farrington's very welcome to share it.' She drew the bow securing her work apron, sighing and shaking her head. 'Country parts are fickle and lawless these days, no place for respectable bodies.' She tapped Nat gently on the arm. 'I fear, young man, you'll have to stay at The Bell.' She studied Nat closely for a moment, glancing briefly at her husband. 'Never mind him. A good heart like your lady's a comfort to one that's grieving. You know that, don't you?'

'Aye, madam and you're very kind.' And perceptive, he thought. 'I hate to ask but my lady has a maid, Sarah, who's sweet with one of my men.'

'*Of course* Miss Farrington must bring her girl.'

'And there's Squire Farrington's manservant and his grandson...'

'I understand perfectly and you're not to worry yourself about servants.' Mrs Wagstaff waved a podgy hand. 'I know how to deal with them.' Nat did not doubt it. 'Miss Farrington must have her girl here. If the old man and his boy are earnest and sober, I'll place them with neighbours. They're all vexed by the war's theft of servants.' She sighed, reflecting on the hardships that she and her circle had been put to. 'And your marriage, Sir, what plans for that?'

'A godly parson in a plain church, a couple of kindly souls for witness and the blessings of the Lord is all we want, ma'am, things being what they are, and soon.' He paused, anticipating the effect his suggestion would have. 'I'm wondering, will your chapel of St Laurence serve?'

Quaking with pleasure, she shot the briefest glance at her husband. 'Well, Sir, Major Wagstaff and I would be delighted to assist in any way.

I'll speak with Miss Farrington and see what's to be done.' She tapped Nat playfully on the arm. 'You're to rely on me *completely.*'

'And the parson. I met your parson, at the chapel. What a fine man,' beamed Nat. 'I'm sure Effam would want him to marry us.'

'Parson, Mr Salt?' Mrs Wagstaff's brow furrowed. 'Oh no, we have no parson at St Lawrence!'

'Ah!' Wagstaff hailed the stout middle-aged officer filling the doorframe. 'Salt, you know our excellent Captain Jeremiah Jones?'

'No, Sir,' said Nat. 'Pleasure to meet you Captain.'

The man smiled absently. 'You'll have to shout, Salt. He's Colonel Hungerford's gunner.' Wagstaff poked the newcomer in the guts. 'Deaf as a post. Welsh too.'

'PLEASED TO MEET YOU, CAP'N JONES.'

'Siege guns!' the man belted back taking a long swig.

'Sir?'

'Siege guns, Sir, sakers and the like, the King's got 'em, we ain't. It'll be the ruin of us bach, you mark me.'

'Spare us your broadside Jones,' retorted the Major. 'Let's eat. We keep a Christian table Salt, none of your papist confections and we *never*,' he glared round the room, 'keep a fish day, for fear of popery. Eh, Mrs Wagstaff?

'Indeed Major we do not!' spluttered the lady.

Wagstaff nodded firmly. 'That's good then.' Another swig, a smack of the lips and he was settling at the head of the table, waving at the high back chairs on either side. 'We'll have our fill then Jones'll tell us about malignants. Show him a papist and he's off, like a ferret down a rat hole, ain't you, Jones?' He raised his voice. 'I say, Jones, you'll tell us about your trip to Longleat House, Sir.'

'Aye, that I will, Major,' barked Jones enthusiastically. 'Brightens a dismal scene, see. What with the battle o' Lansdown and the Devizes fight, '43's going the King's way, there's no disguising it bach. Pray for better, Major, or be hung in the market like a row of cock pheasants.' He tipped his glass at Wagstaff. 'And the tattmonger of Longleat'll be sure you're first for the drop!'

'Captain Jones, I'll not have bawdy talk in my house!' Mrs Wagstaff lashed the Welshman.

'Aw, madam, suffer an old campaigner 'is rough edges,' pleaded Jones.

Wagstaff's fingers found his neck, contemplating the shame of being hanging at his door by Sir James Thynne. 'Longleat be damned.'

A girl began ladling the meal into pewter bowls under her mistress's eye: chopped mutton with turnips and potatoes boiled to a dense soup. The Major rapped the oak table with a bone-handled knife. 'For hearty fare and good company, thank God.'

'Hear your boy Jehu did well at the Devizes fight, Sir.' Nat chewed hard, the mutton tough as boots. 'I spent most of it at the bottom of a stinking ditch.'

'Aw, Captain your modesty does you credit.' Wagstaff scratched a fibre from his teeth, sucking his finger. But aye, man, it's true, I'm the proudest man in England. Edward was in the thick of it too, weren't you, son? Tell us about the derring-do, lad.'

'Well, Sir, you know how old Hopton hauled himself out of Devizes when Prince Rupert's horsemen cantered onto Roundway Down?' Edward Wagstaff moistened his lips. 'Well, we're all lined up, waiting around not knowing what's next. Suddenly a horseman breaks from their lines waving his sword, taunting us like he were the bloody King o' France.'

'Language Edward,' snapped Mrs Wagstaff.

'Aye, well, this went on for a bit. Then Jehu with a great whoop spurs his horse and bursts out of our lines. Up and at the fellow like Henry the Fifth. You should've heard the cheer go up from our boys, Sir. Anyway, the two of them clash, going at each other hammer and tongs. But my brother's strong as an ox, Sir, and the cavalier begins to flag.' The boy's voice faltered, his gaze meeting Nat's, united in the horror of Roundway Down. 'Jehu pulled back a bit, then charged the man side-on. Caught him full under the breastplate. Sword went in so far he had to fairly wrench it out or be unhorsed. The man fell away, foot caught in a stirrup. Horse took fright, dragging the corpse through the dirt between the lines for all to see like a traitor drawn to the gallows.'

The Major was beside himself. 'There Sir, what d'you think of *that,* Sir?'

Mrs Wagstaff placed a hand gently on her son's thigh. 'That's enough.' She stared reproachfully at her husband. 'Mr Salt this war drives a cleaver through us, rips us apart. I've seven sons. Two are strangers since falling in with those who pervert the King's good senses.' Tears welled in the corner of her eyes. 'I pray the good shepherd brings them home. Aye, His Majesty to the dear old religion and my boys back to me.'

The Major grunted, turning to Jones. 'Now then Jeremiah, King's men murdered Salt's children, fired his house and confiscated his lady's dowry. Tell him about Longleat House. It'll cheer him up.'

The gunner wiped his chops, crossed his arms and sat back, studying his audience. 'Well, now after our victory at Edgehill...'

'*Victory,* Sir?'

'Aye, Sir, victory, Sir!'

'Victory if you say so, Sir.' Wagstaff winked across the table.

Jones scowled. 'Well see, after we punched the King's nose at Edgehill, Sir Edward Hungerford turns to me and says, "Jones bach," he says, "James Thynne o' Longleat has spilt our boys' blood and him tucked up all cosy at home. What d'you say to that?" "No justice there at all," says I. "Right you are, Jones!" he says, "best we give him a right good going over, boyo."' Jones sucked claret through the gap in his teeth, spilling some, wiping it with his sleeve. 'Anyway up we trot and bang on the fellow's big oak door, see. Man answers, cool as you like, says his master's not home. Says, "Could we come back?" Come back, my arse, I says, pardon ma'am, and in we go. Well, my boys were feeling sore an' hungry so we carry's off all the vittals we could find and some stuff we sold for that chapel of yours.'

'Captain Jones, I disapprove of riving,' chided Mrs Wagstaff. 'But praise the Lord for Longleat's generosity.'

The gunner sniffed moistly, wiping a sleeve across his nose. 'Aye, well, we fancied summat fresh, see. Happens 'is Lordship's fallow deer trots by. Sergeant says can't get no fresher than that. Four hundred yards off they were, a whole troop of 'em, and we bags three. Roasted one of 'em there and then in his Lordship's park, right in front of his door. Beautiful. Slung the other two in the cart see. Them half starved creatures on the Common had 'em – token of his nib's Christian charity!'

Mrs Wagstaff was unmoved. 'Proverbs 11, verse 25, "A generous person enjoys prosperity, and one who refreshes others will be refreshed."'

'Amen.' Wagstaff banged the table. 'Now, Sir, you want Helions House back, eh?' Sucking his teeth, he passed a hand across his chin. 'I'd rather use my boys against the Thynnes of Longleat.'

Nat sucked on a string of mutton stuck between his teeth. 'You're no friend of Sir James Thynne?'

'No, I'm not!' Wagstaff exploded, spraying spittle. 'The Lord has handed me an opportunity to smite the bastard, or if the Almighty hasn't, Arthur Haselrig has, which is much the same thing.'

Mrs Wagstaff's girl padded over. 'Soldier out the back, Sir,' she whispered. 'Say's it's dispatches from Sergeant Major General Waller an' you're to have it right away.'

Knuckling his forehead, the muddy corporal of horse thrust a fold of paper sealed inelegantly. Wagstaff cracked the red wax and paled. 'Ah, friends, this sets the cat among the pigeons.' He sank back heavily, chair legs rasping on the boards, startling the dogs to their feet. 'Sir William Waller summons me to Bristol with all speed. I'm to take whoever I can. That'll include you, Salt.' He smiled apologetically. 'Mrs Wagstaff'll mind your lady and we'll see about Helions when we can. Jones, the General asks for you *specifically*.' The Gunner paled. 'Round up the men, Jeremiah. Search the whore-houses of the Common before the prayer meetings of the town. Shoot any bastard that refuses.'

X

Parliament's army was losing and Waller felt Westminster's accusatory finger jabbed in his direction. The threadbare army he had recently ordered from the fleshpots and alehouses of Bristol to bivouac on the windswept downs was a cauldron of simmering resentment. Incessant rain and the press of men and material had churned his chosen plot into a sea of mud and misery.

A fortunate minority sheltered under canvas strips. Most simply huddled round damp fires waiting for first light. Apart from an occasional resentful scowl on an upturned hungry face, Wagstaff's company, picking through the mire, attracted little attention

The General's tented headquarters, glowing like a great waxed lantern, was some way from the main encampment. 'See them bach?' Jones nodded at the sentries. 'I'm thinking them's to keep Waller safe from his own side, not the enemy.'

Sergeant Major General Waller stood beneath a swathe of canvas stretched between rough-hewn poles, a small fleshy man with a big nose. A dozen officers crowded round a trestle table and its precious maps. Haselrig, propped up on a stick, tight-lipped, nodded curtly at the new arrivals. The atmosphere was tense, a place for a man to be on his guard.

Wagstaff removed his hat, flicking it dry. Waller, walking his compasses across a map, did not look up. 'Wagstaff, I assume. Late.' The General was peering at Gloucestershire. 'Hope you've brought that Welsh knave Jones with you. Clapped in irons.' The deaf Gunner looked on innocently, Wagstaff raising a finger to his lips, turning him round and packing him out of the tent. 'My people tell me that Jack-a-napes and the rogue Hungerford have been cutting a swathe through the west country like Barbary pirates up the Channel. How can I run a disciplined fighting force if martinets like Jones use my army to rough up honest God-fearing citizens that he fancies papists?' Nat stared at Haselrig, the man who had instructed him to do the same, but the Colonel of Horse avoided his eye. General Waller, red-faced, swung round to catch the Gunner's retreating back. 'Come here, Sir!' Jones halted in his tracks and turned sharply to face the advancing majesty of the Major General. Removing his hat, Hungerford's gunner stood stiffly in the rain. 'Captain Jones. You're a disobedient Welsh pirate. Why should I not shoot you for abandoning Malmesbury?' Waller's ejection of the royalists from the Wiltshire town counted as the General's only notable success of the year.

'Well, General, Colonel Hungerford said Malmesbury was secure, see, and didn't need us.' Jones smiled benignly. 'And the men were restless, Sir, itching to be paid, like. Sir Edward said we could get money in Bath. So we went, Sir.'

'Well, Sir, you'll not desert your post again. You'll stay here until called. At attention, Sir!' Swinging on his heels, the Sergeant Major General beat back to the thin comfort of the tent. 'A plague on all Welshmen.' Leaning over the map, water tipped from the brow of his hat to soak the city of Bristol.

A servant padded between the officers refilling pewter beakers from a jug of small beer. Two fussed with a trestle table and a white cloth, arranging salvers of bread and cheese. 'Gentlemen, since we've suffered such a dismal defeat we must break our fast sparingly.' Waller caught sight of Nat. 'Who the devil are you?'

'General, can I present Captain Nathaniel Salt?' Haselrig piped up. 'Did me great service when I was brought to bay on Roundway Down.'

Waller scowled. 'That Devizes fight was my nadir, y'know.' He shook his head wearily, the rain, matching his mood, beating a tattoo on the canvas. 'Still, obliged to you Captain...' His eyes were red raw. '...Salt, ain't it? Aye, obliged, for rescuing my impetuous Colonel of Horse.' The General turned to a second map, a detailed chart of Bristol. Nat could see that it had been marked up to show the earthworks dug by its puritan inhabitants against Prince Rupert. Waller traced the newly inked line with his damp finger. 'Bristol's key to the west gentlemen, and the west is the key to the country. All hangs on Bristol. Bristol, Bristol, Bristol.' His finger jabbed the city. 'The Governor, our good Colonel Fiennes is here. Where are you, Fiennes?'

'Why's the bugger not in Bristol?' muttered Wagstaff as Fiennes, an unsoldierly middle-aged man, inched forward, tripping over one of the canvas buckets for catching leaks.

'Fiennes here says we've plucked the army out of Bristol, leaving him exposed,' said Waller with a curl of the lip. 'Ain't that so, Fiennes?'

'Aye, General.' The man stood limply in front of his commander. 'I must have my cavalry back and some infantry too.' He shifted uneasily. 'Bristol's defences are pregnable if Prince Rupert chooses to fall on us.'

'But I must have a field army.' Waller ground his finger into the hole worn in the sodden map where Bristol had been. 'What's to be done with Bristol, Wagstaff?'

'I'm neither Bristolian nor tactician, General, but I've a man who's both,' offered the Major, 'stood to attention where you left him. Outside in the rain, General.'

'Huh!' Throwing back the tent flap, Waller bellowed into the night. 'Here Jones. Now, is Bristol safe against the King or must I surrender the army of the west to prop it up?'

Jones stood at the table soaked through, rain water pooling at his feet. Wagstaff handed his friend a jerkin of beer. He downed it, smacked his lips and passed it back for a refill. He noted the little flags pinned in the map marking units of the Parliamentary Navy and that the King had nothing at sea. 'General, you and I have an advantage over these other gentlemen, don't we?'

'Stralsund,' conceded Waller grudgingly.

'*Stralsund.*' Jones scanned the line of blank faces. 'Me and the General served in the late European wars, see. Proper wars, they were. I reckon few here have that distinction?' He sighed, feigning disappointment. 'Well, gentlemen, Stralsund port was captained for the King of Sweden by our godly Scotsman Alexander Leslie, see. Held off a murderous siege by the Emperor's cronies who thought they'd take it in three days.' He smirked. 'Well, after *eleven weeks*, butcher's bill forced the Emperor's crew to give up. The moral, gentlemen?' He peered at them like a schoolmaster. 'The moral, *gentlemen,* is never lay siege to a port from the land alone, see, least of all one blessed with nature's bastions and the bulwarks of the engineers, like Stralsund. Or Bristol.'

Waller nodded, brightening up. 'So Fiennes is bellyaching and I can have my army, eh?'

The Gunner cleared his throat. 'Stralsund had the advantage of General Leslie, Sir. But Bristol?' He shrugged. 'It only has Colonel Fiennes.'

Governor Fiennes glared at Jones, the staff officers sniggering into their sleeves. But Waller's mind was no longer on Bristol but London and the machinations of his superior, Parliament's Lord General, the Earl of Essex. His great rival was rumoured to be making traitorous overtures to the King. Word had reached Waller that the Earl's behaviour might mean a vacancy, to be filled by an officer of the godly disposition. Waller, in other words.

But after the disaster of Roundway Down, Sir William knew he must scamper back to Whitehall quickly to foil attempts by the Earl to blacken his reputation. He had canvassed Haselrig's views already and felt safe in asking for them now. 'Sir Arthur?'

Haselrig dusted off his opinion. 'General, Fiennes here is tucked up well enough behind his earthworks. The army must remain in the field. We should drive north to Gloucester to assess Colonel Massey's preparations. The Prince will as soon lay siege to that city as this.'

'Yes, yes, and in Bristol our ships control the roads, just like Stralsund.' Waller was toying with a small fruit knife, playing it between his fingers, pouring over the map with its heavily inked road to London. He straightened, bringing the knife down hard, impaling the chart where the City of Bristol had been before it had been turned to mush by the rain. 'We're agreed then.' Waller wheeled round to face his staff, all nodding. All, except one.

Nat cleared his throat. Now they were all glaring at him, officers and gentry, important men who knew things. But none of them had more right to have his say. 'Don't reckon there's an earthwork in the whole of Christendom that'll shield your pitchfork militia from Prince Rupert.'

'Oh?' Waller, raised his eyebrows quizzically at the softly spoken country captain. 'Go on, young man.' There was the cruel curl of the lip but the General curbed his impulse to cut the rustic dead.

'Well, I mean, won't Parliament be asking why its godly army gets beaten by the King every time?' Nat reddened. 'What'll you say?' Nat felt hot blood pounding in his temples. *Impertinent oaf,* spat one of the dandies. God, why had he opened his mouth? Now they were all marvelling at the lumbering farm idiot with his borrowed gear picking at the sore of Roundway Down. 'Can't you see why we're losing?'

'Out of the mouths of babes and sucklings,' muttered Haselrig.

'The army's a rabble, Sir. Like its cut from good timber but cheaply joined. And it's armed with what?' Nat scanned the bemused staff for support. 'Pitchforks and billhooks, that's what. I'd sooner have a company of Prince Rupert's Cornishmen at push of pikes than a regiment of unshod farm boys.' Seeing Waller's lip was no longer curled, he pressed on. 'The Parliament must model a new army Sir.'

Jones ended the uneasy silence. 'The Devizes fight was no less than a rout, Sir, a disgrace, Sir. The King will have our heads on spikes unless Parliament can cast a new army in the foundry of our despair.'

All eyes fixed on the General, no other officer was bold enough to say what he knew to be true. Waller said nothing, weighing the rough-shod Captain's words, turning them in a way that might finesse his culpability for the defeat at Devizes. 'Where's my new parson? Sing out, man!' A small figure dressed entirely in black slithered from the shadows. Between leathery talons he clutched the trademark oversized bible. Markham. 'Ah, Reverend, set us on the Gloucester road with a prayer, won't you?' He was staring at Nat intensely. 'Ask Him that shaped us to build new legions from the ranks of the righteous, eh?'

The cleric wet his thin lips, thumbing through the dog-eared volume, finding the prophet Micah.

'*But in the last days it shall come to pass that the mountain of the Lord shall be established in the top of the mountains, and it shall be exalted above the hills; and people shall flow unto it.*'

Nat knew the words by heart and from the movement of their lips could see that much of the general staff knew them too.

'*And he shall judge among many people, and rebuke strong nations afar off; and they shall beat their swords into ploughshares, and their spears into pruning hooks; nation shall not lift sword against nation, neither shall they learn war any more.*'

The words of the Old Testament fell melodically from the priest's twisted mouth.

'*But they shall sit every man under his vine and under his fig tree; and none shall make them afraid; for the mouth of the Lord of hosts has spoken it.*'

'*For all people will walk every one in the name of his god, and we will walk in the name of the Lord our God for ever and ever.*'

The book banged shut. Markham chose his words carefully. 'Lord, protect good Governor Fiennes and our brethren left in Bristol against the violence of the enemy. May Parliament model an army, a new-model army,' he liked how that sounded, and saw Waller did too, 'to smite the King's wicked counsellors and bring His Majesty to the true religion.

Then England shall rise and be exalted among nations and thy will be done. Amen.'

Waller beckoned Nat and Jones. He spoke softly, making sure they were not overheard. 'Jones I should have you disciplined for your rudeness to poor Colonel Fiennes.' He jabbed a finger at Nat. 'You, young man, should be horse-whipped for presumption.' Pulling at his goatee, he smiled conspiratorially. 'But I'm more than a soldier, *gentlemen*, I'm a politician. That means I take a broad view.' Waller looked over his shoulder. 'Take the fastest horses and the London road. Lord General Essex will be putting it about that I'm to blame for the west's misfortunes. We must outflank him.' He drew Jones and Nat close, whispering now. 'Get to Mr John Pym with my despatches, quick as you can. If they call me William the Conqueror they call him King Pym, and with better reason for he's first among the captains of Parliament and a true friend of the army. Tell Pym and his people of our situation. Tell those damned news book writers who give the mob their opinions. Give a good account, mind, before city gossip tittle-tattle and the cussed news sheets cast me as scapegoat for our defeats.' The saturnine Lord General Essex had the ear of Parliament's moderates who would be quick to accept his diagnosis, and his prescription. 'Tell Mr Pym about the war in the west and the Devizes fight and how godly men and leaders like lions are no substitute for...' he hesitated before spitting the words, '...*a proper army*.'

*

'Damn glad to be shot o' that dismal garrison bach.' Captain Jones lifted a buttock to pass wind. 'Shot of Waller too.' He grinned at Nat. 'Even if the price is a hell-for-leather chase down the London road to save the bacon of our God-bothering William the Conqueror.' He patted his saddlebag. 'Dispatches for Pym yes, but dispatches too for the news books of London see. Sir William strokes public opinion like it was his mistress.'

Nat shrugged. He resented the flight to the capital, away from the action, Carew and Effam. 'We'll do as we're told, Jones, then head back fast as we can.' He turned in the saddle, bawling at Jessop, Clegg and Will Porit. 'That's right, lads. Avenge the Devizes fight, eh?'

Jones beamed. 'Oh, but Sir William was insistent bach. We're to await his return to London, massaging his reputation in Whitehall's pretty parlours, see.' He jabbed Nat's ribs. 'Cheer up boyo, we'll have you back on your road to perdition quicker than a papist's prayer meeting.'

Around the bend, a pair of youngsters took fright at the troop of roundheads. 'See 'em run bach. Cock pheasants from a buckthorn bush, eh? Deserters, I expect.'

'First young men we've seen in this poxed country,' said Nat. 'Their mates will be under arms or under the ground, eh?'

'Aye bach, butchered by brethren for a cause they don't understand,' mused Jones. 'Still, ain't no good philosophising when you're a soldier, Salt. Best not to brood. Inclines a man to melancholia see.'

'Oh, I know all about melancholia, friend.' Nat blew out his cheeks, staring despondently across the fields. 'Black dog's always been snapping at my heels.'

'What's that?' The deaf gunner cupped his ear.

'Black dog, Jones. Needs a good kicking or it'll bite your balls off.' He felt for a twist of the apothecary's wort.

'Ah.' Jones pressed a hand to Nat's back. 'Look here bach, the Lord knows you've reason to be pissed off. Young 'uns and all. A lesser man...'

'Aye, but God's promised me a reckoning. So I keep going, one foot after the other,' intoned Nat. '*Jehovah Providebit.*'

'That's the spirit!'

'God promised me Carew.' Nat looked across at the unhearing gunner. 'In St Laurence chapel, he *gave* him to me.'

'Can't blame those runners bach,' said Jones.

'Parson told me,' said Nat. 'Peace'll come at the end, after I've done it, after I've killed Carew.'

'Hungry mouths at home see, crops turning to mush,' barked Jones. 'Here, now won't you look at that, boyo?' He nodded at the unnatural form like an overgrown round barrow. 'They call it Silbury Hill.'

'Looks like a tit. Stuck out all pert an' bosomy,' marvelled Jessop. 'An' it looks like your nag's cast a shoe, Cap'n Jones.'

'Aw, hell's teeth.' Jones was off his horse lifting its foreleg. He nodded at the village down the track surrounded by standing stones. 'That's Avebury. It'll have a farrier.'

The troop halted outside the Red Lion. 'Farrier's away with the army though I'm not sure which one,' snarled Jessop. 'Publican 'ere says he'll send word for the blacksmith but he's a lazy cur so we're to expect a wait.'

'God's blood! Poxed war's made a prince out of every tin pot tradesman.' Jones nodded at the inn. 'Gaff looks cosy enough. Better make the best of it.'

The officers and Jessop awaited the blacksmith's pleasure, supping warm ale in the sun. Nat scribbled a letter, not rating its chances of reaching Warminster.

Sweet heart,

Sir William Waller has sent me to London to prepare for a meeting with Mr John Pym, parliament's leader. The general shouldn't be blamed for our army's defeats but unlucky captains have few friends.

I'll wait for Sir William at my sister's house in Eastcheap. Hope to see my brother there too.

Every moment away from you is a great trial. I pray for orders west to rejoin the fight so I can...' Can what? Nat played the goose feather across cheek stubble. Kill Erasmus Carew? She did not want to hear that. He dipped the pen, *'...be reunited with you.'* Better. *'In the meantime, my sweet love, look after our affairs best you can. Mrs Wagstaff's a good woman. Rely on her for the wedding arrangements but, dearest, make it nice and simple – a great show wouldn't be right.*

I'll write from London where I expect to be the day after tomorrow.

All of my love,

Nat

The innkeeper's boy was belting down the track waving his arms. 'Soldiers! A whole *army* of bleeding soldiers!'

'Where away?' Jones, grabbing his sword, moved surprisingly fast.

'Beyond the stones, heading in.'

'Ours or theirs?'

'Dunno.'

'Upstairs gents 'til we see the colour of their cloth.' The innkeeper nodded at a window set deep in the eaves under the thatch. 'That chamber's best. You'll get an eyeful of the soldiers when they sally forth between the stones. I beg you, if it's the King's men, lie low or they'll put me to the nubbing-post.'

The soldiers bolted to the eyrie with its low beams and tiny casement window. The vantage gave a commanding view of the approach road as it cut through the stone circle. They crouched low, awaiting the first sign of the troops.

The crump, crump of well-shod feet was a bad sign, heralding disciplined, properly kitted out men; King's men. Nat fingered the pommel of his sword and surveyed the room, a cell set in a stone and earthwork trap.

Lilly Burlero, its jaunty Celtic strains scratched out on whistle and fife announcing the arrival of the column, still out of sight. 'Bloody papist ditty, boyo,' hissed Jones. 'Make ready, we're in for a fight.'

The file swung into the stone circle. The standard with its cross of St George, red field and Captain's pile-wavy swallow tails fluttered gaily behind a mounted officer in a great feathered hat and, heaven be praised, parliament's orange-tawny sash.

'It's the Red Regiment, by God!' Jones leapt up, hitting his head. He flung open the casement waving his hat, the company drawing alongside and, in good order, coming to a halt. 'Hurrah, the Red Regiment! Hurrah, you Londoners, victors o' Turnham Green!' The gunner was quite beside himself. 'Hurrah for Colonel Atkin's hearts of oak!'

The mounted officer, a grizzled old man, doffed his hat and bowed gracefully at the window. 'Well, bless my soul, Cap'n Jones. What are you doing cowering in the eaves like a frightened old woman?'

'Cowering, my arse,' spluttered Jones. 'Had you for malignants. This county's got more papists than a tart's parlour.'

'Aye, that it has. We've swept a few of 'em passing through, as you can see.' Captain John Grimston, nodded to the rear of his column where a dozen semi-naked prisoners hopped from foot to foot. 'My canting preacher had me spare their miserable hides.' He raised his voice. 'Though I'm sorely minded to hang the malignant, murdering bastards.' Grimston stuck his boot into the nearest captive. 'Sheep-bothering Cornishmen, bog Irish, pig ignorant farm boys and a brace of the French whore-queen's mercenary frog papists.' He hauled himself down, rubbing the horse's neck. 'Told my preacher, if he wants 'em fed he'll have to miracle up some loaves and fishes. He ain't, and that's why they're so damned thin. Ha! Ha!'

'You'll have to agree terms of bivouac with the innkeeper bach,' said Jones. 'His writ runs here since the two local landowners went to war, in separate directions.'

'Aye, quartermaster'll see to it. An army must live off the land gents but we're not thieves and must mind our good reputation,' Grimston observed. 'A hundred young Londoners take some vittalling and I'm sorely tempted to insist on free quarter which is my right. But my man will lodge promissory notes with these poor souls so all of the godly persuasion and declared for the Parliament will be paid, sooner or later.'

'The husbandmen of Avebury'll think your promissory notes poor dole for their finger-thick turnips and sinewy pullets, Cap'n,' said Nat thinking of Hinton Helions.

'Ah, well, Captain, we all suffer for the cause, though unequally, it must be said.' Grimston, smoothing his beard, peered at the Wiltshire farmer. 'Some men are asked to give up root vegetables, some their lives.'

Nat baulked at the silver-tongued merchant's easy dismissal of the rural poor, born, he suspected, of very little suffering and a belly that was always full.

'What you doing here then bach?'

'On detachment from the Earl of Essex Captain Jones,' replied Grimston. 'The Lord General wants the county scoured for royalists.'

Jones swaggered up and down the line, nodding approval. 'For a troop of 'prentice boys your company makes a pretty picture, Cap'n Grimston.' The sturdy, well equipped men were a million miles from the surly, resentful creatures Waller had pitched outside Bristol. 'They're a credit to you, Sir, a credit.'

'Thank you, Captain Jones, though the flintlocks and buffcoats you see have cut a hole in the bottom of my purse.' Grimston sucked his teeth.

'Flintlocks, eh?' Nat guessed the merchant's purse was deep enough. 'If we'd just matchlocks with enough powder and shot and the lads a penny a day, Waller wouldn't be losing the year to the King.'

'Well, the Earl squeezes us poor London traders like grapes in a press to pay for the army's matchlocks friend.' Grimston was tiring of the upstart.

'London caused this calamity,' Nat retorted. 'Only right it pays up.'

'True,' said Grimston. 'But our livery companies have opened their treasuries to the Parliament, our merchant ships are the very life-blood of the cause and London sends sons and 'prentice boys to rot in your stinking fields just as surely as its grain's turned to corruption for the want of reaping.'

'Aye bach, right enough,' Jones interjected. 'London's the great shop of war and England's fields are soaked with the thin blood of your barrow boys and lumpen merchant men.' He put his arm around Nat's shoulders. 'Our brother here means no offence to your city boys. Saw 'em stand well enough at the Devizes fight. Aye, and with their country cousins taking fright and riding off. Eh, Captain Salt?'

Nat snapped at the innkeeper fretting at his side. 'What?'

'Beg pardon Sirs, farrier's done the Cap'n's horse. Says he'd be obliged for 'is pay.'

Jones slapped Grimston's back. 'Well, I'm mighty glad to run into you and your fine lads, Captain Grimston. It would have been an honour to share the road to London but I mean to add to the day's bag before supper.'

'Godspeed bach. Huzzah, the Red Regiment! Grimston's column marched off through the stones, sun setting at its back.

Jones beamed at Nat, spirits lifted by the encounter and strengthened by the beer. 'Meeting those boys was an unexpected pleasure, Salt, though we'll need to ride hard to make up time.'

'Aye, but be thankful for the cover of darkness.' Nat had not forgotten his narrow escape after Roundway.

'As long as the London road's in good repair and the horses keep their shoes on.' Jones had no more time or money for farriers.

*

A solitary raven shrieked at the glowering sky. 'Bad omen boyo, damned black-hearted crow.' Jones had a Welshman's superstition. 'Harbinger of death, that's what. Here, sling me that pretty pistol brother.' The sleek bird cocked its head at the horsemen. 'Brother, the pistol?' Mindlessly, Nat surrendered the Upton.

Crack! The beauty tumbled to earth.

'No good'll come of that, Jones,' mumbled Nat, the black dog, his old companion, padding in like a wolf on the fold.

'Aw, buck up bach.' Jones nodded at the turn in the road. 'Now then, we'll rest up at that village and have a spot of breakfast.' He turned in the saddle. 'What d'you say, lads?'

Marsh Benham was a settlement of turned backs and sullen faces. 'Kind of place best passed through quick without looking back,' said Nat.

'Aye.' Jones too was weighing the village sympathies. 'Best bivvy over the bridge, across that meadow.'

After breakfast, Nat ambled downriver for a piss and freshen up. Crouching low, he splashed his face with the cool waters of the Kennet then stretched his poisoned leg into the flow, easing off the encrusted dressing. Happy with the wound, he wrang the binding, wrapped it round and dressed up. Whistling contentedly, he wandered further downstream.

Too far.

There were fingerlings in the shallows. Smiling, he leant over.

A flintlock dog drawn from half-cock clicked at his ear. He froze. Slowly, raising his arms, Nat twisted round to the barrel and half a dozen dragoons. 'Hold, Sir.'

The Cornet pulled up his gun. 'Zounds! It's one of their rag-tag officers scratching in the dirt. This bag'll please His Highness.' He looked for the smirking endorsement of his men. 'Name, fellow?' The Cornet raised his heavy bucket-topped boot and slammed the fashionable red heel into Nat's face, spur ripping his cheek.

'Captain Nathaniel Salt. General Waller's staff.' Nat raised his blooded hand. 'Hold now! You've got my parole.'

'Parole be damned,' lisped the youngster. 'I've a mind to stretch your neck right now, *whoreson*.' Nat doubted the pup knew what a whore was. 'Take his sword, corporal, and bind him, tight mind. You're a brave fellow, I'll grant you, travelling the London road alone.' The young man hesitated. 'You are alone?'

Nat shrugged. 'See for yourself.' The corporal pumped his fist into Nat's guts, passed Farrington's sword and the cherished pistol to the Cornet and remounted. With a sneer, he jerked Nat in close to his mount's rear, hemp sheering his wrists. 'Hold up, Sir, I can't be towed like an animal!'

'Arseworm.' The Cornet had learnt his troopers' vocabulary. Nat took the heel of the youth's boot in his face as the troop pulled away along the steep-banked lane, thick on either side with blackthorn and elder.

'Hold on, shit-for-brains.' The Cornet was fingering the Upton. His voice was urgent. 'How d'you come by this?'

'What's it to you?' spat Nat from the corner of his bloodied mouth.

The corporal's blow put Nat on his knees, squinting at the blurred Cornet leaning over the mane of his beast waving the Upton. 'It's my brother's, arseworm, our father's gift to him.'

Nat fell back on his haunches. 'Then you should know the meaning of a war between brothers.'

'What d'you mean?' The boy's face fell. 'He'd never part with this.'

'Course not.' Nat gazed impassively at the fop, pleased to spike him with the news. 'Your brother's numbered among Parliament's dead.'

The boy looked away. 'How so?' He sniffed moistly, passing a sleeve across his face.

'Honourably,' Nat conceded, 'at the Devizes fight.'

At four paces a doglock musket reliably flays a man. The first trooper was dead before hitting the ground. 'Huzzah!' The butt of a matchlock crashed through the hedge smashing the temporal bone of the soldier immediately behind the officer.

'Stand to, stand to!' The horrified Cornet turned to see the ram-rod from a hastily loaded gun piercing the breast of a third man.

Will Porit pushed through the blackthorn, slashing with his long gutting knife. The slaughterman opened the belly of the Corporal's horse then attacked its rider, the two entwined in a hideous, slippery ballet in guts and gore. The Cornet and his remaining horseman made off down the track. 'Look at 'em go! Yella bastards.'

Flinging the dead corporal's saddle across his horse, Nat seized Will Porit's knife and kicked on. Drawing alongside, he sliced the first beast's girth strap, lunging at the petrified trooper. The man slid sideways snapping his neck cleanly on the road.

The Cornet turned his bloodless face to Jones' horse rearing above the bank. The animal, falling on the bewildered youth, bucked the Welshman into the blackthorn. Jones tore away from the hedge, growling, sword poised over the squirming cavalier. 'Prickless streak of piss.'

'Hold man!' Nat pulled up between them.

The Cornet, pawing at blood coursing down his face and into his eyes, fell sobbing against the bank, arm raised to fend off the blow. Jones dragged him to his feet, hissing in his ear, 'God, it's your lucky day boyo!'

Nat retrieved Farrington's sword, drawing the blade. Towering above the snivelling youth, he laid cold steel against downy cheek. The boy flinched. 'I should send you to your maker with the rest.' The youth's mouth opened and shut like a beached fish. Sheathing the sword, Nat turned his back in disgust, nodding at the royalist dead littering the lane. 'Shame to leave those poor bodies on the road, all bloodied and torn, mothers' sons and all.'

'Aye, this rantipole boy can clear up the mess bach. Lay 'em out all neat and tiddly, like soldiers.' Jones took a drag from his flask, passing it round. 'Depending on how he does, we'll either string him up now or give him to our ill-affected Earl of Essex. What's your name, boy?'

'Henry Russell, Sir.' He drew himself half upright against the bank. 'Lord Russell. Cornet, Prince Rupert's Royal Regiment of Horse.'

'Oh I say! Lardi-da.' Jones' face creased. 'Should've kept that quiet boyo. Half a dozen o' Prince Rupert's horse *and* a pocket aristocrat.' The gunner leered over his prisoner. 'M'Lord General will be pleased, eh Salt? Might bring a cheer to the melancholic old get.'

Nat pitied the chinless pup with his massacred troop and dead brother. 'Look boy, tell me straight and I'll spare you from Captain Jones.' He lacked the stomach for tormenting the lad but his intelligence could warn them of better led cavaliers in Berkshire's narrow lanes. 'I want to know what you're up to.'

The young man, wide-eyed, gawped at the officer with his soft, west-country burr. 'The Prince sent me to reconnoitre. Said Lord Essex was making for Newbury.'

'Where's Prince Rupert's army?" The boy said nothing, casting his eyes sullenly to the ground. 'Listen, boy, Cap'n Jones wants you dead and he's in charge. Tell me or crows'll peck your eyes within the hour.' Nat's head began to throb, bile rising in his throat. 'Now, be a good lad, tell us where the Prince is, um?'

Cornet Russell shrugged miserably. 'Supping with the Aldermen of Bristol, I shouldn't wonder.'

Nat swallowed hard, mouth dust dry. The blow from Russell's boot had been worse than he thought. 'What's that, boy?'

Russell glanced between his captors with mounting incredulity. 'Well, honestly, did you expect the Prince to creep back to Oxford after the thrashing he gave you at Devizes?'

'Bristol!' spat Jones. 'I knew it.'

Nat threw up in the hedge, Jones slapping him on the back. 'Better for that bach? Ye Gods, you're white as a shroud.' The gunner lowered his voice but there was no disguising his urgency. 'Listen, that arse Waller's made the wrong call. He'll be closing on Gloucester now when he should be shoring up Fiennes in Bristol!'

'Best head north. Catch up with Waller.' Nat passed a sleeve across his mouth. 'And pray the army turns back in time.'

'I'll send Clegg on Russell's Arab.' Jones chewed his lip, weighing up the fine horse. 'He's a good lad, fast too.'

'But if he's killed or the horse casts a shoe?' Squatting on his haunches, he lowered his head, breathing deeply. 'We should all go.'

The gunner shook his head. 'Waller wants his despatches in Pym's hands right away and London'll need our latest intelligence on Rhineish Rupert.'

Nat was too ill to argue.

Dragging corpses from the road, Lord Russell felt Jessop's boot. Jones was equally sympathetic. 'When your sexton trick's done, Sergeant, I want that canting cock bird trussed up like a spatchcock chicken.' Filling his pipe, the gunner passed his flask to Nat. 'What place is this, Salt?'

Nat pushed the liquor away. 'They call it Marsh Benham.' Nat gulped on another wave of sick.

'Marsh Benham, eh?' Jones fumbled in his saddlebag for paper to write his report. 'Y'know bach, songs'll be writ about Edgehill. Even the Devizes fight. But who'll give a tinker's cuss for our poxy action at Marsh Benham?'

He pulled at the pipe, head shrouded in a malodorous fug. 'I'll tell you who brother, nobody. It'll be like it had never been, like those poor bastards never drew breath.' Captain Jones spat his disgust. 'The German wars bach, now they was real wars with ordinance all lined up and rank on rank of proper soldier men see. But this, *war*, it's a thousand Marsh Benhams, a constellation of twatty little skirmishes played out in narrow lanes for the purpose of mutual ruination. A pox on it!' Jones thrust the note at Clegg. 'To Gloucester boyo like the devil himself was snapping at your heels.' Clegg, grinning astride Lord Russell's gelding, kicked on cuffing the cavalier as he passed.

'Godspeed.' Nat raised his hand. 'Fly like the wind Arthur Clegg.'

Jones was in good voice:

'We be soldiers three

Pardonnez-moi, je vous en prie

Lately come forth from the Low Country

With never a penny of money.'

Nat smiled, running a hand through his hair. The gunner was full of surprises. 'Good jingle friend.'

'Eh?'

'YOU'VE A FINE SINGING VOICE'

'Ah, Welsh see.' Jones nodded, stroking his rough chin. '*We be soldiers three*. Ditty we sang in the late wars bach. You're meant to join in, for the verse, French bit.' He nudged Joe Jessop. 'Come on, sergeant, and you, Porit.'

'Here good fellow, I drink to thee

Pardonnez-moi, je vous en prie

To all good fellows, wherever they be

With never a penny of money'

Nat saw the first musket poked from the hedge. 'Take cover!' A puff of smoke among the briars as the powder took fire and the familiar low crack. The matches of half a dozen muskets ignited their pans, punching a ragged salvo through the air.

But the musketmen had set their trap on exposed ground where horsemen could drive easily through the blackthorn. Across the hedge, the land rose gently towards a long earthwork, the trace of an ancient fort. Hitting the ground behind the shallow bastion, Nat trained his eyeglass on the ambush. 'Should've held their fire, given it full on. Look, they're all over the place, four, five, I think six of 'em.' Thrusting the glass at Jones, he turned for a roll call. Will Porit was hauling Russell from his horse, ashen, pawing a dark stain spreading between his fingers. The boy's eyes lobbed between the men appealing for reassurance they could not give.

'Lost their advantage.' Jones grinned, anticipating an easy mop up. He nodded at Russell choking and spitting blood. 'You're a piss poor field surgeon Will Porit.' Jones rolled back, taking another sweep of the enemy. 'Set him on his bad side boyo and he'll breathe better, maybe live a tad longer.'

Head low, Nat moved to the stricken youngster. Pulling him up by the collar, he ripped the thick doublet and shirt, wringing red. The shot had hit him full square smashing through the forth rib, the breach drawing in air with a hiss on each laboured breath. There was a matching wound at his back, a good sign as the shot was not left to fester. But the coughed blood, bright and frothy, heralded a swifter end than gangrene.

'I beg Sir, a good account,' the cavalier was transfixed by the rib sticking from his chest, splintered and white, 'to a childless old man, if you can pass word to Oxford, for me and my brother.'

'I'll send your father what comforts I can.' Covering the wound, Nat lowered the boy onto his right and scrambled back to Jones.

'Buggers are crouched behind that hedge with muskets sticking out like quills from a hedgehog.' Jones was still scanning the hedgerow with the perspective glass. 'Haven't moved an inch bach, scared shitless shouldn't wonder.' Snapping the glass shut, he nodded at the spinney on their left flank. 'We'll leave his Lordship to finish dying, sweep round the back o' that, fire off a volley and despatch what remains with cold steel.'

The horsemen took a wide arc five hundred yards west swinging behind the trees. Muskets half cocked, they flanked the five men with weapons still pointing at the empty redoubt. Reining in at a hundred paces, Nat wondered dully about the sixth man they had seen from the hill.

'Look at them poor bastards.' Jessop took aim. Too late, the foot soldiers turned, backing up against the hedge, struggling to retrain their clumsy weapons. 'Bagging birds in a henhouse, this.' Three shots and two of the men slumped forward. The horsemen pulled back out of range, the remaining soldiers opening fire uselessly. The horsemen turned again to finish it forcing the foot soldiers to test the razor sharp hedge, bastion turned against them. 'Run you Jabbernowls, run!' Jones' blood was up. The royalists raced along the hedge, clawing for rat-holes. 'Huzzah!' Jones was on top of them. Backed up against the blackthorn, two of the peasants stuck their arms up.

Nat saw the gunner's mortuary sword rise, his face a spittal-flecked contortion. Splitting the first man's head, with a deft flick of the wrist Jones skewered the neck of the second. And Nat was laughing, at the hand, severed by Jones' butchery from the principal part of the first man, fingers curling like a crab.

'Stick 'im, Salt!' Jones was pointing at the last man ripping through the blackthorn, taking off down the lane. Kicking on, Nat took the hedge, his sword's leisured arc slicing through flesh like butter. Circling the twitching corpse, Nat's guts cramped at the bloodied features of a child. 'Bravo Cap'n Salt!' Nat dismounted, falling to his knees. Not much older than his son this *soldier*, some other husbandman's pride.

Regrouping at the redoubt, Jones was flushed with success. Nat crouched by Lord Russell's still form. The Cornet's head was laid against the earth, eyes fixed as if studying the close-cropped turf, a thin line of blood tracking from his mouth. Jones stood on the bank, outlined heroically against the sky, sweeping the horizon with the eye glass. *Get down, Jones.*

'There's a company o' foot swinging round from the east bach. Smart an' soldier-like, so doubt it's ours.' Jones snapped the glass shut, squinting at the lowering sky. 'Weather's closing in.' He stretched with a grunt, thrusting his chest like a cock pheasant.

Crack! A single shot from the road. Too late, Nat remembered the sixth man. Jones was on his knees like he was praying, falling forward, face in the dirt with the black sentinel crow screeching its delight to the heavens.

Pulling at the borrowed flintlock, Nat aimed at the assassin's back; an ambitious shot. 'Got you!'

'Bleedin' good Cap'n.' Crashing into the lane, Will Porit's boot connected with the prostrate soldier. 'Thought so. Bastard's foxing, Sir.' Wrenching the man's head back, he looked for the signal. Nat swallowed hard. 'Sir?'

'Well, *Sir*?' sneered Jessop.

'Just do it, Porit,' snapped Nat.

The practised hand of the butcher's apprentice opened the soldier's neck, Nat's stomach contents joining the gore washing across the road.

'Must've been that bang on the 'ead, Sir.' Jessop was slapping his back, confidence restored.

They scooped a single pit for the dead officers at the redoubt.

'Here, Sir.' Jessop passed Russell's fine chiselled court rapier and Jones' brutal instrument. 'And these.' Nat flicked the pages of Jones' well-thumbed bible with letters stuffed inside. 'The good book can stop a musket ball at a hundred yards,' said Jessop. 'Cap'n Jones wore his on the wrong side, poor sod.'

Nat's hand closed on an engraved locket with a strand of hair, a silver nutmeg grater and a leather purse containing some change. Binding the pathetic collection in Jones' orange sash, he jammed the parcel in his saddlebag. 'We be soldiers three. *Pardonnez-moi, je vous en prie.*'

'Sir?' Will Porit was tying sticks to make a rugged cross.

'Captain's Jones' jingle.' Nat gave a tight, rueful smile. 'We were four, but now we're three.'

'We'll be turning back then?' Jessop's question was met with silence. 'Just I couldn't help hearing you back there, with Cap'n Jones, you know, 'bout warning Waller.' Jessop knew what pulled Nat west and it certainly was not the plight of William Waller.

'Careful, Jessop.' Nat's temper was on a short fuse. 'Waller's orders are clear.' But Nat was sorely tempted to revoke the dead gunner's decision. 'Clegg'll be closing on Sir William by now.' He paused, gulping to keep his guts down. 'We'll press on with Waller's' despatches and Lord Russell's intelligence.'

Jessop shrugged, sucking his teeth. 'Right you are.'

Will Porit closed the grave with a dozen heavy stones, Jessop thrusting the marker into the cairn. With no time for ceremony, the three stood heads bowed, Nat with his bible open at Psalm 23.

It was just as well he knew it by heart, his head spinning and the print dancing irretrievably.

XI

From Psalm 23 to London, hardly a word, but closing on the capital, the three men began to buck up.

'What're they up to?' Jessop nodded at a large work party picking and shovelling.

'Digging banks and ditches against the enemy,' said Will Porit. 'London had a close shave at Turnham Green last year. If the King comes again, we'll be ready.'

A digger straightened painfully. 'Good day, brothers.' Leaning against a wooden spade, he squinted at the horsemen. 'What news?'

'All's well, father.' Will Porit knew his city, how rumours spread faster than sweating sickness. 'Not a papist in a hundred miles on account of your excavations.'

'God bless you, brother!' the ancient chortled, returning to the chorus of tools chiselling the ground.

The tentacles of the metropolis snaked well beyond the city walls to the burgeoning shanties that serviced the fastest growing conurbation on earth. Homecoming Will Porit grinned at the countrymen. 'Who's got the shits now then, Serg?' He nodded at the distant mass of stone rising from a jumbled streetscape of slatted wood and thatch. 'Southwark cathedral, London bridge.' Closer in, he jabbed at a series of long poles set rakishly above the gatehouse, each with a bulbous end, like hatpins. 'What d'you think of that, Sir?' The sentry leaning against his halberd was bracing up to salute the young officer riding into the shadow of the great arch.

'Dear God!' Stomach churning, Nat passed beneath a dozen heads skewered on spikes.

'Traitors, Sir,' said Porit nonchalantly, tipping his chin at the first head, pole slipped forward, pecked eyes glaring at travellers. 'He's yer arch malignant, Thomas Wentworth, Earl of Strafford. Saw him topped I did.' Impaled for more than two years, his Lordship was looking remarkably well. 'Oh yes, what a gay day that was. Gawd how the mob bayed and hollered when that noddle hit the planks.' Will Porit, cock-a-hoop, grinned at his bewildered country Captain. I'm Julius bloody Caesar, he thought, the conquering bleedin' hero.

'Ain't Salisbury, is it, Sir?' Jessop leant over to avoid Porit. 'Nothing like Sarum, not even on a quarter day.'

Nat shook his head. 'This Babylon's no place for countrymen, Joe Jessop.' Pulling up, he snapped at the sentry. 'Turn out the Captain of the Guard.' He rubbed his thigh, hot and tight as a drum. 'Now!'

The duty officer doubled across, buckling his sword as he ran.

'Cap'n Salt, General Waller's staff, with dispatches for Whitehall,' Nat barked. 'D'you have a horseman that'll deliver them, lad? Fast one mind.'

'Aye, Sir.' The officer glanced over the parapet at the swirling maelstrom of the Thames. 'But there's a good flow tide that'll carry you in sooner.'

The journey was uncomfortable and the press of boats jostling for space at Whitehall steps meant a scramble for the floating jetty. The boatman squinted at the coins Nat dropped in his filthy palm. 'Bleedin' pauper.' He spat into the ooze.

'Mind yer bleedin' language, fuck-wit,' snarled Jessop cuffing the man with the flat of his hand.

Nat lunged for the platform, skating on slime like green baize on a table. His foot plunged into a slick of filth with a dead sheep waiting for the turn of the tide. Jessop followed and, more decorously, Will Porit.

'Bumpsy daisy!' Rubbing his bruised ear, the boatman shoved off. 'You mind yourself, Cap'n.' He tipped his chin at the Parliament. 'Only the sure of foot survive in that nest o' vipers. Ha! Ha!'

Hugging the damp wall, Nat edged up. The stink was worse than his festering leg. At the top of the steps, a low stone arch below the slab face of Star Chamber funnelled travellers onto a broad boulevard and the mêlée of New Palace Yard.

'Bloody hell!' Jessop gawped. 'How's a bloke to find his way in a hodgepodge like this?'

'Gatehouse is your first port o' call Sir,' said Will Porit. 'Over there.' A Colonel's colour flapped gently in the breeze from the depot across the yard. Its owner, Colonel Talbot Purefoy, was watching Nat's progress from his office above the arch.

There was a steep climb to Purefoy's rooms but the Colonel's orderly was at hand fussing with a chair. Pinching the tall tapering stem of the Venetian wineglass offered on a salver by the servant, Nat's eye drifted to Purefoy's wooden leg, a burnished peg of oak turned like a stick of furniture. 'Edgehill Captain.' Purefoy tapped the appliance with his riding crop. 'One of Lord Wilmot's troopers took off with it.'

'I'm sorry to hear it, Sir.' Nat raised the glass, sipping sherry from its tiny etched bowl shaped like a trumpet. 'But right now I'd gladly swap my festering leg for yours.

Purefoy stroked his goatee, piercing Haselrig's country captain with deep blue eyes. 'Heard about your great loss, you poor devil.' Foxwood had briefed him on Brook Farm. 'Never a day passes without another outrage by the King's feral militia, though the news books exaggerate, of course.'

Nat cleared his throat. 'Dispatches from Sir William Waller Sir.' He thrust the greased packet, the purpose of his mission. The slightest twist of the Colonel's mouth and Nat knew Waller was right to be worried about his detractors at Westminster. 'And I've intelligence of my own from the Bristol road. Serious stuff, Colonel.'

Purefoy pointed his clerk at the stool. 'This man'll set down your report, Captain.' Putting the delicate glass aside carefully, Nat began with Cornet Russell's intelligence. 'You think your man Clegg caught up with Sir William in time, Salt?'

'If not, Colonel, Bristol falls.' It was obvious.

Purefoy spun on his good leg, the peg's arc narrowly avoiding the scribe. 'West too.'

'Aye, and our back door'll be wide open,' said Nat. 'King'll ship in every last cut-throat Irish Catholic.'

Purefoy's lips tightened sardonically. 'And have our heads on spikes by Michaelmas.' Shaking a tiny hand bell, he re-sealed the clerk's transcript with Waller's papers and a scribbled note of his own, dropping the packet in a leather satchel. 'Committee of Safety *tout de suite*.' He tossed the bag at the runner. 'You're to place it in Foxwood's hands.' Nat's ears pricked at the mention of the odd little man at Tobias Norrington's house. 'Foxwood's, mind, no other. Wait for the reply.' Purefoy turned to Nat, smiling. 'Now, Captain, what's this about a new-model army?'

Nat shifted awkwardly. He was sure the abscess would burst. Then, no more pain but the most awful stink. Talbot Purefoy listened from behind his great desk as Nat's voice broke over the chaos of Roundway Down and Parliament's army destroyed by the King's force, smaller but properly run and officered by men who knew their business.

'We've reminders, you and me, of our inadequacy.' The Edgehill veteran stamped his peg leg on the elm boards, lifting the table bell. 'Get some shut-eye, man, but be ready. John Pym himself will want to see you.'

*

Retrieving the horses from the London Bridge piquet, they crossed the river. Nat fished out Dorothy's crude map to Kettle's Yard, marked up with taverns and churches. The route led up Fish Street Hill and left down Great East Cheap opposite the church of St Leonard's. To the left along the Thames she had written in heavy script 'Alsatia – keep out.' Impatiently he thrust the scrap at Will Porit.

Turning the paper this way and that, the trooper clicked his teeth. 'She's done you a picture o' London, not a map. Lucky you got me for a pilot.' He smiled, showing off. 'She's right about one thing, mind. Alsatia's a regular thieves' kitchen. Makes Warminster Common look like friggin' Hyde Park!'

Nat and Jessop marvelled at the crush of taverns and shops, all sorts and sizes, edging forwards and upwards to crowd out the light. There was a light breeze, enough to lift the brightly coloured signs that swung head high to a horseman. Urbane Will Porit beamed at the cornucopia 'Don't get treats and fancies like this in Sarum, eh?'

'Gawd, look at 'im.' Jessop reined in, captivated by a young man with a small, animated monkey jabbering on his shoulder. 'Black as Hades.'

'Moor,' remarked Porit absently, leaning across the horse's neck with a coin. 'From over the narrow seas. Here.' He broke the purchase in three, thrusting a strip of dried, salted fish at the Sergeant. 'Good, eh?'

Off Eastcheap, the clamour died away quickly. After a few yards, dung-strewn cobbles gave way to packed earth. Jetties stuck out from every floor so that, sagging together like dowdy old women, the tight-packed houses reached across, conspirators in the scheming city of spies.

Fleetingly, the noonday sun should have illuminated the gloom, teasing between buildings like shafts through the monoliths of Stonehenge. But the fug of a city addicted to sea coal put paid to that. The lane surrendered its noonday equinox to the fires of ten thousand hearths.

Kettle's Yard proved to be no more than a bulbous turning at the end of the lane. There were a dozen houses all heavily timbered and with leaded windows, each with a solid, studded front door. These were the hallmark homes of the ascendant merchant class of the most brazen, boisterous trading post in Europe.

An upper casement flew open. 'Nathaniel?' Moments later, Dorothy with a mourning face, beat across the yard. Moist-eyed, she fell into Nat's arms. '*Captain* Salt, now look at you!' she choked, trying to put a brave face on for Nat. 'And all newly betrothed to the lady Euphemia, the lucky morte.' She dabbed her eyes. 'Sword and sash and everything. But what's this?' She turned his head, examining Lord Russell's handiwork.

He looked away 'Fell off my horse.'

Her eyes narrowed. 'You always were a poor liar, Nathaniel Salt.' And me no better, she reminded herself. She held his jaw, moving his head from side to side. Just tired maybe, but where was the sparkle in those famous blue eyes? She could see only lead. A full belly and a feather bed, then she would look again. 'Who are they?' She looked the soldiers up and down. 'I know you, you're Joe Jessop, Squire's man.'

'*Sergeant* Jessop, yes, and Trooper Will Porit,' said Nat. The Londoner tugged his forelock. She liked that. 'If you can find them a stall with a scrap o' hay they'll be happy enough.'

'You're welcome, Sirs, if you're of a godly disposition. We must all put ourselves out for the army.' She sighed. 'Goodness, what sacrifices we make for the cause.' Her chubby arms round Nat's neck, she pulled him down, planting a kiss. 'Now, you'll be hungry and have thirsts to slake. Saltpetre men haven't been, so put up with the stink best you can. Decent country folk never really get used to it. London's such a filthy, godless pot o' flesh.' She looked at him suspiciously. 'You didn't come through Alsatia, did you?'

'No sister, you told me not to,' laughed Nat, combing back his hair. 'The map, remember?'

She nodded gravely. 'Alsatia's a veritable Sodom brother. I've told Etienne – they're going to make him a liveryman you know – Pym should clear it out. The trained bands should be in that papists' paradise like ferrets down a rat-hole.'

'Oh Dorothy, there you go again. Papist in every shadow!' Etienne Le Roux was framed in his doorway looking every inch the apothecary. 'Welcome to Nineveh, *mon ami*. Salvation within the quarter we call Alsatia is my wife's special concern.'

'Etienne,' she shook her head, 'and you spoken for as Common Councilman.'

'Only by you dearest,' observed Le Roux.

'Oh, away now!' said Dorothy. 'Mind you tell your cronies my brother, *Captain* Salt, is staying with us. Eh?'

'See how wretched I've become, Salt, and you so blessed. You should be thanking me for carting her off to London.' Le Roux clapped Nat's shoulder. 'But we'll escape this evening, take a glass of Orotava wine, eh?' He pinched thumb and forefinger to his lips. 'Shipped for £20 a pipe.' Bravado falling away, Le Roux smiled weakly. 'No long faces, Dorothy said.' He shifted uncomfortably, staring at his feet. 'The children, I mean. Just wanted you to know...'

'Enough, brother.' Nat patted his arm. 'The Lord's offered a remedy for my loss. I'm quite settled.'

'Offered you a remedy, has He?' The Apothecary peered at him. 'Well, I can't compete with the Almighty but I'll grind some wort to lift your spirits,' he said, muttering, 'though, *Mon Dieu*, you've every right to your black dog.'

Dorothy bustled Nat into the narrow hall that passed straight through the house to a small courtyard where Will Porit was already rubbing down the horses. On the first floor at the front, jettied above the lane, Dorothy's oak-lined parlour was well lit by a length of mullioned windows. 'Brother, you've the second best chamber, above mine. My girl has the attic.' She closed the parlour door. 'Be careful of the wench, brother, warn your men too. She's distantly related to my husband, but given to licentiousness.' Glancing from side to side, Dorothy lowered her voice. 'I'd be rid of the hussy but the association makes it awkward.' She cracked open the door, hesitating. 'The French pox rips through the city like the plague of '34. Brother, I hope your stay in London will be...'

'Chaste?'

'Aye, chaste,' she shuddered. 'My husband's pox remedies aren't pleasant.'

'I promise,' Nat bent over, planting a kiss. 'But Jessop and Porit'll plough their own furrow.'

'Not under my roof,' scolded Dorothy, hands on hips. 'This isn't a bawdy house, you know.' She waved him away. 'Oh, get on now. Brother Edward's ship's in the river so he'll join us for supper.' She paused, biting her lip. 'Edward's very upset, about the young 'uns. Just so you know.'

'Yes,' he said briskly, turning away. 'Can you rustle up some writing stuff?' Wiping his eyes, he sank into a high back chair at Dorothy's bureau in the window to pen two sad letters.

'I'll leave you to it.' She picked up her pointwork, watching him as the needle rose and fell, brimming with pride at the changed man; her brother, farmer turned officer, confederate of great men.

19 July 1643

My Lord Russell,

It is my sad duty to return the sword of your son Henry who fell yesterday in his action against me at Marsh Benham in Berkshire. It may comfort you to know he died bravely from a single shot doing his duty. He was a gallant and honourable soldier and we laid him to rest with all dignity.

I have further news to add to your cup of sorrow that may not have reached your Lordship. Your son John fell at the Devizes fight, gallantly in defence of the Parliament. I enclose the Upton that I learnt from Henry was John's dearest possession.

Nathaniel Salt

Captain

Gallant, honourable? Nat picked at the encrusted mess left by Henry Russell's boot. His account of the little tosser was over-cooked. But an old man robbed of heirs by a war between brothers wants comfort, not the truth. Nat brushed his teeth with the quill. When the time came, maybe someone would overlook his crimes on the London road and write a nice letter to Effam.

Jones' wife had sensibly left Bristol before the siege to stay with her father in Chepstow. Nat found the address on a slip of paper in the bible.

Madam,

It is my painful duty to report the death of your husband, Captain Jeremiah Jones.

Your husband died instantly in a skirmish on the road from Bristol to London. He was a courageous officer and it was a privilege to serve under his command.

I laid Captain Jones in earth with another noble officer near a place called Marsh Benham in Berkshire. Enclosed are the possessions he carried and his sword.

I hope I may call on you in happier times.

Nathaniel Salt

Captain

Nat had a third letter to write in the privacy of his bedroom. Effam was entitled to a long, lover's letter. He sat on the bed staring at the blank paper wanting to send something to cheer her up, make her smile. It would be unkind to burden her with the horrors filling his head. He settled for reassurance.

Dearest,

I have arrived at my sister's house and am fine though the road to London was not easy and my leg hurts. I have delivered my report to Mr Pym's man at Whitehall and await his summons.

You should tell your girl Sarah that Arthur Clegg was well when I sent him yesterday with dispatches to Gloucester.

I will write again soon.

I am, your love,

Nat

It was not yet dark when he woke in a sweat, struggling to hold the dream receding as fast as an ebb tide over the mudflats of Foulness. Desperately, he clutched at a figure in the red shift of a Catholic martyr. Turning in a vortex, the martyr whirled round and round and with each revolution slipped further beneath the waves. But his face was not choked like a drowning man and he made no attempt to save himself. And the face was clear as day.

Erasmus Carew.

Too soon, the bewitchment and its interpretation were gone as if sucked up the Thames with the evening mist that inched thick as molten lead through the rookeries of Alsatia.

Nat did not know how long the girl had been at the door, studying him. He tugged at the blanket, glowering at the trim, handsome creature. Oh, how well his sister knew his weakness.

'Mistress says your brother's here.' She glanced at the basin. 'I warmed some water Captain, fetched a razor.' The temptress' smile played across her face holding out all possibilities, closing none.

'What's your name, girl?' She had long blonde hair let down, and deep blue eyes, large, seductive.

'It's Clarissa.'

He was surprised his sister tolerated such a minx. 'Well, Clarissa, tell your mistress I'll be down soon. And Clarissa…'

'Captain?' Amusement played across full lips.

He cleared his throat. 'Have my men returned from the parliament house?'

'No, Sir.' She turned, profiling herself unnecessarily against the light.

The girl was having a powerful effect but he remembered Dorothy's warning and the curious way Clarissa came to be under her roof. 'Your master's also your kinsman, yes?'

'My aunt married his cousin.'

'Which means we're related.'

She shrugged. 'If you like.'

He doused his face in the warm water. 'You should be pleased to be connected to a man like Etienne Le Roux.'

'Yes, Sir. Master Le Roux trained as a chirurgeon. Served with my father in the late wars.' She handed him a towel. 'When my father was killed by a French papist and my mother by the plague he took me in. *Of course* I'm pleased to be connected with such a man.'

He buried his face in the coarse woollen cloth. 'I heard only chirurgeons and apothecaries stayed in the plague years.'

'Aye, well, Etienne Le Roux said he owed it to these folk, for sheltering him from the Bishop of Rome. First sniff o' sweating sickness and London's posh doctors, those mountebank physicians, *gentlemen*, flew to the country with nosegays pressed to their pretty faces.' The girl looked away, distracted. 'Sorry, should've answered you plainly, about Master Le Roux, I mean. Sweating sickness was bad in 1630, see. He physicked my mother. Nobody else would.'

149

She smiled as she turned, pulling the door shut. Pulsing with desire, he heard her footsteps retreating fast across the passage, down the stairs. He dressed quickly, knotting the orange sash for Dorothy's benefit. Satisfied, he banged down the passage, pausing at the head of the stairs. A companionable spice of claret and tobacco rose from the parlour but the voices were muted.

There was a young man Nat did not immediately recognise. 'My own brother, is it really you?' He grasped the youth's strong shoulders.

'Sweet Jesu, Nat.'

'Don't.' Nat cradled Edward's face in his hands. 'We'll avenge them both.'

'Yes, yes,' choked Edward. 'How'll we avenge them Nat?'

'*Jehovah Providebit*, remember?' Nat smudged away Edward's tears. 'You know, "*God will provide*."'

Edward nodded, big-eyed, wiping a sleeve across his nose. A boy in a man's body. The wrong son had been sent to London.

'Where's our uncle Abiel Biles then?'

Edward shook his head. 'Sends compliments, Nat. Rheumatics playing up. Blames unwholesome vapours.'

'But the London damp hasn't fogged his mind or his way with business,' observed Le Roux, glancing quickly at Dorothy.

'Indeed not, brother!' Edward had missed the hurried exchange. 'Trade's doing mighty well with God's help.' He nodded enthusiastically. 'Aye, we've bought two more ships this very morning!'

Nat feared Le Roux had plied Edward with too much Orotava wine. 'How's that then with fortunes bumping along like apples at the bottom of a barrel?' Nat asked sweetly. 'Trade can hardly be easy what with all the trouble with the Dutch.'

Edward took more wine from Le Roux, spilling some on the oak boards. 'Better ask uncle. Says you're to step aboard *Deliverance* tomorrow before I take her to Newcastle for more of the sea coal,' he nodded at Dorothy, 'the goodwives of London are so wedded to.'

Nat caught his sister's eye, sensing trouble. It was strange that the old man was prospering because the rest of the sea trade was in the doldrums. And stranger still that their brother, Abiel Biles' apprentice, was so ignorant. He would have to speak with Dorothy before tackling Biles.

'Tell us about the Devizes fight, Nat,' enthused Edward. 'We're all so proud, aren't we, Dorothy?'

'Of what?' retorted Nat. 'Devizes was a rout, Ed.'

'Aw Nat, come on,' protested Edward. 'Old soldiers down the butts are so full of shit. None of 'em been in action, see. Never seen the thick of battle, not like my own brother!'

'Oh, leave him be Edward,' said Dorothy.

'Nah, come on Nat. What was it like, up there in the thick of it?'

'Well, a soldier doesn't ever see the thick of battle,' sighed Nat. 'He smells it, hears it, *feels* it. I've never known such butchery, nor ever want to again. War isn't heroic, Ed. Death in battle isn't glorious. It's brutal, dirty, reeking, hell-on-earth. When you've worn your mates' guts and brains, when you've wiped them off with a flick of your wrist, then you'll understand.' Nat smiled quickly and took a swig, hand shaking.

Edward stared at his feet. Dorothy, looking cross, took Nat's arm. 'Nat's in London to see Mr John Pym, *John Pym*! What d'you say to that, Edward?'

'You'd better hurry, brother. News books say Pym's sick.' Edward was slurring his words. 'Consumption probably, or the French pox. Wormsmeat by Christmas, they say.'

'But the Assembly of Divines banned Christmas,' smiled Le Roux. 'Since it'll never come, Mr Pym can look forward to a very long life.' At which point Edward fell over.

'Edward! Oh husband, you've made him drunk.' Nat hauled the youth up. 'Oh, poor love.'

'If my Orotava wine has made him queer I also have the makings of the hot Turkey drink they call coffa,' said Le Roux, unmoved by Edward's incapacity. 'Black as soot it is, bitter as the cud. I cannot yet vouch for its medicinal properties but I'm told it's good for defluxions and sooths the brain. We'll test the coffa on Edward, *n'est-ce pas*?'

XII

Talbot Purefoy had been insistent. Nat was to hold himself ready for an audience with John Pym at Westminster. But with time on his hands, Nat was determined to illuminate the curious affairs of Abiel Biles and Edward's involvement. In the bay of her sunny parlour, Dorothy willingly poured out her fears.

Dorothy Le Roux had a nose for business and the ear of a village pump gossip. And in the dealings of uncle Abiel, Dorothy sniffed the heady musk of the black market, and worse.

*

With Dorothy's foreboding, Nat picked his way through the human soup of Great East Cheap. Sensing a short cut, he turned left at St Michael's Church into the darkness of Crooked Lane, watching his back. At Fish Street Hill he fell in with the throng towards the hodgepodge of piers and jetties that stabbed the river from the north bank below London Bridge. Here the stink was especially strong, edging from the waterfront, rising from open sewers and cesspits. Nat nodded briskly at the soldier nudging his mates, bracing up as he passed. Flattering eyes under crimped linen bonnets lingered for just a moment too long. A black-clad burgher inclined his head gravely, 'A good day to you, Captain.'

Nat crossed Thames Street where the road ran due south across the bridge to Southwark and the gatehouse with the severed heads. Shops and houses jammed in on either side, leering over the road as if the great river did not exist at all. The Thames itself shone like burnished pewter, the sun burning off the last of the morning haze.

Turning left off Fish Street Hill, Nat dropped down a steep flight of steps to the seaward side of the bridge. The river ran salt below the bridge, smell of the sea diluting the urban fug. The stone embankment was crammed with men and livestock jostling precariously along the thin ledge between the wall of wooden storehouses and the river. He spotted Edward at the waist of a conspicuously well-found vessel among the hulks littering the Pool of London.

Nat smiled at the youth flipping adroitly over the ship's side. 'Uncle's parked his boat in a right stinking pit, Ed,' said Nat.

'Belinsgate.' Edward grinned, tipping his chin downriver. 'Mustn't mind the smell, brother, if you dine on the profits! Half the fish in England's landed in what you call a stinking pit.' He nodded at the watching greybeard. 'Best not keep Uncle Abiel waiting.'

Nat negotiated the thin plank slung between *Deliverance* and the jetty, tipping inboard to the hatch combing. He raised his arm against the bilge stench mixed with the damp earthiness of sea coal sinuating from the open hold.

'Ship without cargo's a bird without song, nephew,' rasped Abiel Biles. Leaning heavily on a stick, crotched beak nose slashed between gimlet eyes. Should be perched on a spar, thought Nat, perfectly still, watching his men scampering like field mice on the deck. 'Come now, Nathaniel Salt, we'll take a glass in the cabin.'

'Will you look at that!' chortled Edward. Two landsmen were negotiating the plank like acrobats on a high-wire. A cloak covered the first man's face although there was no sweating sickness in town. At the ship's brow, the man's thin court sword jammed between fashionable bucket-top boots. Tipping inboard, he bowled into Nat's shoulder.

'I do beg pardon, Sir.' The man's cloak fell to the deck.

Retrieving it, Nat looked up at a man his own height and Edward's age. 'Here's your cloak.' Nat shook it for coal dust, noting the man's soft downy beard fashionably clipped and an unnaturally fine complexion. The second man refastened the cloak at his master's throat, fussing and fretting.

'This way, nephew.' Abiel Biles gripped Nat's arm, steering him towards the cabin beneath the quarterdeck.

'Hang on, uncle.' Nat was sure he had met the stranger before. 'Won't you introduce us?'

'Don't know him,' snapped Biles.

Nat cleared his throat. 'Well then.' He stuck out his hand. 'Captain Nathaniel Salt, Sir. General Waller's staff.'

Glancing at Abiel Biles, the man bowed stiffly. 'Your servant, Sir.' A clipped, privileged voice.

'Oh, get on, nephew.' Biles pressed Nat towards the cabin. 'I haven't all day.'

Half the size of Dorothy's parlour, the low beamed great cabin was dominated by the stern window. Its panes, mullioned and slightly green, refracted coloured light that danced and played across the sparse interior like the oriel windows at Helions.

Casually, Nat brushed off a thin layer of pink dust covering his shoulder, glancing at the deck head. Intrigued, he raised his hand to his nose and tongue. 'Chalk, like ladies' face powder.'

'Eh?' Abiel Biles poured two tumblers, dismissing Edward with a nod at the door. 'Brandy wine, nephew?' Handing the smaller measure to Nat, he swirled the spirit, downing it in one, watching his guest like a hawk.

'Odd gent, that,' said Nat flicking the rest of the powder, 'wearing powder like a morte.'

'Eh?'

'See?' Nat showed Biles his palm. 'Face powder. Must have smudged off your friend's cheek when it hit my shoulder.'

'Well, you're not in the shire now, nephew,' shrugged Biles. 'London's full of strange young men.' Recharging his own glass, Abiel Biles slumped on a narrow bench running the width of the ship below the window, nodding at the cabin's only chair.

Nat eased his leg gratefully, rubbing the tense, throbbing limb. 'Thank you for sponsoring my brother.'

Biles' sunken black eyes gouged Nat over the rim of the glass. 'Ah, well, my sister, your mother, had children. I wasn't blessed.' Nat knew Abiel Biles had buried three wives. 'And, as you can see, I'm not well. O how I suffer!' Streaming in at his back, the light turned the greybeard into an Old Testament prophet. 'I thought the youth might take to business. But...' Only his knitted eyebrows moved, hardly at all. 'And me beyond my biblical span. What am I to do, eh?'

'I'm wondering why the harbour's full of boats looking for work,' said Nat. 'All, except yours.' He nodded at the door. 'And what to make of gents like him on the deck of a collier.' Nat wet his lips with the dregs of the brandy. 'What're you up to, Uncle Abiel?'

Abiel Biles eyed his nephew frostily. 'War brings risk and opportunity in equal measure.' He dug his stick at the toe of Nat's boot. 'After all, haven't you done well, eh?' he sneered. 'As a good puritan,' he spat the word, 'you should seek guidance. Let me think, ah yes, John Chapter 8 verse 7. "Let he that is without sin cast the first stone'" and Mathew Chapter 7, verse 3 I think. "Why beholdest thou the mote that is in thy brother's eye?" Eh?'

'What sin?' Le Roux really would have to let the pus out of his throbbing leg. 'What mote?'

'Well, young man, I mean to say, who's benefitted from this *situation*? The poor merchant become a tad richer, or the farm boy gone for an officer. Just look at you, strutting about with your borrowed sword, *yeoman*!

'The last man to put my great loss in the scales with promotion and reckon a profit is dead,' intoned Nat.

Biles shrugged. 'I'll soon be dead too.' But Abiel Biles was not poor, hapless Thomas Salt.

'Your ships sail freely when the rest of London's stopped up with the blockade,' snapped Nat. 'Why's that?'

'The idle ships you see are those that no underwriter will cover because of size, age or inferior cannon. Some risk it.' Biles swirled the liquor round his glass, tipped it down, smacking his lips. 'The Downs crawl with Dutch and Turkey pirates but if you're fast and well protected you can outrun them. Those that do command a pretty premium. So I buy the best sherry wines for next to nothing and sell at £30 a pipe.' He smiled thinly. 'Easier than farming.'

'Etienne Le Roux's in the trade. His canary wines are very expensive.' Nat stared at the bottom of his glass. 'But his profit's small. Whilst you …'

He felt the old buzzard hovering, poised to take him, effortlessly, like a poor sightless vole. 'Listen Salt, understand me well. I've told your brother and I'll tell you. My business is my own and I'll share it with no man this side of the grave.' He leant forward with his sour breath. 'When I'm laid in earth, sweet Mary make it soon…' Nat's ears pricked at the Catholic invocation '… my kin'll profit, aye profit, from this war beyond their dreams. But cross me, laddie…'

All booted and spurred, the rough hewn farm boy was 'laddie' no longer, not even to a rich uncle without an heir. Fixing on the ships riding at anchor, framed by the great stern window, he fired back. 'Look here, uncle, mother trusted Ed to me on her deathbed. Oh, you've got the measure of him alright. He isn't clever or cunning but he's good and trusting, honest too.' He turned his sights on the merchant. 'Abiel Biles do not stand my brother into danger.'

The merchant sniffed loudly, drawing a sleeve across his face. Pity he'd been sent Edward and not this man. He began hauling himself up. 'Said my piece *boy*. You've done your duty to my poor sainted sister, God rest her, and so have I.' Bare feet slapped on oak boards above Nat's head to strange commands, sounds of a ship preparing for sea. '*Deliverance* sails on the tide and I must regain *terra firma* since it's my heartfelt desire to die in my bed.' Halfway to the door he turned, pivoting unsteadily on the stick. 'I do business in many quarters, with all manner of men.' He turned back, fiddling with the door fastening, voice trailing away. 'Knowledge walks with danger boy; ignorance'll be your best defence. Find what comfort you can in that, young man.'

*

Swinging over the ship's side, Nat hailed Joe Jessop and Will Porit bowling towards *Deliverance*.

'Colonel Purefoy said to give you this,' wheezed Jessop.

Nat cracked open the seal. 'I'm to meet John Pym's clerk Foxwood at one o'clock in the Great Hall at Westminster,' he murmured, still digesting the cabin's cryptic conversation.

Will Porit glanced up and down river, nodding at the swell. 'Tide's on the turn, Sir. Go now or you'll have a rough ride.'

Nat peered suspiciously at the eddying, mercurial Thames. 'With my leg it's that spavvy midden or half an hour boxed up in one of those lurching upright coffins on sticks.' Dismissing Jessop and Porit, he took to the water at Swan Stairs opposite Pewterers' Hall.

Nat's second Westminster landfall was more accomplished than the first. Safely ashore, he made his way across New Palace Yard towards the Great Hall. A crush of petitioners and lawyers in gowns, peddlers and livestock blocked the way, the smell of shit easily penetrating Dorothy's nosegay. Veterans with broken bodies were filling London fast. Nat tossed a coin into the upturned pot helmet of a man without legs. 'God bless you, Cap'n,' croaked the old soldier.

A knot of Talbot Purefoy's troopers loitered beneath the hall's arched entrance. Three had left their halberds resting against the stonework crouching low at dice which they tossed across a square of cobbled yard. The corporal, leaning on his weapon like a shepherd watching sheep, turned a shoulder as Nat approached. Kicking the halberd, Nat sent him sprawling. 'Turn your back on me, Corporal, and I'll have you horsewhipped.'

'Aw Captain, ain't no cause to take up so.' Retrieving his halberd, the man dusted down his surcoat, snarling at the small crowd attracted by the fracas. 'No offence to yer honour.'

'Court of Requests,' Nat barked.

'Aye, Sir, yer honour. Straight through the hall, through the screen and you're in the Court of Wards. Requests leads off it.' The soldier stuck out the halberd pole to clear a path. ''Ere, mind the way for the officer!' He jabbed his chin at the crowd. 'Pig ign'rant round 'ere, Sir.'

'Lord, will you look at that?' marvelled Nat, striding into Westminster Hall. The great hammer beam roof raised on thirteen giant trusses, carved angels in allegoric procession. Sections had been parcelled off by wooden screens to make courtrooms. Hawkers dodged the Keeper's men who depended on rents extracted from the little shops lining the Hall. Nat's delight turned to disgust. 'Poxed market for sweetmeats and keepsakes.'

And Jesus went into the temple of God and cast out all them that sold and bought in the temple and overthrew the tables of the moneychangers and the seats of them that sold doves.

The traffic spilling from the yard congealed around the first of the Hall's three courts; the most junior and first hope for plaintiffs, Court of Common Pleas. A judge in scarlet, grey full-bottomed wig set rakishly, sat perspiring and disinterested behind a long table covered with papers. Clerks in fustian gowns scurried about the scarlet man like dung beetles round a cow pat.

In the centre of the mêlée, a country-clad petitioner stood cap in hand, pathetically hopeful. Nat saw himself as supplicant at the bar with Carew smirking in the stalls and the pockets of the justices well lined. He doubted there was justice here.

Case dismissed, petitioner crumpled and bundled aside, his lordship rose, yawned and farted. His blue bulbous nose, pitted like a pomegranate, twitched moistly, searching for lunch like a Helions hog. The crowd rolled back, only Nat standing in the way, the object of rheumy eyes in a field of blotched skin and broken veins. 'Out the way, damn you, Sir.'

The stink of sweat and stale liquor drove Nat back against the crowd, the big-nosed judge continuing his precarious navigation down the Great Hall, batting away tinkers like flies.

Foxwood on tip-toes was craning his neck for the yeoman who had made such an impression at Tobias Norrington's house. 'Captain Salt, Sir!' Heart fluttering, he waved his good arm. 'Careful, Foxwood,' he muttered, 'Oh, do be careful.' He plucked Nat's sleeve. 'This way, Sir.'

'What's the news from General Waller, Mr Foxwood?' Nat prayed Clegg had been successful. 'What's happening in Bristol?

Foxwood shook his head. 'Your dispatches were our last word.' He paused. 'I hope you don't mind, Sir, but I'm Foxwood, plain Foxwood, if you please.'

'Foxwood, then.'

'I'm sure your man, Clegg, was it? Well, I'm sure he got through.' Foxwood gave a crooked smile. 'Now, Sir, we're in the crypt under the Parliament House. Chapel of the Virgin Mary it was.' He sneered. 'But virginity ain't fashionable.' He jerked his withered arm at the desecration. 'See? Work of our Committee for the Removal of Superstitious Monuments.' The wall paintings had been whitewashed giving the faint impression of saintly figures advancing through fog.

'This way, Sir.' Hitching his gown higher on slanting shoulders, Foxwood led on. 'Mr Pym read your dispatches and Colonel Purefoy's briefed him too. Hope I'm not speaking out of turn, Sir, if I say he likes your conclusions.' He coughed weakly. 'In fact he likes them very much.'

Nat had the feeling that nothing got to or from John Pym without Foxwood. '*My* conclusions, Foxwood?

'*Your* conclusions, Sir,' insisted Foxwood. 'Now, I hope this will be adequate?' He rapped an oak trestle with a chair facing the wall with the saintly figures. There was a pewter inkpot and pen already set up with some paper and a small pot of sand.

'For what, Foxwood?'

'Your account, Captain.' The clerk seemed surprised. 'Colonel Purefoy was most insistent. A full report of the disaster at Devizes, if you please, and your remedy.'

'Remedy?'

'Of course, Westminster's abuzz with it. The Parliament's New-Model Army.' Foxwood rolled each syllable, pleased with the effect. He tapped the side of his nose. 'And we know who to thank for it, don't we?'

So, here was Foxwood the fixer, spinning an obscure west-country farmer's accidental turn of phrase. New-Model Army? Nat knew he should be flattered. But it was only words, this thing Foxwood was so pleased with. Nat felt like he had missed his footing in a mill stream, a drudge in Pym and Waller's political game with the Earl of Essex. Sir William Waller was using the poor state of Parliament's army to deflect responsibility for defeat in the west. Waller, the magician, had breathed life into the inchoate ramblings of a yeoman farmer and given it form. The New-Model Army had become Waller's path to redemption, his ticket to preferment at the Earl's expense.

'Be sure to write it, mind.' Foxwood tested the pen's nib with his forefinger. 'Write it lots – *New-Model Army*. Got that?' He scurried away like a sewer rat leaving Nat to compose his thoughts in the violated chapel beneath the chamber of the House of Commons.

Nat got to work. He wrote about the Devizes fight and the war in the west. He spoke of soldiers with little food and less pay slipping away to their fields under a harvest moon. He asked how cities could be held without powder and shot and whether peasants with pitchforks would ever triumph over dragoons with flintlocks. He talked of Parliament's loose confederations commanded by sectarian fops and unreliable politicians pitted against the King's professional, battle-ready officers with their regiments and modern, continental ways. He argued for a new parliamentary army. He argued for The New-Model Army.

Tossing the blunted quill aside, he scattered sand over his signature and slumped back. What was the point of it? A clumsy turn of phrase and heavy yeoman hand would have Pym and his University men pitch the paper laughing into the fire.

*

'Been here half a day with only them for company.' Nat nodded at the spectral figures beneath the chapel's whitewash. The damp was playing havoc with his leg and the tell-tale stink meant a lancing.

Foxwood was all contrition. 'I had thought to stand you down, Sir. But my master…' He shrugged, more a cringe, mustering a resigned smile. God's blood, how the yeoman stirred his loins. But there was more than manly beauty in Captain Salt to excite a complicated man like Foxwood. The author of the gritty document in its unlettered copy book style that he had put in front of John Pym had a nobility that set him apart from the fops that congealed around the Palace of Westminster. 'I must warn you Sir, Mr Pym isn't well.' Foxwood lowered his voice. 'A contusion of the bowels puts him in a lot of pain. I hope you'll not think badly of him if he's a bit short.'

A narrow stone staircase twisted from the chapel's altar end. It dawned on Nat that he was about to meet the most powerful man in England after the King. Blinking out of the gloom, he found to his surprise a formal garden boxed in by the Parliament House, a collection of low buildings clinging to the Great Hall and the high walled embankment of the Thames. Trees had been planted along two gravel paths crossing at a stone pineapple on a plinth. Foxwood steered his charge down one of these towards the river. 'Ah, here's my master.'

John Pym, *de facto* head of the Parliament, propped against the pineapple, leathery skin pulled taught with the waxy yellow signature of impending death. 'My good friend Farrington, is he really dead? Aye, and your young 'uns, terrible, terrible.' He shook his big head. 'But now you're betrothed to sweet little Effam, eh?' He tapped his nose. 'Clever man.' Nat understood why Pym was known as the Ox. Despite his illness, he was a great, jowly bull of a man. 'Read your report, Captain Salt. Agree with it.' Plucking a large scarlet handkerchief from his sleeve, the Ox coughed and spat. 'Haselrig and Talbot Purefoy speak highly of you.' He tipped his head at Foxwood. 'So does he.' The Ox steered Nat slowly down the lavender-lined avenue towards a wall of grainy yellow sandstone running along the Thames. Pausing at the iron water-gate, they stood for a while watching boats manoeuvre artfully on the tide.

'What's Waller up to, wandering the west country like Moses in the desert, eh?' Pym sucked his teeth. 'Essex'll have him, you know.' He clicked his fingers at Foxwood. 'Any news?'

'No, Sir, not since Captain Salt's intelligence.' The clerk fussed with his papers in the light breeze.

Pym grunted. 'Then what detains the House today?'

Foxwood thumbed through his notes, pinning the portfolio artfully with his withered arm. 'After prayers, Sir, Honourable Members considered advances for the Army. Resolved on £522 for my Lord Willoughby to maintain Lincoln.'

'Willoughby's an ass. Not worth a groat but you'd think money for the Army was filched from the privy purses of those we are forced to call Honourable Members,' he paused to catch his breath, 'but which privately I call something different.'

Foxwood played a discreet note in the back of his throat. 'The House considered a document called the Popish Hierarchy in England, appointed the godly preacher Mr Bridges to sermonise at St Margaret's next Friday…'

'I'm mighty pleased I won't be there to hear it,' said Pym.

'… and decided to release poor Colonel Farre.'

'Farre, yes, make sure he calls on me. That all?'

'Pretty well, Sir.'

'Seems hardly worth getting out of bed for.' Pym hunched over to cough into the red handkerchief. 'These days this place ain't worth a tinker's cuss, Captain Salt. All gone away, see.' Farre would have to be quick, thought Nat, or he would be calling on a corpse. 'Still, devil makes work for idle hands, no point in having them mope around, getting in the way. Ain't that so, Foxwood?'

'It is as you say, Sir.'

'Lords, Commons, Bishops and the Bench, off to the King in Oxford like Israelites to the Promised Land.' Pym dug the clerk's ribs with his stick. 'Foxwood's got a list of fence-sitters too, ain't you, Foxwood?

'Well, Sir,' lisped Foxwood, wiping his brow. 'It's true there are certain *gentlemen* taking the opportunity of this unseasonable weather to slip our tinder-box capital for the obscurity of their estates.' Sensible, though Nat, longing to fly across the Thames to the green fields glimpsed briefly through the water-gate.

Pym flicked idly at the gravel with his cane. 'So, Foxwood, what's to be done with our capable Captain Salt?' The Ox and his secretary stared quizzically at the officer. Nat sensed that at Westminster nobody asked a question for which he did not already have the answer. 'You see, Captain, Parliament's split like a withy. Two factions. Whining Presbyterians wanting to parley with the King,' he leant forward on his stick, grimacing cadaverically, 'and us, God-fearing folk, backed by the army, united with our Scottish Covenanter brethren.' Foxwood maintained his unnerving scrutiny, tracking Nat for dissent. 'Our army demands strong leadership from the Parliament or the matter of religion will never be resolved and the King'll return to unpick everything. Parliament needs leaders, Nathaniel Salt, blooded men o' war, who'll lend it spunk, forge the new army you speak of.'

Nat stared blankly at the two men. Foxwood, wringing his hands, glanced briefly at his master. 'If I may, Sirs, on the question of Captain Salt's employment? I think Mr Pym would want to point out that an office has arisen, very tragically arisen, in the room of the late Colonel Farrington.'

Nat jammed a finger in his collar, brow creasing. 'Wiltshire's plenty of gentlemen to fill the Colonel's boots on the bench, Sir.'

The schemers smiled at him, sweetly. 'Oh no, Captain, I don't believe Mr Pym has you marked down as a *magistrate*.' The clerk raised a crooked index finger to his lips. 'I, that is Mr Pym, would rather like to have you here,' lisped Foxwood, counting the ways he would like to have the young officer.

'Here?'

'Westminster, Sir.'

'Jesu, you want *me* to put up for Parliament?' Ah, now they were teasing. He waited for the laugh and the friendly slap on the back.

Amusement did play fleetingly across the clerk's thin lips, but Foxwood's mirth was always sardonic. 'Well, Sir, it's more a case of being nominated for Parliament since Mr Pym controls the seat. You see, England's richest seam of *obliging* parliamentary divisions runs straight through the county of Wiltshire. Why, the glorious constituency of Old Sarum has no electors at all, just coney rabbits hopping among the ruins. Hoppity hop they go all day long,' Foxwood illustrated with his fingers, 'but somehow they still manage to return two members to the Parliament.'

'What about Hinton?' snapped Nat. 'It's got voters, Foxwood. I had the vote when I owned Brook Farm.'

'Yes, it's a bugger,' huffed the clerk. 'Hinton does have actual voters. But there ain't too many and I've every reason to suppose they're, eh, *biddable*.' He winked at Pym. 'As it were.'

Tight lipped, Nat shook his head. 'Absolutely not. Gentlemen, find a *gentleman* to fill your vacancy. Won't be difficult.' But his bemused interlocutors had decided his future and that was that. Any further debate was an indulgence. They would wait, patiently but not too long, whilst he exhausted the last of his energy, a fly caught in their web. 'Look here, Sir, I can't believe how far the war's advanced me, becoming an officer and all, up in London, talking to you *here*. But I'm a farmer, a yeoman, just a frigging yeoman.'

'Oh my dear fellow, we can't hardly go backwards, can we?' Pym wagged his index finger. 'None of us, least of all you. Least of all, if I may say, the fine Captain picking up that band of slovenly vagabonds masquerading as soldiers in New Palace Yard this afternoon, for which, Sir, I'm in your debt. Least of all the Parliament Officer laying into those jabbernowls like he'd be born to it.'

'But Sir...'

Pym raised his hand. 'Young man, when you fastened that borrowed sword and tied the tawny scarf of our persuasion, it was like...'

'...Transubstantiation, Sir,' said Foxwood. 'Turnip grubbing peasant one minute, then, puff...!'

'...An officer!' said the Ox, 'and so, a gentleman. Like bread and wine, it's a sacrament that once taken can't be undone.' Lowering his voice, he took Nat's arm, making a play of speaking privately, away from the secretary. 'Your lady knows it. Did you expect proud Farrington's daughter to wed a sod-turning farmer, spend the rest of her days rearing chickens, baking bread? D'you believe for one moment my good friend Miles Farrington would bless such an improvident union or *his* friend...' he jabbed his chest, 'fail to advance the happy consort to his proper place?' The Ox swung on his stick, face uncomfortably close. 'Buck up, man, snatch the chance fickle fate's shoved under your nose.'

'Sooner return to our Army in the west,' muttered Nat.

'Bravo! I'd expect nothing else from a soldier.' Pym's breath had the rancid taint of the deathbed. 'But there are battle honours to be won here too, and laurels of sorts.' He tapped his nose. 'Not to mention emoluments to maintain a man and his missus in their proper state. Eh?' Nat did not doubt that Pym's patronage came with sinecures and money, enough to keep Effam and Helions. 'War's like the plague, a blessing on survivors. Exploit it, or watch your wife grow old with the disappointments of a yeoman's hearth and the scorn of her peers.' Pym hacked into his handkerchief and Nat saw why it was red. 'Take my charge and fulfil the greatness Miles Farrington spied. But cross me, young man, and you'll pay the price, by God you will.'

The secretary coughed discretely. 'Perhaps, Sirs, I may assist? The Captain may not realise that there are, in fact, two vacancies at Hinton.'

'Oh?' said the Ox. Nat thought he saw Pym wink. 'Do tell, Foxwood.'

The double act's other half responding with a show of hand wringing. 'Indeed, Sir. The papist Carew's estates now lie within the Parliament's control.' Foxwood cocked his head slightly, smiling comfortlessly. 'He's to be dispossessed, declared malignant by the House. Don't you see?' Nat did not. 'Well, it means he'll no longer be a Member of this House. Though what he gets up to in the King's toy Oxford assembly is his affair.'

'Now you're egging me to take Carew's seat,' Nat observed petulantly as they looked on like a pair of maiden aunts inspecting a dim child. 'You're chucking a gauntlet at me.'

'Exactly so,' purred Foxwood. 'Now Sir, Colonel Cromwell's here.' The clerk tipped his head at a squat middle-aged man at the stone pineapple.

'Behold the dour Member for Cambridge, stood all alone like a revenue man come for the Ship Money.' Pym smiled at the newcomer. 'Mark him well, Nathaniel Salt,' he whispered, 'find common cause with *that* gentleman for he'll be a power in the land.'

Cromwell, buff-coated and booted, crunched through the gravel. Nodding curtly at Pym, he glared at Nat. 'Who are you?'

Pym's lips twitched; the man's boorishness was legendary. 'Colonel Oliver Cromwell, Captain Nathaniel Salt. Mr Salt has condescended to join us as Member for Hinton.' He winked at Nat. 'The Captain's been telling us how to remodel the army. How regiments of unshod farm boys led by clueless gentlemen are bound to fail against the mighty legions of the King.'

'Remodelling, eh?' Cromwell looked Nat up and down.

'Oliver, I'm away to my bed. Will you walk with me?' Pym turned to Nat, spare flesh swinging from his chin like a turkey's wattle. 'Foxwood's at your disposal Captain Salt. Rely on him, totally.' He tossed an afterthought over his shoulder. 'Have a care though for he's an inveterate diarist. The Foxwood journals will record your doings for all eternity. Eh, Foxwood?'

The Ox steered Cromwell towards Star Chamber. 'You keep an eye on that fellow Salt, Oliver,' he murmured. 'I'm thinking he's more than just another of our russet-coated country captains.'

'Aye, John, I've heard his story,' said Cromwell. 'You're right to mark him out.'

Nat glared at the backs of the two great men. 'Well, Foxwood, you and Mr Pym have me cornered like a boar on market day. Looks like I'm in your hands, doesn't it?'

'Yes, Sir, it does,' lisped the clerk, aching at the thought. 'Now, Captain, I've prepared a brief on your situation.'

'Listen, Foxwood, I'll play your game as long as it gives me what I want,' snapped Nat. 'Understood?'

'A knife between Erasmus Carew's ribs?'

'Yes.'

'And Euphemia Farrington,' smiled Foxwood. 'I understand perfectly. Now Sir, please pay attention.' He took a deep breath. 'Farrington and Carew entered Parliament as Burgesses for the Hinton constituency in 1640, not so much unopposed as by prior arrangement.' Foxwood was confident that the same would apply at the by-election. 'Normally writs get served without delay and the ballot's shortly after. But the times ain't normal.' Foxwood knew his business. 'The town's worthies'll be rubbing their hands at the prospect of election swag.' Let Foxwood blather on, thought Nat, imagining he's in charge, so long as this circus leads to Carew. 'The Burgess role for Hinton holds forty-four voters,' intoned Foxwood. 'If I may suggest you call on as many as possible? It's the done thing and they do so appreciate it.' Nat scowled at the prospect of prostrating himself before his neighbours. Foxwood smiled thinly. 'Captain, if I may suggest...?' Nat shrugged. 'You need an agent, Sir. That is, someone who knows the ropes, a fixer.'

'But Mr Pym says he's got the borough in his pocket,' said Nat. 'So why bother?'

'Oh no, Sir, that won't do.' Foxwood was appalled. 'We must turn out the vote, even in a rotten borough.'

'Bloody hell,' huffed Nat. Joe Jessop was right; after the fight at Marsh Benham he should have turned his back on London and chased west after Waller. 'Will you be my agent, Foxwood?'

'Yes, Sir.' The clerk took the commission solemnly, though his heart was racing. 'I'd be delighted.'

*

The servant Clarissa let him in, following him upstairs, checking for Dorothy. 'Here, Sir, let me help.' Kneeling, she took a boot under her arm, pulling gently. 'Very stiff, Sir.' The temptress' fingers began their seduction.

'No, madam.'

She sat back on her haunches, pouting. 'Your brother was far more willing Sir.' Taking the least scuffed boot, she fingered the hole in its sole. 'Will Porit too, though much too quick.' She sighed, turning to his feet and calves, pressing her thumbs in. 'How does that feel?' Casually, the Siren threw back her long golden hair and drew the cords to unwrap the ripe objects of his desire.

Opening the laced bodice to free paps smooth as Silbury hill, Nat was pumping lust. 'Clarissa.' He dropped to his knees, biting his lip, pulling the garment back.

She pulled away, eyes flashing defiance. 'Captain warrants a finer trollop is it?'

'Lord no, madam.' He looked away, thigh throbbing in time with his tumescence. 'I'd respond, as a man should, but...'

'I know.' She sighed, covering herself. 'You protest the scruples of one bound to another.'

'Aye, that's it.'

There was a commotion in the hall. Dorothy, distraught, busted in, ignoring the servant relacing her bodice. 'Oh stir yourself, Nathaniel Salt.' She would deal with the girl later. 'Uncle's arrested, carted off in a wagon *like a common criminal.*' She slumped on the edge of the bed, wringing her hands. 'It's as I feared. The ships he sends to Newcastle to fetch back sea coal take twice as long as they should. What does that say to you, brother?'

Nat retied the strings on his doublet. 'That Abiel Biles needs to get his hulls scraped, or his captains don't know their business?'

'No, you dolt!' She shook him hard. 'The old goat has the best-found craft on the Thames, fast ships, seasoned commanders.'

Nat removed her hands gently from his shoulders, trying to make sense of the news. What was Abiel Biles telling him in the stern cabin of the *Deliverance*?

Dorothy, beside herself, paced up and down. 'The old devil's been sending his ships to Newcastle, yes, but not before dog-legging across the narrow seas. To Holland!' The cogs in Nat's fuddled mind turned to the chilling consequences of what he was being told. 'How d'you think he's done so well when half the Exchange rots in the Clink, up to their necks in debt? In league with the whore-Queen's gang, that's how, or at least trading with it, which is the same thing.'

Nat combed his fingers through his hair, still distracted by the girl slipping from the room. 'Where's the *Deliverance*, where's Edward?'

'I don't know.' Dorothy at the window, wiped a smeared pane with her sleeve. 'I've sent Etienne to get what he can from the gossips at the quay.' She spun round tugging at his arms. 'Nat, you'll have to go to the Constable, tell him Edward had nothing to do with it. They'll listen to you, Nat. You can, can't you?'

Nat felt the burden of Dorothy's damp-eyed faith. Nat the magnificent, her brother, communicant of great men, wished more than anything he was at home behind the plough. 'Our brother would never treat with malignants. He hasn't the wit.'

Dorothy stared across the City's crooked rooftops. 'I knew something was up, Abiel Biles with all that money.' She unhooked the casement, cool air flooding in. 'Fine new ships, stone warehouses and a town house that's as near the Strand as makes no difference.'

'*C'est le plus mauvais.*' Etienne Le Roux wheezed up the stairs. 'Abiel Biles is in the Fleet gaol. It's bad. Warehouse, ships, house, impounded, all of it.' He slumped against the door jamb. 'Charge of treason. Up before King's Bench. Tomorrow, maybe.'

Dorothy cupped her face. 'Edward?'

Le Roux pulled the drawstrings at his throat, whipping away the lace collar, wiping his brow. 'Biles' people cleared off like rats from a sinking ship but I found one of his clerks down the Angel, well into his cups. Reckons Deliverance'll be off Harwich by now.'

'Harwich, you say?' Dorothy brightened up. 'Then there's time. Send a boat, take him off. You can do that, can't you, Nat?' He turned away, impotent in the face of her expectations.

Le Roux held out little hope. 'She'll be in the roads by sunset, alongside tonight if the wind holds. Between here and *Deliverance*, fifty miles of the busiest waters in Europe.'

'So we wait, at the quay with the constable's men, the gaoler with his leg irons?' Dorothy's wide eyes shot desperately between the two men. 'This isn't scrumping for apples, Etienne. Nat, we're talking about treason. D'you know what that means? Have you any idea what they'll do to him?'

'Nothing,' said Nat. 'He's innocent.'

Dorothy snorted. 'I'm glad, brother, you've such high confidence in the King's Bench, for it's no less cruel than Star Chamber.' She thrust her blotched, crimson face at him, arms thrown back. 'Have you seen what those *Justices* do to traitors, Nathaniel Salt, have you?'

'Edward's no traitor,' whispered Nat.

She batted him away. 'Let me tell you what they do. If you're noble you're lucky. That is, if the headsman's sober. For the rest it's hanging till you're not yet dead.' She swallowed hard. 'Then they tear off your privy parts with a butcher's knife and hoist you up on a meat hook to slit open your belly. That means your guts spill out. Finally they slice off your limbs, one by one. After all that, if you still draw breath, they cut off your head.' She gripped her brother's arms, hissing at him. 'That's what your King's Bench does, brother. If you trust in its justice you're a fool – as well as a fornicator.'

*

Inside the Fleet gaol, Nat was sized by the clerk for what he could be touched for. Not much. 'Abiel Biles, you say?' His forefinger travelled down the list of names in his ledger. 'Ah, yes.' Nat followed the clerk down a short corridor with cells on either side. 'Biles has one of our less expensive rooms, Captain,' smiled the official. 'Now, here's the gentleman looking after him.' A gaoler loomed out of the shadows. 'Visitor for Mr Biles.' Scowling, the brute heaved open the trapdoor, gaoler and clerk backing off artfully as the dungeon belched. Nat raised an arm to the sticky miasma of excrement and death.

'Ain't no spring meadow, is it, yer honour?' The gaoler grinned toothlessly. He jabbed a club doused in pitch at the brazier, lighting up slimed steps tumbling into the abyss, wringing wet.

'Now do be careful, Captain,' fussed the clerk. 'I'm afraid the spring tide washes through those quarters like the Nile through Egypt.'

At the bottom, three iron-grilled cells led off a wide passage. The gaoler swung his torch at semi-naked inmates groping through the bars. At the far end of the passage there was a corpse on a stone bier, feet jutting from a filthy blanket. 'Tight purse bastards at Company o' Barber-Surgeons didn't want that,' spat the gaoler. 'We'll heave him out on the tide.' He ran his stick across the bars. 'Biles! Got a visitor, arseworm. Sing out, damn yer eyes.'

Propped against the back wall of the third pit, Nat spotted the tortured form of Abiel Biles clawing blindly at the light. 'Open it and get out.' The wretch stuck out a filthy paw. Snatching the torch, Nat threw some money to the floor. 'Now get out.'

The man pawed the black straw for the coins. 'Two pennies,' he spat, rubbing them together, 'buys five minutes.' Turning the heavy key in the lock, he pushed Nat in, slamming the gate. 'Any trouble with them prisoners, General, just whack 'em.'

Nat crouched low to catch the old man's words. 'Don't bother yourself, nephew. I'm wormsmeat, shriven and ready for God.'

There were rats. Sleek, arrogant and well fed. 'The charges?'

'All true.' Wincing, he shifted his bones against the cold damp wall. 'My ships have been engaged in Her Majesty's service. Profitable business, but I'd serve my Queen for nothing. It's been my Catholic duty.'

'Edward?'

'Safe. Remember what I told you.' Biles spat, fresh blood. 'Ignorance is bliss and I've made a deposition.'

'Here.' Nat fumbled with the cloak fastening. 'I'll get you out of this stinking hole.'

Abiel Biles shook his head. 'In my condition, I'll likely cheat the hangman, like him.' He nodded at the corpse. 'If not, these lodgings'll fit me for a short measure at Tyburn.' He shook Nat's cloak from his shoulders, thrusting a bent finger at the wraith-like figures in the gloom. 'And you'd best keep this. Those poor bastards would kill for it.'

The gaoler was shambling towards the gate.' 'Time's up, yer honour.'

Nat needed no encouragement, feeling his way to the sweet air and grey light of the upper level. 'Your prisoner will die tonight down there.'

'Well,' said the clerk, pinch-lipped. 'If that's so he won't be troubling the hangman, now will he, *Captain*?'

Instantly, the functionary was up against the wall, strong fingers closing round his throat. 'Lock him up here with bread, ale and a blanket, arseworm.' Nat rummaged for the last of his money. 'Here's for your charity. Mind, if I come back and he's still down there, you'll answer to John Pym himself. D'you understand me?'

*

The blue-nosed justice peered at Biles' deposition and the terrified prisoner at the bar. 'Abiel Biles dead, you say?'

The Constable braced up before the bench. 'Aye Sir. Gaoler tended him like he was 'is own father, Sir, so he'd be fit to stand before your honour, like.' He sniffed, wiping snot with his sleeve. 'But 'e pegged it, Sir, this very morning. This here's 'is accomplice, Sir. Nephew, Sir.'

The judge grunted. 'Hangman cheated, eh?' Grubby fingers scratched close-cropped scalp under the wig.

'Yessir!' The Constable tipped his chin at Edward. 'He'll do just as well.'

'A dying man on peril of his soul says not.' Sucking his teeth, the Justice squinted at the affidavit. 'Where's your evidence? Must have evidence, y'know.'

'Lying's easy at death's door.' The Constable scratched his balls and shrugged. ''Specially if you're a scheming papist bastard. Beg pardon, Sir.'

'Aye, that's true.' The judge brushed a goose feather quill across his blackened tooth stumps, raising his eyes to a carved apostle in the roof. 'But I can't draw a man for the sins of his uncle now, can I? Where's your evidence?'

''Ere 'tis, yer honour.' The Constable, grinning triumphantly, tossed a box of documents at the clerk. 'Taken from the dead man's house. Me mate what knows 'is letters says them papers bangs Biles to rights. Nephew's guilty...', he sniffed and wiped again, '...by association, like.'

'I'll have to read 'em, damn your eyes.' The judge thrust his pen messily into the inkwell. 'Court adjourned 'til half past four o'clock.'

XIII

The uniform and a shilling got Nat past the Justice's clerk. Peering into the dark, airless recess, he spied the shaven-headed figure in scarlet robes muttering behind Abiel Biles' unopened box of papers. Nat's bowels turned to water. The man sitting in judgement on his brother was the beak from the Court of Common Pleas.

'I'm busy, Captain.'

'Yes, Sir, your honour.' Nat caught the tap-room whiff of liquor and stale piss. 'But I've got a petition for mercy.'

'What? You Army fellows! Too bold, Sir, too bold.' The Justice dislodged a hand bell and a sheaf of papers. 'What petition?'

'Case of Edward Salt, Sir,' said Nat. 'My brother.'

'You mustn't importune a Justice in his chambers, Sir.' Blue-nose flicked his wrist. 'Now get out.'

'Listen to me, Sir.' Nat whipped off his hat. 'I have bled for our godly cause, my home's been razed and two sweet children butchered by malignants. Hear me out, for mercy's sake.' Scowling, the Judge slouched back, waving acquiescence. 'My brother's a simple, trusting soul,' Nat pleaded. 'Wasn't born with the senses to plot and scheme. I curse the day our mother sent the boy to Abiel Biles.'

'That's as may be but the sins of the father will be visited on the sons, on the sons, Sir!' The Justice half-rose, farting. 'The law demands a necking for such despicable treason. Oh yes, Sir,' he wagged a crooked finger at Nat, 'for it's struck at the very heart of our godly city.' He collapsed back, catching his breath, sweating like cheese on a hot day.

Nat met the judge's rant with forced moderation. 'Your honour, the mob's justice is the lore of the wildwood. It would see each of us at the nubbing post.'

'Got a way with words, haven't you, Captain?' The Justice squinted at Nat suspiciously. 'Might have been a lawyer, had you not been whelped in some turd-bound hovel, eh?'

Nat swallowed hard. 'Sir, Tyburn's mob is kept busy by the bench. It won't miss my brother.'

'Ha!' Blue-nose glanced anxiously at the shuttered window. 'The mob always needs more.'

'But not as badly as the army,' pleaded Nat. 'Send Edward to the Lord General.'

'The Lord General, you say?' The Justice sucked noisily on mucus at the back of his throat. 'Abiel Biles' confession would have bought him a quick death at the end of a rope. I'd have been hard pressed to draw him though Lord knows the mob likes the job done proper.' The Judge rubbed his bloodshot eyes, peering at the paper. 'Biles says the boy had no knowledge of his doings, that he always followed the true religion, mustered with the Trained Bands, cussed malignants at every opportunity and professed his love of the Parliament and the godly cause.' The judge's brow unfurled. 'Good, *good*,' he intoned.

Nat pressed his advantage. 'A man facing his maker tells the truth.'

Blue nose shrugged. 'Maybe, maybe not.' Spitting into the grey linen hanging limply at his wrist, he smacked his lips and tapped the desk, gazing vacantly round the room. 'Captain Salt, I know you.' Only from their brief, unsatisfactory encounter in Westminster Hall, Nat felt sure. 'That is, *I know your kind*. Your brother's lucky to have you as his champion.' He twitched at the racket outside. 'But it's the mob, Captain Salt, don't you see?' He jabbed a finger at the window. 'There's blood spilt and that makes all the difference. The fire of sin must be doused with blood. Your brother's all I can give for this sin. See here…'

He pushed a copy of *Mercurius Civicus* across the table. The news book's main story – Prince Rupert had laid siege to Bristol – barely registered. Of more immediate interest to him, and the judge, was a lively account of the misdeeds of the *Deliverance*.

The Justice beckoned Nat into his fetid miasma. Lowering his voice, he glanced anxiously at the door. 'Can't be too careful lad. Spies see – London's crawling with 'em.' Nat gagged at the gout of hot rancid breath. 'Slip away, young man. Land's stuffed with families split like withies by this uncivil war but your traitor kin spread about the news books'll be bad for you, mark my words.'

'So he's condemned already?'

*

Nat found Clarissa alone at Kettle's Yard. Seizing her wrist, he made for the hayloft above the stables. They coupled without a word.

*

Edward was awaiting justice in a stinking hole no better than the Fleet gaol. The boy was wedged into a green-slimed corner where he crouched bleeding from heavy irons cutting him at the wrists and ankles. 'They mean to martyr me for a cause that isn't mine.'

Nat shook his head without conviction. 'There's no evidence.'

'Does it matter?'

Nat knew it hardly did. 'What happened?'

'I was learning ship craft, how to conduct the sea trade, nothing more. Lord knows, I was happy enough with that.' Edward sniffed, pressing the back of his hand across his nose. 'Sometimes we beat to the low country on our way north, delivering stuff.' Nat's heart sank. The Justice's paranoia could make only one thing of that. 'Sometimes it was letters, or crates, sometimes travellers keeping counsel with the skipper. Like that gent who bowled into you. We dropped him at Scheveningen.' Shaking his head at Edward's credulity, Nat remembered the strange, powdered young man on the deck of the *Deliverance* and Abiel Biles' evasion. 'When I asked uncle what's up he scowls and says "ask no questions, tell you no lies". That was that.' Edward was crestfallen. 'You think I'm soft, don't you?'

'No, of course not.' Nat tried to sound convincing.

'Well, you didn't know our uncle,' said Edward bitterly. 'Now he's cheated the hangman, the Justice will want my blood to quieten the mob.'

'What happened to the skipper and his mate?'

'Sniffed trouble. Took off in the boat towards Southwark.' Leaving gullible Edward in charge, thought Nat. 'But the revenue cutter puts out to intercept. Skipper starts shooting and gets it back, both barrels.' The boy turned his moistening gaze to the damp brick vaulting. 'They got their just deserts. I'm next in line though as God is my witness I never did anything.' He began to sob. ''Cept shame you.'

Nat put his hand on Edward's heaving shoulder. As the key rasped in the lock, the youth backed into the wall like a cornered animal.

'On yer feet.' A rough arm hauled him up.

Standing by helplessly as his brother lost his composure, Nat followed the halberdiers bundling Edward blinking into the light and clamour of the courtroom.

173

The raucous crowd spilling from the wooden stalls piped down as the Justice stamped in, bowing at the court. A crone jabbed her talon at the wide-eyed prisoner. 'Hang him, my lord. Justice!'

The blue-nosed judge cleared his gizzard, finger dragging across the page trailing grime like slime from a snail. 'Edward Salt, I have listened to the evidence and studied the papers seized from the noisome malignant Abiel Biles, may he burn in the fire that is eternal. I've weighed the deposition made in the hours before his death by your uncle, said traitor Biles.' Sucking his teeth, the Judge gave a little shrug. 'Aye, and minded your past good character; above all the steadfastness of your gallant brother, Captain Nathaniel Salt.'

Blue-nose smiled, inclining his head at Nat. Warmed by the benevolence beamed from the bench, Nat called down blessings on the sage sitting in judgement. 'Praise the Lord!' He squeezed Dorothy's hand excitedly, mouth dry, heart beating like a drum. 'See? It's a capital sentence defrayed to military service, just like I said.' He was pleased with himself, and so was Dorothy, puffed-up by the success of his intervention and the influence he had used so cleverly.

An ominous silence from the public gallery set blue nose anxiously scanning the crowd. 'And yet.'

'Death, my lord.' The verdict of the livid readership of *Mercurius Civicus* crashed through the court. Now they were busting over the stalls, jabbing fingers and fists at the defendant. 'Neck 'im, papist bastard!'

The Justice's pig-eyes whipped round the courthouse. 'And yet ignorance is no defence!' He coughed, spitting into his sleeve. 'Sin must be expunged!'

'Aye, hang the Laudian cock-sucker!' The crowd banged and kicked the stalls in a cacophony of righteousness. 'Draw the papist, my Lord. Quarter 'im.'

'Therefore,' the Judge waved his expectant audience silent, 'therefore, you will be taken from here to a place of lawful execution and there hanged by the neck until dead. And may the Lord have mercy on your soul.'

A great cheer from the crowd. Nat hung his head, unable to watch terrified, bug-eyed Edward who, frozen, was being lifted out of the dock. Le Roux leant across urgently. 'I've a remedy.'

Nat looked round at the tortured apothecary. 'Not now, brother.' Since the unfortunate replacing Edward in the dock was not *Mercurius* material, the crowd was dispersing noisily to catch the last of the entertainment at Tyburn.

Le Roux persisted. 'May God forgive me for what I'm about to tell you, *mon frère*.'

Nat dismissed the apothecary with a tight smile and quick shake of the head. He knew what he must do and it involved his new circle, Pym, Cromwell, Purefoy. And he needed to enlist them fast.

'Listen to me,' Le Roux implored. 'The man sending your brother to the gallows is known to me, *professionally*.' Nat stared at him blankly. 'Brother, that creature is one of my patients.' Le Roux's hand was covering his mouth, concealing the betrayal. 'His mind's addled, completely shot, raving when I see him.'

'Brother, please.' Nat was struggling with his scheme.

'Be quiet you foolish man, *écoutez bien*,' Le Roux snapped. 'Now, the physicks administer cantharides to the scalp and other horrors that make him worse, of course. Then he comes to me.' Le Roux bit his lip. 'A dish of laudanum with a peck of wormwood improves his humour, but his intellect...'

'How so?'

'Fornication in Alsatia, *mon frère*, invites what your countrymen call the French pox. Most recover from the immediate distemper, but that's a cruel deception.' He shook his head sadly. 'Years later back it comes in a virulent, shocking form, mashing the brain. Makes a man frightened of his own shadow so the Judge'll be terrified of the mob. You saw it just then, eh?' Le Roux hesitated, grappling with what he must do. 'And there's more, enough to save Edward's life. You see, I know where he goes to indulge his passion, and what his passions are.' Le Roux fell silent, knowing he must divulge everything to save Edward Salt.

Nat, planning how his great men could remove Edward from the shadow of the triple tree, laid a hand on the tortured apothecary's shoulder; 'Etienne, my brother will swing tomorrow on the orders of a man you say is a lunatic?' He combed his hand through his hair. 'But I reckon madness never stopped a man being put on the King's bench.'

'*Alors*.' Glancing anxiously at Dorothy, Le Roux bent over to whisper in Nat's ear. 'You and I; men of the world, yes?' Nat shrugged. 'Then I must tell you there exist, deep in the licentious precincts of Alsatia, inns of pleasure, dark, *unnatural* pleasure, practices beyond your wildest imaginings.' Le Roux swallowed hard. 'The pox is there, always, and so is the man sitting in judgement over poor Edward. *Comprenez-vous?*'

'*Unlawful* practices?'

'Enough to fill *Mercurius* for months.' Le Roux snatched away the apothecary skullcap as if defrocked already. 'But use my intelligence sparingly, Captain. The worshipful company would expel me for my incontinent tongue.'

Squeezing Le Roux's shoulder, Nat rose to seek out the man who would know precisely how to exploit the apothecary's revelation.

*

Foxwood was brusque. Unfazed by Nat's account of the compromised Justice, he regretted his master would be unable to help. Indeed, it was unclear whether John Pym would see another day.

But the nobs still fawning on Pym's gatekeeper would, Foxwood knew, drop him like hot coals before the great man was cold in his grave. And Pym's sharp overnight decline meant he must find a new situation fast. Maybe Captain Salt was worth a punt. And what a pleasure, being alongside such a man.

As one patron lay dying, Foxwood was sizing the opportunity to become indispensable to another. He hoped the means of achieving the transfer had not yet left for East Anglia.

He must find Cromwell.

*

The Colonel of Horse slammed into the Justice's quarters, batting away his clerk's choked protestation. 'Your mind's turned to mush, Sir. You are unfit, a bloody disgrace.' Cromwell did not spare the blue-nosed Judge. 'You've wickedly condemned the brother of a very great officer. I will have it undone, Sir. Or I will undo you.'

Piecrust tumbled from the Justice's lips. 'What about the mob, Sir? All screaming and hollering, baying for blood.' He glanced anxiously at the shutters, spittle and bits of food spraying across the desk. 'They will have it, you know, Sir. Oh, they will have it!'

Cromwell leant across the table, his warty face in the Justice's. 'Visited Alsatia recently, *Mr Justice?*'

'Eh?' The man's pig eyes narrowed. 'What's that?'

'Oh don't deny it, you canting hypocrite.' The judge, jaw-dropping, shrank from Colonel Cromwell's invective. 'Your Lordship takes his carnal delights in the morning, then sits in judgement after noon. I've a full account of what you get up to and *Mercurius* gagging for a story.'

'But the mob, Sir. Can't you hear it?' The Justice twitched at the window. 'It's to be assuaged, Sir, with blood. You know it, being a soldier, Sir.'

'Pah!' Cromwell yanked the door, sending the ear-wigging clerk sprawling. 'Write.' The man scratched Cromwell's dictation.

To all and singular,

In the matter of Edward Salt, apprentice, be it know that the sentence of death passed this day is commuted to army service with Colonel Oliver Cromwell of the Eastern Association. The prisoner is therefore delivered into the custody of the said Colonel Cromwell.

Witness my hand in the Court of King's Bench at Westminster this the 24th day of July in the Year of Our Lord 1643

The judge needed little persuasion to add his arachnid mark. Scattering sand on the paper, Cromwell seized the man's ring finger, thrusting his device into a splash of blood red sealing wax. 'Good. Now you.' He jabbed at the clerk. 'Witness it and fetch the prisoner to Palace Yard.'

Cromwell towered over the Justice with a bellyful of invective. But another broadside at a man already reduced to gibberish would be a waste of breath. Turning on his heels, he stormed out, Nat in his wake, through Westminster Hall to the yard and a dozen mounted troopers. 'Fortune favours the brave friend but the bench is famously vindictive and we've really pissed them off.' Cromwell clapped Nat on the shoulder. 'Take a sojourn in the country, young man.' He lowered his voice. 'But remember, my good turn demands one from you, Captain Salt. After you've cooled your heels I want you here, in the Commons, minding my back.' Cromwell had saved Edward's life, but anything involving Foxwood came with a price. Cromwell leant low across the horse's neck, dark eyes drilling. '*Do you understand me?*'

Nat understood alright. Foxwood had used Nat's trouble to bind him to the scheme mapped out with Pym in the garden by the Thames. 'I do, Sir.' In three words Nat was Cromwell's bondsman, indentured Member of Parliament in the army interest.

Cromwell twisted in the saddle. 'Well, here's your brother.' A gaoler was dragging Edward blinking from the bowels of Star Chamber. 'Strike those irons, damn your eyes.' The turnkey fumbled with the prisoner's bindings. 'Quickly man, we've sixty miles to Huntingdon.'

Edward, dazed and filthy from the Clink, could barely speak. Covering his shoulders with his coat, Nat pressed his last few coins in the boy's palm. 'God keep you, Edward.'

The corporal hauled him up like a sack of coals. With the crowd's huzzahs and a casual wave of the hand, Colonel Oliver Cromwell, the people's darling, led his troopers from the yard and left past the Abbey.

*

The bells of St Clements banged into Nat's fuddled mind, thick with Le Roux's Orotava wine. *Sunday, praise be.* He rolled over, pulling the bolster over his head. *But it's Thursday; something's up.* Unlatching the casement, he squinted at Porit in the yard. 'Is it Bristol, Will?'

'Nay, Sir! It's General Waller,' grinned the trooper saddling up. 'All London's turned out. Thought you'd want to take a mosey down the Strand too,' he said, rubbing the mare's rump, 'to see William the bloomin' Conqueror.'

'What about Bristol?' If Clegg had got through, Waller would surely have turned around to lift Prince Rupert's siege and relieve Governor Fiennes. Or returned in disgrace, ragged and blood shod, not in triumph like Caesar entering Rome.

'Don't know, Sir.' Cannon touched off away to the east. 'It's the Tower, Sir.' Porit came to attention, knuckling his forehead theatrically. 'A city salute!'

Taking stairs two at a time, Nat bowled into Dorothy, arms full of linen. 'It's my chief. Back to save his name from Lord Essex's hatchet job.'

'Oh *do* be careful, Nat.' She put her hands to her face. 'Or he'll pluck you from the Parliament before you've even been elected.'

'If that man put as much effort into war fighting as protecting his reputation...' Nat bundled the linen back into Dorothy's arms, planting a kiss. 'Don't worry; whilst I'm on his staff, I'll be loyal as you like to William the so-called Conqueror.'

When Nat and Will Porit arrived at Colonel Purefoy's depot, soldiers were already forming up in Palace Yard, clearing a route to Westminster Hall with their halberds.

Someone raised a cheer above the great bells of the Abbey, the crowd followed and then a great sea of adulation for the City's very own general. William the Conqueror swept through the gate, a company of gilded officers in his wake. As he reached the great north door he spotted Nat in the press. 'Captain Nathaniel Salt! To me, man.'

Nat saw Arthur Clegg among Waller's horsemen. 'Get him, Will Porit. I want to know what happened.'

'Captain Salt, where are you man?' boomed Waller but Nat wanted Arthur Clegg first.

'Well, Clegg?' snapped Nat.

Clegg knuckled his forehead. 'General Waller was half way to Gloucester Sir, when I caught up. But he wouldn't turn back to Bristol.' Clegg shrugged apologetically. 'Said Governor Fiennes'd save the day.'

'Bloody idiot.'

'Salt!' Waller was insistent. 'Clear a path there!' Halberdiers forced a channel. 'Ah, Salt. You seen Pym? You tell him?'

'Aye, Sir. Told him straight.' Waller looked uncertain. 'About *your* New-Model Army.' He swept an arm towards the crowds. 'Anyway, fears for your reputation were groundless. Eh?'

'Ah, but the mob's fickle as a French tart.' Waller, bemused by the reception, glanced over his shoulder, waving at the ecstatic crowd. 'And Essex?'

'Is sulking. But what about Bristol, Sir? I sent a man.' Nat could not believe William the Conqueror had left the back door open. 'Why aren't you with Governor Fiennes?'

'Fiennes'll take care of himself,' snapped Waller. 'Boorish of you, Salt, to bother with Bristol on a day like this. Stralsund, remember. Captain Jones' prescription. Eh?'

But Nat remembered the gunner's words precisely. *Stralsund had the advantage of General Leslie, Sir. But Bristol? It only has Colonel Fiennes.* 'Sir, there's talk of an inquest into the losses in the west.'

'That'll be the Lord General's work.' A star struck burgher pushed his son forward, Waller bending down to ruffle the lad's hair. 'Essex's paw marks on that, I'm thinking.'

'But the City's with you.' Nat's residual enthusiasm for Sir William Waller was evaporating faster than the morning mist. 'There's talk of new regiments to make a flying army. Likely you'll get command.'

'Independently of Essex?'

'No, Sir. The Earl remains Lord General, for now.' And I wouldn't give the man who abandoned Bristol command of a piquet, thought Nat. God's blood where was Cromwell? Foxwood slid alongside. 'Sir William this is Foxwood, John Pym's clerk.'

'Oh, I know Foxwood. *Everyone* knows Foxwood!' He slapped the agent's back, too hard. 'Foxwood beckons William the Conqueror to pay homage at the feet of King Pym. Ain't that so, Foxwood?'

'That's right, Sir. This way, Sir.' Shaking his head, he gave Nat a wan smile. The Captain must understand the agent's worth. 'Not you, Sir.'

*

Smarting from Foxwood's rebuff, Nat had pushed into the Red Lion for lunch. Lamprey pie and anchovies.

It was easy to blame fish from the Thames for the billowing waves of nausea. He needed his bed in Kettle's Yard but the press at the water gate was too great. With no hope of a boat, he headed back down Whitehall on foot. The crush along the Strand pushed him along until, sick and faint, he ducked into the Blue Boar. 'Ere, ain't you had enough, soldier?' A big-breasted woman barred the way. 'You don't half look queer.'

'Clarissa?'

'I'm whoever you want, dearie, when you're in a fit state.' Jamming hands on hips, she jerked her head at the privy. 'Out there, lover, before you show us your lunch.'

Nat pushed through the crowd, following the stink. 'You alright brother?' A tatmonger rehousing his member glanced anxiously at Nat, pale and sweating, pushing against the green-slimed wall trying to piss.

'Aye, friend.' Nat lied, bladder of blackthorns spitting against the stones.

*

Le Roux cracked open the door, peering down the corridor. Satisfied, he touched it shut and returned to the three-legged stool watching his patient perched miserably at the foot of his bed. 'I think you ignored my wife's warning, *mon frère*.'

'Yes.' Nat nodded glumly. Clarissa had sat where Le Roux was now, treading the foothills of seduction leading to the hayloft.

There was no mistaking the apothecary's disappointment. 'When did you last couple?'

'Four days.' Nat flushed, praying his brother-in-law would not demand the lady's identity. 'Just once.'

Le Roux snorted. 'In this cess pit that's once too many.' He began his gentle admonishment. 'Dorothy told you about Alsatia. You've not been dipping your wick there, I hope.' The apothecary sucked his teeth. 'Was it a whore?'

'No!' Perhaps Dorothy had not told him about the interruption of his intimacy with Clarissa as she crashed in with news of their uncle's arrest.

Le Roux shrugged. 'Well, whore or not, the affliction's the same. It's the chaudepiss.'

Nat paled. 'Like the Justice?'

Le Roux's lips twitched. 'No, the Justice has syphilis. You have chaudepiss.' He grinned ruefully. 'Be thankful for that.'

'Will it mash my brains?'

The apothecary shook his head. 'Syphilis and the chaudepiss are French. Afflictions of the nether regions always are, *malheureusement*,' he sighed. 'But provenance is all they have in common.'

'And the remedy?' Nat chewed his lip. 'I heard cures for ailments below the belt are worse than the illness.'

'Only quack cures,' snapped Le Roux. 'Drink plenty. Small beer's best.' There were footfalls on the stairs. 'I'll prepare an application of sandalwood oil. Use it and the malady will pass in a week.' Nat glanced anxiously at the door. 'You must be continent for a month. D'you think you can manage that?'

Nat eyed Le Roux sheepishly. 'Hope this stays between us, brother?' He felt chastised, like a randy youth.

'You mean, will I tell your sister? You don't need to ask.' He smiled thinly, eyeing the door. 'Remember, *mon ami*, I've broken confidence just once, to save the life of brother Edward.'

'The infection's just deserts for betraying Effam.' Nat knew self-loathing would endure long after the sickness had passed. 'I'm no better than the Justice.'

'*Non*. The Justice is a sodomite. The law says he's an irredeemable sinner. Your lapse is a minor fall from grace. I was a soldier too, remember.' He winked conspiratorially. 'But be constant after you're married, though temptation of the flesh is rarely dissolved by matrimony.'

*

'A pox on this weather.' Talbot Purefoy, easing his peg leg on a three-legged stool, was fanning himself, scowling at his colours hanging limply above the depot. 'A pox on Waller too.'

'Colonel?' Nat sipped from the fine glass offered by Purefoy's servant.

'Well, him and his staff, yourself excepted Nat, strutting round London,' huffed Purefoy, 'basking in the glory of William the Conqueror *sans* conquest.'

'Aye, well, Devizes was a complete disaster,' conceded Nat. 'Still, Sir William's doing a fine job with his flying army down at Merchant Taylor's Hall.'

'Ah yes, I hear London's young gallants have been pressing forward to enlist even faster than their pot-bellied merchant fathers have been opening their purses,' mused Purefoy, 'to the capital's very own general. Garlanded by the City like Caesar, no wonder he's cock-a-hoop. Meanwhile, our saturnine Lord General, Robert Devereux, Earl of Essex, scowls from the shadows with his constant companion.' Purefoy stroked his lip. 'You know what that is Nat?'

'I heard the Lord General never moves without his coffin Colonel.'

'What, oh!' Purefoy sprang to the window with surprising agility. 'It's Redmayne!' An officer Nat recognised as Governor Fiennes' man from the Bristol council of war was beating towards the depot through the crush of Palace Yard. 'What news Redmayne?'

The captain of dragoons looked up, shaking his pale, disfigured head. Seconds later he burst into the room. 'Bristol's fallen!'

'No!' Purefoy slumped back in his chair.

'I was lucky to escape with my life Colonel,' blustered Redmayne. A contortion of teeth and tissue grinned through a livid slash in his face, saliva scoring a red-raw path down his neck. 'You see, Bristol was like Ireland in the rebellion of '41. Our soldiers paraded in the bollocky buff at the point of a pike.' He pressed a napkin to the dribble. 'Prince Rupert dubbed all godly women whores. Told his men to dip their wicks. Truly, God's forsaken Bristol.'

'Redmayne's a brother-in-arms from the German wars Nat.' Purefoy pointed at the dragoon's cropped ear. 'Beneficiary of the King's mercy, as you can see. He won the gash that cleaves his face at Edgehill. Badges of honour, eh Redmayne?'

'With Bristol lost the King commands the west,' said Nat absorbing Redmayne's report. 'Now he'll sweep north to threaten Colonel Massey at Gloucester. Rupert'll take our four warships and two score merchantmen penned up in Bristol and beat across the Irish Sea.'

'Aye, ships with holds full of papists,' said Redmayne. 'Those Irish cut-throats'll find a warm welcome in Wales. Then they'll spill out through the marches to Gloucester and the godly towns of the midlands.'

'What about Governor Fiennes?' Nat wondered why Redmayne was not with his master.

'Spewing excuses,' sneered Redmayne. 'It doesn't look good for him does it, Colonel?' Despite his noble injuries, the officer of dragoons was ratting on his commander.

'Doesn't look good for Waller,' muttered Purefoy. 'Wasting the Bristol garrison at Devizes then marching off what's left to leave a great and godly city to its fate. God's blood, Waller's every bit as culpable as poor, hapless Governor Fiennes.'

'The west's lost because that miserable canting toad Nathaniel Fiennes ran out of powder,' spat Redmayne. 'In a sea port!' The dragoon was enjoying the denouncement, his mangled face twitching.

'Rupert's a good quartermaster,' observed Nat. 'He'll not run short of powder and shot like Fiennes.'

'Still, the governor's neck will be saved by Essex who'll side with Fiennes against Waller.' Purefoy, soldier-politician, was considering where the turn of events placed the key players. 'Either way I fear the news is bad for Sir William.' He flipped the lid of a silver inkwell. 'Redmayne, Salt, you're to find Foxwood.' He sealed the note and thrust it at Nat. 'Pym's to have this immediately. And, Nat, you'd better tell Waller, quickly.'

'Aye, Colonel,' said Nat. 'Sir William must prepare his flying army for Gloucester's relief before the Lord General seizes the opportunity created by this disaster.'

*

Cheapside

10 September 1643

My dearest sweet heart,

Every bell in London's ringing out. Gloucester's relieved by Lord General Essex. Will it be the turning point in our fortunes?

The news for Sir William Waller is bitter-sweet. After Gloucester, he'll be replaced in the people's affections by the Lord General.

Sweet heart, you deserve better but could you settle for a simple country swain? I've had a bellyful of politicking.

Waller says it's my duty to take your father's seat to help the army at Westminster. But he thinks I'm his creature and will do his bidding when I'm elected. He's wrong. I'm beholden to Colonel Cromwell for saving Edward from the gallows and have given him certain undertakings that make me his bondsman. It's a nobler position than Waller's lickspittle.

I hope the wedding is ready because I have some good news. I'm to be recruiter in the west for our new army and will shake the dust of London from my boots within the week.

Your ever loving,

Nat

*

Leaving Kettle's Yard early, happily anticipating an easy ride home, Nat was leading Jessop, Porit, Clegg and Foxwood straight into the eye of a storm.

Newbury had just fallen to the King.

'Listen,' said Will Porit. 'Thunder?'

'That ain't thunder mate,' said Jessop.

Nat kicked on to a rise in the road, standing in his stirrups with the perspective glass. 'Artillery, lots of it, down there in the meadows beneath the town.' He snapped the glass shut. 'Come on!'

The piquet, a detachment of the Red Regiment, stood to, Nat's party trotting towards the standards marking the HQ of the Lord General, Robert Devereux, Third Earl of Essex. There had been plenty of action in the narrow lanes surrounding Newbury and the guards were on edge. But their Sergeant had been with Grimston's company at the Avebury encounter. 'I see you Cap'n Salt Zur.' He waved the horsemen through,

184

grinning broadly. 'You've fetched up in a right bugger's muddle an' no mistake.'

The Lord General peered at the plainly clothed officer and his odd little clerk with a mixture of contempt and indifference. His legendary short temper had not been lengthened by his victory at Gloucester. Nat's appointment as recruiter for the New-Model Army and his association with Sir William Waller prompted a vicious tirade against both. 'You've seen the carping against me in the news books, and my remonstrance in *The Scout*?'

Nat had read the Earl's rebuttal, blaming Waller for the losses in the west. But Foxwood said London's wagging tongues were more interested in the Lord General's alleged difficulty between the sheets. 'Gloucester's done your reputation a power of good my Lord.' Nat tried to sound convincing.

Essex was barely listening. 'They even say I'm in league with the King!'

Nat had not expected to be confessor to a morose, self-pitying Lord General fretting over the news books of London in the middle of a battle.

'I'll publish my remonstrance in full Salt; insist on my inquest. I will not be blamed for Sir William's manifold failings, neither will poor Governor Fiennes be his scapegoat.' Essex spun on his heels. 'And all the while your master Waller persists with this, this,' he spat the words, 'New-Model Army *thing*. Know what they're calling it Salt, eh, eh?' He jabbed Nat's chest with each syllable. 'New *noddle* army! Aye, that's it. What d'you think of that?' He turned to a trestle table covered with papers. With mounting contempt, Nat saw city news books and political pamphlets obscuring campaign maps dotted with pins.

The general's secretary coughed discreetly. The interview was over. Bowing at the Lord General's back, Nat caught sight of a long black box. The gossips were right then. Essex travelled light, except for a coffin.

The secretary took Nat's arm, steering him away. 'Don't mind his Lordship Captain Salt. The battle's quite overwhelmed him.'

'He's more vexed by Sir William and the scribblers of London than the enemy.'

'Not so!' The secretary's was an aesthetic figure, prematurely bald, Nat suspected, beneath the wide brimmed hat. 'It's been a savage fight on top of two days hard marching and a cold wet night bivouacked in these poxed fields.' Smiling wanly, he pulled off his hat, confirming Nat's suspicion. 'We're just all done in, friend, that's all.'

'Well, I didn't see any stripes on his Lordship and his horse will have done his marching,' observed Nat tartly. 'And the Lord General can always kip down in that damned box. His poor boys must take their chances under a hedge.'

With a click of the secretary's fingers, an orderly appeared with bread and ale. 'Isn't much Captain but there are plenty of empty bellies under the stars tonight.' Nat guessed the un-soldierly figure with his inked stained hands had been the Earl's man of business before the war. 'This poxy fight has been a right higgledy piggledy affair, units swinging hither and thither all day long.' He prodded the fire angrily. 'Very devil to keep track with these high banked lanes and tight little fields.' Hissing and spitting, there was little warmth in the flames. 'Artillery's done the most damage, to both sides. Surgeons are overwhelmed.'

In the shadows, Foxwood's wet nose was twitching. 'There's mischief afoot,' he muttered, hugging his arms.

Nat squatted at the fire with half a dozen of the Earl's staff. 'Your boys look beat. Doubt there's much fight left in them.'

'Aye friend, but the enemy's the same,' replied an elderly captain of dragoons.' 'Pummelled each other to a standstill we have.' Pulling a clay pipe from his coat, he rolled a plug of tobacco, thumbing it into the bowl. 'His Lordship intends to rest and review the situation at first light.'

'Well the *situation* is threatening my wedding day,' quipped Nat. 'Didn't expect the road to be blocked by cavaliers.'

'And it wouldn't have been friend if Rupert's cavalry hadn't intercepted us at Aldbourne. Still, we'll punch a hole in the enemy and be back in London by the weekend.' The dragoon sucked noisily on his pipe. 'Indeed, the city regiments'll brook nothing else. Desertion is sapping their strength by the hour.' He streamed blue smoke from the corner of his mouth. 'Sorry about your nuptials. Who's the girl?'

'Euphemia Farrington,' Nat boasted. 'Late Colonel Farrington's daughter.'

'No!' The officer coughed and spluttered.

'Oh, you know her?'

'Good lord, yes.' He winked at the secretary who rolled his eyes. 'Everyone on the staff knows Miss Farrington.'

'The hell they do!'

'Oh, I swear it,' chuckled the dragoon. 'She's been the Earl's great tribulation.' Nat stared at him blankly. 'God's bones, you don't know, do you? Christ, laddie, should've locked her up before you came away.'

'What d'you mean?' Nat was not sharing in the amusement around the fire.

'Well, Miss Farrington poled up about a month back demanding an audience with his Lordship. She and another gentlewoman, major's wife.'

'Lord have mercy, that'll be Mrs Wagstaff.' Nat braced himself for the details.

'Aye, that's the morte, Wagstaff,' the secretary chipped in. 'Came with maids and cartloads of stuff. Wanted to help.'

'Christ Almighty.' Effam and her crew had entered the war.

'Just as well the Lord General didn't know his great tribulation was your affianced.' The old dragoon poked him in the ribs. 'He'd have had you horse-whipped, m'boy.'

'So, where are they now?' Nat fumed, red-faced and furious.

'Last saw them at the Aldbourne fight outside Hungerford. Rupert's dragoons gave us a drubbing there a week back. Those ladies nursed the injured like they were their own. Men loved them. No work for gentle mortes though, scandalous really. I'm sorry.'

'You've no idea where they are then?'

'Not really.' Tamping the tobacco, the captain of dragoons played a taper into the fire, raising it to the bowl of his pipe. 'The Earl had them removed. Said bloody carnage was no place for ladies and he owed it to Colonel Farrington and Major Wagstaff.' He leant over, nostrils venting. 'Truth is he was tired of their hectoring. Doctors were about to revolt.' He patted Nat's arm. 'A couple of my boys escorted them back along the high road. They'll be fine laddie.'

Cursing Essex and distracted by Effam, Nat found his troop on the edge of the bivouac.

'That Foxwood's a queer un, Sir,' said Joe Jessop tipping his chin at the clerk. 'Keeps 'imself to 'imself, pads about the place, won't say nothing. That's right ain't it, Will Porit?'

'Pretty much.' Porit sucked his teeth. 'I'd be leery of him if I was you, Cap'n.'

Nat grunted and fished out his bible, the full moon illuminating Leviticus 16. But The Day of Atonement with the goat carrying off the sins of the world into the desert was too close to the dead curate and the swine of Gadara. Nat felt for a twist of Le Roux's wort, prayed for his headstrong fiancé and, rolling into his blanket, fell into a troubled sleep punctured by the cries of dying men.

*

Foxwood shook him, finger to his lips, nodding at the arched back of the Earl's secretary pushing through the furze. Nat rubbed his eyes. 'What?'

'Something's up.'

Nat sighed, passing a hand through his matted hair. 'The man's going for a piss.' Pulling at the blanket, he turned his back. 'Go to sleep, Foxwood.'

'Bastard's up to no good,' Foxwood hissed.

'Alright, Foxwood.' Time to test the clerk's nose, and maybe send him packing. 'Shake Joe Jessop.' Pulling on his boots, he hauled the blanket across his shoulders.

The battle lines were indistinct but a thousand campfires shone like stars in the pitch black. From the hedgerow, Nat spotted the General's secretary moving swiftly and sure-footed, hugging the contour of Round Hill. Pausing at a stile through the hedge, the man struggled with a box draped with a cloth like the fashionable canary cage Nat had seen outside a shop in Fish Street. Balancing the object on the gate, with a glance over his shoulder, he half removed the cloth. The beam of light pierced the gloom like the Pharos of Alexandria. Quickly, the secretary covered the lantern, repeating the action again, and again.

The man glanced around. Satisfied, he returned to the lantern. Jessop saw the response first, pointing at the flickering light slightly uphill in the hedge. Essex's secretary advanced clumsily over the stile, Nat and Jessop pressing forward. They could see the Lord General's man and another talking in the middle of the field. A packet passed between them, quickly pocketed.

Jessop circled the hedge line finding the weak point where the mystery figure had barged through to rendezvous with the secretary. He did not have to wait long. His quarry, pressing back through the hedge, felt the full force of Jessop's musket, knocking him senseless to the ground.

At the other side of the field Nat waited for the secretary, crouched low beneath the stile. Over came the lamp, one long leg, and the other, about to launch off when Nat seized his ankles. Squealing like a girl, the secretary tumbled over and was silenced by a fist to the head.

'Truss them up against that hedge,' hissed Nat, 'then we'll find out what skulduggery's been going on here.' Reaching into the cavalier's doublet, Nat retrieved the letter with a flourish. The document was in cipher. Foxwood's business. He turned to Essex's secretary. 'What's it say?'

The man got the butt of Jessop's musket. 'Spit it out, whoreson, or rue the day yer mother opened her legs.'

'Alright!' The secretary flinched beneath Jessop's raised fist. 'It's a line of communication kept open with the King,' he spat blood and teeth, 'to facilitate the exchange of prisoners.'

'D'you take us for fools?' lisped Foxwood. 'Moonlight trysts, ciphers and signal lanterns – *prisoner exchange?'* He tipped the secretary's head with his boot, so their eyes met. 'The message is in cipher, not code, so we will have its meaning, eventually. If we don't, I'll rack you.'

Another well-placed blow from Jessop. 'I don't know, I'm just his secretary.' Dazed and blooded, he would not resist interrogation for long. 'Please, you must ask the Lord General.'

Nose vindicated, Foxwood smirked triumphantly. 'So, it's as I thought!' He crouched on his haunches, seizing a fistful of the secretary's thin hair, yanking his head back. 'Essex treats with the King.'

The secretary struggled with a mouthful of blood and a swollen tongue. 'I just do what the Lord General tells me.'

'And you think that lizard's pizzle will back you?' Nat snorted. 'You're in deep trouble friend.' He turned to the cavalier. The boy had the disagreeable air of a patrician's whelp. 'Who the hell are you?

The pup's lip curled. 'I'm surprised you don't know, farm boy.'

'God's blood.' Nat's eyes narrowed. 'Surely not?'

Jessop squinted at the lad. 'You know this little tosser Sir?'

Nat nodded grimly. *'Jehovah Providebit.'*

'Sir?'

'God will provide,' Nat intoned impassively. The boy Carew glared at Nat with the sullen assurance of a captive expecting the usual treatment, an early exchange of officers. But there was no chance of that. The hand of God had delivered Erasmus Carew's heir. The boy was bound to die. 'It's Carew's brat, Jonathan Carew.'

'Bugger me, so it is.' Jessop understood the dire implications for the young man and issued a taster, a smack to the head. 'That's for the kicking your old man gave me and for cussing my lady.' He grinned ominously. 'But there's much worse to come, arseworm, for doing in my Emma.'

The pup's fate was sealed but Essex's secretary and his secrets presented a dilemma. Nat drew the agent out of earshot. 'You've a nose like a bloodhound Foxwood but it's got me in a fix. What'll I to do with your powder keg?'

'Take the secretary and his encryption to London.' Essex's allegiance had always been questionable but the intercepted material would surely put the matter beyond doubt. 'Waller will be heavily in our debt.'

Nat shook his head. 'Sir William's need for evidence against the Earl doesn't excuse us from behaving like soldiers. We've pitched into the middle of a battle. I'll not be leaving until its over.' He left Foxwood with Jessop standing guard, moving back to the Parliament lines to wake Porit and Clegg, still weighing his duty and Effam with the encryption and London.

Dawn without birdsong was breaking across the battlefield, obscured by a misty pall hiding its horror from heaven. Sergeant Foster of the Red Regiment lurched from the gloom. 'Sing praises, Captain! King's left the field.' He flung an arm towards Newbury. 'Bugger's gone. Halle-bloody-lujah!' Glancing from side to side, he lowered his voice. 'Though you can't believe all you're told, Sir. Truth is, we've took a right beating. Reckon His Majesty'll be marching back to Oxford in good order boasting of our bloody nose. Still, my city boys'll be cock-a-hoop on the London road again. You'll see the Red Regiment with a spring in its step the morning, Cap'n Salt.'

Dimly, through the mist, Nat saw the preacher setting up on the back of a wagon, soldiers moving in like ghosts. The cleric's tone was jubilant despite the night's ministry to the dying. Nat knew the voice, as he knew the passage, Exodus 15:

Thy right hand O Lord, is become glorious in power. Thy right hand, O Lord, hath dashed in pieces the enemy. And in the greatness of thine excellency Thou hast overthrown them that rose up against thee. Thou didst send forth thy wrath, which consumed them as stubble.

Apparitions in a sea of souls slid from the white morning shroud, pulled by the parson.

'Ol' tub-thumper's name's Markham,' whispered Sergeant Foster to Nat.

'*Markham.*'

'Aye, that's it. Men call him the half-pike parson. Short-arse get but fierce as a forest fire; second only to the reverend dragoon, old Hugh Peters himself.' Encouraged by the turn-out, the charismatic belted his injunctions; Leviticus, Deuteronomy, Psalms. 'You don't mess with either of them parsons. When they're not preaching at you, they're talking about you and they don't talk to anyone less than full Colonel.'

Nat returned to find his prisoners had not done well in Jessop's custody. 'Can't leave you gentlemen with our tricksy Lord General so I'm seeking higher authority, in London,' he said, crouched beside the Carew boy. 'Now you listen, son, my Sergeant's had a bellyful of your bloody family. He'll gladly do you in if you piss him about.'

Jonathan Carew scowled. 'Untie me, Salt.' The lad had spirit. 'You've got my parole.' Nat slit his bindings, turning to help hoist Essex's secretary on his horse. But the boy was too quick. Nat spun round. Carew was poised for freedom at the top of the stile. Jessop took aim. The secretary, seeing his chance, slipped his muzzle, alarm forming in his throat. Six inches of thin steel glinted and disappeared into the man's larynx with Foxwood's surgical precision.

Jessop spat, steadying his weapon on the stile. Crack! Clean kill.

Face down, brains glistening in the wet grass, the youth with the broken parole lay twitching. Nat dropped to his knees in the spreading gore.

'Robbing a corpse, Sir?'

'No, Joe Jessop.' Nat had his hand deep in the dead man's buff coat. 'Here, this'll do.' He pulled out a monogrammed handkerchief and a locket. 'For the boy's father.'

'Thoughtful.' Jessop shrugged.

'You think so?' Nat folded the effects into his doublet. 'I doubt Erasmus Carew will when he gets these trinkets,' he patted his chest, 'with a note from me.'

The commotion brought half a dozen soldiers bowling through the mist, muskets ready. Their corporal drew up, seeing the captain.

'The secretary's been killed.' Foxwood flopped a hand towards Jessop, strapping the bloody corpse across the neck of his horse. 'And we've dealt with his assailant.' He nodded at the crows working on Jonathan Carew.

The corporal sucked his teeth, eyes shifting between Foxwood and the officer. Something was up, but what was it to him? 'Come on, lads, Sir's got this covered.'

Nat found Essex breakfasting alone at a trestle in front of his tent. The man looked up, dabbing egg from his mouth. Nat heaved the secretary to the ground, raised a finger to his lips, turned his back on the dumbstruck Lord General and left without a word.

*

The Red Regiment, buoyed up by what was being sold to them as victory, was straining for the London road as Nat's group made its unhurried exit through the mist. Passing the standards, Nat swept off his hat. 'Godspeed the Red Regiment! Godspeed city boys!'

'God keep you, Captain Salt.' Grimston returned the salute with a grin and a flourish. 'Huzzah, country cousins!'

*

The Captain of dragoon's assurances had done little to placate Nat's concern for Effam's welfare. Now his search had been complicated by the need to safely deliver the captured encryption. With elements of the King's army likely to be on the London road and the duplicitous Lord General wanting his material back, the chances of getting the incriminating papers to Waller looked slim. But at the crossroads of the Hungerford-Thatcham highway a solution was emerging from the clearing mist in the unlikely form of the Reverend Daniel Markham.

The energetic half-pike parson was helping troopers to the Soldier's Pocket Bible, just published in London by Edmund Calamy. 'A very good day, *Captain* Salt.' Pressing a copy of the crudely printed volume into Jessop's reluctant palm, the preacher's eyes hovered on Nat's sword and sash. 'Where you bound, brother?'

'West, Reverend.' He turned in the saddle, winking at Foxwood. 'But this gentleman's clerk to John Pym. He's bound for London.'

'Pym's clerk, you say?' The half-pike parson scratched his chin. 'I hear the poor man's grievously sick.'

'Aye, needful of a godly sermon, like you gave our boys back there.' Foxwood winked at Nat. 'Will you come to Whitehall with me and counsel the man that runs the Parliament?'

'Parson travelling with his clerk,' muttered Nat. 'Perfect.'

Foxwood began helping himself to the bibles. Turning his back, the agent carefully tore the middle pages from one of the books. Inserting the encrypted papers, he tamped the volume gently until satisfied with the alteration. 'I'll have the cipher broken by Sunday.' He stuffed the ripped pages into his pocket. 'Pym and Waller *will* be pleased, Sir. The evidence will surely do for the canting Earl of Essex.'

The odd couple disappeared at speed down the London road.

'Good,' said Nat. 'That's sorted then, Joe Jessop. Now all we have to do is rescue your mistress from whatever fix she's got herself in, eh?'

*

'Hello, Nathaniel.'

Nat spun round. The small figure marching up the hill might have been the Queen of Sheba. 'In the bowels of Christ, woman, what're you doing?'

Wiping her hands, Effam combed fingers through tussled hair. 'God's work, same as you.' Insouciance with just the hint of a pout.

'But Essex sent you away,' Nat blustered, 'with an escort.'

'You mean the dragoons?' Her lips twitched. 'Gave them the slip, easily.' She smiled, head cocked slightly. 'Needed here, you see. I can't begin to tell you how busy we've been.' Her long apron, once bleached white, was soiled and bloody. She nodded at the river. 'Mrs Wagstaff's down there, washing with the girls.'

'Girls?'

'Yes, of course, servants. Sarah too, my maid, remember?' The hands jammed on her hips were red-raw. 'Better than emptying chamber pots, don't you think?' She shrugged. 'Well, they do. And that's all that matters.'

He passed a hand over rough stubble. 'God's teeth, you've pluck, Euphemia Farrington, but the Lord General's right, damn him, nursing's peasant work, *male* peasants' work, not a pastime for gentlemortes.'

'Rubbish,' she exclaimed. 'Those poor boys need a woman's touch, not the indifference of those jabbernowls Essex hires.'

'Well, it just isn't right, Effam.'

'What isn't right, *Nathaniel*?'

'Squire's daughter pawing common men in the blood and guts of a battlefield,' remonstrated Nat. '*That* isn't right!'

'Oh, my poor booby, what have I done to you?' She smiled, reaching up to touch his face. 'You're thinking, "what's this frightful Amazon I've fetched up with?"' She bit her lip, wondering how much to tell him. 'Look,' she sighed, 'its time you knew the truth.'

'What truth?'

'Well, I wrote to Uncle John. That's John Pym, father's friend.' He stared at her blankly. 'Well, look here *Captain* Salt, truth is, I told him to offer you something.'

'Offer what?' Barely reconciled to Pym and Foxwood's manipulation, his exhausted mind tumbled to the spider in the web. '*You*? Putting me up for Parliament – God's blood, it was you, wasn't it?'

'I suggested it to Uncle John.' Her eyes burned defiantly, meeting his rising ire. 'Look, you dolt, father held Helions in the Parliament. As I would now, had I been born with balls.' She tugged at her apron strings, shaking her hair free. 'But I wasn't, more's the pity,' she fumed tossing the garment on the back of the wagon. 'Look, Pym agreed that if Colonel Farrington's daughter was to marry poor Nat Salt the yeoman must be advanced.' She pursed her lips. 'Oh dear, my intrigue's upset you. Then you should know the rest,' she smiled. 'Dear, beautiful Nat, the truth is I simply couldn't play moll to a dung raking peasant. You see that, don't you?' The hurt in his eyes was ripping her apart. Every sinew pressed her forward into his arms where she could mouth the pretty platitudes he yearned for, and that she would spend eternity regretting. 'I'm thinking...' she glanced away, towards the river. 'I'm thinking maybe my country lad's better fitted to...' She glared at him, acting the part, but through his bewilderment he thought he could see tears winking like diamonds, '...someone else.'

Joe Jessop crashed in. 'Trouble, Sir.' The Sergeant wielded Nat's perspective glass like a general's baton. 'Dozen troopers coming on like the hounds o' hell.' He whipped off his hat, passing an arm across his brow. 'Reckon Lord General's got his head round our little night shift.'

Effam snapped to. 'Break out in this terrain and you'll be like a fox on a ridge. And I'll give odds for the doglocks the Lord General's troop carries.' She barked orders at the river. 'Time to go, ladies. Now!' The colonel's daughter turned on her country captain. 'You always bring me trouble, Nathaniel Salt. Slip those horses, Jessop.' She raised the edge of the cart's tarpaulin. 'Now get in!'

The three men, cowed and sweating among Effam's poultices and liniments, crouched low as Essex's troop pulled up. Nat recognised the commander's drawl from the campfire. 'Zounds lady, thought we'd sent you packing,' grinned the captain of dragoons. 'His Lordship won't be pleased, y'know.' Spotting the horses settling to graze, his eyes lingered on the cart. 'Fine beasts, ma'am.'

Effam shrugged. 'Not mine.'

The captain was circling the wagon now. 'No, they're certainly not yours, lady. Five horsemen passed through. D'you see them Miss Farrington?'

'One officer, villainous looking cove, three soldiers and a crook-backed clerk.' She smiled up at him coquettishly.

'Aye, lady, that's it.' He grinned, drawing his sword with a rasp to catch the edge of the tarpaulin. 'And I'm wondering what's in this box o' tricks.' A shaft of daylight illuminated the fugitives. The old soldier scanned his fireside companion, jaw tightening. 'Ah!'

The sheet flopped back. He bent low over the horse's neck. 'Aye, lady, villainous looking cove's about right.' He winked, straightening up, scanning the horizon theatrically. 'Now, those villains, where away d'you reckon?'

She pointed north. 'Ruffians'll be half way to Oxford by now.'

'Best get at 'em then.' The captain kicked on. 'Good luck lady,' he said and, *sotto voce*, 'Godspeed ye both.'

Part Two – Republic

XIV

The Lamb Inn
Hinton
6 June 1645
Dear Captain Farrington,

I must apologise for the delay in arranging your election. Lord knows how difficult it is to arrange anything at the moment but, with the King now at bay and equanimity restored in the west country, we can proceed.

We have been beset with troubles. Firstly, the gentleman we intended to run with you has mysteriously been consigned to the Fleet debtor's gaol. In his place has emerged Captain Tobias Norrington of Lavington who we both know. As an army man he enjoys the confidence of our patrons, if not ourselves...

'Pah!' Nat banged down the length of the hall. Running a hand distractedly through his mane, he shook the letter at Effam. 'I'll not line up with your poxed cousin Norrington,' he fumed. 'Or deal with Erasmus Carew except at the point of a sword.'

...The malignant Carew, believed to be with the King in Oxford, engaged cunning lawyers to delay the tabling of the election writ. Nevertheless, the instrument has now been served so the Sheriff can instruct bailiffs to proceed with the vote. I suspect it will be on the Saturday two weeks from now as is the custom.

As you can see, I'm in The Lamb at Hinton where I've established a headquarters. I'd be mighty pleased to see you here.

I remain, Sir
Your most humble and obedient
Servant
Foxwood
Clerk

'Porit! Saddle up the gelding.' Nat tossed the crumpled letter into the grate. 'At least I won't have to face Pym, God rest his soul.' And *she* would just have to lump being married to a farmer, he thought with satisfaction, for all her scheming with Pym. 'I'm off to tell Foxwood he'll have to send for some other poor sap.'

Mrs Nathaniel Farrington, sitting in the south oriel, did not bother to look up from her accounts. She knew her husband's needs and she had the measure of Foxwood. The clerk would persuade him easily and if he did not there was Cromwell and Nat's promise to the great man.

'God's teeth, where's Porit?' Nat stamped off to find his horse.

Effam flipped the inkwell lid shut, scanning the portraits re-hung in the hall and the bright rectangle where her mother's picture, now lining the bottom of the moat, used to be. She was grateful for Carew's brief tenure and the mark it had left, most of it for the better. He had redeemed the mortgage to the money lenders of Bristol, her father's preoccupation. There was a new roof, stout buttresses to shore up sagging walls and work begun on two handsome wings that would have doubled the hall's footprint in Carew's quest to veneer his questionable escutcheon.

The maid Sarah scampered through with warm milk flecked with nutmeg. 'Told him your news then, lady?'

'It's much too soon, child,' said Effam stroking her belly.

*

Nat found Foxwood in the The Lamb's front parlour. The agent had wasted no time in securing the best chamber overlooking the green for his candidate and a back room as headquarters. Nat learnt that Foxwood and his servant would occupy a single room across the landing.

'You must try these oysters, Sir. Salted, of course, but really very good.' Nat wondered why such a small man had to eat so much. 'Captain Norrington will not be visiting as such but he's prepared an address which I'm to put about.'

Nat stared bleakly at the note shoved across the table as Foxwood wiped juice from his chin with the back of his hand. 'The Hinton constituency, you know, comprises Hinton Helions, with six burgage plots in your pocket, and the electorally more significant hamlet of Hinton Champflower, a piss-pot sort of place.' Foxwood shifted in his chair, scratching his arse. 'Manor's held by the Bishop of Winchester but Sir Thomas Wraxall at Champflower House holds sway. He has the freehold of twelve burgage plots, controls ten more and used them all to return his mucker, Colonel Farrington.' The servant replaced the oyster shells with chicken pie and turnips. 'The other seat was taken by Carew in the election of 1640, by mutual consent, with his ten and a half burgage plots in Champflower and six in Helions.' Foxwood thrust deep in the pie, twisting the knife out and flicking his long tongue across the blade, eyes fixed on Nat. 'I've identified nine voters as what you might call independents, that is to say, not obliged to any particular Lord or influence, other than the obvious pecuniary inducements that we'll come to shortly.'

'What's that fellow doing?' Nat peered at the constable on the green.

'Ah!' Flipping the casement, Foxwood sat back for the oration, arms folded. 'Announcing the writ.' He smirked, tongue touring the recesses of his mouth.

'County constituency of Hinton (to wit). By order of the High Sheriff of the County of Wiltshire, under the seal of his office to the Bailiffs of the said constituency of Hinton in the said County, directed and delivered for the Election of two members for the said constituency to serve in the Parliament in the room of Miles Farrington Esq deceased and Erasmus Carew, delinquent. We, Jeremiah Norris and Joseph Bates, Bailiffs of the said constituency, do hereby give notice that we shall proceed to the Election of two members, to serve in Parliament for the constituency aforesaid, on Saturday the twentieth day of this instant at eleven o'clock in the forenoon of the same day, at The Lamb in the main street of Hinton Helions being the usual and accustomed place. Given this day under our hands, Jeremiah Norris and Joseph Bates, Bailiffs.' The fat man finished with a flourish. 'And Godspeed Captain Nathaniel Farrington o' Helions!'

With a low bow at The Lamb he pinned his proclamation to the whipping post. Nat glowered at his agent across the table. 'I quit.'

'Eh?' Foxwood picked chicken fibres from needle-like teeth, a bead of fat inching from the corner of his mouth.

The unwilling candidate pushed his chair back. 'Tobias Norrington's the double-dealing crony of Erasmus Carew. I'll not stand with him.' He began to rise. 'Find another jabbernowl for your election.'

The agent's greasy talon cuffed Nat's wrist. 'Too late.' Foxwood prepared his bluff, eyes narrowing. 'Writ's posted, see. Can't be undone.' He shrugged. 'Election law. Once posted, that's it, you're the candidate.'

Nat screwed up Norrington's address, tossing it angrily at the grate. Wrenching his arm away, he slumped back like a truculent schoolboy.

'Anyway, you promised Cromwell. *Oliver bleeding Cromwell*!' Foxwood puffed his cheeks. 'And him snatching your brother from the shadow of Tyburn tree and all.' He shook his head mournfully, tongue clicking against teeth. 'Bad form, bad form.' With a heavy sigh, the clerk continued his lunch.

'Alright, Foxwood.' Nat had a solution. 'Norrington and me, two candidates, two vacancies, yes? Foxwood, shrugged. 'So, fix the Burgesses a dozen hogsheads, supper for the Bailiffs and send me a note when it's done.' Foxwood was silent for too long. 'There's a problem, isn't there?'

'There might be, Sir, but only a small one and nothing that can't be fixed.' Foxwood passed his little finger over his teeth, scraping and sucking. 'Took a stroll last night to that piss-house.' He tipped his chin at the inn across the green.

'The Angel.'

'Aye. Don't know why they call it that, full of high pads and bung-nippers. Anyway, fell in with one or two of the better sort, to get the lie of the land. There was talk of another candidate, two actually, Percival Arkell and Miles Compton.'

'A contest then,' said Nat flatly.

Foxwood wiped the greasy residue on his plate with a scrap of rye bread. 'Seems so, yes,' he said, licking the pewter plate like a dog.

'But *you* told me the election was a formality.' The agent shrugged, looking hopefully at the kitchen. 'I blame you, Foxwood. You're a damned, scheming mongrel.'

'Yes Sir.' Foxwood waited, for the Captain to calm down and for pudding.

'Percival Arkell.' Nat fumed, chewing on the name. 'Yes, he's one of those blood-sucker lawyers at the Court of Common Pleas.'

'Quite. The Angel reckons he's Carew's man sent to mind the seat whilst his master's in Oxford.' Foxwood belched. 'That'll be the oysters.' He exhaled theatrically, patting his skinny shanks. 'And Miles Compton's another Carew crony.'

Nat's patience snapped. 'I'll deal with Carew *properly* when he crawls from his Oxford cess-pit. Aye, and any of his whelps still drawing breath.' Leaning forward, he fingered the pommel of his sword, jaw-jutting, jabbing the agent's sunken chest. 'Politics is for charlatans and mountebanks. I'll have no part in it.'

'Well, there's no retreat. Walk away and your adversary'll bag both vacancies,' said Foxwood. 'Anyway, what about Cromwell?'

Nat threw up his hands. 'Look, Foxwood, I came to take Hinton, not fight for it.'

'Oh, now you're sounding like Marcus Antonius, Sir.' Julius Caesar really, thought Foxwood. The triumvirate: Pym, himself and Euphemia Farrington, had lined the new Squire Farrington up for a scrap that was meant to be a coronation. 'Cornered, but not stabbed,' he murmured.

'Eh?'

'Thought you wanted to knife Carew,' shrugged Foxwood, wiping his chops with the back of his hand. 'And keep your promise to Cromwell.'

Nat glared at the agent.

'*But* we are in a quandary that risks both. You see the number of voters in each camp is finely balanced.' Foxwood, giving up on pudding, clicked his fingers at the servant, pointing at his glass. 'Carew still has a following.'

'Oh, how's that?' Nat contemplated the grisly prospect of selling himself like a sack of corn to his neighbours, the doubting burgesses of Hinton. 'You told me Court of Sequestration seized the bastard's property. Got no land, got no patronage, eh?'

'I said the court *would* do so.' The clerk smiled. 'Conditional tense, you see. Until it does, Carew's placemen can manipulate his burgages at will.'

Nat scraped his chair back. 'Then bring the matter to court, now! With your reputation Foxwood, I'm disappointed Carew's goose isn't cooked already.'

'You and Cromwell assaulting that judge, springing your brother from the Clink, didn't help.' Foxwood shook his head mournfully. 'Thicker than an Anabaptist's prayer meeting those lawyers and that Percy Arkell takes his dinners at the Inner Temple. No, we'll buy what we need.' The servant slopped more claret into his master's glass. 'God's blood, I swear the landlord brews this puke from potatoes,' Foxwood winced. 'Though there are votes to be had without a penny piece.'

'How so?'

'Faggots, Sir.'

'Eh?'

'Faggots. Created by summoning the Court Baron to admit burgesses and allowing them to do homage.' He shrugged, casually. Nat needed to know how effortlessly he could fix things. 'I've arranged the court two days from now, here in The Lamb.'

'And the faggots?'

'Are votes Sir, faggot votes.' Foxwood saw he was going to have to be patient with Nat. 'Sir Thomas sells burgage plots and dwelling places, each carrying a vote, to yokels he can trust. Only he doesn't *really* sell and they don't *really* buy.' He paused, allowing Nat to catch up. 'It's a pretty fraud see, got up by artful lawyers to baffle knuckle-dragging bailiffs.' Foxwood swirled the dregs, tipping them down his neck, slamming the glass on the table. 'Now then, our fake burgesses present themselves at the Court Baron clutching fake freeholds – we call 'em snatch papers – in their sweaty palms. They pay the tuppence we've tipped 'em, make an act of obeisance before the Steward and *Voilà*!' Foxwood thumped the table, 'they're on the Burgage roll, *and they're a voter*.' Foxwood looked pleased with himself. 'There, Sir, I see my explanation's restored your heart to its proper place, above your girdle.'

Foxwood tapped his glass at the servant, pointing at Nat. Reluctantly, Nat drew up his chair and took the offered glass. The agent was right, the wine was tart, even to his untutored palate, but The Lamb's patrons drank beer and cider, not claret. 'Except Carew's weasels are likely as conniving as you.'

Foxwood doubted they were. 'We'll tell the electors they'll keep their scraps and hovels after the sequestration order if they vote the right way. Our army's victory at Cheriton'll concentrate minds.' Foxwood smirked because he was getting to the business that made life worthwhile. 'Then there's the matter of patronage, Sir. Minor offices and the like. We have 'em, Carew doesn't since the reversal of the King's fortunes.' He thumbed his small black leather book. 'Here, for example, is John Meddlicott, yeoman, holder of one whole burgage. One vote. Happily John Junior is after an Army position, a lucrative one, and he'll get it, as a quartermaster, if his father votes right.' He jammed his tongue in his cheek, finger working down the page. 'Ah, Richard Blunt, carrier of this parish. One vote costing five shillings up front and another five when the result's declared for us.' Foxwood turned the page, shaking his head in a grotesque parody of regret. 'I'm *so* sorry William Hopkins felt it necessary to bad-mouth yourself, and him being a debtor and all. He'll spend polling day in custody.'

'But I've known Will Hopkins all my life,' Nat protested. 'Now you're doing him in.'

'Not at all,' protested Foxwood. 'A day and a night with Sarum's drunks and pickpockets will neutralise Hopkins' vote *and* teach him his manners.'

*

'How many of these men tipping my beer down their necks actually have the vote, Foxwood?' Nat's mood had not improved for polling day.

And neither had Foxwood's at the early appearance of his candidate. 'Oh buck up, Sir. Voters want a jolly member, not some long-faced get. Anyway, since your canting vicar shut down church ales and saints' days, there ain't much entertainment in an arse-end place like this.'

Foxwood's set-up at The Lamb was matched by his opponent at The Angel. The two inns glared across the green like pugilists in a ring, puffed-up voters rolling from one to the other. But traditionally polling was held in The Lamb's front parlour.

And tradition in Hinton Helions was greatly prized, the village's sense of itself acute as any cathedral city. The two bailiffs Norris and Hunter marched up the high street from the church, constable in front with the great leather-bound burgess roll and poll book. A knot of barefoot ragamuffins danced behind.

'Just look at that,' sneered Foxwood, fingering his pledge list. 'That little toss pot Norris worries me though.'

'Aye, I know Jeremiah Norris,' said Nat. 'Cut me dead when I tried to say hello.' The encounter had not been pleasant. 'Hinton gave him a Skimmington ride, couple of years back, hounding him out of town, him and his missus. Bad business, though Lord knows, I did my best for him.'

'Well, pasty little bat's pizzle was in his cups at The Angel last night with Arkell and Compton.' Foxwood passed a finger round his gums. 'Problem is, he's presiding over this clown's court. If he's taken against you he'll need watching.'

The Lamb's patrons cheered the pompous party bustling into the parlour. 'Give me that.' Norris seized the burgess roll and poll book, throwing them onto a trestle table in front of the fire as the church bell struck eleven. 'Right, who's first then?'

A faggot voter elbowed through. Norris thumbed his way to the place in the ledger, squinting at the grubby deed offered as proof of tenure. 'This seems in order, Mr Meldrum, who'll I put you down for, eh?' He marked the poll book without waiting. 'Next!'

'I'd like to see *Mister* Meldrum's papers,' barked Foxwood. The bailiff pursed his lips, eyes flicking between Nat and his agent, reluctantly pushing the deeds across the desk. Foxwood barely glanced at them. 'It's a faggot vote. Meldrum you're a faggot, a fraud.' Meldrum raised a ham fist but got the constable's wand across his chest.

Nat winced. 'How many of my neighbours d'you plan to piss off before high-tailing back to London Foxwood?'

'They're not neighbours, Sir, they're voters. Peasants mostly, illiterate jabbernowls,' hissed Foxwood. 'Now, you leave this to me.'

'Faggot, you say?' Norris flicked the paper, conferring with Hunter. 'Mr Meldrum attended the Court Baron and these papers were accepted by his Grace's steward. Vote's good.'

Gesturing obscenely at Foxwood, Meldrum retired in triumph. A small queue built up behind John Blunt, one of Foxwood's faggot voters, brandishing snatch papers for one burgage plot, an acre of perpetually sodden meadow. Jeremiah Norris peered at the deeds. 'How much d'you pay for this then?'

'Says how much on them papers.' The ruffian leant over the table, thrusting his beery face at the bailiff. 'Can't you read?'

'Yes, but you can't.' Norris screwed his face against the hot, stale breath. 'If you could you'd know how much.' Eyes narrowed, he tapped the deeds. 'What's this property then, where is it, eh? Tell me now, John Blunt, are you the master of a meadow or pasture, a tidy wee cottage or...' he smirked at the audience, '...a manor house?'

'Tis a field up yonder.' The man waved expansively.

'You don't know, do you Blunt?' Norris cradled his head in his hands. 'I suggest no money changed hands for this property.' He dismissed the man with a flick of his head. 'Your vote's invalid.'

'What!' Foxwood would not be outsmarted at his own game.

'The deeds are obviously snatch papers,' declared Norris. 'I'm sending them to the Court Baron since his Grace's steward has clearly entered this faggot voter by mistake.' Norris jerked his head towards the door. ' Now clear off, Blunt.'

William Hopkins barged his way to the bailiffs and was checked off against the burgage roll. 'He's a friggin' debtor,' Foxwood snarled and spat. 'I saw him carried off yesterday, by the sheriff's man.'

The man sneered. 'You saw me carried off alright. Spent the night in Sarum gaol I did for 'aving twenty pounds owing these past five years. Five years, Sirs, and I gets pressed for it now. Why? Well, to keep me from casting my vote, Sirs, that's why.' He glared menacingly at Foxwood. 'Now I wonder who to thank for them rough lodgings, eh? But some kind body pitches up this morning with twenty gold sovereigns to buy me out.' He beamed triumphantly. 'And here I am to cast my vote. Mark me down for Mr Arkell and Mr Compton boys, if you please.'

'Lunch.' Norris drained his tankard and the official party began its unsteady navigation to the back parlour. Norris stumbled, lurching towards Foxwood.

Foxwood stepped smartly away. 'Pissed as a fart.'

Nat caught the bailiff before he hit the floor. 'Easy, Jeremiah.'

Norris shook him off. 'Reckoned to get even with you *Captain*, and so I will, you'll see,' he snarled.

Wiping spit from his face, Nat grabbed Foxwood, propelling him towards the makeshift HQ. 'Votes evenly cast and a bailiff with a grudge, Lord knows why.' He kicked the door shut. 'You promised an anointing, Foxwood, not a bare-knuckle fight.'

'You've an enemy in Norris's wife.' The agent shrugged unhappily. 'Something about a fracas in church and that Skimmington ride?'

'God's blood!' Nat combed his fingers through his hair. 'I was the only one sticking up for him that day!'

'Well, he's referring our faggots back to the Court Baron for adjudication and accepting Carew's. Since the Court Baron won't meet 'til after the election, your only remedy if this goes on is to petition Parliament.' Foxwood knew that meant a long delay and an unpredictable outcome. He doubted Nat would stay the course.

Nat planted himself uncomfortably in one of the room's two high-backed chairs, the familiar ache in his thigh promising trouble, sharpening his temper. 'Norris's taking a big risk, given Carew's prospects.'

Foxwood took the other seat, tugging off his boots. 'He just wants to poleaxe you.' Straightening his thin shanks, he flexed the big toes poked through their stockings. 'Raw emotion, you see, often gets in the way of good sense.' The servant appeared at the door. 'Ah, good, sustenance. Hungry business, democracy.' He pointed to the table. 'And my boots need buffing.'

'I won't lose to Carew, Foxwood.' Nat leant forward, hands clasped, jaw jutting. 'I'm sure you understand.'

'Oh, I do, Sir.' Sucking his teeth, Foxwood dragged a chair to the table. 'A good agent knew his master's mind and his opponent's better. That's why I've never lost an election and why I'll be visiting Norris tonight.' He fished an iron knife from his waistcoat. 'Now, what's this?' Splitting the piecrust, he thrust his long nose in the steam. 'Mmmm. Pickled oysters, anchovies.' He poked a finger at the pie. 'You know Captain, this dump's a damned good bill o' fare, except the wine which is cat's pizzle. Want some?'

'Perhaps I'll talk to him,' said Nat. 'Norris that is, ease his mind, about the Skimmington.'

'Oh, no, that would never do, Sir.' Foxwood licked the knife on both sides. 'You leave the bailiff to me. One way or another he'll be dancing to a different tune tomorrow.'

'Foxwood.' Nat wagged a finger, labouring each word. 'I don't want him hurt.'

Foxwood pursed his lips. 'My methods are my own, *Sir.*'

*

'It wasn't me,' said Foxwood.

Norris had appeared for the second day of polling dishevelled, left eye swollen and red. Mutely, he began taking Foxwood's faggot votes.

'Well, explain that,' hissed Nat.

'Really Sir, the bailiff's stripes are none of *my* doing, although his long face probably is,' smirked Foxwood. 'All you need to know is today's faggot votes are secure.'

'How's that then, Foxwood?'

Foxwood sighed. 'Well, I called by and his moll did the talking. Seems the old harpy's learnt nothing from the Skimmington. I explained the

Skimmity ride, how you tried to intervene on their behalf and how much his slight yesterday had upset you. Mrs Norris rolls her arms at that and screws her face. Not pretty.'

Nat shook his head. 'Its her fault poor Norris ended up in the dungheap.'

'Indeed,' Foxwood shook his head mournfully. 'Women are so often the root of a man's tribulations, ain't they? Anyway, the old bag's truculence led to a nice chat about the last wretch to be tried by the Commons for abusing electoral office. The miscreant, Sir, was bailiff of some poxed Kentish borough.' Foxwood stroked his lips, contemplating the Medway towns. 'Anyway, Committee of Privileges found he'd been accepting snatch papers from one candidate, rejecting faggots from the other. Sound familiar?' The agent fingered the tuft of thick black hair sprouting from his nose. 'Well, bailiff ferments in the Clink for a bit then he's dragged to the bar of the House for a tongue lashing, on his knees. Now some say Speaker Lenthal is a weak old fool. But he strikes like the hammer of hell when crossed.'

'Was that it?' A dressing down did not seem much of a penalty.

Foxwood shrugged. 'Scoundrel was undone, disgraced, turned out, dismissed. Hung himself from a meat hook.' Screwing his face, he pinched and plucked a nasal hair, holding it to the light. 'His old dear was quite unhinged. Followed hubby to a painful death at the rope's end, hanged as a witch to general approval.' Foxwood shook his head, eyes raised to the yellow ceiling. 'I could see Mistress Norris beginning to make the connection. But we were not there yet.' Foxwood paused for effect. He had put a lot into fixing the Norris couple and wanted Nat to appreciate his workmanship. 'Old cow began to petition for a bribe. Can you believe that? Told her we'd allow them the quiet enjoyment of their home which, in the circumstances, I thought mighty generous.'

'The bluff worked?'

'No bluff. I've acquired Norris's freehold.' He patted his left breast. 'Mistress Norris went white as a Michaelmas goose when I showed her and, sweet Jesu, the language after I left. Whole street got the benefit of it.' He nodded at the black-eyed bailiff. 'And I don't think we've far to look for his assailant. Reckon Jeremiah Norris's heading for another Skimmity ride!'

On the cusp of noon, Foxwood's servant slunk in through the back, whispering urgently in his master's ear. The agent scowled. 'It's damnably close. Two of our electors, bribed ones, voted for Carew. Bastards. My man's been knocking up three firm pledges but they've gone to ground.' Foxwood chewed his lip, glancing anxiously at the increasingly excited Carew ensemble. 'One Jacques drank his bribe last night. Cracked his head and is now *in extremis*.' He sighed unhappily. 'The poxed reverend told me in a roundabout way he'd vote for you, but he's been called to a parishioner, apparently. Housekeeper can't say when he'll be home.' Foxwood checked the numbers, knowing them perfectly well. With another furtive glance at Carew's leering supporters, he steered Nat into the back room. 'Seems it's in the hands of the Almighty, if you believe in that stuff.'

Nat's boot sent a stool crashing across the room. 'I'll not be beaten by Carew!'

'Well, by my reckoning he's one up, 22 to 21.' Foxwood was pacing the room, wringing his hands. 'Sir, I fear you must prepare for defeat.' And I, he thought, must look for another position.

'Preacher's here!' Foxwood's boy burst into the room.

The elegant retired archdeacon was carrying a package wrapped in brown hessian and tied with string. 'Yours, Captain.' He offered the package to Nat. 'Now then, let's see, what a choice we have, gentlemen,' he beamed at the rustic inebriates. Nat drew the strings as Foxwood computed the significance of the unexpected voter's arrival. 'What fine candidates. Indeed, a person can hardly choose.' Foxwood's gimlet eyes narrowed. 'Two votes, are there not, Mr Norris?'

The bailiff nodded gravely. 'And a minute to cast 'em, Reverend.'

'Well, I'll vote for Mr Compton.' Eyes closed, the picture of piety raised a hand like he was blessing the company. 'In remembrance of his dear father, the late Bishop of Truro.'

A gasp from the assembly, a 'huzzah!' from Carew's camp and Foxwood, the master fixer, was spitting tacks. 'Shitty death, the bugger's switched. A pox on all blatherskite, sanctimonious parsons!'

But Nat, impervious to the drama, had spotted the man who could only be triumphant Miles Compton. Across the fug-filled parlour, grinning modestly, pressing the flesh, the candidate's fine boned features were etched in the deep recesses of Nat's mind. But as their eyes met across the sea of ruddy drinking faces he strained to remember.

Now Foxwood was hissing in his ear. 'Best get you out the back, Sir.' Magnanimity was not the agent's way.

'I've to cast another, eh Mr Norris?' The reverend pursed his lips.

'Don't have to, Reverend,' said the bailiff slyly. Foxwood steered Nat away. The turned parson was bound to vote for Compton's running mate.

'Then I endorse...,' the archdeacon's finger hovered, '... Captain Farrington! Sir your kindness amidst the hurt of this terrible war fits you well for the Parliament.' He waved at the package in Nat's hands, the hessian falling away. It was the pistol and a note.

My Dear Captain,

I trust the vote of my good friend will be of assistance to you. Please accept the Upton with my thanks for the kindness of a stranger.

I am etc.

Russell

Nat gulped, wiping a hand across his face. In Foxwood's septic world of intrigue and double-dealing, amidst the swirling hatred of his great adversary, the ballot was turning on a simple act of human decency.

'Ye gods.' Foxwood looked like a man reprieved on the steps of the scaffold. 'That's set cat among the pigeons.'

Nat was not listening. 'Foxwood, I know that man, Miles Compton.'

'You meet many people, Sir,' sighed Foxwood. 'Pay attention now, it's a split vote.'

The bailiffs were making a great show of checking ballots. Then Norris stood up, clearing his throat. 'I, Jeremiah Norris, merchant, do declare the number of votes cast to be 82. For Mr Compton, 22 votes.' There was a great roar from Miles Compton's rabble. 'For Mr Arkell 21, for Captain Norrington 18 and for Captain Farrington...' he paused, moistening his lips, spitting the score, '21'.

'What now, Foxwood?' hissed Nat.

'We toss for it.'

'Oh, good grief.' Nat threw up his hands.

'Fifty-fifty,' said Foxwood. 'But let's see if we can narrow the odds, eh?'

Nat reached into his doublet for the talisman, slamming it on the desk. 'Here, use this.' The constable examined the silver penny suspiciously, biting it from habit. 'King gave it me when he passed through.' There was a low murmur and nodding of heads. After two decades, Hinton Helions remembered King Charles' visit like it was yesterday. 'What can be fairer than that?'

'Here. I do the tossing.' Norris seized the coin, held it high, describing an arc so everyone could see the King's money. 'A comes before F so its Mr Arkell's shout. Heads or tails, Sir?'

A farmer's lad piped up. 'Be it the King's head, Mr Bailiff?' He waved his leather flagon wildly, beer slopping. 'If 'tis, take it, Mr Arkell, or Cap'n Farrington'll cut bugger off!'

Arkell scowled. 'Tails, damn it!'

The bailiff tossed the piece high. Down it fell, all eyes on it, spinning in the dull light with the constable holding the crowd back. The two bailiffs crouched low, Foxwood behind them. In the gloom Nat thought he could see a flash of steel at Norris's back, saw the man start and heard the agent hiss in his ear. Norris whipped back snatching the coin.

'Heads!'

Norris struggling to be heard. 'Gentlemen, gentlemen.' The constable called for order. 'Gentlemen. I do declare Mr Compton and Captain Farrington elected to serve in the Parliament as members for Hinton.' A bovine roar of approval, and now Miles Compton was closing on Nat, hand outstretched.

'Well, Sir, we'll serve in the Parliament together.' The man's face lit up, boyishly enthusiastic.

Nat's heart missed a beat, the cogs and levers of his mind tripping to the truth. Here was the King's officer trotting down the lane after the Devizes fight *and* the enigma on the deck of *Deliverance*. God's blood, they were one and the same. Compton blushed. 'Well, Sir, that is to say, I'm looking forward to serving with you, Captain, in Hinton's interests.'

Nat stared at the man's hand aghast. 'You were at the Devizes fight.'

The man's brow creased. 'No, Sir.'

'Yes, you were.' Nat was sure of it. 'And we met in London, on my uncle's ship.'

Compton shook his head vigorously. 'No, Sir!'

The man was a damned good actor. Nat struggled to make sense of it. The officer of the King's Lifeguard on the road from Devizes had a livid purple stain across his face. This man's complexion was unblemished.

He raised his hand, but not to shake his adversary's but for the powder he felt sure the man was wearing. Compton recoiled and Foxwood was at Nat's arm, sensing trouble. Shaking off the agent, he advanced on the puzzled young man. 'Well, *placeman*, you'll be out by Michaelmas on account of Erasmus Carew's attempt to rig the election.'

'Well, Captain Farrington, I'll endeavour to be restored in your good opinion.' He flushed, swallowing hard, cartilage in his thin neck bobbing up and down. 'Until then permit me to congratulate you on the honour bestowed on us by these good people.' He finished with a tight little bow.

Nat turned his back. Soiled by his elevation, product of the artful manipulation by Pym, Foxwood and Effam of a damn fool farmer with a score to settle, his solace was the paradox of Lord Russell's note and the treasured Upton. 'Foxwood!' Nat's suspicion, the flash of cold steel at Norris's back and the snatch of the coin, demanded an answer that only Foxwood could give. Now, like a sack of corn, he was being hauled in the air. He twisted to find the agent. '*Was* it heads, Foxwood?'

The arch-fixer, snatcher of victory, smiled inscrutably, already composing the day's entry for his journal of secrets. 'Congratulations, Sir.'

XV

Helions House

June 1645

At the south oriel, white chemise, cuffs drawn tight but open necked, index finger sliding across his lips like a bow on a fiddle, Nat was thinking.

Effam smiled absently at his back. Was it the right time? She had dismissed the sickness; venison hung too long, she thought. 'Bed.' She tapped the arms of the chair and rose, carefully, padding across to kiss him. Preoccupied, Nat watched the last of the light playing on the lawn. With a glance at the screen to be sure she was gone, he felt for the grubby paper delivered earlier by military courier.

'What's that?' Effam had asked.

'Nothing sweet heart.' He had quickly pocketed the letter, knowing where it had come from. Now, alone, he studied the packet, passing his thumb over the heavy red wax seal pitted deeply with its author's badge. Fumbling among Effam's writing things, his fingers closed on a fruit knife. He paused for a moment, playing the tool between his fingers before sliding the blade between the papers.

Naseby June 15th 1645

My dear Captain Farrington,

Of the many letters I write today after our great victory few are more painful than this. It is my sad duty to inform you that yesterday your brother Edward Salt fell in defence of our godly cause when the Army under my command joined with the King outside Naseby in Leicestershire. It will comfort you to know that he acquitted himself well in the Lord's work and died quickly and as handsomely as may be. Indeed, his death has brought credit to your family which in life he feared he had denied it. Your brother lies in the lee of Mill Hill a half mile from Naseby where he was laid to rest with all tribute.

I felt it my particular duty to learn from Colonel Okey the circumstances of your brother's death. I have to tell you that Trooper Salt fell during the cavalry engagement at Sulby Hedges at the hand of a colonel of dragoons in the van of Prince Rupert's horse. Okey is acquainted with the officer, Erasmus Carew, who I recall is a Wiltshire gentleman known to you.

I pray for you in your adversity and remain
Your good friend,
Oliver Cromwell
Lieutenant General

Effam awoke cold and felt across for him. Pulling her linen shawl around her shoulders, she slipped downstairs. The letter lay where it had fallen like an autumn leaf. In the moonlight she glimpsed the signature, a fusion of curves and spikes, guessing the rest. 'Oh, Nat, sweet heart.'

Nat's brow was furrowed like a winter field, eyes black as mourning stones, and his strangled words, half prayer, half curse, grating like a hurdle drawn to Tyburn, pierced her soul. 'Charles Stuart, damned Carew, I lay my eye upon you. Aye, even to the tenth generation.' She was back in her carriage watching the yeoman calling down she knew not what among the ashes of Brook Farm for the murder of his children. 'Dark men of blood, you foul, ungodly creatures, as God's my witness I'll not rest.' He fixed on her, unseeing. 'Eye for an eye, Lord. Give me the blood tribute you promised. *Jehovah* Providebit' A cold smack across her shoulders and her stomach knotted, like the forest clearing and the smell of blood, men and women grunting and heaving like a child should not see, and she was crashing back through the trees, wide-eyed and gibbering into her father's arms. 'Or I'll seal my oath with the gods of the greenwood.'

'Nat! Her hand shot to her face. 'May the Lord forgive you!' She knew her sweet man danced with demons, the old ways pricking his soul, but this dark communion... 'Gentle husband, the Good Shepherd offered retribution to the multitude to teach us to turn the other cheek, blessing our adversaries.' Now, the news she had waited so long to share would bring him back to the Lord. 'Nat, dearest, I have something that'll sooth your poor grieving soul. Sweet heart, this terrible war has robbed you of a brother but, God willing, by Christmas you'll have a son.'

*

The widow Banks came on horseback. Helions was expecting her, but not Foxwood. Nobody ever expected Foxwood. The two met in the kitchen, striking an easy confederacy. The agent poured the midwife another restorative whilst she trotted out her secrets to the master of secrets.

Beans spilt, Mrs Wagstaff, who did not approve of Foxwood or his restorative, bundled the midwife into Effam's bedroom. 'My dear, here's good Mrs Banks. She's delivered me eight healthy children and attends all the gentlewomen in the county. Isn't that so, Mrs Banks?'

The old sow grunted, tossing her great leather saddlebag onto the chest at the bottom of the bed. 'Aye, and dragged a fair number of them self same gentry morts into this world withal, ma'am.'

The midwife shot a sly glance at both ladies. 'I did all them Carews. Aye, and on both sides of the blanket.' She hesitated, but Foxwood's restorative made her bold. 'Cap'n Farrington too an' his cousin Thomas. If you take my meaning. She winked lewdly at Mrs Wagstaff, testing the bedstead, plumping up the soft duck pillows. 'Girt big nipper, the Cap'n. Never did see such a one, coming to this world two months before his time an' all.' Discretion overcame the restorative and she muttered the rest into her sleeve. But downstairs Foxwood was committing every detail to his journal. 'Right, missy, up here if you will.'

'The doctor?' Effam protested.

'Ain't available.'

'Mrs Wagstaff, please get the doctor,' said Effam. 'Now.'

'There, there, dear.' Mrs Wagstaff bustled around the room. 'Mrs Banks knows what she's doing, don't you, Mrs Banks?'

'The doctor...' Effam felt her strength draining away.

Now the old woman was dousing her hands with sweet smelling oil from the leather bag. She parted Effam's legs roughly, scanning the room. 'Madam fetch me that,' she nodded at a three-legged stool, 'and put it 'tween Missy's thighs to rest me bones on. Stick one of them bolsters under her arse. That's it. Here we go, deary.'

Effam gasped, the woman beginning her intimate examination. She looked down to see the grizzled head between her legs, arm moving to the left and right. 'Get out!'

Mrs Wagstaff held Effams's shoulders as the widow Banks completed her examination. 'You're as ripe as a pomegranate, missy. All you need's a tonic and my Spanish root to bring you on some.' She rummaged in the bag for more oil, this time dark brown and smelling of liquorice, applying it with her fingers, liberally. 'Birth chute's tight as a clergyman's purse string ducks.' She sniffed, wiping a brawny forearm across her nose. 'But my magical root will make it as broad as the gates of Hades so yer infant can pass. There now.' She pulled out her fingers, wiping them with satisfaction. 'Now here's the restorative that'll make you strong.'

Effam caught a whiff of the concoction and recoiled. 'What's in it?' Newbury had doubled her suspicion of quacks.

'Oh, you needn't worry your head about it, missy. Just some burnt claret with a pennyworth of saffron, a little sugar and an ingredient known only to the apothecary what I bought it off.' Too weak, Effam swallowed the sticky elixir before her body was convulsed with another contraction. 'Very well, deary, push now like you was doing the ordinary deeds of nature.' The midwife pressed down hard on her belly until the contraction passed. With a swig of tonic, she stood back slamming hands on hips. 'You'll have to move on, dear. I've got the curate's wife at Imber on the boil and it's a murderous long ride for an old woman.'

Effam's head was spinning from the elixir but she could tell the last contraction had been weaker than before and knew what it meant.

The old woman was becoming impatient, eyeing the rapidly failing light. 'I'm going to break your waters, missy. Law won't allow me the hooks and crochets the chirurgeons use so I've to rely on the instrument God gave me.' Brandishing her left hand, the crone grinned toothlessly. Effam could see that the nail on her index finger was hornier and much longer than the rest.

'No! Please God!' She pulled back but Mrs Wagstaff was on top of her. Plunging in, the old woman fumbled about until warm liquid spilled between Effam's legs, fingernail snagging the membrane. The midwife's fingers remained in with the contraction passing quickly and feebly, then she pulled them out and her manner was changed. 'Look, deary, I'm going to stick you with more Spanish root and you must finish this bottle o' tonic. I'll be back when I'm done with the curate's wife.' She was wiping her hands, packing up. 'Meantime I'll send for the chirurgeon. He says he's a man-midwife, whatever that is, on account of his iron instruments what we poor women can't have.' Effam's head was spinning with the alcohol. The old woman threw the last of her things in the bag, making for the door.

'My baby?'

215

She half turned. 'Your baby's stuck like a cork in a bottle. The chirurgeon must winkle it out with his tools as best he can.' Effam heard the aside meant only for Mrs Wagstaff. 'If she lives, she'll bring forth no live 'uns, Madam, for her parts are as narrow as the Straits o' Dover. It's a wonder her hubby could sow his seed.' She heaved the saddlebag across her shoulders. 'Must 'ave a dick like a darning needle.'

Biting her lip, Effam turned away, grieving for the last of her line.

XVI

Helions House

May 1646

Effam led the party out through the side door. The red-bricked terrace overlooked a walled enclosure, generously planted by Erasmus Carew. The sun, beating off the grey-green stone, created a warm arbour, full of lavender scent and industrious bees.

'Oh, it's a sort of secret garden. Really, you wouldn't know it was here,' gushed Mrs Wagstaff, cupping one of the vivid red flowers spilling from terracotta pots.

'Cranesbills from Africa,' Effam remarked absently. 'Carew planted them. My botanical calls them geraniums.'

Wagstaff bent stiffly, snorting the blooms like he was taking snuff. 'Uggh! Carew's left 'em to poison you.' He plucked an oversize handkerchief from his sleeve, blowing hard. 'Bloody red see, King's colour. Tip 'em out, man!' He wiped his nostrils, scowling. 'Aye, and our Scotch brethren can keep Charles bloody Stuart. Don't want the scoundrel back.'

'Too right,' said Nat, eyeing Carew's blooms suspiciously. Town criers across the country had been belting out news of the King's flight from Oxford to the chilly embrace of Parliament's Scottish Presbyterian allies. 'A trick up north'll cool those fancy red heels.'

'Hear you've been civilianised.' Major Wagstaff, reduced to a pot-bellied study in broken veins with jowls like mutton chops wedged his buttocks into the small space left by his wife on the stone bench, glaring at the geraniums.

Nat grinned ruefully. 'Yes, Harry, it's true.' Perched on the terrace's low wall, he plucked idly at tufts of grass poking between the coping stones. 'Parliament's Self Denying Ordinance means MPs can't do politicking *and* soldiering. So I'm out of the Army.'

'Well, soldiering's for young 'uns,' observed the Major. 'And now the south's secure, pray God we'll have peace. But mind that conniving weasel Charles Stuart,' Wagstaff admonished him, 'and those Scotch sourbellies.'

'Oh, we've the measure of our gruel-supping brethren.' Nat made a note to have Jessop deal with the geraniums. 'As for the King, he's sent proposals for his restoration.'

'Has he, by Jove?' Bursting more veins, Wagstaff hurled his fist into the air. 'Then sling 'em back, the brute!'

Mrs Wagstaff coughed disapproval. 'England's suffered grievously from this war and the King's to blame. But he's still the Lord's anointed.' She laid a hand on Effam's knee. 'Now, dear, haven't you done well in the garden?'

Effam surveyed with a mixture of indifference and dismay the pots of bright terrace plants and the lavender laced lawn ringed by a gravel path. 'Carew's legacy. But the means to keep it went with him.' She nodded at a wicker basket loaded with freshly cut lavender sprigs. 'So the mistress of Helions turns from huntsman to horticulturalist.'

Effam's surgeon had completed the midwife's grisly work, blood loss and sepsis almost killing her. The same man-midwife confirmed the widow Banks' opinion on Effam's fertility. On hearing the prognosis she had taken to bed and would not be comforted.

But lately Nat had begun to detect weary resignation, a form of settled contentment at Helions among the lavender. Life as the wife of a minor country gentleman did not seem so bad, organising servants, riding to church on Sunday, good works among the poor like she was tending troopers at Newbury. For her sake, he bottled emptiness that often conspired with the black dog to overwhelm him.

Effam twisted the single strand of pearls at her neck, her mother's jewels, thrown on before the Wagstaffs' arrival because Nat liked her in them. 'I hear Sarah Clegg's with child?' After the Newbury fight Effam's maid had found a billet in Mrs Wagstaff's household.

'Yes, I'm afraid so.' Peace had not resolved Mrs Wagstaff's perpetual servant difficulties. 'And her husband's made Sergeant in Colonel Purefoy's regiment so she'll be leaving me, I suppose.'

Wagstaff shuffled uncomfortably on the bench. 'How's old Joe Jessop?'

'Much improved. Learnt his letters and promoted to steward.' Nat grinned, running his fingers through his hair. 'Become quite a figure down the village has, *Mister* Jessop. They'll be electing him sideman next.'

'And I see you've tamed Will Porit,' said Wagstaff.

'Not really.' Nat winked at the Major. 'Will has an eye for the ladies. Given the widow Banks a great deal of work.'

Wagstaff sucked his teeth. 'Well, war's cut the competition.'

'You're right there, Harry.' Nat shook his head, each loss keenly felt. 'Grim reaper's swung his scythe broad and long in these acres. My old ploughman fell at Langport and two stockmen died at the siege of Basing House.'

'What's become of the Earl of Essex?' There were rumours at the Red Lion of Nat's involvement in the Lord General's denouement.

Nat smiled at his part in the Cromwell-inspired army clear out. 'Well, you know my man Foxwood exposed the Earl's double-dealing with the King at Newbury?'

'Foxwood!' Mrs Wagstaff's ears pricked. 'That ghastly little man?' She leant across to Effam. 'My dear, I found him drinking with the midwife Banks. Here. *That* night. Thick as thieves, they were.'

'We hoped the papers we intercepted at Newbury would be the Earl's death warrant.' Nat shrugged. General Waller had tried so hard to indict his rival with the encryption. 'Essex kept his head but not his reputation. He's been allowed to withdraw, so to speak.'

Mrs Wagstaff pursed her lips. Her host collected questionable characters and here was another edging in, snatching away his cap. 'Will Porit.'

'Man here with a message, Cap'n.' Porit eyed Mrs Wagstaff warily. 'Fellow wouldn't give it me, Sir, said you was to have it direct.'

Wagstaff drank up, smacking his lips. 'Well, we'd best be off, Farrington.' He held out a hand to his wife. 'Must be clear of the Common by dusk. It's bad, you know, with the typhus and quartan ague.' Nat heard the burghers of Warminster were bleating about the cost of burials. 'All on account of this unseasonable weather.'

Nat shot the bolts home, pausing with his back against the door. The message, he supposed, would be from Foxwood. But the man he found in the kitchen was not from London.

'Been on the road all day, Cap'n.' The courier sniffed loudly, nodding at the table. 'With not a scrap of pannum or scrape of spreadum to keep a poor body together.'

'Will Porit'll sort you out.' Nat turned to the note marinaded in its sender's venom.

*

He wandered back through the hall and onto the terrace where he stood unable to speak with the paper limply at his side. Effam, happily plucking weeds from the geraniums, was glowing in the warm residue of the evening. 'Good Lord, what's up?'

She took the note, reading swiftly. 'Effam, sweet heart, as God's my witness it was before the Devizes fight,' he stammered. 'Before any understanding passed between us.' She raised a finger, reading and re-reading the scrawl.

Farrington,

You will recall, I hope with as little pleasure as I do, your brief sojourn under my roof, if only for your tumble with my maidservant.

Well, you've a bastard now two years or thereabouts.

My housekeeper, Mrs Cotton, has neglected her proper duties to mind the brat since its mother died and is now widowed. She insists the child's parentage is beyond question and you should know the mother quit this life with an oath in the presence of a parson that she had lain with no other. I too am confident that this is so from my knowledge of the strapper, or lack thereof, if I make myself plain.

The text was indistinct, obscured by blotches of what she assumed was claret.

You'll understand the trouble your incontinence has put me to. It has heightened my distaste for the most regrettable connection we have through my kinswoman, your wife.

I have no wish to support any bastard of yours further so await instructions on what to do with it by return or else I shall be obliged to turn it out.

I am,

Etc.

Tobias Norrington

'I swear there's been no other...' he paused at the painful memory of Le Roux's servant and the chaudepiss, '...since we wed.'

Effam spun away. He reached out, touching her shoulder, feeling her tense, backing off. She stood, head bowed, letter clutched tight. 'This changes everything, Nathaniel, doesn't it?' He shrugged unhappily, wrapped in misery and recrimination. His arms half raised flopped helplessly to his side. She took a while, on the terrace among the geraniums, watching the bees in the lavender.

'You're to send for the child. Quickly, mind, Norrington *will* turn him out.' She turned, taking his stricken face in her hands. 'The Lord's chosen to make me barren but this woman's given the child you long for.'

He knew the protest slipping his lips was unconvincing. 'Sweet heart, truly, I'm content as long as I have you.'

'Ah my poor booby, don't I know you better than you know yourself? You'll resent my empty womb and, in time, you will resent me.' She smiled tightly. 'Don't you see?'

'No. You're wrong. Never.'

'Destroy this.' She handed the letter back. 'Now, listen to me Nathaniel. Taking this child's mother, the Lord's passed her burden to you. That means me. My duty's clear. And no man stands between a Farrington and her duty.'

Effam's hand lingered on his cheek. 'Write to my cousin.' She turned back to the geraniums. 'I'll look after this child as if it was my own.' The snap of scissors in the warm stillness of the evening was the very mildest reproach.

Nat rifled through the flask of pens at Effam's writing table. He thought of their stillborn; a son, although she had never asked. The widow Banks had taken the mangled remains in a box to the sexton and the reverend had concluded the business at night at the foot of the churchyard wall.

Dear Norrington,

I'm grateful for your message. Please send the child to us, with the widow Cotton if she'll come. We'll raise the child as our own, my wife's health being uncertain.

I remain,

Nathaniel Farrington

Nat found the courier with Joe Jessop filling his face. The peasant grunted at the officer thrusting the letter. 'Soon as you're done, take this to your master.'

The man sneered. 'Tomorrow, Cap'n, by your leave, 'cos I reckon to find a bit o' comfort tonight on the Common.' He winked lewdly. 'If you take my meaning, which I'm sure *you* do.'

Jessop lost his patience. Deftly he pulled the chair sending the man sprawling on the stone flags. 'Go now and mind your bleedin' manners.'

'Oh, one thing, before you go.' Nat dug in his pocket, the messenger brightening at the silver penny. 'Norrington's maid, the one dead in childbed two years back, d'you know her?'

The brute shrugged, surprised at the gentleman's interest. 'A rum mort she was, proper lady, unlike 'er mate what was a right little prick-teaser.' The man grinned hideously, mouth a slash of gum and blackened stumps. 'So when she gets up the chuff nobody could work it out. Anyway, took 'er secret to the grave, poor cow.' He passed a grimy fist, one finger missing, across his mouth and leered. 'Ere, Cap'n, weren't you what tupped her, was it?' Nat said nothing, Joe Jessop pursing his lips, eyes on the floor. 'Course not, 'spectable married gent, an' all.' Jamming the letter into his coat pocket, he headed for the yard. 'Probably some young soldier passing through.'

'Yes,' murmured Nat, 'a young soldier passing through.'

XVII

Helions House
Spring 1647
'I spy a break in the weather.' At the south oriel Effam squinted optimistically at a faint clearing in clouds that had been piling in for days. 'Nathaniel, why not ask Will Porit to get the trap out?' Boxed in, she was at her wit's end.

*

Nat unclipped the door, handing her up. 'Where's Oliver?'
Effam was expecting this. 'With Mrs Cotton and a head cold.' She would have to be firm. 'The apothecary's sent liquorice and ordered rest.'
'You can't leave him alone *in the house*, with the housekeeper!'
'Why not?' She knew why not.
He combed a hand through his hair looking up at the smiling face of Helions. 'Sometimes I see flames licking at those eaves, wrapping around the mullions, with Old Ma screaming into the night.'
'You think I don't know? Sweet heart, don't I watch you at night railing against phantoms, comfort you when you jerk awake soaking wet? I know the captain of all your terrors, Nat, the torment of a family left to burn with the housekeeper. But Helions isn't Brook Farm, Nathaniel.'
'And you, as always,' he sighed, 'are right, my love.'
'That's settled then,' she smiled, patting his hand. 'Anyway, how can any harm befall General Cromwell's godson?'
'Aye, I suppose that's right,' said Nat staring anxiously at the house. 'Drive on, Will Porit.'
'Speaking of demons, I often think of my mother,' she said as the coach trundled over the moat, 'with her portrait rotting down there, brooding in the mire like a malign water spirit.' The carriage kicked its heels through the gate and into a blaze of spring sunshine. 'But there comes a time to exorcise our demons.'

Nat's route had celandines, wild daffodils and crimson-tipped daisies brightening the banks and early crimson elm blossom. Pulling over beneath a coppice overlooking strip lynchets clinging to the side of the downs, Will Porit uncoupled the horse, leading it away.

The southerly breeze carried the slightest hint of the sea from just beyond the rolling chalk downland tumbling towards the Dorset coast. Nat picked a posy of dog violet and wood anemone. She smiled at the tiny, delicate blooms, azure and creamy white. 'They're so fragile, transient, a metaphor for life itself.'

'Don't say that,' Nat said. 'It's tempting fate.'

'Silly!' She planted a kiss. 'I'll press them for a keepsake, remembrance of this instant, snatched upon a grassy knoll with my love.'

*

The carriage swerved back through the gates, onto the drive, and chaos.

'What's going on, Nat?' The front of the house was jammed with carts unloading booty under Joe Jessop's supervision.

Nat struck the carriage floor with his cane. 'Oh, blast the man. Told him to have the carriers take the stuff round the back.' He looked at her shame-faced. 'It's my share of loot from Carew's place.' She began picking through the plunder, shaking her head.

'Ah, here's the best bit.' Nat found Jessop puzzling over the trigonometry of a staircase laid out in rough assembly order. 'It'll replace that crude stone arrangement behind the screen. Just need a carpenter to knock it into shape.' Idly Effam's fingers explored the crevices of the foliate head of the green man carved deep in the burnished wood. She marvelled at the entrails of another woman's house laid out in front of her own. Here were panes of subtly tinted glass ready to be tapped into Helions' stone mullions. She imagined sunlight streaming through, dancing merrily on the floor of Carew's mansion. Would it dance on hers?

'You can be sure every gentleman, yeoman and husbandman for miles has been at it.' Nat felt like a schoolboy, mouthing excuses. 'Erasmus Carew'll have four walls and not much else, generous given what he's done to me.' He threw back a tarpaulin revealing the richness of his plunder like a merchant in a souk. Coldly, she inspected strings of plaster relief and stone corbels with rose motifs and petals picked out in red ochre and gold. He turned to face her silent reproach. 'Well, fine,' he fumed. 'Actually I've no more appetite than you for raising Oliver amongst Carew's fancy ware.'

Stooping low and smiling, getting her way without a word, Effam fingered the inscription on the lintel of a stone fireplace partly reconstructed on the grass, translating easily. '*Caelum non animum mutant qui trans mare currunt*. You're sulking.'

'I'm *not* sulking.'

Her lips twitched. 'Well, don't you want to know what it means?' He shrugged. 'Well, it means those who cross the sea change the sky, not themselves.' She squeezed his arm. 'It's from Horace's Epistles. He insists we're unchanged by our journey through life.'

'Lord, I wish it was true.' Nat kicked angrily at the stone. 'Horace, eh? Well, I tell you, *Horace*, that animal Carew and his butcher King would've changed you, my friend.'

'Hush now, sweet heart.' Effam put a finger on his lips. 'The Roman was a poet, not a sage, and England's catastrophe has made a great man of my poor, tongue-tied booby.' She straightened, counting the ways he had changed. 'Anyway, when we're cosy in front of the fire, wind whipping off the downs, I'll not want to gaze on Mr Carew's flummery, however exquisite.'

'Then we'll have it on the terrace,' Nat grinned. 'Park our bottoms on Horace and watch the changing sky.'

Jessop coughed his apologies. 'Mason's here, Sir. You wanted him to fix Carew's spot o' vandalism.' He nodded at the scar in the soft stone above the door. Carew had taken a chisel to the Farrington coat of arms, planning to replace it with the slash of his own crescent moon.

Nat unclipped the signet from the string around his neck, tossing it to the artisan. 'Can you restore the Colonel's badge to its proper place?' He winked the surprise at Effam, sure she would approve.

'No!' She pressed her hands against her mouth. Nat, oblivious to her lonely reconciliation with the end of her line, crushed between the blades of a surgeon's forceps, mutely awaited an explanation. 'No, sweet heart, it was enough you took his name.'

The mason looked on, bemused. 'What'll we fix above your door then, Cap'n?' Nat shrugged. 'A badge, Sir, from your family's coat of arms. It'll be my pleasure to carve it.'

'Got no badge,' Nat snorted, angrily. She had, inexplicably, snubbed a scheme designed for her pleasure and made him look awkward in front of the mason. 'We've always been yeomen with no need for arms. No entitlement either.'

The stonemason struggled to hide his disappointment. 'If you apply, Sir, the heralds won't refuse. You being so distinguished and with a son and a house that's proper handsome,' the mason's practised eye scanned the face of Helions, 'and with such a fine lady on your arm.'

'Can you carve this?' She plucked a tiny anemone from Nat's bouquet. 'A simple Wessex spring flower. What could be better? Yes, let it be the badge of our house.'

The artisan grinned toothlessly. 'Aye, lady, that I can do, and a right pretty one it'll be an' all.'

XVIII

'God's Blood.' Dark, damp and depressing, a trick in the Parliament House and the black dog was snapping at his heels. Nat reached for a twist of the apothecary's wort.

The chamber was pierced by thin light falling in narrow corridors of dust from high windows. And, always, the stink of the river impregnating every pore of the narrow, airless chamber. Two dozen Members who had managed to haul themselves from bed slept on against the hard wood benches on either side. A troika of wigged clerks sat at their table below Speaker Lenthal. Below them the mace, glinting obscenely like a rock on a Spaniard's finger.

A curt nod at Mr Speaker and Nat Farrington, army man, took his place next to Colonel Talbot Purefoy. William Lenthal glared at the two confederates, braced for trouble. A Member in a wide-brimmed hat prodded his neighbour. 'Wake up, it's Cromwell's firebrand.'

Lenthal cleared his throat. 'I have a message petitioning the loan of two hundred thousand pounds in support of the Army.' He glared across the chamber for objections, cursing the man who rose in his place. 'Mr Herbert,' he sighed and muttered, *sotto voce*, 'if you must.'

'City can't extend funds wi' no security,' Herbert whined, rubbing flabby hands. 'What man o' business would contemplate such a thing?'

A ripple of anticipation swept through the chamber. Captain Farrington was on his feet. 'Mr Speaker, the honourable gentleman is a money-grubbing grocer...'

Lenthal leapt up. 'Order! The hon gentleman can't say that.' Though it's true enough, he thought. '*Money-grubbing*; indecorous Sir, unparliamentary. Apologise, Sir.'

'I will not, Sir, apologise to a fat man demanding collateral to prise his fingers from moneybags needed for our army.' Nat sat down heavily, arms folded.

'Order, order.' Lenthal must face down Cromwell's stormy protégé. 'Now, Sir, clement language, and an apology for Mr Herbert.'

Nat, unrepentant, rose again, glaring across the chamber at Herbert. 'I said the honourable gentleman was a money-grubbing grocer. I didn't *need* to say "money-grubbing". I say the honourable gentleman's a grocer, and leave it at that.'

The army faction erupted. 'Bravo!' Nat was their undisputed champion. Talbot Purefoy thumped his back, reckoning John Pym plucked a winner from Wiltshire obscurity and Cromwell was right to promote him.

'Order!' barked Speaker Lenthal. The rough-hewn country captain really had become very good.

Purefoy winked at Nat, hauling up on his good leg. 'If it helps the House, there's the property of papists-in-arms remaining unsequestered. Offer that to secure the merchants' loan.'

'My friend's right,' Nat enthused. 'There are too many delinquents with intact estates and uncollected fines.'

Purefoy continued the double act. 'For example, there's the arch-malignant Erasmus Carew, murderer, arsonist. Army's yet to benefit from his estates.'

'Order!' Lenthal could not allow that. 'The estate of the malignant Carew is not listed in the day's business.'

Nat sat back in his place, arms folded belligerently. Word of Cromwell's fiery young Captain twisting the tail of the City merchants was attracting Members to the chamber. Lenthal called Mr Trenchard. 'Further to the loan, Mr Speaker, there's the matter of the great brass horse of Roehampton, a wicked, malignant relic hauled down by our committee of sequestration.' He beamed around the chamber. 'The army might have the benefit of that.'

A low murmur of approval was cut by Nat's expletive. Rubbing the stubble on his face as he rose, he grinned broadly at his confederates, laying it on thick. 'Army's fortune won't likely turn on a brass nag from Surrey, now will 'e?'

'Order, order!' Lenthal struggled to keep a straight face. 'Is it the wish of the House that the Roehampton property be seized for the benefit of the army?'

'Aye, aye.'

Nat slouched back muttering darkly to his neighbour. 'Cheapskates like Herbert'll pull purse strings tighter than a duck's arse for as long as the Army lacks a majority.'

'Aye.' Talbot Purefoy massaged his mangled thigh, twisting the bindings that held the peg-leg in place. 'Suit those blood suckers to have the King back tomorrow.'

Nat winced at the red-raw stump beneath the Colonel's breeches. 'Those clowns,' he nodded at the benches opposite, 'blame evil counsellors, creatures like Carew. Chop 'em, they say, and Charles'll be a good 'un like his father.'

'Plenty still believe it, Nat.' Purefoy lifted the reseated prosthetic so it jutted into the aisle to send the unwary tumbling into the pit. Nat had seen him deftly remove the obstruction from the path of his friends and his face crease at his opponents prostrated in front of the clerk's table. 'There's even some on our own side saying Charles might yet rule again with a godly Parliament pressing a knife to his back.' He lowered his voice. 'Others mutter into their cups that he must die.'

Nat nodded gravely, but said nothing. Just one man knew his thinking on Charles Stuart; that it was as hard as gritstone since his brother's death at Naseby.

That man, Nat's constant admirer, kept to the shadows. He was admiring Nat now. From his eyrie the watchman cast a jaundiced eye over the Long Parliament. 'Windbags and petty-foggers,' muttered Foxwood. 'Set me a pretty task, you did, John Pym, navigating this sea of hereditary half-wits with my Adonis.'

But there was a secret known only to Foxwood, a twist that had tumbled from the mouth of a drunken midwife preparing to botch the birth of an only child.

The conjoint object of the watcher's desire and ambition rose in his place, moving towards the bar of the House. As Nat left the chamber, his admirer padded from the shadows to his side.

'Ah, Foxwood, you're never far away.' With a nod at the sentry, Nat swung the heavy black cloak around his shoulders, clipping a silver fastening beneath his chin. 'What d'you want? I'm in a crashing hurry.'

'Indeed you are, Sir.' The clerk fussed like a spaniel under Nat's heels, papers clamped under his bad arm. 'You're away to the Red Lion to parley with the committee of sequestration.'

'Then you'll know why.' Barging through the chaos of Westminster Hall, Nat's leg had shortened his temper. 'God's blood, Foxwood, wish I'd left this thing at Devizes like peg-leg Purefoy.' Le Roux's pus-letting knife would do the trick but the apothecary would only intervene if there was fever.

A tatmonger peddling ribbons and laces sent Foxwood flying. 'Look where you're going, bleedin' cripple,' snarled the tradesman.

Cursing, Nat heaved Foxwood to his feet, dusting him down. 'Mind your manners, oaf, or I'll put you out.'

The tatmonger paled, seeing the cripple was Nat's man and, worse, who the cripple was. 'Oh, Sirs, pardon me.' Knuckling his forehead, he grovelled for the scattered papers.

'Now Sir, you're off to strip Carew's estate, like you said in the Commons,' said Foxwood snatching the papers.

'Aye, troupe of Jesuit-loving charlatans.' They were at the great north door, shoving through the crush of New Palace Yard. 'This blatherskite House thinks the Army'll be palmed off with a brass trinket from Roehampton!'

'Erasmus Carew's lobbyists have been most persuasive.' Foxwood had to shout. 'But, if I may, Sir, I've taken the liberty of obtaining a copy of the relevant ordinance.' He fussed with the papers, losing control of them again, the precious file disappearing under the feet of the crowd pressing towards Whitehall. 'Fuck off!' He was scratching in the dirt. 'Go on, get out the way. Tossers!' Flicking muck from the binding, he fished a page from the file. 'Here, I have it.' Inching though the press, he brandished the statute like a weapon. 'You'll see it lays out the sequestering of malignants' estates for the army's benefit.'

Nat batted the paper away. 'Don't need your ordinance to know Carew's estate should be vit'ling the army, not keeping him in claret. Why's the committee not done its duty, eh?' He grinned at the little man sheltering in his lee. 'Aw, my blood's too hot. Come on, Foxwood, your lawyerly ways'll appeal to these *gentlemen* when an ill-tempered farmer cannot.'

'Thank you, Sir,' lisped Foxwood. Lord, how his loins ached for Nathaniel Farrington. He wondered if he should spill the secrets winkled from the midwife Banks. But the old cow's testimony might dampen the feud with Erasmus Carew and it was serving him well. Best keep quiet, for now.

After they had elbowed through Purefoy's gatehouse onto Whitehall, the traffic eased a bit and Foxwood no longer had to shout. 'The procedure's this, Sir. The county sequestration committee applies to the Commons committee in respect of those considered delinquent and those believed papists.' He paused. It was important Nat understood. 'If deemed papists their property can be sold and that's an end of it. If they're considered merely delinquent they may compound with the committee and simply pay a fine.'

A string of donkeys with sacks of corn slung on either side blocked the way. 'God's blood!' Nat's boot sank in a pile of shit. He kicked against the cobbles, scraping away the muck. 'Carew's a papist, a fine's no good. I want his estate parcelled up, sold to arm Fairfax and Cromwell. Got it?'

Foxwood shook his head. 'That's for the gents of the county committee. Here's the list.'

Nat scanned fifteen names but only one interested him. 'Bloody Tobias Norrington,' he snarled, crumpling and tossing the paper. 'So now we know why the county committee hasn't done for Carew.'

'Indeed. The Wiltshire committee sequestration's thin as gossamer. Its capricious gentlemen have a high reputation for self-service,' said Foxwood. 'Look out, Sir, more shit.' Nat stepped short, avoiding another steaming obstruction.

The Red Lion's landlord nodded Foxwood to the fug at the end of the room. In its furthest recess two high-backed benches lined a rough table. Against the wall perched three members of the committee eyeing the arrival beneath stiff, wide brimmed hats.

'Good day, gentlemen.' None of the members rose as Nat squeezed himself onto the empty bench. 'Sequestration, Sirs. The Army expects better, *demands* better.' He leant forward, menacingly, rapping out frustration on the table. 'Cromwell keeps a tally of committee *gentlemen* whose receipts disappoint him.' The committee said nothing. 'And you laggards leave the murdering papist Erasmus Carew unmolested.' Nat jammed his face at the president, jabbing a finger on the table beneath the man's nose. 'I'm wondering what inducements have been offered...'

Pelham's icy glare fixed the yeoman upstart from the shadow of his hat. 'Papist, eh? Evidence, young man, of communion with Rome or

Carew'll be fined for delinquency, and nought else,' he sneered. 'As for inducement, *Captain*, look to your own morals before doubting those of a gentleman.' The hat twitched slighted, left and right. 'We learn you've been through Carew's house like a maggot through a cider apple. Bad form, Sir, badly done.' Pelham shook his head sorrowfully, fiddling with a letter in a familiar hand. 'And, Sir, what's this about your interest in the land you'd have us confiscate? Fields, Norrington says, grubbed by you, *personally*.' His nose twitched. 'And recently too, judging by the stink. Have you stepped in something, Sir?'

'A soldier needs no lectures from soft-skinned so-called gentlemen.' Nat slammed his palm over Norrington's report, curling his fingers, grinding the heavy bond into a ball. 'Look to your duty, man, as better men have to theirs. Such men as have *grubbed* their fields, bled too, keeping the likes of you safe in bed.' Tossing the paper into Pelham's lap, he towered over the Commons committee. 'I'll see Erasmus Carew's estate carved up, sold to the highest bidder. Be sure of it!'

'Well I think we're done.' Pelham sucked his teeth, unwrapping the paper ball, smoothing it. 'And we've others to hear before supper.'

Nat turned on his heels. In the press he had not seen Compton loitering at the door. But Foxwood, who missed nothing, had. Foxwood, the agent, with his notes and files and skein of contacts, had learnt a great deal about Compton. Limping in Nat's wake, he twisted to see the committee rise to greet Hinton's other Member of Parliament.

Through the fog of the Red Lion, Foxwood laid his black mark on Compton. But such a well-connected gentleman must be taken apart carefully, in the shadows without any suspicion of his master's hand in it. Foxwood's clients always had spotless hands.

XIX

Helions House

Summer 1648

Effam reached for a small, stoppered bottle of greenish glass on a piece of twine nailed to the kitchen door.

'Tis a witch bottle, Madam,' said Mrs Cotton casually as she pummelled more flour into the dough. 'Put there so the hags and harpies go a-riding on some other poor body. Filled it, I have, with vervain root from the foot of Calvary's cross.'

'I'm not sure I approve.'

'Ah, well, Madam, there's dark 'uns out there, see.' She sniffed, nodding into the gloom. 'Like the Cap'n's man Foxwood.' She lowered her voice, fists deep in the dough. 'He's a tankerabogus Ma'am, make no mistake, sliding in here after dark without a by-your-leave, a regular boggart.' Face tightening, she rolled the preparation, thumping it down hard. 'You keep that boy away from him.'

Effam shook her head, but left the charm where it was. 'Dear me, mustn't fill Oliver's head with country nonsense.' She scooped the boy up, smothering him with love.

'Careful, Madam.' Mrs Cotton turned from the bread mix, banging her hands together in a cloud of flour, judging the lady's colour. Yellow, that's what, and skin like gossamer pulled tight over those high cheekbones. Aye, that's it, all skin and bones. 'The doctor, remember?'

'Oh, doctors, what do they know?' But lifting Oliver had sapped her strength. 'Mama had her fill of chirurgeons on Newbury field, didn't she?'

Nat had rescued Foxwood from the kitchen where he was pinned by Mrs Cotton's disapproving eye. In the evening half-light they walked from the yard to the walled garden through the postern gate. Dealing briskly with events swirling and eddying about Whitehall, the agent indulged him in the habitual prelude to his master's preoccupation, the purpose of his visit, Erasmus Carew.

'You're the master of dispatches, Foxwood.' He could not know the reports sent from London were drafted in a lover's hand. 'But apparently I'm not your only correspondent.' Nat plucked a sprig of lavender, rubbing it between thumb and forefinger. 'It's said you feed half the news books of London.'

'No Sir!' The gossip annoyed Foxwood because it was true. An agent must live in the shadows.

'It's said you keep a journal.' Nat raised the crushed herb to his nose. 'Foxwood's diary of secrets.'

'Ah, now that's true. But it's a flimsy, inconsequential tome. Weather, what I ate, that kind of thing.' If only his Captain knew the mischief sealed between the tooled leather covers of slim volumes deposited with the goldsmith in his Cheapside strongroom.

'You're a liar, Foxwood,' said Nat.

Foxwood smiled, a semblance of sweetness. 'Whatever you say, Sir.'

Nat passed his hand through his hair. 'You know, Foxwood, even with your dispatches I'm struggling to keep up with events.'

'Aye, well, with Essex finally nailed up in his mobile coffin and Sir William Waller exiled, things have changed whilst you've been languishing in this poxed backwater,' said Foxwood. 'You're missing the Cromwell ascendancy.'

'Well then, I've got some good news,' beamed Nat. 'I'm coming back to Westminster.'

Foxwood's hands flew to his face. 'Oh, *Sir*, how pleased I am!' He resented his Adonis rotting in shit-shovelling obscurity beneath the thumb of the stuck-up bitch Euphemia Farrington. For all the distractions of 1648, Nat, object of Foxwood's unrequited love, was the unwavering point in his constellation. In his mind they were lovers among the lavender, striding out in the twilight at Helions. But as the year tipped into summer, he knew that Nat's preoccupation remained the fulfilment of his oath and that five years was a long time to wait.

'Sir, I've got news too.' Foxwood was itching to tell him.

'Indeed.'

'Oh yes,' gloated Foxwood. 'You see, Miles Compton's been interfering with the Board of Sequestration, on Carew's behalf. Compton's your lodestar, Sir. My list of disaffected persons revolves around him.' He smiled, composing his intelligence, enough to hang a man. 'And Mr Compton has a younger brother.'

Nat shrugged. 'People do. I did.' He pulled a run of ivy from the wall. 'Put to earth at Naseby, by that *bastard*.'

Sweet innocent, thought Foxwood. The midwife's intelligence on his master's pedigree was a treat in store, tucked away in the goldsmith's vault. 'Ah, but Miles and Benedict are like two peas in a pod, excepting the cruel birthmark smeared across the face of the younger man. And young Benedict Compton has been a very busy boy.'

'Tell me.' Foxwood now had his full attention. Nat was sure the cavalier he narrowly escaped after the Devizes fight and the gallant bowling into him on the *Deliverance* was the same Miles Compton that offered his hand on polling day. But Foxwood's inquiries had confirmed that Miles could not have been at either place. Benedict, however …

'Benedict Compton was recognised on the quayside at Lymington by a soldier who once worked for the family. He was boarding a vessel, for Yarmouth *on the Isle of Wight*.' Foxwood gripped Nat's arm. 'You appreciate the sensitivity, Sir?'

'Of course,' snapped Nat. 'The Wight holds the most important prisoner in the land.' Some warships had mutinied off the Downs and there were rumours of plans to spring His Majesty from the island.

'Quite.' Foxwood shook a large cotton square from his sleeve, blowing loudly. 'Pollen, Sir, always starts me off. Your poxed countryside's no good for me, really it isn't.' He dabbed his eyes, blew again, spinning it out. 'Anyway, my soldier knuckled his forehead saying "Good morning Mr Compton, Sir" as you'd expect. But the gentleman turned away. Said he didn't know him.'

The evening had turned cold, the hall's warm tallow lights and congenial chit-chat beckoning. 'How can you be sure it was the brother and not the man?'

Foxwood sneezed, cleared his throat and fired a gobbet of phlegm at the lavender. 'Because Miles was in London building the best defence in the world.' He paused dramatically, enjoying the suspense. 'What d'you think that was?' Nat shrugged. 'Well, blighter's holding forth in the Commons, of course! Each friggin' word faithfully scratched by the clerks and a dozen unimpeachable witnesses looking on.'

'D'you say Benedict Compton had some sort of birthmark? Bloody hell, Foxwood, I'd forgotten the face powder!' Pleased with the epiphany, Nat scythed his cane through the lavender. 'Bloke on the *Deliverance* was wearing powder. Like a woman.' He raised the silver pommel to his lips. 'Reckon it hid a mighty inconvenient badge for a King's agent.'

'Yes, but that's just the start,' smirked Foxwood. 'Next day Charles Stuart receives a book with an escape plan leafed inside.' He thrust a paper at Nat. '*Voilà!*' Dark eyes plumbed for a reaction. 'Perhaps you'll recognise the hand?'

'Carew.'

'I believe so, yes, but unsigned and unsealed, of course, so on its own it'll stretch no necks.' Foxwood carefully folded and replaced the document. 'And the King pours cold water on the scheme in the reply sent by courier to Yarmouth.' He patted the breast of his doublet. Carew's letter might yet bluff a confession. 'The courier's place was taken by Governor Hammond's sergeant who made the rendezvous.'

'And the Comptons?'

Foxwood held up a finger, coming to the clever part. 'In Yarmouth a villain dressed as a seaman receives the message but the sergeant's too slow and the bastard gets a way.'

'Compton?'

'Benedict Compton. Hammond thought he'd foiled a ruse by another cavalier romantic, but he lacked my Lymington intelligence.' Foxwood smiled viperously. 'For a few pennies my informant identified Compton's vessel. Its skipper was less helpful. Had to be coaxed.'

Nat ignored the nature of Foxwood's encouragement. 'Nobody else privy to this?' Foxwood shook his head. 'Make sure it gets no further than your damned journal.'

'Aye, Sir.' But a plot to spring the King was leagues from a feud between two country gentlemen. Foxwood would prosecute his master's dark business, but with an eye to a much bigger prize: the indictment of Charles Stuart. 'By your leave, Sir, I'm away to squeeze those Comptons, like grapes in a press.'

'Keep it lawful, Foxwood.' Nat winced. 'D'you understand?'

'Oh, Sir, I understand. *Perfectly.*'

Nat rounded on him. 'You're thinking what lily-livered poltroon wills the ends but not the means, eh?'

'You know *what* I'll do,' said Foxwood wearily, plucking the cloth from his sleeve, rubbing his eyes. '*How* I do it is my business.'

Nat turned his back. 'Just do it, Foxwood.'

'Aye.' Unseen, the cold-blooded schemer's mouth contorted sardonically. 'Thank you, Sir.'

'Supper, Foxwood?' Say no, say no, he begged silently, willing the man to slip away in the night. 'Major Wagstaff is dining with us.'

'No. My servant's secured lodgings in Blandford.' He grinned. 'Busy day, tomorrow.'

Nat watched the saturnine clerk vanish into the gloom and shuddered, throwing the bolts across. Oliver bowled into him. 'Steady, trooper!' He threw his giggling, golden boy into the air. General Cromwell's godson, spinning around in Nat's arms and planted at Effam's feet.

She held her tussle-headed boy tight, wiped her eyes and packed him off with a kiss. 'God keep you, sweet heart.' Oliver Farrington, smiling brightly, padded through the screen with Mrs Cotton. Wagstaff, beetroot red on Nat's liquor, clapped his host on the back, too hard. 'Fine lad, Farrington. You're a lucky cove.'

Nat caught his wife's eye. 'Aye, I am that.'

*

Foxwood arrived at the Comptons' New Forest estate with his commission, servant, a platoon from Hurst Castle and two artisans with their gear.

'Our stock in trade should extract the means of destroying Mr Carew and his circle,' said Foxwood to his man. The brothers' fate hung in the balance of the agent's lurid imagination.

'Blackmail?' sneered the servant.

'Aye.' He tipped his chin at the artisans. 'If not, we'll unleash them. Doubt the brothers will resist long but if they do I'll draw them to the Tower on a tumbrel. Constable can press them for evidence admissible at the King's trial. With care and the devil's luck we'll skewer Carew and the King today.'

Pale-faced Benedict Compton answered the door, ushering the party into the hall. Foxwood's eyes widening at the breakfast table. 'I'll overlook your exploits at Devizes.' He plunged a corner of white bread in a beaker of whey, waving in his servant. 'That was a fight with honour and ignominy, on both sides.' Foxwood continued his survey of the Compton's table, plunging a finger into some oats and warmed milk. 'Needs a scrape of nutmeg that.' He shoved the bowl away. 'But communing with the traitor Biles, running errands for the whore-Queen...' Wagging the licked finger, his face set in a rictus grin with a scrap of anchovy between his teeth. 'And now this...' He flipped Carew's escape plan from his doublet. 'Your contrivance to spring Charles Stuart. Bungled, of course, but incompetence never saved a man.' Miles Compton's protest was dismissed with a cut of the agent's hand. 'My master's a fair man. Says I should act *appropriately*. So, gentlemen, here's the plan.' The Comptons were hanging on his words. 'Word must reach me by Lammastide that the Board of Sequestration has appropriated Erasmus Carew's estates, all of them, and those of his bitch wife.'

Miles Compton shook his head, eyeing the artisans. Foxwood hacked off a wedge of turkey pie. 'Haven't you got anything stronger than whey?'

'Small beer or a glass of claret?' suggested Benedict.

'Nah, you're alright. My lads are better when they're sober,' said Foxwood grinning at the artisans. 'Look, I want a list of Carew's confederates too. Oh, and the cunts involved in His Majesty's attempt to escape Hampton Court and the Isle of Wight fiasco.' He tipped his chin at the artisans. 'These two gents'll help.' With their blocks and ratchets, the sort of assistance the craftsmen offered was plain to see. 'And my man'll scribe for you.' Foxwood's servant was rooting in his satchel for pen and paper. 'Once I've got my list and word's passed about the sequestration, you can leave the country.' Faux smile evaporating, he measured each word carefully. 'But know this, if either of you whoresons falter, I'll personally impale the other's head on a spike, by God I will.' He paused, contemplating Benedict stripped and wriggling under the knife of the public executioner. Letting the lithe little bird fly would be a shame. 'Oh, and my master would want Colonel Carew to know the author of his misfortune. Yes, yes, I'm quite sure he would.'

Ashen-faced, the Comptons weighed their situation and Foxwood's reputation. 'Carew's very run down, you know,' spluttered Miles Compton. 'Gristle and bone really. And his son still warm in the ground from consumption, just one still drawing breath. Your gentle master might show some... compassion?'

'Compassion, *compassion*?' spat Foxwood, food spraying across the table. 'On the contrary, if what you say's true, the consumption marches in step with my master. You see, gentlemen, Carew's death at the snatch of a rope ain't good enough. Your friend, cowering in his damp Dutch squalor, should know my patron's bent on the complete annihilation of his line. If misadventure's left just one rat in the nest, it's one too many!'

Miles Compton bowed his head. 'And who is this poor tortured soul with a heart as black as sea coal?'

'Surely you're not so blind?' Foxwood was disappointed the brothers' cooperation had been secured so easily, without the assistance of his artisans. Noisily sucking each fingertip in turn, he leered at Miles. 'My special care these past months has been the honourable and gallant member who sits with you at Westminster.'

*

The Squire and his lady sat in the front pew on the right with Oliver, fractious after the Reverend Nicholas Sedgwick's epic. The newly installed fresh-faced vicar glanced nervously at the Member of Parliament and the formidable Mrs Farrington. Stony-faced, she hissed in Nat's ear. 'Two hours and none the wiser.'

Nat's throat made a noise like a horse on a hot day. 'Well, it's a damned sight better than three hours of Markham. God rest him.'

'True,' she conceded, nodding at Carew's smashed window, sparkling with the plain glass installed by her father before he rode to his death at Devizes. 'Doesn't it look well in this light?'

Nat grunted. He privately disapproved of the original violation. 'Time to eat.' Ruffling the boy's hair, he gathered up their prayer books.

The mellow, golden summer had brought peace to England and to Nat unimagined happiness, gently husbanding Helions with the help of sinecures awarded by Pym and Cromwell. But in London, Parliament's failure to bring the King to trial had fractured the army's patience. Nat had risen in the House to press the Army Remonstrance demanding Charles be charged with high treason. The die was cast.

In the porch Nat pressed Nicholas Sedgwick's hand. 'Nice sermon, Reverend.' The parson gulped thanks.

'But too long,' barked Effam, whispering to Nat; 'Westminster's taken my farmer's plain speaking for a politician's silver tongue.'

Restoring the vicar's spirits in a glance, Nat took Oliver's hand and the family tripped off towards the carriage. But a pale young man was skulking at the lynch gate.

'Uggh!' barked Effam. 'What's he doing here?' It was Foxwood's servant with a note. Nat flicked it open.

Westminster

10 December 1648

Sir,

Today the Board of Sequestration forfeited the estates of the recusant Erasmus Carew and his wife. Praise be.

Nat smacked the page. 'God be praised!'

As I write London is abuzz with the arrest last night of a dozen disaffected persons from Compton's list. They are all confederates of your great enemy and implicated in schemes to restore the King. I fear the headsman will be busy.

Nat sensed the agent's relish, and the irony in what came next.

It is my painful duty to report that among this company is your wife's cousin, Tobias Norrington, who yesterday was admitted to the Tower through that gate from whence there is no return.

Messrs Miles and Benedict Compton were reported to have slipped past our guards in Ramsgate on a cutter bound for the Low Countries, in accordance with my undertaking.

However, on 6th inst Colonel Pride purged the Parliament of the weaker sort. The Rump, as the news books have it, is resolved to impeach the King for treason.

'Your cousin Norrington's been arrested. It looks bad for him. And the King's set for the scaffold. Praise be.'

Given the change in political weather, I felt it expedient to advise the Constable of the Comptons' flight which bears witness to their guilt. I'm told the brothers are now on their way to the Tower to await interview in the matter of the King.

I trust this meets with your approval and that we will have the pleasure of seeing you in London soon.

I remain etc

Foxwood

'I don't give a damn for Norrington or those Compton saps,' grinned Nat. 'Dead meat, they were, the moment they crossed Foxwood.'

The warmth of her Sunday passed in a shiver. 'Nat, be careful, of Foxwood.'

'O Foxwood, wonderful, artful, Foxwood,' Nat kissed the letter, bouncing with glee on the ball of his toes. 'Don't you see? Now we've nailed the bastard.' He continued his jig as she looked on askance, hands plunged deep in her fur. 'I must return to London, but first to Carew's.'

'What'll you do there?' The long summer had reduced Nat's reliance on Le Roux's wort and the obsession with Carew, though never far from the surface, was dormant, she thought. Now, his wild-eyed joy at Foxwood's news gripped her with a new and terrible foreboding. She pulled Oliver close, shielding him from Nat's unbottled insanity.

'Why, parcel up the Carew estate for sale to as many London merchants as I can find.' He clamped her tense form in his arms. 'Don't you see? Once they're reassigned, he'll never prise those burghers' sticky fingers off his acres. Whoreson and his tribe are as good as in the gutter!'

XX

Westminster

29 January 1649

John Bradshaw took his duties grimly. Before him, the death warrant, awaiting seals and signatures to send its subject to the scaffold.

With the exception of the Lord President, those assembled in the Painted Chamber were united in a nervous skittishness, a silliness cloaking the burden they all felt. The act itself was inconsequential enough. Several of them had sent men to die more horribly than the manner prescribed for the unfortunate named in the warrant. But to kill a King, God's anointed, was a very grave matter indeed.

And the grand families of the Commissioners owed their dignity to a hierarchy topped with a King. Burdened by the conservatism of having something to lose, their obsession was the mob. Some of those gathered in the January gloom saw in the King's predicament a foreshadowing of their own. They felt for their necks and wondered if in a world turned upside down it would be the mob or a prince's revenge that would do for them. Indeed, several of those commissioned to try the King had absented themselves. A mark withheld might save a man's life, fortune and posterity. And relinquish his honour.

There were men there familiar enough with the atmosphere of fragile, nervous merriment that bound them together in shared adversity. It had salved the desperate, gut-wrenching fear that froze men facing off across the fields of Naseby, Marston Moor, Devizes and the decade's hundred battles and skirmishes.

Even Cromwell larked about, uncharacteristically. On a whimsy he reached over the shoulder of Richard Ingolsby, stabbed his forefinger in the pewter inkwell and dabbed Henry Marten on the nose and forehead amusing everyone except dour, unbending John Bradshaw.

Lord President Bradshaw, disliked and mistrusted, longed to surrender an office he had never sought and return to the country. He had always struggled with his fractious Commission but now, at the end of it, with his soft voice breaking over the grim document, the room was quiet as the grave. 'At the High Court of Justice for the trying and judging of Charles Stuart King of England January 29 in the year of our Lord 1649.' Bradshaw paused, tugging at his unyielding collar, scanning the sixty great men packed in tight. 'Whereas Charles Stuart, King of England, is and standeth convicted attained and condemned of High Treason and other High Crimes. And sentence upon Saturday last was pronounced against him by this Court, to be put to death by the severing of his head from his body. Of which sentence yet remains to be done. These are therefore to will and require you to see the said sentence executed in the open street before Whitehall upon the morrow, being the thirtieth day of this instant month of January between the hours of ten in the morning and five in the afternoon of the same day with full effect. And for so doing this shall be your sufficient warrant. And these are to require all officers and soldiers and other the good people of this nation to be assisting unto you in this service. Given under our hands and seals.'

Again, Bradshaw glanced along the line of pale, expectant faces, the instrument of regicide hovering over the warrant, inked up, ready to condemn them all. All eyes were drawn to it, the Lord President scratching his cramped signature, top left. A clerk fussed with wax at his shoulder dripping it to the right of the mark. Bradshaw sunk his seal defiantly and, staring straight ahead, shifted the paper to his right. Thomas Gray grasped at it, looping his signature with a swagger. Cromwell, taking the pen, paused, theatrically. 'Gentlemen, this is but a cruel necessity.'

One by one they fixed their mark. There were men that had seen too much blood shed on English soil. Nat knew them. They signed with jaw-clenching resolve and soldiers' tight-lipped conviction. The others, lawyers and soft, cunning men viewed the King's sins in abstract, and wavered. Edmund Harvey, Alderman Pennington and William Heveningham each passed the document unmarked and left the room uncomfortably. Against their marks, the seals of gentlemen spotted the paper like drops of blood making it stiff. Round it went, coming to rest before irresolute John Downes and Thomas Waite. Rising heavily from his place, Cromwell moved behind them, hissing in Downes' ear. The man paled, shaking his head mournfully at the dangerous instrument. 'Gentlemen, our court's an exceptional thing. It does not follow the ancient laws of England and, on my life, I fear the King is right to question its legitimacy. His Majesty should be allowed to address the Lords and Commons.'

Cromwell slammed the table setting the inkpot dancing, its contents creeping towards the parchment like dark venous blood. 'Is he guilty?'

The wretched man could hardly be heard. 'Yes.'

'IS HE GUILTY?'

'Yes, yes.'

'Then sign. Or be damned!'

Downes scratched his mark. Absently, Nat noted the white cuff at his wrist blacken, its fabric sucking up the spilt ink.

Cromwell was now leaning over poor Thomas Waite. With a furtive glance at Downes, he too added his signature. Nat was next. He seized the pen, the clerk setting down the paper and inkwell. 'The traitor Charles Stuart burned my farm, spilt my blood. This *King* brought my dear ones to dust.' In great bold letters he made his mark. *Nathaniel Salt...* 'Damnation!' He poked at the ink and wrote again, striking out the slip. *Farrington.* 'There, gentlemen, I do this with all my heart, for all my kind.' He rose unsteadily, leg raw and stinking despite Le Roux's embrocation. 'You, popinjays, with your fancy ways and nice distinctions, can spit in the eyes of common soldiers. But remember, *gentlemen*, us dirt poor farmers, city 'prentices, decayed serving men, tumbledown tapsters, you snigger at behind pretty nosegays. *We* delivered our godly common wealth. I may be a simple yeoman, the son and grandson of yeomen, we may be rough in our ways, clumsy in speech, but I tell you such men are the hammer and anvil in the forge of our nation. And only the blood of a King can cure the blade.' Nat slammed the new seal into hot red wax. His device, a simple anemone plucked from a Wiltshire field on a spring morning for his love, was there with all the rest. Oliver Cromwell, silently, moved behind his country Captain and, gently, pressed his shoulders.

The last man, Corbet, fixing his seal, Cromwell snatched the paper triumphantly, thrusting it at Edward Dendy, Sergeant-at-Arms. 'There man, it is done. Now do your duty.'

Bradshaw rose for the last act of his commission. 'With the leave of the Commission established for the trying of the traitor Charles Stuart the Sergeant will repair with our warrant to the Lieutenant of the Tower in whose custody the bright execution axe for the executing of malefactors is, there to command him to deliver unto the said Edward Dendy Esquire, Sergeant at Arms attending this Court, the said axe and for his so doing this shall be our warrant.'

Beyond the Painted Chamber, in the maelstrom of retainers waiting for their masters, two men stood uncompanionably.

'Hear you're newly wed, friend,' lisped Foxwood. 'To the widow Clegg.'

'Aye, to my Sarah.' Joe Jessop blew into his hands and turned away.

'That'll be *Arthur* Clegg's wife then.'

'Arthur's dead.'

'Clearly.'

The door crashed open for the Sergeant at Arms on his commission. Foxwood and Jessop looked for Nat and their instructions.

*

The business drawing Members across London in the early morning mist was substantial. The House must approve an Act against the acclamation of Charles Prince of Wales following the deed to follow later in the day that Parliament had already endorsed. After all, there was little to be gained by striking the head from a King if another emerged like Hydra from damp exile in the Low Countries.

The House had heard politely and refused emissaries from the continent petitioning for the King's life. Each Ambassador in turn filed in with his appeal, knowing the hopelessness of his quest. Actually, few could care less for the welfare of Charles Stuart. But the sensibilities of their uncomfortable guest Queen Henrietta Maria and her bloated family must be accommodated. Job done, they retired to their fires and their claret and sent servants to stand in the cold below the scaffold in order to inform their dispatches.

'It's midday and I'm thinking the Act won't be passed today,' said Nat. 'And without third reading the King's head'll stay on his shoulders.' Nat limped from the Commons picking up Foxwood and Jessop in the lobby. 'Come on, I must brief Cromwell.'

Commissary General Henry Ireton had chilly premises among the warren of sets in the palace of Whitehall that had been occupied by courtiers during the reign of the man they were intent on killing. Nat found the trinity, Cromwell, Fairfax and Ireton, bunched glumly at the window, overlooking the frozen expanse of the Thames.

'God's blood, Farrington, it'll be dark by four and the mob's grown restive right down Whitehall,' said Ireton. 'The King must not see another dawn yet we cannot permit this execution until the Bill has been read thrice.'

'But, Ireton, there's something else, isn't there?' said Cromwell. 'The small matter of the King's executioner.'

Nat was surprised the arrangements he had seen underway that morning outside the Banqueting House had not been completed. Where was the public executioner, the notorious Richard Brandon?

'Aye, Oliver.' Sheathed in a thick blanket, Ireton glared at Cromwell. 'My man found Brandon in his lodgings. Blind drunk, swearing he'd sooner do the Tyburn jig than separate the King from his head.' He drew the blanket tight across hunched shoulders, condensation shaping his breath. 'Fetched him back with his apprentice and their apparatus, but neither can be relied upon. We're trawling for good strong fellows to take their place.' A woodsman or countryman, thought Nat, someone whose axe would do the business at first strike. Across Ireton's shoulder he hovered dreamily over the river winterscape. Lads skimmed across the glistening grey esplanade. Tradesman had been tempted onto the thickening ice with braziers but were now touting mainly on Whitehall among the expectant crowds.

'Offered forty sergeants a hundred for a headsman but each blackguard refused,' grumbled Ireton. 'What d'you make of that?'

'Damn Brandon!' Cromwell hit the stone column. 'There's none finer.' He sucked his skinned knuckles. 'Did for Strafford with utmost facility and, damn me, he'll do the same for the King, or hang.'

Fairfax pursed his lips sardonically. 'Hugh Peters volunteered.'

'Of course he has,' scoffed Cromwell. 'Reverend gentleman's mad as a box of frogs. But he'd have difficulty slicing through butter, ain't that so, Farrington?'

'General?' Run, run, he thought, on your poisoned leg, across the frozen river, south and home. 'Eh, well, all of London and all the Princes of Europe are watching, Sirs. We can't afford Brandon messing up.'

'Aye,' wheezed Ireton, 'get this wrong and it'll be our heads on the block.'

'Out of my way.' Colonel Hacker, fresh from the Commons, barged through the anteroom clerks. 'General, they've passed third reading. We can go.'

'With what, Hacker?' Ireton gave a small hysterical laugh, like a girl. 'Unless you've got a man that can swing an axe.'

Cromwell turned on the two hardened soldiers. 'Colonel Hacker, Captain Farrington, *you're* to do it. It's no business of any other gentleman here.' Seizing a pen from the clerk, Cromwell wasted little time scribbling the death instruction. 'Here, find a headsman, or do it yourself.' The men charged with the day's grim business exchanged anxious glances. 'Fairfax thinks the King's head can remain where it is,' hissed Cromwell to no-one in particular. 'But for as long as this man remains alive, we'll have no peace, no respite and no sanctuary. All, together or separately, will take his place on that scaffold.' Cromwell banged out into the corridor, spinning round to bark his final injunction. 'I charge you both with the orderly and decorous removal of the head of Charles Stuart before the day's out.'

'Well, old mate,' blusterous Colonel Hacker gripped Nat's arm, 'looks like Parliament's grand affair's been dumped in our laps like a barrow o' hot, steaming turds. Come on, let's get this thing done.'

Nat fingered the sodden binding, praying his leg would hold out. 'You're going to have to hold me up, Joe Jessop,' he winced, limping after Hacker.

Across the frozen expanse of New Palace Yard, the guardroom holding Brandon and his mate was heavily protected by Hacker's men. 'Look lively, lads.' The soldiers pulled up sharply from the brazier. 'Evenin', Sirs. Come to see Mr Brandon, 'ave you?'

Hacker grunted at the Sergeant, drawing him into the room. Nat saw the grisly tools of Brandon's trade stacked against the wall of the antechamber. Foxwood too noted everything, for his journal and the news sellers. Nat kicked the heavy wooden block painted black with carrying handles sunk on either side. Maybe three foot high, sufficient to allow a man to kneel, like a clergyman, more or less upright. Hempen rope lay in a bugger's muddle with a pulley of the sort used by seamen and a bucket of sand. A pine carrying chest with its lid ajar contained two black woollen smocks, leather face-masks and caps. There were crude false beards and a wig to protect the identity of the headsman in sensitive cases, like this. Selecting one of the foul-smelling garments, Joe Jessop pressed the fur to his chin, grinning broadly. 'It's a perfect disguise, Sirs, for the job in hand. Even my Sarah wouldn't recognise me in this!'

Hacker scowled, spitting through the bars at the executioners. 'If these two piss-artists don't tread the boards today, they'll be dancing in thin air tomorrow, at Tyburn.'

One of Hacker's troopers staggered in with a log eighteen inches by six. Flat bottomed, it was rounded on top like a jewel casket. 'This do you, Sir?'

'That's better.' Hacker grunted satisfaction, nodding at the block. 'Lay it down there boys and get rid of that one. I want to see Charles Stuart grovelling in the dirt, not kneeling prim and proper like he's taking communion.'

Part hidden under sacking, resting against the block was the axe that Bradshaw had ordered from the Tower. Joe Jessop grasped the handle, lifting the blade a few inches. The weapon was alarmingly short, not much longer than the block was high. 'Christ, I wouldn't rely on this bastard for chopping wood at Helions.'

Nat closed the pine chest, slumping down before he fainted. He was pleased the cell stank, disguising the whiff from his thigh. Le Roux must open the wound.

Brandon and his man were slumped in either corner. The apprentice was snoring loudly and the public executioner, eyes glazed, waved a hand disconsolately at the officers and their clerk. 'Sod off, gentl'men. I ain't topping no King.'

Hacker advanced on the executioner, Jessop grabbing his fist before it fell. 'Beggin' yer pardon Colonel, he's pissed as a fart. Don't want to be on no scaffold with 'im lunging around.' He spat into the straw. 'Likely strike the wrong 'ed.'

'Aye, right you are,' Hacker grunted, reaching inside his doublet for the bottle. 'Here.'

The liquor drew the executioner like a rat to a sewer. ''Ere Colonel, ain't laced, is it?'

Hacker smiled menacingly. 'No, Master Brandon. Good sherry wine, so it is, liberated by my own hands from His Majesty's cellar.'

The rogue bit the stopper, features contorting as he sniffed and swigged. Hacker turned to Nat with an appalling grin. 'Now then, brother, is it thee or me that'll part the King of England from his head today?'

XXI

Driving south across the Thames, the great bulk of Southwark cathedral loomed above the smoke of a thousand chimneys. Nat squinted downriver.

There were rumours of an invasion. There were always rumours. Rumours in London snaked through the narrow lanes and hemmed-in yards of the city like the stench of the Fleet River. They were, for once, well founded. The new republic was a pariah in whose failure every crowned head and every settled order in Europe had a stake. When they came, England's enemies would strike at her heart, up the leaden river, carried perhaps on this easterly wind, to London.

Nat hoped Joe Jessop had got away safely and was tucked up at Helions with his new wife. His last words to Dorothy were to bolt and bar the door behind him. The cold would keep simmering tempers off the boil but the city apprentices were fickle and the mob unpredictable.

According to Foxwood, the King's body had been taken to Windsor in one piece, head sewn back by Cromwell's own surgeon. Nat prayed he would be as reconciled with his part in the week's events as the principal parts of the King's person.

*

The Red Lion at Salisbury was a beacon on the long, miserable slog down the London road. The coach yard was lit up with tar torches and a central brazier that roared and spat.

Nat thrust the reins at the ostler lumbering from the shadows. 'She'll need a good wipe down, boy, and a warm blanket.' He rubbed life into his thigh, drying up nicely thanks to Le Roux's embrocation. 'I'm worried about that shank. You got liniment and a binding?' He patted the animal's withers, tossing a penny at the lad. Knuckling his forehead, the youth began to lead the horse away. 'Wait.' The boy turned, exposing his wound to the brazier's flickering light. Nat nodded at the livid scar. Etched deep in his forehead, it swept across a stove-in cheekbone to his chin. 'You're young for a stripe like that, soldier.'

The boy's grin was a contortion of broken bone and severed muscle on one side and a fair remembrance of a face to make a mother proud on the other. 'Naseby, master, with General Cromwell. Took a swipe from a dragoon's sabre.' The young veteran tapped his heavy brow. 'Surgeon said if I weren't so thick I'd have lost me eye.'

And you'd be closer to the gutter, thought Nat. 'Naseby, you say. D'you come across my brother there?' Nat blurted out. 'Edward Salt. Colonel Okey's regiment.' The youth stared at him blankly. 'No, course not.'

The innkeeper, Edgehill veteran of Lord John Robarte's Regiment of Foot, sailed through his sea of drinkers. 'Welcome, welcome, Sir! Come sit by the fire.' He batted away clerks with their leather tankards and fugging clay pipes. 'It ain't every day the piss-pot patrons of the Red Lion have such famous company.' He glared at the regulars, clipping his fingers at the buxom serving girl. 'Our mutual friend Major Wagstaff dropped in last week.' Nat remembered Wagstaff's company had been part of Robarte's Regiment. 'We were saying how well you've done in London. Get the news books here at the Red Lion, see, to follow events. Other folk don't know what's going on a mile from their own front door.' The full bosomed servant was back refilling his tankard, preening herself. He could overnight at the Red Lion. But last time he was tempted he ended up with the chaudepiss and a lifetime of self-loathing. He would never be unfaithful to Effam. 'You know the Major's got a commission in Colonel Dove's Wiltshire militia? Means he don't have to go far in defence of the good old cause.'

'Ah. No further than the taproom, I'm thinking,' grinned Nat. 'Look, friend, my horse is done in and I have to get home to my wife.'

The publican tapped his nose, winking lewdly. 'Me old mare'll carry you home and I've an embrocation that'll physick your lame 'un.' He nodded at Nat's leg. 'Probably do you an' all.'

*

Nat forced the animal hard along the bleak slash of drove road. Soon the familiar stones of the henge were breaking the horizon like the cogs of a mill wheel.

Squinting, Nat made out two forms at a fire away off in the lee of a round barrow and a tinker's wagon pulled up off the road. The first souls since Salisbury, the forlorn creatures in such a spot gave him no comfort at all. He kicked on, hard.

The mare, wide-eyed, bucked and whinnied. In an instant, she was on her knees, tipping forward, pitching into darkness and in his fuddled mind he was falling into the curate's bottomless pit. He heard his head crack and fought to keep his senses.

Coming to, Nat hit a wall of pain, tortured leg pinned between the horse and the frozen ground. Sobbing, he fought free, the terrified beast, wide-eyed and snorting. He cried out as the leg took his weight. It would not carry him far. Cursing his stupidity in forcing her, he examined the beast's damaged foreleg, moving his fingers expertly up and down, feeling for a break. Pulling the saddlebags free, he coaxed her gently and she took the weight, moving ahead, but her eyes told him any more would put her in the knacker's yard. 'Damnation!'

He spun round, searching for the shadows at the fire. They'd be eyeing him up with his bags and crippled horse. There, moving closer, as his vision blurred. He fingered the pommel of his sword, felt for the Upton pistol.

Now they were on him, bearing down out of the gloom: a great hulk of a man and a stooped old woman in black weeds. The giant lunged forward, Nat pulling at his sword. 'Steady, master. My son means no harm.' The crone rattled a command in her tongue and the man backed off. 'Come, master, you'll not get far with that lame 'un.' She tugged his sleeve. 'Come now, I'll see what can be done, if you'll let me.' Pulling a square of clean white cotton from her sleeve, the woman pressed her hand to his head, searching his eyes. Nat felt the warm tackiness at his thigh and raised a blooded palm. 'Aye, that's a cruel wound, Sir, and an old one, I'm thinking. Come, mind yourself by our fire for a while.'

The son tossed Nat's saddlebags onto his back as if they were feather pillows and took the reins, whispering softly to the animal. The ancient looped her arm in his, guiding him to the fire. She had the creviced, mud-brown complexion of her kind and smelt of horse and wood-smoke. He felt the bile rise in his throat and the world spinning. As he fell he saw the man, square lantern jaw, great fists, towering. So he was worm's meat at a tinker's hands, stripped by thieves, his body tossed in a sodden ditch and his tortured flesh picked by the black carrion crow screaming anticipation.

*

The woman's elder embrocation brought him round as the low morning light was starting to finger the great stones. He struggled to make sense of his situation but could remember nothing more than the Red Lion. Instinctively he felt for his leg and found the cold balm of a poultice.

Nat turned his head painfully. The woman, cross-legged by the fire, was ladling broth from the skillet. Their eyes met through the smoke. She nodded gently without breaking her baleful song. He tried to get up.

'Steady, now, master.' The woman was at his side, the heady brew wafting under his nose. 'The magic winter roots'll restore your senses.' He sipped the thin fluid wondering why his throat had not been cut. 'Took quite a turn so you did, Master Farrington. I've tied a healing bandage o' sweet herbs to your animal's leg and my son's bound it.'

The mare was grazing contentedly, leg tidily bound. 'You know my name.' He screwed his eyes, wood smoke blowing across his face. 'How's that?'

'Aw, master, there's much I know. The brew makes all things clear, see, for them that's got the arts.' She poked absently at the fire. 'The magic tells things that should remain the secret of a crabbit old woman, I daresay.' Her brown eyes bored into his. 'Like the death of a King and the men that wield the axe. Aye, we see their faces.'

'What faces?'

A black-eyed bird took off, noisily, circling the bivouac. 'I see a battle, a terrible fight, and a father's letter to his daughter.' She squatted on a stool by the fire, gazing through the smoke. 'And there's a sweet bastard child in the arms of a barren woman, its dead mother withal. All these things, back and forth like the tides of the sea. Back and forth, master, fain to make a poor body spin.'

The plane simmered like midsummer and he felt the ground buck and bend. 'You speak of the past, but d'you see the future?'

Shaking her head, she lowered her eyes, inestimably sad. 'Aye, master, I see it. But I do not profess it. For that would make me a witch.'

The stones, burning with bright, unnatural colour, spun round and round. He tossed the brew away. 'Tell me this and I'll reward you well. Tell me...'

She raised a finger to her lips. 'Hush now, I know what you seek. There's dark hatred burning in your breast and an oath twice sworn, even against your own flesh.'

'Own flesh – that's not right!' A tattoo in his head and beads of sweat squeezed like water from a cheese cloth. 'If you'd seen the secrets of my heart, woman, you'd know. It's the devil Carew I'm after, not any flesh of mine.'

She said nothing.

'Wait, I had a cousin,' Nat gawped. 'Folk reckoned Thomas was old Carew's bastard.' That's it! Desperately he fitted Thomas Salt's inconsequential death to the shadows she saw, imploring her to crush the dark spore of suspicion.

'Hush now, sweet master. The shades sing of an oath 'gainst Erasmus Carew.' Head cupped in her hands, she stared dolefully at the heart of the fire. 'What's to become of it? That's your question, isn't it?' He nodded mutely but she was shaking her head. 'I know, master, but I must keep my counsel, since prophesy would see me burn.'

Nat blacked out. Tipping her head to the heavens, she screamed her catharsis in her own language. 'Twisted iron, and mud, seas of mud, and men with muskets that fire on and on.' Now she was scanning the plane like a cornered beast. 'They're here, all around, can't you see? Soldiers, around the stones, look, *look*. Mud, oh great oceans of it, across the seas, fire and blood, an ocean of despair.' Her head flopped forward, long, matted hair hanging like tendrils. 'I see two upon their blood feud lying in that great ooze, pretty they are, gentle-born, last of their lines, last of their *line*.' Breathless, she swept away hair and sweat, staring defiance at her unconscious guest. 'Aye, and the years they're numbered threescore and three hundred. There now, that's my prophesy Nathaniel Farrington o' Helions, may I burn for the telling of it.'

*

There was a boy from Hinton at the kitchen door with a story about a giant with a hatchet face and would they fetch back the master. When Joe Jessop and the stockman arrived they found Nat asleep behind the barrow with the horse and his gear. Of the odd couple, there was no sign.

'Heavy session was it, Sir?' Jessop shook him awake. 'Bit like my wedding breakfast. *That you missed.*'

Nat squinted at Jessop, moving in and out of focus. 'There was a pair of tinkers. Old crone and her son...' he rasped, waving blindly at the stones. 'You got spliced, Joe?'

'Aw, you know it.' Jessop and the stockman bundled their charge into the saddle. 'Easy now. Had a bit of a skinful, that's all, and a wee crack on the head.'

'... great square head, paws like spades.' Nat waved the palms of his hands at Jessop. 'D'you know them?'

'Reckon *I* knows 'em,' the rustic piped up. 'When I were a nipper, me ma said there was this old witch an' a cut-throat giant wi' big spade hands an' beetle brows that'd be after us if we was bad. But that were a few year ago, mind, an' I ain't seen neither of 'em since.'

'Get on, you silly old get,' Jessop snorted. 'You're two score year and ten, if you're a day. The reason you ain't seen 'em is 'cos they'd be dead.'

'So a dead woman bound my wounds and her son applied that poultice...' Nat pointed at the mare trailing behind. The stockman looked aghast. 'What?' He felt his head for the bandage but fingered no more than a mess of matted hair and congealed blood. His thigh, he realised dully, no longer hurt like hell and when he felt down for the crone's poultice he found only Le Roux's lint dressing. Shifting in the saddle, he screwed his eyes, focussing on the horse. Her foreleg was bare.

'Blimey, it *was* a good night, Sir!' Jessop grinned, winking at the stockman. But the rustic did not laugh and, as Nat drew the blanket tightly, he knew the chill had nothing to do with the cold.

Skinful or no, Joe Jessop had to tell him, before he got home, so he was prepared. 'Mistress ain't been too good, Sir.' The soft aside cleared Nat's head in an instant. 'Mrs Jessop sent for the doctor, couple of days back.' Nat was already kicking on. 'Just so as you know.'

*

On watch at the south oriel, Effam saw him canter up the drive and gave thanks, beckoning Sarah Jessop to help her to the door. The maid threw back the bolts as Nat fell from the horse. Batting Jessop away, he staggered up the steps to his love framed in the archway. 'The Doctor?'

'Says I'm improving.' She stood on her toes, pecking him on the cheek. 'He's cupped me and prescribed pulmonaria and a dish of aurum potabile. But you know what I think of doctors.'

He held her tight for an instant then pulled away, anxiously scouring her face. Thin, he thought, pale from cupping. She stroked his furrowed brow. 'Husband, I'm very well, really.' The widow Cotton, fussing at the screen, coughed dissent. 'Come, sweet heart, there's a good fire lit.'

He glanced absently at the hearth where the logs had settled low in the grate. Mrs Cotton was hovering. 'I'll make you up a warm sack posset with some bread and cheese. There's a mutton tart with turnips, if you've a mind to it. And I'll send the boy to help with your boots. Then I'll bring your son.' She turned, tight lipped. 'Oliver's been asking for you.'

'Oh, Nat, she's been such a treasure during my sickness.' Effam smiled fondly at the old woman retreating to the kitchen. 'I can't begin to tell you.'

Nat sniffed the air. 'Well, she's not got the chimney to draw any better.' He unclipped his sword, glad to be rid of it. 'Which physick's attending you, my love?'

'Dr Farrar of Salisbury. He's been good enough. Says I have, *had*, a distemper of the chest.' She planted a kiss on his lips. 'From which I'm quite recovered.'

They pulled apart as the servant appeared with a cup. Wine and curdled cream, dusted with a rasp of nutmeg. He threw fresh logs, greenwood and lumps of Carew's house, into the grate speeding embers up the chimney. 'Mrs Cotton says I'm to help with your boots, Sir.'

Nat collapsed in a wingchair, sipping the confection. He heaved the injured leg gratefully onto the three-legged stool. The rejuvenated fire hissed and spat in the grate. 'Thank 'e, lad.'

After a while Mrs Cotton appeared at the passage screen clutching a small boy he barely recognised. 'Off you go.' The scrap in nightclothes danced across the flagstones. Nat hugged the sturdy lad, face buried in thick, golden hair with the scent of freshly mown hay.

'Have you killed him, father?'

Blinking, he held the wide-eyed boy, befuddled mind grappled with the interrogation, and what to say. 'Yes, my son, I killed the King, may God forgive me. Me and sixty other gentlemen, each in equal part.'

Oliver settled nonchalantly on his father's lap. 'How did you kill him?'

Nat stared into the well of the boy's blue eyes. 'With a great, sharp axe brought specially from the Tower of London.'

His son's eyes widened further. 'But who chopped him with the great sharp axe?'

Nat looked away at the flames dancing in the grate. 'Ah my son, that's a secret for a man to take to his grave.' He glanced quickly at Effam through misting eyes. 'There now, enough, trooper! There'll be nightmares. In the morning you can tell me how you've looked after Mama and Helions whilst I've been kicking my heels with Uncle Cromwell in London.'

'Papa, are you going away again?'

'No, son. Never.'

XXII

Nat pulled Etienne and Dorothy into the hall. 'God's blood, I'm so very glad to see you.'

Le Roux lost no time. '*Mon frère*, we thought I could help, with Effam.'

Nat was close to tears. 'Oh, my dears, how pleased I am to see a proper medical man. She's so very weak, you see.'

'Then I'll attend her immediately.' Le Roux made for the stairs with his saddlebags. 'Send the widow Cotton brother, *s'il vous plaît*.'

*

Dorothy returned from the kitchen with a sack of posset and a tart with artichokes. 'You look like death, brother. Here, eat.'

'Not now, Dorothy.'

She shrugged, tucking in, watching him between mouthfuls pacing the hall, waiting for the apothecary's prognosis.

Le Roux appeared at the screen. '*Mon dieu*, this has taken its toll on you.'

Nat's rheumy eyes implored him. 'Tell me.'

'People fear the sweating sickness and the spotted fever, which is to say the same thing, plague, though I don't know why. There's no plague in my parish Bills of Mortality. In London, as here, the Captain of the Men of Death is the consumption. And it's that distemper threatening the life of your dear wife, *mon ami*.'

'Father died coughing his lungs,' said Dorothy.

Le Roux nodded grimly. 'It would have been the consumption.'

'Aye, but his attendant was just a wise woman from the village,' implored Nat. 'You can physik her, can't you, Etienne, *can't you*?'

The apothecary gave a shallow, unhappy shrug. 'I've already overstepped myself. The physicians would have me up before the beak on a charge of practising. As for a prescription, you must consult a doctor of physik.'

Nat shook his head. 'Dr Farrar of Salisbury has diagnosed a suffusion of the lungs. He's cupped her and ordered a dish of a stinking weed he called pulmonaria.'

'Farrar, I know him.' Le Roux scowled. 'He's a disciple of the mountebank Simon Baskervill who preys on the parishes I serve, damn his eyes. They believe plants can treat parts of the body they look like, so each herb has its own signature, if you will. Thus walnuts are good for the brain simply because they look like a brain, at least one that's been pickled. Childish, *n'est-ce pas*? Likewise the weed pulmonaria is said to look like a man's lungs. Not that either *gentleman* would know, since they understand these things only from their school books. If they saw a man's entrails spewed out as we poor artisans have they would know a man's brains are a mess of porridge. Not a spavined walnut!' Le Roux threw up his hands. 'My dear friend, whatever the physicians say, your wife is brought very low by her illness. It is, without doubt, the consumption. And I fear the affliction is far advanced.' He paused, hoping Nat would understand. 'But I'm just an apothecary, not a physik, though I've observed the condition more than most of their worships, and stayed to see it run its course.'

'I'm putting my faith in you, Etienne.'

'No.' Le Roux shook his head. 'Put your faith in the Almighty, brother. But what I tell you is true, friend, for I see the consumption every day of my life. It's a sad thing for a man to say, but it keeps me in business. The malady often takes an indolent course with patients spared for many years, perhaps even being carried off by something else.' He smiled with the compassion of the best of his calling. 'Though your poor wife is so terribly weak. I fear there is no remedy save that in the hands of God. But I will ease her discomfort as best I can.' He gripped Nat's arm with a solemn intensity. 'I carry a sweet cordial made from the juice of wild choke pears that I've found to be a comfort and a quantity of the Lac Sulphuris which was much favoured by the King's doctor. But, please, no more cupping, for the poor creature has already coughed away too much blood. I fear the leaches would bear her clean away.'

Nat buried his face in his hands, massaging the red swollen orbs. 'No cupping then.'

The old man lowered his voice. 'There are those that say the illness is caused by evil vapours or witchcraft. It is not. I'm convinced the consumption is spread from one person to the next.'

Nat looked around to be sure he was not overheard. 'Like the chaudepiss?'

Busy Dorothy re-appeared from the kitchen with posset and left over tart, placing it noisily in front of her husband. He waited for her to go. 'Yes, like the chaudepiss, in a way, but through the air. Thus.' He raised a hand to his mouth. 'Put your fist here and cough on it.'

Nat did as he was told. 'And what did you feel?' He shrugged. 'You felt the breath forced from your lungs, where the consumption lies.' Nat looked blank. 'So, the breath that has aired the consumption floats on the ether and is drawn in...' Le Roux took a deep breath and exhaled. '... by the consumptive's attendants.' A talon fastened on Nat's arm. 'Be mindful of my theorem, *mon ami*, for the sake of your son.'

Nat nodded bleakly, getting up to make the unhappy ascent. He hesitated before entering the sick room, wanting to cheer her up. Mrs Cotton, fretting with the bed linen, followed his gaze to the windows. 'Master Le Roux flung them open, Sir. Most partic'lar he was. Dr Farrar won't be pleased, mind.'

Effam smiled weakly, holding out her hand. But as he took it, she rolled away, coughing and spitting bright red froth in a cup already half full. The horrors of Devizes and Newbury were nothing to this. Searching his face for reassurance, she saw only her fate in his desperation, sensing her rock's helplessness. She was drowning and he, reaching out, could not catch her as she drifted. But there was something she must say to him and she could not trust her strength to delay. 'Nat, sweet heart, our time's been shorter than I hoped.' The words were difficult so she chose them well. 'But I've loved you more than you ever knew. Far more than I thought possible to love a man.' His tears fell unchecked. 'Nat, listen to me. There are three pledges I must have. *Three*.' The wasting disease had turned her hand into a claw. It gripped him now with all her remaining strength as she braced for what she must say. 'Death fractures our union, breaks the contract. Marry again, Nat, if the Lord sees fit.' She reached up to sweep away his tears, fingers combing the mane flecked with grey. 'But Oliver's your sole heir, yes? Promise me.'

'With all my heart. I ask only to see our son a man.' Stroking her forehead, he choked his response, half pledge, half prayer. 'Then, pray God, I'll be called to your side for all eternity.'

She looked away, passing the back of her hand across her eyes. 'There is the other matter, dear, that's been unspoken.'

'Let it remain so.' The stillborn, last of its line, waited beneath the north wall to be reunited. 'Sweet heart, it will be done.'

She pulled him close, summoning strength for the third, most earnest of her demands. 'Nat, I'm shriven, ready for the Lord. Although my sins are more plentiful than birds in the sky, I've always walked with Him. But, Nat, though you're the gentlest of men, there's a canker keeping you from God.' He wanted to interrupt but she persisted. 'We've lived the darkest of days. But unless there's forgiveness in your heart we'll never be reunited. You know what I ask.'

'Sweet, you mustn't ask what you know I can't give.'

'Husband, I *demand* it.' She tried to claw upright. 'I see the portent as clearly as the augurs of Rome. The blood feud must end or it will destroy you.' Effam fell back exhausted. 'Upon my soul, if you refuse, you'll find no peace in this world, or the next. And I can't pass eternity without you.'

He shook his head. 'Twice sworn, I am, for the murder of my children and brother. They must be avenged. Dearest, they *will* be, eye for eye.' His jaw tightened. 'There can be no peace, no contentment, no honour 'til I've sheathed my sword in Carew's bowels.' He smiled, gently stroking her cheek with his finger, trying for all the world to assuage her horror. '*Then*, sweet heart, I'll be reconciled with the Lord and we'll be together 'til the end of time.'

'We'll speak of this again.' Releasing her grip, she turned her face away. 'Go now, husband.'

Part Three – Restoration

XXIII

Hinton Helions

February 1660

It had been nicely done.

Sacred to the memory of Euphemia Farrington of Helions, beloved wife of Nathaniel Farrington, Gent. and only child of Miles Farrington, Esq. She departed this life 1650 in the 30th year of her life.

Nat had arranged for the tomb to be cut in the side chapel by the Farrington monument. His device, registered by the heralds, chiselled in stone, a wood anemone plucked for his love on the morning that Effam wanted to preserve forever. Lovingly, his fingers traced the inscription, lingering over the space below. There was room for another, when the time came. 'God, let it be soon.'

The Reverend Nicholas Sedgwick had complied readily with Effam's instruction. The small parcel had been removed from beneath the north wall and now rested in its casket on her coffin.

Nat crouched as low as his knees allowed, whispering to the cold stone. In the spring he would lay the posy of wild flowers laced with the hedgerow's pale crimson betony he had brought for a decade.

*

'Dear God, it's a physick you need, not a lawyer.' Gaskell stood at the screen, appalled by the gowned and slippered figure shuffling down the hall. 'Should I send for Dr Farrar?' It was an arduous ride from Gaskell's Salisbury chambers to Hinton Helions but the attorney charged by the quarter hour. 'You obviously need a good will writer, though.'

Nat waved Gaskell to a wingchair by the unlit fire. 'She was very sick but I never thought she'd be taken so soon.' Eyes misting, he watched Oliver and Joe Jessop on the drive wrestling with the dapple grey. Knife out, the youth was expertly assessing the uncooperative beast's foreleg. 'I expect she's caught another stone.'

'Eh?'

'She died at peace just before sunrise, y'know,' said Nat. 'That night my beloved made three demands of me. First, rebury our son. The second's impossible; I'll answer to God for it soon, I'm thinking. You're here for the third.'

'May I?' Gaskell looked meaningfully at the claret. The attorney drank too much. 'Seems to me the first charge is the sexton's business, the second the Almighty's, but if a poor lawyer can help with the third, he will.'

'Hinton Helions belonged to Effam, you see,' said Nat.

'Not in law,' sniffed Gaskell. 'You see, a widower continues in title to all that in life a wife might fondly regard her own. Remarkable though your dear lady was, the death of Euphemia Farrington is a legal irrelevance.'

'Helions was Effam's,' Nat insisted.

'Except that, but for the bad fortune of your recusant neighbour Carew, the moneylenders would have foreclosed on Helions years ago.' Gaskell tapped his teeth, wishing he could tell Nat who had bought Brook Farm after the fire on such generous terms. 'It pains me to see neighbours feuding. So wasteful. I act for Mr Carew too, you know. It's my duty to advise an olive branch.'

'Ha! My retribution's been thin as field poppies given Carew's trespass against me which is as bloody red,' snapped Nat. 'You forget my twins, my brother, my farm, my wounds!'

'I'm sorry, Captain, for my inelegant tongue,' said Gaskell coughing on his claret. 'I was simply pointing out that the fingers of my godly clients, including your fingers, are sunk deep in the estates of their royalist neighbours.'

'Rightly so.'

'Indeed,' said Gaskell. 'And isn't it also true that the purses of Cromwell's more reliable gentlemen have been filled by sinecures and emoluments these past ten years, yours included, eh? The war's made you a rich man, not Miles Farrington's decrepit estate.'

Nat shrugged. 'Remarry, my lady said.' He waved an admonishing finger. 'I'll sooner bump down the aisle in my coffin than a wedding coat. But...'

'Oh, come now.'

'Oliver's position is unusual, some would say challengeable.'

Gaskell met his client's eye as it fixed through the oriel window on the young man. Nat passed a hand across his face, over swollen eyes and stubble. 'So, I'll anticipate my joyful release by signing Helions and all else I've laboured for to the boy, now. Can you do that?'

The lawyer sat back, pointing fingers like a steeple to his nose. 'The admonition of the prophet Isaiah doesn't apply in common law, you know.'

Nat gave Gaskell a bitter smile. 'Sin of the father visited on the son?' The attorney's fees were high but so was his perception. 'Isaiah and Exodus are both clear on the matter.'

'You think Charles Stuart'll smite you for your part in the late troubles.' Gaskell sensed his client could not care less for himself.

'Perhaps, but not quite for the reason you think.' He was fumbling with papers on Effam's desk. 'You see, my recusant uncle Abiel Biles may have doused the King's ire.' Smoothing the paper, he offered it to the lawyer. 'Here.'

Breda, Holland

14 November 1659

Dear Captain Farrington,

The King commands me to write to certain gentlemen with his thinking on the late rebellion.

Whereas his Majesty is resolved to censure felons involved in the murder of his beloved father, he is persuaded that particular sufferings may have forfeited the judgement of some subjects.

The Queen has made the King aware of your uncle Master Abiel Biles and his sacrifice in her service. My Lord Russell has similarly petitioned on your behalf.

I hope this will comfort you in the knowledge of his merciful and benevolent Majesty.

I remain,

Edward Hyde

Puffing his cheeks, Gaskell sat back heavily, thumb flicking a corner of the stiff paper. 'Well, Sir Edward's certificate's a mighty shield.' He poured another glass. 'The word of Charles Stuart's chief counsellor will surely save your neck, perhaps your estate.'

'Not so,' rasped Nat, blowing noisily into his handkerchief. 'There's more.' The lawyer said nothing waiting for the great confession, the biggest. 'My enemy'll discover to the court things to seal my fate. Terrible things, borne on the tide of the times.' Gaskell leant forward on the edge of his seat, sure of what was coming. 'I was a soldier, you understand. I commanded and was commanded to do all sorts of things. But my conduct seemed right, at the time it did.' Nat saw Will Porit baring his captive's neck on the road from Marsh Benham, looking to him for the sign. The soldier's gore washed across the dirt, sharp earthy tang heavy in the air so rich he could still taste it. 'Changing skies, Gaskell.'

'Eh?'

'Changing skies. A man's deeds take on a different hue after so many years.' His back to the great stone fireplace, Nat stared bleakly at his absent mother-in-law's place on the wall. 'And there's a particular one that'll want me arraigned.'

Gaskell knew all about Erasmus Carew, his other client. 'On what charge?' A drop of claret fell from the base of the glass, spotting his white lace collar. 'Not the death of that spavined curate?' Miles Farrington's instructions to the spotty apprentice Gaskell taking depositions on a three-legged stool by the Wylye river had been clear. *The evidence must be helpful.* 'You mustn't worry about that curate. I was there, remember?'

Nat shook his head. The attorney did not need to know it all. 'Carew's stock with Charles'll be high. He'll return to Wiltshire in triumph, taking his revenge.' Nat passed a hand through his lifeless grey mane. 'If violence is offered, best it's catastrophic. Avoids retribution, see, lets you sleep. Carew'll get me. He'll succeed where I've failed.'

'But any charge must have a basis in law.' Gaskell tapped his pursed lips. There were rumours. His ears pricked in the taproom of the Red Lion, men hunched darkly over their drink sharing confidences. 'Now here's a thing, Captain, news books are debating the identity of the King's executioner,' he said casually, eyeing his client for the response that did not come. 'Westcountryman they say, a farmer. Apparently, usual headsman was blind drunk, nobody else would do it and ...' Joe Jessop was at the screen, stock still, staring intently. Why was the fellow in the hall, rough-shod, glaring like that? Over the rim of his glass Gaskell caught Nat glancing at Jessop, sharp as knives, the steward silently turning on his heels. Now his most enigmatic client was behind him, bending low, hissing in his ear. 'Is there a name among the tittle-tattle of your news books?'

Gaskell turned in his seat, searching for a clue. He was used to winkling truths. Good at it. 'Well, it's just your name's on the death warrant. You were at Whitehall for the execution. Thought you might be interested, that's all.'

'God's blood, lawyer, you've been paying too much attention to tap room chit-chat down the Red Lion.' Nat slouched in the chair opposite. 'Stick to what you *know*, eh?'

The attorney was patient, waiting for the old soldier staring blankly into his cold hearth. But Nat was climbing the chalk path above the farm with Billy Burrows. He was at the top of the hill, standing with Carew watching the gathering clouds of civil war.

'My fork in the road,' said Nat. 'Different conversation with Carew and I'd have stayed a Wiltshire yeoman, buried and forgotten as if I'd never been. But there'd have been children, the twins of course, and more I daresay with a comfortable wife. Contentment.'

'Ah, but the Lady Effam and Oliver, Helions and the arms above your door,' said Gaskell, 'all of them because you chose the right course, the proper path, eh?' He smiled sweetly. 'But, if there's something your attorney should know, something to share, *consequences* a legal draughtsman might help avoid...?'

'No,' snapped Nat. 'You can whistle for all your probing, Gaskell. I simply ask that what my love and I brought together be put beyond those who would have it back.'

Without further comment, the lawyer plucked a sheaf of paper from his satchel, a pen and a small bottle of ink. And with a smile, he began to craft an instrument that would confound the Court of Star Chamber itself.

XXIV

The Jewel House, Westminster

April 10 1660

'Bloody immaculate, Charles Stuart's timing.' Colonel Francis Hacker, brandishing a well-thumbed *Mercurius Britannicus*, glowered down the long table at the line of gentry sitting like apostles at the Last Supper. 'Masterful document, this proclamation from Holland. Have you seen it, sirs, eh?' He waved the news book at the glum assembly. 'Well, you should. You'll learn all a citizen needs about what to expect from His Majesty.' Another glass of claret tipped down his neck. 'Mark you, gentlemen, though it carries the signature of an ambitious young man, there's a scrawny old goat behind this, and a damnably clever one too. It's the stink of that black rat Edward Hyde that's carrying across the narrow seas.' He wiped his lips. 'Charles' puppet-master says the army's arrears'll be paid, *in full*. Now, where's the soldier simple enough to believe that?'

'They'll believe their turncoat general,' spat Major General Whalley. 'They'll believe George Monck.'

'This *proclamation* promises mercy for tender consciences.' Hacker cursed, shoving the *Mercurius* at Edward Whalley. 'Papist scoundrels, bog Irish and the like. I'll be bound.'

'No, Francis, it's the King's olive branch,' Whalley protested, stabbing the paper with his index finger. 'See here, no appropriation of property we've *redistributed.*'

'Ah my gullible friend, how many popish popinjays with gay ribbons and false airs'll land with Charles?' Hacker wagged his finger, his slurred voiced laced with sarcasm. 'The bastards we've compounded and taxed for delinquency, licking their wounds for a full ten years, will crawl from Dutch obscurity to take their revenge.'

'Well, what d'you expect,' Sir Edmund Ludlow fingered his collar, 'from that papist harpie and font of all our misery? What d'you think the widow queen'll be whispering in her son's ear?'

'Ah well now that's the cunning part of it, Hyde's part no doubt. Charles offers all a free and general pardon...' Hacker cast his eyes around the table at a dozen glum men staring at the scaffold, '...apart from fifty persons, most with their marks on his father's death warrant or...' he glared at Nat, '...*intimately* involved in his execution.'

'Well, I wish you gentleman Godspeed.' Ludlow banged his empty glass on the table. 'Me, I'll cart off what I can to my dear Swiss canton which is as far from the perfidious agents of any King as it's possible for a Christian soul to be.'

Whalley shook his head. 'You're a fool, Edmund, if you think you can hide. Can't you feel Hyde's spite, smell the bitter vengeance of the delinquent French whore you and I widowed?' He stood heavily. 'Whenever you hear the gallop of hooves on a dark night and with every rustle of the wind, you'll be twitching at the window, braced for the fury of the King's agents. He won't let up 'til the severed heads of the chief architects of his misfortune are spiked on Tower Bridge.' Turning at the door, the Major General offered parting advice to his friends of twenty years. 'Take ship for the colonies, brethren, sharply too. In New England we'll rekindle the good old cause among godly folk and pray for England's deliverance.'

Hacker sneered, attempting with difficulty to focus on the silent brooding officer at the foot of the table. 'And you, dear Cap'n Farrington, what'll you do? Writhe and squirm at the dauphin's feet for your part in killing Cock Robin?'

The two men glared at each other bound by an oath sworn in the Church of St Margaret in the lee of the Abbey on the frozen morning of the King's execution, fever from his festering leg taking hold of Nat. He remembered their desperate conversation huddled off the south aisle under the basalt skulls of Haughton's grim memorial, Joe Jessop hovering in the nave. But Hacker had become a dangerous liability and the regime they served was done for. He must shelter his family from the new King's agents. Quickly.

'Oh come now, *brother*, don't recall you being so coy when Cromwell thrust Charles' death warrant at you. Oh, so willing we were, quite the orator.' Hacker, spittle-mouthed, banged down the line of confederates. 'Those papists have grounds for doing you in a hundred times over. Their damned news books still want you for killing one of their canting priests in '43. That alone's sufficient to have you dancing at the end of a rope, *without the rest.*'

'The man fell, damn you,' muttered Nat. 'Hit his head on a tombstone, in his own churchyard.' He lifted his face to stare into Hacker's watery eyes. 'Have a care, old man.'

Hacker knew. King's death warrant and the curate apart, there was another, inestimably more serious, matter, known only to five men. Cromwell had already taken the secret to his grave. It was a secret that, divulged, was bound to attract the severest, most horrible penalty imaginable.

*

'Foxwood, you still here?' Nat was halfway down the stone steps. 'Everyone else is clearing out.'

'Ah, Sir, you can rely on me.' Wrapped in a black cloak, the crook-back agent looked like a Tower raven hopping along.

'Sand's racing through the glass, Foxwood.' Nat steered his man through an archway leading off the staircase into an empty room, slamming the door. 'We must act fast to conclude my great matter.'

'Erasmus Carew's paid heavily for his crimes already, Sir,' said Foxwood. 'But he'll want your head. It would be sensible to strike first.' He toyed with the secret of the midwife Banks and what it might do to his master's state of mind, to his relationship with Carew. But there was nothing for Foxwood in purging the black hatred fermenting in his master's bowels for twenty years. The feud fed him and, in its final days, he intended to squeeze a pension from it. 'My people say Carew's in a ruinous state, Sir, utterly undone.'

'Where is he?' Nat stared at the Abbey Chapter House from a thin arrow slit, the room's only window. Don't trust Foxwood, Effam had said. How uncharacteristically wrong she was about him.

'Penned up in the Low Countries with his son since the Compton scandal we got up.' The agent shivered, drawing the cloak more closely around his uneven shoulders. The Jewel House was as damp as the Fleet gaol. 'Lodging with a tradesman near Breda. Keeps the closest company with Charles Stuart.'

'I was wrong, Foxwood, to spend all my energy bringing that man to justice.' Nat shook his head, full of recrimination. 'Cromwell said traitors must be brought to book with a halter about their neck.' He pawed his injured limb, throbbing, hot and stinking beneath the binding. 'Better if I'd let your man slip a stiletto between Carew's ribs.'

'It would have been a pleasure, Sir, though by all accounts poverty and damp digs have been doing the assassin's work.' The cell was completely bare, so Foxwood leant against the wall. Ten years ago and half a mile down the road – he could almost see the spot through the slit window – he had scribbled the scoop of his life. How the news books fought, fought like cats, for his lurid account of the King's death. But their editors would be selling their own mothers for his journal entry that day, his pension safe and secure in the goldsmith's strongroom. 'Remember Carew's already lost his wife and a son to the consumption and another spread his brains across Newbury field. The Carew estates in Wiltshire and his wife's in Lancashire have been irredeemably dispersed.'

Nat at the slit window smiled at the Abbey choristers tripping behind their master, surplices billowing in the light air. 'Little white ducklings.'

'Eh?'

Nat shook his head. 'Charles Stuart's cronies cling to his coat tails because they want their estates back.' He wondered why Effam had taken so strongly against Foxwood. She *was* wrong about him. 'Whalley's olive branch ain't worth a tinker's cuss.'

'The army's receipts from Carew's lands were modest because I made the sales murderously complex. Erasmus Carew will need an army of lawyers to unpick my handiwork,' boasted Foxwood. 'He hasn't the money.'

'But what about my oath, the absolution that parson gave me in St Lawrence's chapel, eh?' Nat slumped against the cold stone wall. 'Dutch squalor and the consumption haven't worked, have they?'

'If you mean to kill Carew...' Foxwood had been planning for this.

'...It must be done before Carew crosses the narrow seas, whilst he's weak.' Nat nodded grimly. 'Can't trust Edward Hyde. Those addlepates just now are going to learn that hell has no fury like an exile returned. And that bastard Carew will hunt me down.'

Foxwood smiled. *Bastard*? Nathaniel Farrington, of all men, should be choosy with his expletives. 'Then I must do it personally. Though the risks are great and,' he hesitated, shrugging apologetically, 'I have responsibilities.' Nat looked down at him bleakly. It was said Foxwood had a woman and a couple of bastards. 'I've taken the liberty of setting a consideration.' Foxwood handed him a note inscribed with a sum worthy of the job.

'Alright.' Nat swallowed hard. 'Sail on the evening tide. Swan steps, eight o'clock. Money'll be ready.'

*

Foxwood pawed at the heavy purses and bills of exchange, grinning satisfaction. 'It'll be done.' Hitching up his cape, he flopped into the boat with his gear. 'Goodbye, Sir.' As the boatman pushed off, the assassin turned to wave at the faded object of his desire but Nat had turned his back and was already retreating into the gloom. Clearing his throat noisily, the clerk curled his long tongue to fire a plug of mucus at the black, seething Thames.

'Tosser.' Foxwood was already computing the value of secrets to the exile of Breda.

XXV

Harwich

Autumn 1660

The town was en fête. *Royal Charles*, first-rate ship of the line, rode proudly at anchor in the roads, mother goose to the squadron waiting to return the new king from exile.

Harwich had much to be thankful for. The republic had become too much even for this most godly of boroughs. Now it was fizzling out like a lit match on a damp day.

The revellers spilling into the town's narrow lanes from the Three Cups to the brothels by the dockyard gate had set their faces resolutely against the late troubles. Why not? Even General George Monck had turned royalist. The signwriters had lost no time on the transom of Monck's flagship, dabbing out *Naseby*, picking out *Royal Charles* in bold gilt. But the jubilation of the poor swains of Harwich was lost on the sad little party gathered on a lick of sand under the watchful eye of a sleek black bird.

There was a boat with two oarsmen and an impatient coxswain holding fast on the shingle. Further up, Etienne and Dorothy Le Roux sat stiff and grim-faced in the carriage waiting with the door open for Oliver.

The coxswain, with an eye on the tide, called out anxiously. Nat held Oliver in a mist of tears. 'Here.' The signet ring with its anemone device that he had thrust angrily into hot wax on the King's death warrant, he now pressed into the youth's palm. 'Your mother chose our badge.' He spun on his good leg to face the sea and his transport, the old *Matthew* riding uncomfortably downwind of the flagship. 'Carry it, boy, to remember.'

The coxswain pushed off, cursing as the vessel bit the surf, grabbing his wringing wet passenger. Nat bunched miserably in the sternsheets, eyes screwed against the spray to find the solitary figure on the beach. He must turn back, while there was still time. 'Too late now, master! Skipper won't have it. Tide's on the turn, see.' The seaman grinned toothlessly. 'We'll next tread God's good earth in Massachusetts, Lord love us!'

Matthew's starboard side rising up on the swell, Nat struggled to scale the greasy wall, guts churning. The crew was already heaving at the anchor and loosing the tallies that bagged the sails to their spars. The grey canvas broke free, spanking the wind, anchor lifting clear. The *Matthew* drew abreast his Britannic Majesty's fleet and began to punch her way, anonymously, out to sea.

Rounding the point, the skipper called the boatswain to harden up. Nat felt the antique merchantman heave over on the starboard tack, sheets cracking sharp as a hangman's rope. Abaft the beam, the tower of St Nicholas passed unnoticed as, staggering to leeward, he threw up. Between convulsions through watering eyes he took a last glimpse of England.

*

Erasmus Carew and his son stood on the bluff above the town as the *Matthew* prepared to beat out to sea. Foxwood, the dispenser of secrets, pulled at his new master's coat. 'I must send the cutter now, Sir, if it's to intercept.'

Carew leant on his stick. The hireling was right. Send the cutter to fetch Farrington back. 'Have the boatswain make ready. I'll go myself.' Foxwood's protest and the cries of a circling black crow were lost in the gathering wind.

*

Matthew's skipper cursed as he saw the cutter with the King's ensign beating towards him. No seaman would willingly heave to with a lee shore and a running tide.

The cutter's boatswain was at the prow. '*Matthew,* heave to in the King's name. Heave to and turn out Nathaniel Farrington.'

Nat saw Carew jammed uncomfortably amidships, clutching the mast. His fist closed round Foxwood's note from Holland. '*Jehovah Providebit.*'

'Look lively now,' the skipper snapped at his men, shrugging apologetically. 'Family in Harwich, Sir. I daren't cross 'em.'

Foxwood's letter had arrived at Kettle's Yard the day before. Fifteen years too late, the agent had spilt the intelligence gathered over the kitchen table at Helions from the drunken midwife Mrs Banks as she prepared to destroy Effam's child. Dorothy read the note and lifted the dark veil on their parent's secret. The widow Banks was right, she said. Nat's father was Erasmus Carew's, not hers.

Nat hauled himself over the side, dropping heavily into the boat's stern. Creased with his suppurating limb, he squinted up at the heels of the *Matthew* beating away to windward and the safety of the New World.

'Ready to face the King's justice Farrington? snarled Carew from the bowsprit.

Unnatural weather slammed the cutter like a hammer from hell. With a backing wind, the boatswain shortened sail but his slight vessel was shipping water fast. 'God have mercy!' The darkening firmament and the gathering violence of the sea sent his crew whining to the bottom boards.

'Effam!' Nat screamed across the foaming deep. As the sea made matchwood of the cutter, Nat saw the price of their reunion, the third pledge, her deathbed pleading: the forgiveness of Erasmus Carew. He would do it, and confound the curate's curse.

He would have his redemption.

Nathaniel Farrington opened his arms and cried above the tumult, 'God rest you, Erasmus Carew! God rest you, *my brother*!'

'Go to hell,' spat Carew. 'You killed God's anointed, *brother*.'

'No, Erasmus!' They were all going to drown so the executioner and his family would be beyond the new King's malice, unless Foxwood knew.

'Liar!'

'Raving I was, when Charles died,' yelled Nat. 'Cripple, spewing pus under a surgeon's knife.' Carew's brow furrowed and Nat knew the rat Foxwood had missed the switch.

'Who then?'

'Ha!' Nat laughed into the storm. 'We'll die here, brother, and my secret with us.'

'Who killed the King?'

'Joe Jessop.'

'*Jessop*?'

'Aye, Charles died with me crippled, sweating out the fever,' he ripped the bindings from his suppurating, red-raw leg, 'because of this.'

Erasmus Carew weighed sins like St Peter as the cutter corkscrewed. Brook Farm, the twins, Edward Salt, his son, his estate. As he prepared to answer to an authority higher than the King, he judged them finely balanced. 'Forgive me, Nathaniel?' Releasing his grip on the bowsprit, he tumbled into Nat's arms.

'With all my heart, brother,' sobbed Nat. 'If you'll forgive me.'

In the very moment of their redemption, the men were pitched into the watery chaos like the Swine of Gadara, the raven shrieking absolution to the skies.

From the bluff, Foxwood and the two young kinsmen watched in horror as the cutter plunged into the foaming abyss of the Rolling Ground.

And was gone.

Epilogue

XXVI

Helions House
July 1914
'Yo fella!'

The young man squinted at the car from his rose bed. Straightening, he pinched the woodbine, exhaling with practised ease through the corner of his mouth, taking the measure of the wide-lapelled stranger prising himself from the back seat. American.

'You live here, pal?'

'Nope.' The gardener had work to do.

'OK.' The American scanned the crumbling, kindly face of Helions. 'But you're local, right?'

The gardener flicked his fag end into the roses. 'Born an' bred.' He began patting his overalls. The bloke looked good for a smoke.

'Oh, here you go.' The stranger pulled a silver case of Camel Straights and a box of lucifers from his jacket, lighting the smokes with practised yellow fingers. 'Nice old place you got here.'

'Suppose.'

'I love old things,' smiled the American. 'Bit of a history buff, you follow me? Matter of fact, I'm kinda researching my folks, going way, way back. Fella I'm looking for left the old country in the fall of 1666.' He scratched the side of his nose. 'In a hurry.'

'Yeh?' The young man decided the smooth tobacco was worth his time.

'Yep. Big cheese in your English Civil War.' The gardener said nothing, savouring his fag. 'Wrote it down, every day, *every* detail.' The stranger waved a small leather volume. 'This one puts him right here. Working for a Captain Nathaniel Farrington, and another fella, name of Carew.' The American squinted through pebble glasses. 'Mean anything to you, son?'

The gardener thought for a while, waiting for another Yank cigarette. 'Sir James Farrington owns this place but he ain't never here.' He trod the butt into the gravel. 'Carews are at the other end of the village.' He tipped his chin at the gate. 'But they're in London mostly.'

Sucking his teeth, the American felt for the cigarettes. 'Well, ain't that a bummer? Wanted to meet those folks, show my books and all.' He kicked the gravel. 'My great, great, whatever, granddaddy, what a guy; fixer see, kinda like a private investigator, you understand?' He winked theatrically, patting the book. 'Reckon this'd spice up the ol' family tree.' A hint of malice and the gardener was on his guard. 'Son, there're more skeletons in these books than Gettysburg.' A black sentinel crow lifted heavily from the stack, beating low, cawing displeasure. 'D'you think the boss'd be interested in my diaries, pal?'

The gardener shrugged. 'Dunno, maybe.'

'Tell you what, fella, here's my card. Maybe you'll pass it on and the boss'll call me?' The American grasped the gardener's hand, pressing the card and a half-crown, slapping him gently on the shoulder. 'Yeah?' With a half wave, half salute, he was gone, across the little moat bridge in a cloud of dust towards Salisbury.

The gardener flicked the sliver of pasteboard, lit another woodbine and plunged the card into the oblivion of his trouser pocket. In that dark recess, his thumb found the heavy embossed lettering. Fishing it out, he squinted, half-interested, at the Yank's name through the smoke of the rough tobacco.

Foxwood.

Printed in Great Britain
by Amazon